THE
UNBOUND
WITCH

COPYRIGHT

Unmarked
© 2022, Miranda Lyn
All rights reserved.

No part of this publication may be reproduced, stored in a retrieval system, stored in a database and/or published in any form or by any means, electronic, mechanical, photocopying, recording or otherwise, without the prior written permission of the publisher. This book is a work of fiction. The names, characters, places, and incidents are products of the writer's imagination. Any resemblance to persons, living or dead, is entirely coincidental.

Cover Designer – Tairelei – www.facebook.com/Tairelei/

Copy Editor – The Khans/ Second Pass Editing

Sensitivity Reader -@sarahinwanderland (Instagram)

CONTENT WARNING Violence, Language, Sexual Content, Death

ALSO BY MIRANDA LYN

FAE RISING:

BLOOD AND PROMISE
CHAOS AND DESTINY
FATE AND FLAME

TIDES AND RUIN

UNMARKED:
THE UNMARKED WITCH

www.authormirandalyn.com

FOR THE **WITCHES**

THE ONES THAT **BURN**
THE ONES THAT **BLEED**
THE ONES THAT **RISE**
THE ONES THAT **NEED**

MAY YOUR **SPELLS** BE AS **WILD**
AS YOUR **DREAMS**

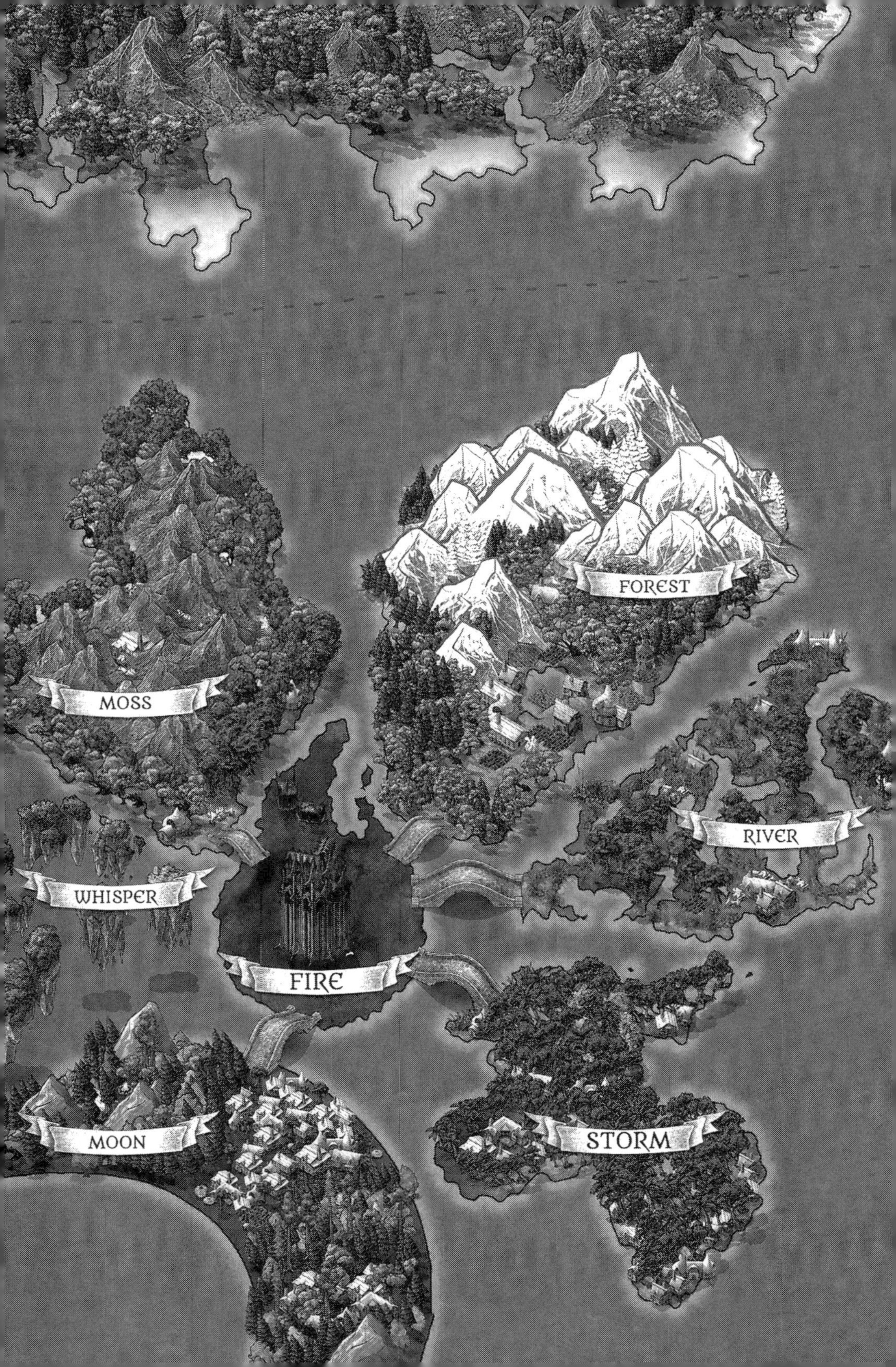
FOREST
MOSS
RIVER
WHISPER
FIRE
MOON
STORM

RECAP

Need a recap from book one?

Let me help you out. We started with the death of Tasa, the beloved Moon Coven leader. Her funeral gave Raven flashbacks to her grandmother's funeral and basically brought us up to speed on all things "Evil Dark King." Her asshole boyfriend, Nikos, got a little pushy and she left him in the dust to traipse off to the dark castle with her bestie Kirsi after being selected for the Witch Trials.

The competition is going about as well as one could hope. Kirsi and Raven are doing okay, but they've got some competition if they want to win the coven leader spot. Onyx is a dick, Willow is out for blood, and the Dark King has eyes for one person only, much to her dismay. But then shit gets real and people start dropping like flies. Grey, the Dark King's cousin, forms a friendship with the girls, but when he catches Raven in the secret Grimoire room, all bets are off. Bastian sends Raven love notes that eventually warm her heart-ish...

But the night of the ball, everything changes. Nikos shows up to find her in the arms of the Dark King, and the other coven leaders force a death spell on her that takes her ability to gain more spells and well... Kirsi is mysteriously killed the next morning.

RECAP

With the Dark King's dagger as the murder weapon, Raven loses her shit and wreaks havoc on the black castle as she's hunting for Bastian. He traps her in the time-out room. Once she's somewhat calm and has his promise that he hasn't had anything to do with it, she wants nothing more than to go home, back to Crescent Cottage, Scoop in tow.

When Nikos shows his face, she tells him she wants nothing to do with him. At the funeral, he gets a little handsy and our king puts him in his place, then whisks her off to dead people's reflection mountain where things get a bit cold and then hot. Then hotter.

The final trial happens, chaos ensues, people die and we find out who the real villain is, just as our beloved Kirsi is wished back into this witchy realm. But that doesn't matter because Raven is forced to do the unthinkable and now Bastian is dead, and she and Kir are banished to the human lands with an angry Grey in tow and no magic.

1

KIRSI

There was life and death and then there was somewhere fucked up in between, and that's where I was sitting. Or not sitting, but hovering, because my soul was ripped from the afterlife and plopped back into this lukewarm existence.

Shored up on the mysterious border of the human lands, after one night only, I'd kill to feel the white sand between my toes, to leap into the cold autumn water and be able to feel it chill me to the bone. But as a wraith, that would never happen. The only thing I could feel was the overwhelming presence of sorrow deep within my gut. Haunted. Which made sense, because that's exactly what I was. Haunted by the reality of my future. Missing my familiar; the tie to Scoop had been completely severed by an unknown hand.

Whoever had killed me deserved a fate worse than death, and I'd be the one to deliver justice. For as much as Raven was responsible for disturbing my afterlife, so was that person for damning me to it.

Slipping away from Grey and Raven for solace, I hovered above the ground, my ghostly being a far cry from graceful as I swooped low, curious to see if I could manipulate the sand. I couldn't. Not a trace left behind as I wandered away from my gloomy companions.

Again, I tried. Descending to the beach in a frantic dive, the world became dark as I crossed the barrier of earth with nothing but silt around me. Twisting back and forth, panicking, I shoved myself out of the ground and thought only of catching my breath, of clutching my chest as the fear subsided, but there was no breath. There was no heartbeat. Everything was different.

Frustrated, I plunged again, intending to claw at the sand I couldn't move, couldn't leave a single mark upon. But within my fury, I jostled the tiny hill, sending several grains tumbling sideways.

It was nothing, really. It was the saddest victory of my existence, but the only one I had now. So, nestled close to the ground, making myself invisible so no one could watch my shame, I tried again and again and again.

As if my body were entirely numb, the rough texture of the sand nonexistent, I shoved my arm toward an abandoned sandcastle, sheer will and cold determination driving me forward. Nothing.

I crept closer to Grey and Raven, both content to brood in silence on the beach. She'd condemned me to this ethereal body. Letting anger swell within until I managed to grasp a small rock, I paused, tumbling it through my fingers, pretending I could feel the bit of lichen on the side, the cool temperature of the stone.

My mouth twisted as an idea sparked in my mind. I was invisible. Long gone, as far as Grey and Raven were concerned. Pulling my arm back, the pebble floated in midair. I chucked it forward, pelting Grey right in the thigh.

"What the fuck?" He jumped to his feet, whipping around, as he rubbed the spot where the rock had hit until it dawned on him. "One day in and you've discovered how to be a dick in a different form. That has to be some kind of record."

"It's a skill." I flicked his ear, but my finger passed through, not making any sort of contact.

Damnit. I'd have to practice.

I sighed. "Are we going to sit here and stare at this water forever, or are we actually going to do something?"

Grey lifted one massive shoulder, content to speak to me though he couldn't see me. "We have no magic. How do you propose we do that?"

Raven sat hunched, holding her knees to her chest, those black curls of hers blowing in the wind. She'd killed the Dark King and had to live with it for the rest of her life. Maybe that was punishment enough.

I reappeared before them. "There are these things called ships that float on water and carry you from one place to another."

"Oh, hey. Glad to see the smart ass came back from the afterlife as well as the asshole," Grey answered, finally looking at me.

"They only let me pick two attributes. I felt like those were key." If I'd had it in me, I might have smirked, but it wasn't there. Only the haunting sorrow and the rage burrowed deep down. I didn't want to be here. I'd seen Raven begging me to live before I was taken, but I'd accepted my death on that castle floor.

The ocean waves roared as they tumbled forward, stretching as far as they could toward Grey and Raven before retreating, as if they were afraid of the witches upon the shoreline. I couldn't be sucked into the lull of the tide, couldn't just stay here. A line of trees, painted in a thousand different shades of autumn, created a barrier between us and whatever lay beyond in a land with no magic.

"How am I here?" I asked quietly.

Raven stiffened, turning to glance at me with red ringed eyes. "Because I made a mistake. Because I thought I couldn't bring you back, so I was careless with my words. You were only supposed to answer the question and then return to the afterlife, but Nikos killed the deja before she could send you back."

"Careless? That's the lightest word I'd use, but that's not what I meant. Are wraiths not magical? If there's no magic here, how am I?"

Grey dusted the sand from his black pants as he answered. "They call them...er... you, ghosts more frequently here, but they exist all the same. Being a wraith is the nature of who you are. Just as a shifter can shift in the human lands, you can exist here. It's not magic. However, the rules work differently here. You have to conceal yourself like you were a minute ago. The humans question your existence, but most don't believe it."

"How do you know that?" Raven asked, pushing herself from the ground.

"There're these things called books that people open and read for knowledge," he said, imitating my earlier tone.

Her eyes lit with fury, but she did what she had always done. Held her tongue and kept absolute composure. She was nothing if not predictable when it came to conflict. Bastian Firepool was the only one I'd ever seen her stand up to, and that had ended poorly, to say the least.

"Don't be a dick, Grey." The words left my mouth before I could filter them. I was infuriated with Raven, but deep down, I would always protect her. I loved her.

He pushed his hands into his pockets. "Are we all friends again now?"

Before I looked into her face, before I could witness myself shattering that hope she would have, I said, "No," and floated toward that line of trees.

"I guess we're moving," Grey said in response.

Footsteps followed me deep into the forest until sand became dirt and dirt became rock and somewhere on the other side, a whole new world awaited. But it would take forever to discover because Raven's progress was slow, lagging behind Grey. She wasn't bleeding, but if the tears in her pants and the dried blood on her legs weren't enough to know she was suffering, beyond her mental state, the limp was. Something that must have happened in the final Trial before Nikos compelled her to kill the Dark King.

"What will we do?" Raven asked, her voice a whisper, though it could have been a shout after the aching silence we'd let settle among us.

"Well," Grey said as we pushed forward, "Everything's broken now. Willow is the Moon Coven leader. The Trials are over. We could stay here together or go our separate ways."

"We can't split up," Raven protested. "You can be pissed at me all you want, but we have to stay together until we have a plan. We can't assume it's safe for us here, and we have nothing to survive on."

"As it turns out," I fired back, "I need nothing. I simply exist now."

She didn't reply as Grey quickened the pace. "We'll find the first town and figure it out from there."

"Fine," I huffed, floating forward.

"Fine," she echoed.

Hours passed as we continued. I'd heard the rumble in Raven's stomach and wished it were mine. Wished with all my being that I could long for anything but the peace I'd felt before.

"You look different without your markings," I said to fill the silence.

"More handsome or less?" Grey asked, plucking a stone from the ground and throwing it into the barren land before us, full of nothing but billowing clouds above and long blades of grass over rolling hills.

"Less. I prefer the sign of a witch."

Peeking down to my own translucent arms, I scowled. My markings were gone as well. Another robbery.

"You're going to be such a joy on this journey," he said.

"I've been a joy my whole fucking life. I don't see a need to change now."

"Where are we going?" Raven asked, ignoring the banter.

Grey stopped, pivoting as he placed his hands in his pockets. "I've got a friend here that might help us. But the problem is, I only know the name of the town where she lives. No idea how to find it."

"How do you know anyone in the human lands?" she asked, shifting from one foot to the other, as if trying to ease the pain without drawing too much attention to her wounds.

"We've never formally met, but we've been in contact. I'm hoping that's enough to find a way back."

"Sounds less than promising," I mumbled, floating back and forth between them.

Grey ran his fingers through his cropped blond hair. "Well, let's just say she owes my family a favor."

"I guess it's better than no plan at all," Raven answered, still very much a shadow of who I'd known her to be.

I was far nosier. "So, who is it?"

He lifted an eyebrow, testing the tension between us before answering, "Eden Mossbrook."

2

RAVEN

I wanted to react. To feel anything but the loss of Bastian, the loss of my friendship with Kirsi, the loss of my entire world, but I couldn't push past the gaping void in my chest that longed for lingering shadows and his beautiful face inches from mine.

When I closed my eyes, he was there before me, reaching as the death spell took and took and took from me, until I thought I'd perish with him. And then I was here, banished to this land of sorrow. Grey wouldn't look me in the face. Had taken active measures to avoid me altogether, it seemed. Kirsi was no better.

Eden Mossbrook had always been no more than a lingering story, something akin to a fairytale. The witch that had vanished in the night, taking the Moss Coven Grimoire with her. Endora, her mother, had condemned Bastian's family for thirty years, proclaiming his father had killed Eden and hidden their Grimoire.

"What the fuck? You know where she is? Why wouldn't your family have told the witches about her?" Kirsi asked the questions I couldn't, always the more indomitable and brave between us.

"Because we're protecting her."

Kirsi moved in front of Grey, stopping him despite her vacant form. "Eden Mossbrook's disappearance is half the reason the witches are mad at your royal family. Why would they let that go on?"

Grey simply sidestepped and kept moving. "You're foolish if you think that's true. Endora Mossbrook may use that as justification, but she has only ever had one goal, and it's never been to liberate her daughter, who, by the way, ran away from her. Endora wants to see the end of the shifters in her lifetime, and she'll stop at nothing to achieve that."

I didn't see the hole until it was too late. Twisting my ankle, I fell forward, squeezing my eyes shut to brace for impact. The wounds in my legs from Willow's arrow and Onyx's blood-bound knife screamed, though I wouldn't make a peep about it.

But Grey's arms were around me before I hit the ground. I stopped breathing. From pain or shock, I wasn't sure. Our eyes met for the first time since the beach, when he'd been poised over the top of me, ready to take my life, as I'd taken his cousin's.

Everything in the world stopped as he held me firm, something deep and mysterious within his lingering gaze. I opened my mouth to thank him, to say anything really, but the words didn't come. He kept me there longer than needed, no doubt trying to work out his hatred for me. But Kirsi cleared her throat behind us, breaking the spell, and we flew apart.

"Thank you," I muttered, my eyes dropping to the ground.

I'd killed two men. One I'd thought would be with me forever, and one that had hated me since I was a child. Irrevocably damaged, I couldn't be trusted to understand anything about them anymore.

"We'll see if we can find a passage back," Grey said, pushing onward. "There's a barrier in the sea. A division placed by the goddess to keep magic in the south. The storms along the border there are dangerous, and not all who attempt to cross make it out alive."

Kir looked at me then, a deep question in her hollow eyes. I shook my head, content to keep my secrets to myself. But as I caught Grey's curious glance, I surrendered. He'd never trust me again if he knew I was withholding something from him.

"That night in the castle... after Kirsi was murdered..." I held her stare as I spoke to him. "When it felt like I'd bring the whole castle down, throwing the shifters like scattered pebbles and racing for … Bastian." His name was like a thousand needles upon my skin. Painful, but bringing me to life in a way I didn't know I needed. "I cast those storms, moved the earth. When I was younger, maybe fifteen or sixteen, I started receiving magic most witches had never heard of. Powerful spells, though there wasn't enough intensity for them to be more than a prick of magic.

"I could make it rain if I felt sad. I could slam doors. I could push a blanket off a bed. But something has been changing. The day we did the mind Trial, I think the coven leaders realized the depth of my power. I shook the room then, but when I fought against Onyx and Willow, I shook the world. I'm quite certain that with enough… *provocation*, I could burn it all. Maybe I could control those storms, crack this world."

Kirsi stared at me, her eyes narrowed. I wasn't sure if she could cry or feel anything beyond anger, but at least she knew now what her death had done to me.

"So, the coven leaders picked the most powerful witch they could find and gave her a spell that could slaughter, even though it broke the laws of magic. That's fucking spectacular." Grey's words dripped in unhinged sarcasm.

I kept his pace as I continued, ignoring the tone. "Unfortunately, yes, but what they did, it was under the blood moon, a seance. They conjured Death into the receiving realm and sent me there. And now, I'll never get another spell." I pulled my tousled hair forward, letting my fingers twist it into a simple braid as my mind wandered. "Maybe I should just stay here, far, far away from them."

Kirsi appeared before me in an instant. I wasn't quick enough to stop and stepped right through her. *Sorrow*. So much aching sadness wracked my body the second we collided. Unsure if it was an amplification of my own feelings or the reality of hers, but either way, as I rushed away, shivers crawling down my spine, I immediately regretted my words.

"At least you have a choice." She surged forward, vanishing over a hill in the distance.

"She's not wrong," Grey added, his words clipped. "Just because you can end lives now doesn't mean you have to give up on your own."

I paused, but he continued marching forward, trying to catch up to Kirsi. Nothing tied me to either of them anymore. But they had each other.

Afraid to be left behind, I hurried, hobbling on wounded legs, wondering when we'd find people in these lands. As I caught up, I found them immersed in a hushed conversation.

"So what? We're going to—" Kirsi's words were cut short as we crested a hill, bringing the little town in the valley below into sight.

"Better do that vanishing thing," Grey said, taking a large stride forward, straight toward the cluster of buildings.

Kir huffed but disappeared as we descended the grassy slope with the sun setting to the west of the village, painting the sky in a variety of watercolor pastels. The air here was stale and dull, the colors less vibrant, the sounds slightly muffled. Our lands were a different world. As different as this place seemed, it could have been a million miles away, nestled in a different realm.

Grey lifted a shoulder to his ear and then shook his head twice before halting. "Knock it off, Kir."

"I'm practicing," she replied.

"Practicing what?" I asked.

"Touching."

Of course. I hadn't realized she'd be faced with a whole world of changes in a new form. Guilt swept through me once more as we closed the distance to the town.

Vines crept up the sides of the homes packed so close together, if not for the varying finishes on the outside, I would have imagined they were all one building. Looking down onto the town, people came and went, some with carts, others with their families, casually strolling the narrow brick walkways between the towering buildings.

The streets were free of debris and packed with humans. Just the sort of place we could sleep for a night without drawing too much attention. I stayed well behind Grey as he approached an older man with a long pole, lighting an oil-fueled street lantern. The concept of living without magic was jarring to witness.

The men talked for several minutes, Grey pointing back to me and then continuing his conversation. Several wary glances later, the old man shook his head and turned away, continuing his work as Grey returned, his chin down.

"We're not going to get anywhere with you looking like that," he said, gesturing to the rips in my pants.

"Willow shot me with an arrow and Onyx stabbed me with a knife in the final Trial. Sorry if that's inconvenient for you."

I'd meant to snap at him, to release some of the fire within me, but it didn't come out that way. It was far more of a sincere apology than I'd intended it to be.

Grey tilted his head to the side, raising a shoulder. Kirsi was still pestering him.

"Kirsi, for the love of all things holy, if you don't stop flicking my ear, I'm going to send you back to the afterlife myself."

"Oh! Promise?" Her voice came from right beside me, though I'd had no idea she was there.

He looked to the sky and took a deep breath. "Do you want to try your hand at being useful?"

"No," she answered, and he jumped again.

"Raven needs something different to wear. Preferably long and warm. Can you manage it?"

"I can barely manage to touch you. Do you really think I can steal clothing?"

"You'll never know unless you try," he said, drawing out the last word as if it would entice her.

"No, I'm pretty confident already."

I crossed my arms over my chest. My body protested the gesture with pain I ignored. "It's fine. I can do it myself."

"You limp. You don't have magic, and your stomach keeps growling. You'll give yourself away in a heartbeat," Grey pointed out, shooting me a hard look.

"I don't need a caretaker." I walked away before he could stop me, letting the anger surge through my veins as if it were a balm, soothing me.

Not many women would leave their clothing on a line overnight, especially in autumn. With limited options, I sank into a small space between two buildings, hoping it was dark enough to conceal me as I watched the passersby.

Several horse-drawn carts meandered down the road, carrying wares and people from one place to another. Listening to the hushed tones of lilting voices, I waited. Their accents differed from ours, though the language was the same. Taking a moment of peace, I closed my eyes as the cool breeze brushed my cheeks, feeling so much more than I wanted to, from the wounds in my legs to the scar on my soul. The ache, Goddess be damned, the ache of that look in his eyes, the betrayal as the spell ripped from me. Bastian may have died, but his memory would always be a living nightmare in every breath I took.

I didn't think I'd ever truly live again. Not without the heaviness of shame and horror that came with what had happened. It didn't matter that I wasn't in control. I'd suffer with the guilt every single day; the pain of missing him.

I could have crumpled to the ground as grief swept in, completely renewed and vengeful. But I couldn't let them see how broken I was. Not when Kirsi had died, and Grey had lost his family. No. These feelings were mine alone to bear. My burden to carry.

The snap of a rock shooting from beneath an old wagon wheel wrenched me from my despondent thoughts. A towering woman hustled her daughters across the street, her hands firmly on their backs as she hurried them along.

"Julia, darling, don't fidget. The Seeker is always watching."

"Yes, Mother," the girl whispered in a sheepish tone, looking over her shoulder toward a large building at the end of the road.

A cast iron circle topped the edifice of the stone structure, branding it the crown jewel of the odd town. Twice the height of the other buildings, with arched windows encased in detailed carvings, one could even say it was beautiful, if not for the overseer standing watch on the immense steps. Dressed in a long black robe with a thick book tucked under his arm, he surveyed the movement on the street as if he were Lord and High Executioner of the village. His dark, keen eyes locked onto the girl and watched her like a predator as she trailed her vigilant mother.

Once the girl had vanished, his pointed nose turned to me. He shouldn't have been able to see me in the shadows, but I was confident those black eyes could find me like a beacon in the night.

He took three steps forward, rubbing his stubbled jaw, until he finally turned away, looking over the evening crowd. I used that opportunity to sprint through the gap between the buildings, content to just wear what I'd come in, judgmental humans be damned.

Stepping out from the houses, I wove my way back to where I'd left Grey standing, though I shied away from the bright orange glow of the lamppost.

He was gone.

"See that wagon over there?" Kirsi's hushed voice startled me.

Swallowing my gasp, I nodded, eyeing the overflowing cart, loaded with an entire home full of items. Rocking chairs stacked on top of trunks, pots and pans dangling from the thick, coarse rope tying it all down.

"There's a black trunk in the back, close to the edge. It's got women's clothing packed within."

"How do you—"

"Don't ask. I'll keep watch, just be quick about it. This town gives me the creeps, and I'm already dead."

I couldn't force a smile at her words as I moved, attempting to make it seem like the items on the wagon were my own. In one motion, I unlatched the chest, swiped the plain black dress on top, closed it and walked away with my chin high, aiming straight for the alley between the buildings again.

"Kir?" I hated that I couldn't see her.

"Present," she answered. "I'll watch the other end, but hurry."

She spoke to me as kindly as she had to Shayva Stormridge, a witch who had pestered us for a fertility spell for years. I shrugged off her tone, removing the ripped clothing, stepping quickly into the black dress.

As I fastened the final button, Kirsi hissed in my ear. "Incoming."

Those same hard eyes from before peered at me from around the corner. The Seeker, he'd been called. Unsure what to do with the clothes I'd been wearing, I grabbed them from the ground, heart racing, as he moved with the strides of a shifter toward me.

"The regime is always open to those who need penance," he said, his voice thick with condemnation.

I was certain he'd somehow seen me steal the cotton dress, baring myself in a narrow alley to change. I opened my mouth to speak, not knowing what I would say, when Grey rounded the opposite end of the gap.

"There you are, my love. I've been looking everywhere for you."

3

RAVEN

I backed away from the man, looking for safety beside Bastian's cousin as he took my hand, eyes flicking to the Seeker at the other end of the tight alley. That basic contact, the single brush of his thumb across the back of my hand, lit my skin on fire. I hadn't known how badly I needed to feel something besides pain. But even then, it was short lived as Grey tugged me toward him, dipped his chin to the mysterious man, and directed me out of the alley.

"That's a dangerous person for a witch," he warned. "They don't know about real magic here. They only know tales, and the humans of the regime don't like witches. They find anything out of order with their neighbors, claim they are witches, and condemn them accordingly. He'd see you dead, burned at the stake or drawn and quartered, before he helped you."

"He came out of nowhere," I explained, the ball of shredded clothes still tucked under my arm.

Grey kept his pace quick, his long strides forcing me into a painful, light jog. Though he was definitely the largest man around, at least his simple slacks and black collared shirt fit right in. "I've found us a place to stay. It's not much."

"We cannot stay here," Kirsi hissed from Grey's other side. "This town isn't safe."

"We don't have a choice. It's too dark to travel in unknown territory at night, and we're going to have to eat eventually."

My stomach rumbled at the mention of food. I ignored it, remembering the eyes of the Seeker. "I'm not hungry. I'd rather sleep in a field than stay here."

"There's a barn just outside of town. I saw it while I was asking around for directions. We can sneak in, rest for a few hours, and leave before dawn. But there's no negotiating. Tomorrow we will be walking and, if we don't sleep, we won't get far."

"Fair." I loosened my hair from the braid behind me, letting it warm my neck as we moved.

The eyes that watched us were wary, as if the Seeker had spread the word of strangers in the village. We hurried, leaving the peculiar seaside town behind us, headed straight for the broad silhouette of a large barn in the distance, lit only by the final seconds of dusk.

Halfway there, hushed voices sliced through the chilly air. Two figures, cloaked in the shadow of night, struggled on the side of the road. A man grunted, attempting to lift the side of his wagon hitched to a single horse. Grey dashed forward, taking the space beside the man to stretch his muscles and hoist the wagon with far more ease than he likely should have in this unremarkable world.

The woman, short in stature and graced with wrinkles that showed even in the darkness, rolled a wagon wheel forward and attempted to lift it onto the axle. She strained, twisting her face, so I followed Grey's lead, dropping my clothing to slide my hands between the spokes and help her.

"I've got this if you can put the hub on," Grey offered the old man.

"You sure, son? It's a loaded wagon."

"Yes, sir."

The man stepped away, grabbing the hub from the ground and shoving it onto the spoke. He reached around to the front of the wagon. With a grunt, he carried back a hefty metal wrench to secure the wheel. The woman and I slid out of the way just in time for him to spin the wheel once, making sure it'd been set straight before giving Grey a nod.

Grey slowly released the wagon, and the horse nickered, kicking at the gravel road as he neighed.

Grabbing the reins, the couple took their seat on the bench ahead of the coach. "I sure thank you, stranger. Seems something's got my horse spooked, though. We best be on our way up to the old barn. Where are you headed this time of day?"

"We're traveling to Bluestem, but our mare was stolen overnight, along with all of our provisions."

"Oh, you poor dears," the woman said, cleaning her hands with her apron. "And you're walking the road this late at night, with your wife, no less."

"I'm—"

Grey swooped in next to me, taking my arm. "We're newly married. Off to visit my aunt. Hoping to settle down before the baby comes."

"The baby?" The woman's gasp covered Kirsi's snort and my own shock at his easy lie.

"Henry," she said, turning to her husband, nearly faint.

"It takes a decent man to help a stranger on the road in the dark during these dangerous times. We'd like to return the favor. Come on up to the house, and we'll see you fed and in a warm bed for the night."

"Oh no, really, we couldn't impose." Grey played this game so well, if I didn't know any better, I'd say he'd performed his fair share of twisted roles in his lifetime.

"Don't be silly," the elderly woman said. "We'll have supper and visit like old friends."

The woman, Victoria, I'd learned, had insisted I ride in the wagon, claiming my condition meant I needed rest. Grey walked behind, far away from the horse, and probably with Kirsi, while the man led us to his home.

Several times, the horse neighed and jerked. I wondered if Kirsi was messing with the animal instead of staying with Grey in the back.

The short trip brought us to a modest home far grander than the cottage Kirsi and I had shared.

Within minutes, Victoria had lit her heavy iron stove, shoving small bits of wood inside its belly to heat the top. Grey and Henry had gone to the barn to put the horse in his stall and unhitch the wagon. Based on the way he'd lifted his shoulder to his ear, as they walked out, I guessed Kirsi had gone with him.

"If you go up the steps, your room is there on the right. I'll call when supper is ready if you'd like to get settled in."

"Thank you so much for your kindness." I didn't hesitate, eager to hide myself away rather than continue the lie these people didn't deserve.

I wondered whether they would have turned us away if we'd been honest. Maybe not mentioning we were witches and had a wraith in tow, only that we were merely traveling companions. But I hadn't missed the same book that the Seeker had been carrying, a golden circle painted onto the cover, on the woman's kitchen table. They had their books, and we had ours. If the witches hadn't yet gotten to them since Bastian's d… I couldn't even think the word.

The door swung open, and Grey stepped into the room, waiting a few seconds before shutting it behind him. Kirsi popped into view, and I nearly jumped, still not used to her new form.

Lifting a dusty pillow from the small bed, I threw it at Grey, who let it fall to the ground. "Married? Pregnant?"

He slid his hands into his pocket, rocking back on his heels. "You need to eat, Raven. And we both need sleep. The lie is harmless. It was the only way I could make sure we were allowed to room together."

I flung my hands into the air. "What difference does that make?"

He took a step toward me. "We're safer off the road this close to that town, and you know it. We need to stay together. We could have slept in the barn but probably not have eaten." He paused, his massive shoulders rising and falling. "I would have warned you, but we came upon them in the dark, and I didn't have time to think it through."

"It's ridiculous. I don't even look like I'm expecting." I jammed my hands on my hips, narrowing my eyes. "It feels wrong to lie to hospitable people."

Kirsi floated between us, her back to Grey as she snapped at me. "Calm down, Rave. You've got dinner and a safe place to sleep. That's not a bad deal for someone who murdered two people today."

The words struck like a fist to my gut. I stumbled backwards, clutching the skirt of my stolen dress in my fingers as I fought the tears that threatened to come forward. I didn't have the right to those tears; not a single one.

"Woah." Grey walked around Kirsi to stand between us, facing her. "That's too far. She's going to carry the weight of those lives for the rest of hers, and if you're going to pin them on her, then I'd ask you what you would have done differently. Onyx was going to kill her. Would you rather he lived?" His voice lowered, taking a dangerous tone. "You cannot condemn her for what happened with Bastian. His blood is not on her hands. Let that shit go, Kir."

My world rocked at his defense of me; his forgiveness.

The wraith's face was hard as stone as she burrowed deeper and deeper into her own feelings. "This isn't about Onyx. It's not about a king who carried his own fair share of guilt. It's about her and me. So, stay out of it."

"How many times do you want me to apologize? The deja said you couldn't return. I didn't know that wishing for you to answer a question would be a loophole."

She sank to the floor, half fading away, the blurry edges of her form still visible. "Ask me," she whispered.

I froze, the ringing in my ears, the fury in my veins melting as the entire atmosphere changed. "What?"

She pushed forward until I could have taken her hands, had they been corporeal. Kirsi and I had fought from time to time. We'd spent so much of our lives in each other's space, it was inevitable. We knew when to push and when to back off. We knew every button; every boundary; every sign of discontent. Resignation.

"What are you asking me to do?" I muttered, eyebrows drawn together, pushing past Grey to settle onto the ground beside her.

She kept her chin tucked to her chest, the haunted sound of her surrender vibrating her words. "If I answer the question, maybe I can go back."

Grey rounded the edge of the bed and sat on the corner, facing us as the mattress squeaked. "What will you be going back to? What is there beyond death?"

She looked up at him, her large gray eyes so full of emotion she was on the verge of breaking down. "Peace." A heavy pause hung in the stale farmhouse air as we waited. "There is no war between the shifters and witches, no coven leaders, no... anything beyond a pure sense of peace and acceptance. I just want that back. Please."

Studying my nails, running my fingers along my hem, doing anything but looking into her face, I confessed. "I'd gotten away from Onyx and Willow, and my mind was addled. When the deja asked for my wish, I realized I hadn't taken a second to consider what I should do. And before I knew it, my heart spoke words before my brain could process. I didn't think at all. I casually wished to ask what you would have asked the deja for. Because losing you was so heavy on my heart, Kir. I promise, it was an accident."

She sat with that for a long time. Grey and I exchanged several glances as we watched her, waiting to see if she would answer.

"I love you, Rave. I'm sorry I've been so hard on you. Things are just different now." She met my eyes then, the hurt behind her stare so raw I could nearly feel it. "If I'm not angry or sad, I'm nothing. I can't feel."

"I love you, too, Kir. When I made that wish, it was such a natural train of thought for me. When you died, you took a piece of me with you. But that piece was always yours to take. I'll miss you."

Nodding slowly, she forced a smile before turning her ashen face to Grey. "I'll miss you too, asshole. Take care of my sister."

Sister. After all we'd been through, the pain I'd caused her, she still thought of me so. My heart ached all over again, and I accepted that this was her choice. She deserved whatever eternity she wanted.

"You're sure?" Grey lifted a single brow, eyes fixed on Kir as she nodded slowly. "Alright, Moondance. Rest easy. Save a spot for us when this all goes to hell."

The old house had gone completely still, as if the owners, fussing around with dinner below, had known we'd needed this moment. I studied Kirsi's face. The way her long hair caught the candlelight, the way her eyes held a mischievous gleam no matter what her feelings were. The way she worked her hands in her lap as she looked at me with that final goodbye on her lips.

She didn't turn away as she whispered, "I would have wished for your happiness, Raven Moonstone."

4

RAVEN

Squeezing my eyes shut, the world vanished as fresh tears fell down my flushed cheeks. I couldn't breathe as I wished with all my heart she'd find her happiness, too. That she'd be welcomed back to the afterlife because that was her choice and what she wanted, no matter how much I would miss her.

I opened my eyes, and she was gone. That was it. Grey rose from his place on the bed, the stiff blankets hardly disturbed by his presence. Taking my hand, he pulled me into a solid hug, holding me as I sobbed. For Kir. For Bastian. For everything. I needed that emotional release. I stepped back as he reached for my face, wiping the tears from my cheeks.

"Losing her once sucked. I'll never recover from losing her twice."

Grey tucked a finger under my chin and forced me to look up at him. And for a moment, a sliver of a second, it was Bastian standing before me, forcing my eyes to his as he so loved to do. But the memory was gone as quickly as it had come, and Grey jerked away from me, no doubt remembering that I was the murderer.

"I'm sorry," I breathed. "I thought … I just …"

"That's the last apology you get, Moonstone. Put some fire back into those veins. Ignite the world if you must, but stop cowering. You are not weak. You are not broken. You are not a victim. You're the most powerful witch of our generation, and it's time to start acting like it."

"Well, that was dramatic." Kirsi popped back into the room, and, this time, there was no hiding my scream.

"What the hell, Kir?" I shouted, clutching my chest.

"Yeah, it didn't work. But it's nice to know you'll never survive my second death. Really touching stuff."

"I hate you."

A smile. A real Kirsi smile crossed her face, forcing one of my own.

"No, you don't."

Grey cleared his throat. "Well, I do. The wedding is definitely off."

She flew toward Grey, flicking his ear. "Good thing, since you're already married. By the way, the oldies downstairs were just feeling each other up, but dinner's ready. Have fun with that."

"I can bring you something up?" Grey offered as I wiped the remnants of tears from my face.

"Don't bother. I don't need sustenance anymore."

"Sorry, Kir," he answered.

She shook her head. "Don't be. At this point, we can only blame two people. Whoever killed me, and Nikos fucking Moonfield."

"Dinner is ready, dears," a smooth feminine voice called up the stairs.

"You don't know who killed you?" Grey asked, moving toward the door to grip the black metal knob.

She shook her head. "I was in the Trial speaking to a very distant relative, and then I was swept away. Slammed back into a broken, dying body with Raven stooped over the top of me."

"I wanted to save you. I tried."

Kirsi lifted a shoulder. "I know."

My stomach rumbled again, and Grey swung the door open, gesturing for me to go first. He kept his warm hand on the small of my back as we navigated the hall and moved down the narrow, creaking stairs.

"Ah. You have that lovely newly wedded glow," Victoria said, her wrinkled hands clasped below her chin as she stared at us with flush red cheeks from the table. "I hope you're hungry."

"Famished," Grey answered, his hand burning a mark onto my back.

Victoria stood. "I need to grab the bread. Seat yourselves."

Henry leaned over the table to shake Grey's outstretched hand. "My God, that's a grip, son. What was it you said you did for work?"

"Ironwork, sir," he answered, sliding my chair out for me.

I sat, surveying the roast, inhaling the scent of rosemary dusting the potatoes. The handmade table had been carefully crafted. Each stretch of wood planed to perfection with no divots, no rough texture below the polished finish. You could set a marble on that table, and it wouldn't have moved. It was the nicest item I'd seen in the home.

"Beautiful, isn't it?" Henry asked, stealing my attention. "It was my first piece after we were married some fifty years ago."

"Fifty years?" I gasped.

He nodded, a gleam in his eye as he gazed at his wife entering the room with a basket of bread in one hand and a pitcher of water in the other. Grey shot from his seat, taking the items from the old woman and finding homes for them on the table before reclaiming his seat and wrapping his long arm around the back of my chair.

"Thank you, dear." Henry lifted his chin to Victoria as she leaned over and pecked his cheek without a thought.

"Such an old coquet." She giggled.

A flush painted my face as we intruded on their intimate moment. As the old man leaned over to his wife and whispered something that made her laugh.

Grey's attention flicked to me, and I couldn't help but look away. I'd wanted that once. Had laid in bed with a man who'd promised it to me as he stroked my body and whispered our future into my ear. Those moments were so fragile between him and me, so fresh and delicate, we'd dared not speak of them loud enough for the goddess to protest.

Lost in an abyss of sorrowful memories, I hadn't noticed Grey filling my plate. I'd been so hungry when we came down, I'd nearly sat on my own hands to keep them back. But now, it was all I could do to shovel the meal into my mouth, and remember to chew, swallow, repeat.

"Are you alright, dear?" Victoria asked, the wisps of her white hair glowing in the candlelight.

"Yes. Thank you. I—"

"No need for explanation. It's just the babe protesting a full meal after a long day of travel, I'm sure."

Grey wrapped his arm around my shoulder, an easy smile showcasing his dimple as he looked down at me.

"Just the babe, my darling. Try the bread."

I kicked him below the table as I reached across it for the basket. His dimple deepened, but he said nothing else. I wondered if he knew that Bastian was the only man I'd ever see when I looked at him. That every word he spoke and each look we shared was laced with remnants of guilty memories that could never be forgotten.

Setting the basket down, I waited for Victoria to finish her bite before asking, "Do you have children?"

A wave of sadness crossed both of their faces, and their hands instinctively found each other's.

"We lost a son in childbirth in our first year of marriage. Our daughter was..." Henry cleared his throat as if it would make the words easier to say. "She was taken from us three years ago."

"You might've heard the whispers in town. They love to gossip," Victoria bit out, "But our Elizabeth wasn't a witch. She wasn't."

"There, there," Henry said, pushing out of his chair to wrap his arms around his elderly wife. "There's no need for that on such a lovely day."

Her sniffles faded away after a few moments. Henry moved back to his seat but never took his hand from his wife. The word 'witch' hung in the air as if it had been painted in blood on the wall, and I wanted nothing more than to assure Victoria that there was no shame in being one.

Grey shifted, moving slightly closer as he gripped my hand on top of the table, rubbing lazy circles with his thumb as the old woman continued.

"We were blessed with Beth late in life. We thought we wouldn't bear children. She was such a joy, Raven. You would have loved her. Everyone did. She had the most precious blonde ringlets. She'd beg Henry for a new yellow ribbon every year to tie her hair up."

She smiled, dabbing her brown eyes with a handkerchief as she continued. "She was a dream in the garden. Born with the purest green thumb. We'd grow pumpkins the size of wagon wheels and enough tomatoes to feed the village. She grew into that role, her knowledge of herbs and flowers growing as fast as she did. And then one day, Henry got the cough. But she knew what to brew to make it go away. Half the village got it. Most that did, died. But our Elizabeth saved her dad. He was right as rain in just a few days."

She paused then, lost in thought. I knew that place well. The one you wished you could stay in. Pleading with the goddess to let you see how precious those moments were. Grey must have followed my trail of thought, because he squeezed my hand once more, pressing his thigh against mine.

I didn't know how to pull away, even as the room became smaller and he became so much bigger. He meant well, I told myself. Meant to soothe my tender heart and maybe even a bit of his own.

When Victoria spoke again, I could barely hear her. "They said it was witchcraft. Said there was no way Henry could have healed that fast. Then an angry mob came and took her away. Her screams were the last sound we ever heard from her."

"And you stayed here?" The sound of my voice startled her. She must have forgotten we were sitting here.

"Oh, heavens." She placed over-worked hands on the beautiful table and shoved, pushing herself up. "What a sad story for a sweet couple to hear. Please forgive me."

"There's no forgiveness needed," Grey said. "We're very sorry for the loss of your daughter."

She moved quickly from the room all the same.

Henry shook his head, taking a long drink of something that certainly wasn't water. "Take it from me, kids. There are some deaths a person will never recover from."

Grey wrapped his arm around the back of my chair again, his hand settling heavily onto my shoulder. It was a façade, and I knew it. A husband comforting his wife after a sad tale. It was wrong, though.

I needed him to stop touching me. Needed the panic of that lingering stroke to go away. Needed to stop pretending that I belonged to anyone but a fallen king with pitch black wings and a dangerous temper. But he was there, in the room, in the shadows of the home, watching me, hating me, gripping my throat.

Henry stood, his body slow and steady. He'd said something, but I couldn't hear it over the ringing in my ears, the rush of panic as Grey's careful fingers became Bastian's firm grasp. As the room grew smaller. The shadows crept toward me. His shadows. His magic. His anger and passion and everything I'd ever wanted from him.

Fear is the darkness that calls to you.

Voices muffled as Grey moved into my blurred vision. He said my name, but it echoed off a wall somewhere far, far away. I nearly fell from my chair, scrambling through the small house and straight for the door, wrenching it open to take in the cool night air. Gasping, I tried to let that sliver of milky moonlight give me comfort as I hurtled past the garden-lined path, flinging open the little white gate to escape.

One breath. Two Breaths. I could do this. Control. Focus.

My stomach rolled, threatening to lose its contents. I sucked in short, sharp breaths. Every muscle stretched and ached with tension. Every sound from miles away pounded into my head. I was certain I could still hear the ocean, the forest we'd walked through, and even the voice of that young girl the monster in the town had stalked.

"Easy." Grey's voice was careful, as if approaching a wild animal. His hand slid onto my back, and I jerked away.

"Please," I whispered. "Please don't touch me."

He knelt until he could look me in the eye. "What happened?"

I let my feet slide from under me, landing on the gravel. I'd made it all the way to the road without realizing it. Pulling my knees to my chest, I looked away. "I... I don't know. It's been a long day."

Another breath. One and two. Control. Focus. "Remember when you said I wasn't broken? I think you were wrong."

He huffed a laugh. "It's been known to happen from time to time."

The gravel crunched below Grey as he, too, sat upon the road beside me. Brushing his palm over the rocks, he gripped a handful and let the sharp pebbles fall one by one as crickets sang a cacophony of chirps, a breeze poured over the hills behind the home, and the moon slowly trekked across the sky. He remained steadfast and patient. Calm.

"You ever wonder what life would be like if we were born into different roles?"

I opened my mouth to say something. What, exactly, I didn't know, but Grey went on.

"I mean, Bastian and I never had it easy. There were no comforts living in the castle beyond simple pleasures. It was hard knowing every day we were always going to be someone's adversary. I think we grew up faster than we were supposed to, and maybe because of that, we grew up differently. Broken, like you said."

I sat silently, listening to his thoughts, if only to escape my own.

"I never thought I'd be good at it, you know? Working in the castle. But it was in my blood, and my father never once doubted me."

"Where are your parents now?" I held my knees closer to me, rubbing warmth into them as he spoke.

"They died when I was young. The Fire Coven has never been a safe place to be."

"I'm sorry."

Green eyes glanced at mine before looking away. "Everyone can become an enemy when you lose something you love. Do you miss him?" he finally asked, a quiet vulnerability to his tone, as if afraid I'd give him the wrong answer.

"I miss planning the future we might have had. I miss the daydream. I'm not sure I have the right to miss the man. Not when I …" my voice trailed off.

"You didn't. Not really. The weapon is not to blame for the action of the wielder. I don't think he would have blamed you. But if you let those thoughts fester, every memory you had with him will turn sour. You'll never trust yourself."

"I think we both know Bastian would have never trusted me again."

He smirked, that single dimple showing through. "He always was a suspicious bastard."

No one but Grey could have said that and gotten away with it. Even now, I thought it was only to grasp for that relationship they'd had. Where Bastian might have answered something ruthless back to him.

"What do you think he would do if he was stuck here?"

He shrugged, swiping at the gravel again. "Probably the same thing we're doing."

"No." I smiled. "He'd have already been four steps ahead of the plan and would likely be halfway home."

"I think you give him way too much credit. He'd probably still be on that fucking beach, contemplating a swim back." He chucked a rock he'd been holding before looking up at the dark sky.

I was certain a thousand memories of his cousin swarmed his mind as we sat there. Bastian's firm command, his easy smile when he thought no one was watching, his fierce loyalty.

"Raven, I need to tell—"

"Did you hear that?" I jumped to my feet, whipping around to look down the road.

We were close enough to the town to see the silhouette of the people between the gathering of lanterns, angry voices growing from distant murmurs to rumbles of strong disgust.

"Time to go," Grey said, leaping from the ground and grabbing my hand as we dashed for the house.

5

RAVEN

I chased Grey into the humble home, bolting up the stairs to warn Kirsi that we needed to leave. The room was empty.

"Kir, if you're invisible, it's time to go."

No response.

I ran back down to find Grey helping the old couple gather provisions.

"Fill your arms with whatever you can manage," Victoria yelled, grabbing her book. "We've been waiting for this day."

I couldn't process those words as I rushed around the house, snatching anything I thought they may want. Blankets and a painting of a little blonde girl with great big eyes. Everyone else had grabbed food.

"We'll need to get the horse out of the barn and hitch him to the other wagon," Henry said. "Can you help me, son?"

Grey flinched at the final word. Only a split-second reaction to the endearment, but enough for me to register. He'd opened up tonight, and that place inside of him was still raw.

"I tried to get the horse," Kirsi whispered from beside me. "But the asshole was too spooked."

My shoulders dropped with relief. "It's fine, Kir. Just stay close."

"You can't see me, but I'm with you," she assured me, and it was the first time I really felt like she was the Kirsi I'd known my whole life.

Pushing out the door, the chant of the mob marching up the hill grew louder.

"Burn the witches! Burn the witches!"

We rushed to the barn, passing Victoria as she ran back into the house. I turned to help her, but Henry grabbed my arm.

"That'll be no place for you," he said, his eyes flicking to my stomach.

I'd almost forgotten the lie. Had it not been dark, he might have seen the red flush of my cheeks as guilt slammed into me. We'd brought the mob, and they would suffer for it. Just because they were good people. Kind even.

"Grey," I hissed. "We have to do something."

He'd led the horse out of the barn, though it neighed and protested, likely still spooked from Kirsi's attempted help.

"I'm thinking," he snapped. "That mob is going to be here within the next five minutes. That's not a lot of time for genius masterminding."

"Not to worry, my boy." Henry clapped him on the shoulder. "We've got a plan already. The second wagon is on the north side of the barn. Get old Hank hooked up and we'll be along."

"What does that even mean?" I asked, rushing beside Grey.

Kirsi's voice popped up out of nowhere, quiet, so as not to be overheard. "You guys aren't very observant. Did you not see all the dried herbs and vials in the house?"

"Everyone has that, Kir." I looked over my shoulder as Grey backed the horse up to a wagon we hadn't seen before, covered in stretched canvas. The crowd of humans, though still only walking, grew closer. "Three minutes, max."

"Not here. Weren't you listening? That's a sign of witchcraft. The old couple are pretending to be witches. Something fun is about to happen."

She beamed, and if I could have swatted her arm, I would have.

"Your idea of fun is creepy," Grey said, hooking the last belt into place.

Kirsi swirled around him, near giddy, but my head began to pound, and I couldn't concentrate on her excitement. The lack of sleep and single meal, alongside the heavy emotions, caught up to me. I swayed, and Grey caught my elbow.

"Okay?" His green eyes narrowed as he held onto my arm.

I sighed. "I'm fine."

"Here they come," Kirsi whispered, vanishing again.

The backdoor to Henry and Victoria's house slammed open, one side falling off the hinges as their small forms moved backward, watching the house. The mob couldn't see us from the road, but they'd find us soon.

"Shouldn't we be racing off?" I asked the old man. "Wait, what is that?"

"It's a fuse." He unwound the bulky spool in his hand, the rope dripping wet, as he continued his hurried backward steps.

"Into the wagon, dears," Victoria called, the panic in her voice barely audible.

Grey's eyes glistened, and I couldn't help but see a hint of his cousin within them. Vengeance was always excusable in the Fire Coven, and these humans had a score to settle with their daughter's executioners.

He took the reins, hopping onto the bench seat behind the horse. I worried that a single stallion wouldn't get us out of there fast enough while pulling a wagon, and we sat atop the hill, staring down the descent. Hopefully, he could keep up with the heavy load barreling forward. Victoria slid to the middle, and I scooted in along the edge, but half my bottom hung off as I braced myself.

The reins rippled through the air before a single snap sent us flying, with Henry on the back of the wagon, holding onto his spool as he fed a line of saturated rope down the hill.

Squeezing my eyes shut, I prayed to the goddess we'd live to see the bottom. The wagon surged faster and faster and faster until I was sure the horse was running for his life; confident he was about to be trampled by the cargo he hauled.

"Woah," Henry called from behind us. "Slow it down."

Grey reached to the side of him, pushing down on the metal lever, the brake squealing and protesting against the friction of the wheel. Struggling, he tossed the reins to me so he could grab the bar with two hands. I pulled back on the smooth leather straps, hardly able to see in the dark and worried sick for the horse as he threw his head back, still dashing, but fighting the harness.

"Kir?" I hissed, aware Victoria would hear, but what choice did we have if the horse didn't stop?

"On it," she whispered into my ear.

One moment the horse was running for his life, the brake in Grey's strong arms ready to snap, the next he whinnied, slowing considerably before rising up on his hind legs and kicking at the space before him.

Terrifying as it was, we came to a stop. Grey leapt from his seat, dashing toward Henry, who must have jumped from the wagon.

"Come on." Victoria patted my leg. "It's time."

Sharp pain shot through my thigh at the hidden stab wound, but she didn't see me wince as she climbed down, lifting a satchel from over her head. At the top of the hill, the orange glow of lanterns surrounded the house before disappearing within the backdoor Henry had kept ajar.

"They don't know we've left. Hurry," Victoria pleaded.

"I've lost the damn rope," Henry growled. "The horse was too fast."

I didn't want to imagine what would have happened to the elderly couple had Grey not been there to handle that dangerous brake. But there was no time to think of that as he grabbed the shard of flint from the woman's hands and darted up the steep hill.

"Grey, no," I cried, taking one step and then two after him.

But it was too late. As stubborn as Bastian, he would see this through. Vengeance for the people that had shown us kindness. The pounding in my head continued as I watched him move like a shadow, powerful legs carrying him up the hill until he jerked to the right, bending to grab the rope he'd found.

"They'll leave soon. We weren't quick enough," Victoria cried, the devastation in her old voice so overwhelmingly sad. "We failed."

"No. Look," Henry said, pointing.

Grey's silhouette hid most of the details, but he'd stopped, crouching. Within seconds, the fuse sparked to life, the flame he'd thrown from the flint racing for the house.

"We've doused the place in the same oil," Victoria explained. "The dried flowers all over will catch fire, causing enough smoke to blind them until they can't get out."

"You really thought this through," I whispered, watching for only seconds before the house became engulfed in flames.

The witch hunters screamed. Grey raced back down the hill to my side, looping his arm with mine, as he deliberately turned and walked me back to the wagon as the shrieking grew louder. The initial smell of smoke and ash filled the air. My stomach turned.

"We need to go," he mumbled into my ear. "This isn't going to end well."

"I have a feeling it's already over," I said, jutting my chin toward the old couple, who'd turned as well, hustling toward us.

"There's more of 'em out front than I'd thought," Henry said. "Best be off before they come after us."

"Let them come," Victoria sneered, eyes glued to the house once more.

I knew that look, the one of wild abandon and no regrets. She'd die here, just to prove to them they could no longer hurt her. I couldn't say I blamed her, but the shouts of the burning people should have shaken her more than it did.

"They'll be coming after us, no matter what," Grey said, pointing toward the shapes of two men stumbling down the hill.

"Can you get in the back?" Henry shouted, scurrying to Victoria to pull her toward the wagon's front.

"We'll manage," Grey answered, yanking me toward the opposite side.

We were no more than halfway in when the snap of the reins rang through the air and the stallion was moving, slowly to start, thank the goddess, but it was still a scramble. Crammed in between pieces of disassembled furniture and trunks with clothes, the ride would be rough and without comfort.

The voices bellowing at us faded into the distance, and only then did I realize we had no idea where we were headed, and I hadn't thought to make sure Kir was there.

"Kirsi?" I whispered.

No answer.

I gave Grey a wide-eyed look and whipped open the cloth panel, hissing her name. "Kirsi!"

"I'm here. Watching the humans. Just in case."

Grey sank back into the small amount of space we had, lifting a copper pot from below his elbow, and then the arm of a rocking chair from behind his back, so he could shuffle, letting me sit sandwiched between him and a crate of food. The canvas over the top of us flapped in the wind, and I had to believe Grey and Victoria would trade spots, leaving the men up front, as soon as we could stop to arrange for any comfort. Or maybe they would drop us on the side of the road, content to proceed with their plan without strangers. I would have been completely fine with that option.

Pressing both of my palms to my temple, I prayed to ease the pain of the headache that continued to plague me. So much pressure had built behind my eyes, trying to focus on anything for too long caused immeasurable agony. I swiped at a small trickle from my nose, pulling my fingers away to see blood.

Grey sucked in a breath. "What the hell, Raven?"

"I ... I don't know," I said, plucking a cloth from an abandoned drawer. "You don't think it could be the Harrowing, do you? Coming back for me?"

He shook his head, swallowing hard. "There's no magic here. The panic attacks, the headache earlier, the bloody nose now... I don't think you're supposed to be in the human lands, Raven."

6

KIRSI

He was there, among the men barreling down the hill. The man with pitch black eyes who'd seen Raven in the alley seconds after she changed into the stolen dress. His towering form, larger than life, was made more severe as he strode forward, steps heaving and determined. Unlike the others, he held no lantern and did not scream. The shadows and darkness of night were a companion to his severity.

He couldn't see me. No one here could when I chose to be invisible. But those cold eyes pierced the night as we raced away. A very small part of me wanted to stop running. To let him reach me and see what he would do with that damnation within his soul. But I worried I wouldn't find the others if I abandoned them.

"Kir, get in here," Grey demanded.

"Honestly, Grey. I'm probably the safe—What the fuck happened?" I jerked to a stop, darting toward Raven who held a folded cloth to her nose. It was too dark to see the color, but light enough to see the handkerchief was covered in blood.

"Something's wrong," Raven whispered, her voice muffled behind the fabric she pressed to her face.

"I feel fine," Grey said. "Does it make you feel sick to be here?"

Shaking my head, I lifted my hand to her brow, worried. Just before touching her, I remembered I couldn't feel her anyway and backed off. "I wouldn't know the difference. I was only back home for minutes before Raven stormed the castle and..." My voice broke, refusing to say the words that might hurt her further, knowing I'd been too hard on her before. "You know."

He nodded.

"But I feel whole. No aches or pains beyond the numbness I believe all wraiths have, and the desolation."

Memories of Raven standing in the forest with blood pouring from her eyes, ears and nose came flooding back to me. Her shooting into the air as if suspended by ropes, her head falling back. The scream that might've broken the world as she hung, arms outstretched. The witches that swarmed and pushed and pushed and pushed to save her. I thought she'd die that night. A thousand witches witnessing the Harrowing strike again.

"Could it be..." my voice faded away when Grey shook his head.

"There's no magic here at all. I can't even begin to feel the pit of my power. The markings are all gone. It can't be the Harrowing. It's something else."

"Do you think we should get out of the wagon?" Raven asked, her soft blue eyes searching both of ours for answers.

"We've left the mob behind, but they will chase this couple. If we don't want to be tied up with them, we need to part ways." Grey ran his fingers through his hair, shifting as if the wooden floor below him might be more comfortable in a different position.

"I saw the look in that man's eyes," I said quietly. "It's the same look Scoop would get while hunting. He's never going to stop. And he knows what you look like. We should put a little more space between us before we split up."

"Okay," Raven whispered, her voice a near rasp. "I think I'll sleep now."

She nearly fell onto Grey's shoulder as her eyes closed. We shared a wary glance, but said nothing more as her breathing slowed.

THE UNBOUND WITCH

"A DAY'S WALK?" GREY ASKED HENRY AGAIN AS THE SUN PEEKED OVER the mountain on the horizon, pushing away the final remnants of the fog we'd traveled through in the early morning hours.

We stood next to a small stream, cascading over slick rocks, the landscape of grassy hills, splattered with sparse clusters of trees. The air didn't hold a trace of smoke, embers, or even ash. I wasn't sure how far we'd gone during the night, but Raven had only woken long enough for Grey to shift some items around in the back of the wagon so she could lay down on some of the stiff blankets we'd grabbed from the old people's death trap of a home. Even when Victoria had swapped places and I'd taken guard over her, she'd barely shifted.

"A long day's walk," Henry confirmed. "Just follow the stream north. You'll come to a crossroads, continue on the northeast path and you'll find it."

Grey held out a stiff arm, but Henry pulled him into a hug. "You saved our lives, son. Thank you."

"Don't burn any more houses down with a getaway plan you haven't practiced."

It was odd to watch him with the old-timer, looking down at him as if he'd been the one in command. He might have been the high and mighty cousin to King 'Do As I Say', but he carried himself as if he'd been giving commands for years. But then I supposed he had, representing the king to the witches for most of his life.

"You gonna die?" I asked Raven as soon as the oldies were gone.

"No." She pressed her wrist to her forehead. "I'm feeling better now that we've eaten again, and I had a chance to rest. I think it was just the stress of the last couple of days."

"Oh yes," I teased. "I always get stress nosebleeds. How 'bout you, Grey?"

"At least once a day."

Raven rolled her eyes. "You know what? I think I liked it better when you two didn't get along."

I reached forward, flicking the back of Grey's ear. "I'm pretty sure we've always gotten along."

"How are the legs?" he asked, eyes looking down at Raven's thighs.

"I'll manage. Just as long as you stop reminding me about it."

We strode in silence, confident we'd find the town with Eden Mossbrook by the end of the day. Within ten minutes, I was already bored of swaying back and forth and around them as they walked. I'd stopped in front of Grey three times, forcing him to pass through my figure. I felt a swirl of his emotions in each instance. The final time I'd done it, he'd threatened to expose me to the humans. When I'd begged him to do it for sheer entertainment, he ceased talking altogether.

"Let's play a game," I offered, hoping to pass the time.

Raven's hair swirled around her in the wind. She grabbed the loose tendrils, twisting her hair into a simple long braid as she asked, "What kind of game?"

"Majority vote wins. Who do you think would win in a footrace? Ophelia or Endora?"

Grey snorted. "Ophelia, hands down."

"What?" Raven gasped. "No way. She nearly died in the poison Trial. It'd be Endora for sure."

"Endora would never in her life run a footrace anyway," he retorted.

"That's not the point of the game, Firewing. And I'm with Rave. Endora would kick her ass, cane or no cane. That's a point for each of us, and you're in last place. Your question."

He remained quiet for a long time, picking up stones and throwing them as he thought it through. "Okay, Storm Coven, Moss Coven and River Coven are all in a three-way battle. Who wins?"

"Are we going based on numbers or skill?" I asked.

"Both for sure. All things considered, who wins?"

"Moss Coven," Raven and I blurted simultaneously.

Grey threw another flat rock as we shared a smile. It was genuine and beautiful, and something within this moment felt like everything would be okay. That we could find a new normal, and I needed that.

"I would have gone with Storm," he answered.

I drew back. "Why Storm?"

"You know," he said, waving his fingers through the air. "What with all the lightning and stuff."

Raven swatted his arm. "You know as well as we do that just because they are from the Storm Coven doesn't mean they would have a higher affinity for lightning than a witch from the Moss Coven. It's bigger than that. Endora is far more cunning, and she's been grooming her coven longer."

"Exactly," I said. "And the Moss Coven's power is stronger when they are just barefoot. They can ground themselves anywhere. Storm Coven has to be in the middle of the storm for that kind of amplification."

He shook his head. "No. I still think Moss is out. They haven't had their Grimoire for a long time. I'm pretty sure they are losing their power."

Raven and I both slammed to a stop. "Is that confirmed?"

He dropped the rocks in his hands, eyes widening as he took in our shocked faces. "Yes."

Raven slowly shook her head. "I mean, we wondered, but didn't know for sure. Endora hides everything."

"Some of the Fire Coven elders are confident. It makes sense, though. We think if a Grimoire is destroyed, all of the witches in that coven lose their power. But she's been so desperate to get into the castle, the attacks have grown in number." He lifted a shoulder. "Like I said, it makes sense."

Raven started walking again, her steps careful. "If the Moss Coven is losing their power, why haven't they actually said anything to anyone else? Asked for help?"

I swooped to her side. "Because then they'd be the weakest, and Endora would never approve. I guarantee she gaslights her coven about it."

"Willow and Nym arm wrestling," Grey said to change the subject. "No magic. Who wins?"

"Nym," we answered again in unison.

That name... that single mention hollowed me. It took me straight back to stolen kisses and budding love. And then to Scoop, a topic I immediately shut out of my mind. I couldn't go there or grieve for him. I just wasn't ready. I let myself be swept back into our game, if for no other reason than reality was far more gutting.

He clicked his tongue. "You guys are cheating. Just because you love her."

The sorrow deepened within me. I couldn't think of that golden witch, or her soft touches and lingering gazes, without feeling sadness or regret or something somewhere in between. Part of me longed to see her face and the other felt so embarrassed to be… like this, I couldn't even imagine it.

"I have a real question," I answered with a smile. "Who is in charge, now that…"

"Bastian's gone?" Grey asked. "It's okay, you can say it. And the answer is not much of one. There's always been a plan in place, but with no heirs, anyone is able to rival what's happening. The Old Barren will take charge for now, securing the castle alongside the Fire Coven. But there's no telling how long that will hold if the witches descend."

"So basically, we have no idea?" Raven slowed her pace.

He looked up at the sky, as if the clouds would orientate him in a new world. "Basically."

"But the Thrashings will stop now? Or will The Old Barren keep those up?"

"The Thrashings were nicknamed that to make them something unforgivable."

If I had a heartbeat, I think it would have ceased beating. "They were unforgivable in more than just a name, Grey."

"No, Kir." Raven cut in. "The Thrashings were not the king. Well, not entirely."

"Then what were they?"

Grey cleared his throat, his gaze a million miles away as he swooped down and picked up another rock. "It started in the Fire Coven. The other coven leaders had been trying to kidnap the witches in our family to force them to give all the information about Bastian they could. To map out the castle and explain how to get to the Grimoires. It got so bad, he stopped visiting any relatives." His chin dropped as quickly as his voice. "Except me."

"But people died."

"Bastian would send soldiers, or go in himself, to rescue the witches that'd been taken. He would save them by any means necessary, which sometimes meant a death. But it was never a massacre. Never what they made it out to be."

I shook my head. "But people witnessed them."

"No," Raven said with a somber voice. "People only saw the aftermath. What the coven leaders did to those that lived but lost the other witches."

"But you can't possibly think *every* other coven leader is in on this. We met them. They weren't all bad. Endora was an asshole, but all of them?"

Raven jerked to a stop, her hands twisting into the skirt of her black gown. "All five of those witches stood on the points of that star and forced death upon me. All five watched me writhe in pain and did nothing. Collectively, they saw your death through, knowing it would be the one thing that could have forced me to kill Bastian. And only when I refused with my own free will did they reveal their hidden plan. They are all guilty."

I couldn't believe the conviction in her voice as she spoke those vengeful words. Raven had always been the levelheaded one. The one that searched for reason and held her composure, even when the world around her shattered. She'd never condemn an innocent party. If her opinion was absolute, then so was mine.

"How long?" I asked, staring at the edge of the village in the distance.

The trees grew thicker here, further away from the sea. The village resembled one we'd find at home much more than the previous one. Quaint cottages were placed on an even grid of cobblestone streets. No stories to the homes, just simple wooden planks, deep green lawns and a plethora of scattered gardens. No wonder Eden had chosen to reside in this town.

"I wish I knew, Kir," Grey said. "But we can't take any chances with witch hunters again. Invisible or stay here."

"I hate being a wraith," I grumbled.

"Aw. Come on. It's not so bad. Look at all the fun stuff you can do. You can be invisible whenever you want. You can walk through walls. Eavesdrop like a pro. And probably a bunch of other cool shit we don't even know about."

"You're talking to me like a child right now, Firewing."

He wiggled his eyebrows. "Is it working?"

"No!" I huffed, going invisible.

"When you two are done …" Raven cut in, her hands on her hips.

She tried to have a firm tone, but I'd been watching her closely. Her breathing had grown more labored, dark circles had formed under her eyes, her steps had become slower. She hadn't once complained. Still, the evidence was clear. The human lands were rejecting her for some reason we couldn't understand. If we stayed here, it was likely we'd be lighting her funeral pyre within a week.

Grey rubbed his hands together. "Okay, for the plan. I know Eden doesn't live in that town. She's somewhere around here, though, and I'm guessing if there are witch hunters, she's lying low. She's easy to identify. Half of her hair is black, and half is white. She has one light eye and one dark. So, she will be cloaked if she is in the village at all. But I think she's going to be nestled into that forest on the side of the mountain. It's similar enough to the Moss Coven, she'd feel at home there."

"So, why do we need to go to the town?" I asked, still pissed about having to hide.

Grey shot me a look, his eyes shifting to Raven and back to me. "We need a horse. There's no way we're going to make it before dark otherwise."

Of course. By we, he meant her. And he wasn't wrong. She'd begun to sway as she walked, as if drunk and not sick. We carried on cautiously. Scarred from our previous experience. But as we approached, with still a good bit of daylight left, we walked through the town with a purpose.

"See the horse, darling?" Grey asked, speaking to me under the guise of a conversation with Raven.

He'd want me to spook it, chase it off to where he'd catch him. But the horse was tied up to a half-broken post outside the tavern and, spooked or not, it wasn't going anywhere.

"Let me go investigate," I whispered into his ear.

He nodded, glancing over to Raven with that same concern in his eyes. I didn't wait around, dashing into the tavern through the wall and scouring the drunks inside. The room was full of unbathed men hunched over their tankards. My eyes followed the fat, tabby cat taking careful steps along the bar as its gaze landed on me. I shifted behind a pillar stained with vomit and ale, never more grateful that I couldn't smell whatever the cesspool of an establishment might be leaking. Confident most of the men had spent their day's wages on ale, it didn't take long to find the only one with spurs on his boots and leather gloves tucked into his pocket. He was undoubtedly the one the horse belonged to. And lucky for us, based on his drooling, he was also the drunkest oaf in the bar. I smiled, concocting a simple plan of chaos.

Thinking of Raven and how desperately we needed to find safety, I concentrated with all my might as I shoved the oversized bloke into another man that was attempting to weave through the tightly packed tables. He fell directly off the wooden stool, his tankard crashing to the ground as hard as he did. Those sober enough to notice laughed as the barmaid left her post to grab a mop, grumbling.

While the two men began to bicker back and forth, one shoved the other, and before I could even stir more trouble, the whole place erupted into a brawl. Elbows flew, fists raged forward, and I was pretty sure I saw a tooth knocked out of a mouth.

Hatred bred tension, and in a town where half the population was crammed into a disease-ridden tavern just to escape reality, rocking the proverbial boat had been easier than I could have imagined. Thank the goddess.

"Take him," I told Grey, who waited against the wall outside the back of the tavern. "No need to cause a scene. Just grab the reins, and let's go. No one in there is going to notice."

"What about the people in the town?" Raven asked, her voice stronger than when I'd left her.

"No one is paying any attention to him. Feeling better?"

She nodded, pushing off the wall. "Just needed a little rest."

"Wait here." Grey circled the building and was back minutes later with the beast he'd freed from the post out front. "We'll take him out of town the way we came instead of directly through, so we aren't drawing attention."

I kept my distance as they mounted the horse and ambled back toward the edge of the village. They would have been far more inconspicuous if not for Grey's massive size, but at least we'd accomplished something. Or, I had, as a wraith. Stealing a horse was no small feat, and I'd helped. A tiny kernel of pride swept through me. An emotion I hadn't experienced yet, trapped in this ethereal body. It was only a horse, but as we continued on the path toward Eden Mossbrook, I knew it wasn't. How many people could have done what I did today? Not one. I'd passed through a wall.

7

RAVEN

"How many people have you killed?"

I whipped my head toward Kirsi's wild question, preparing for dizziness or tracers in my vision to follow, but whatever had plagued me was fading away, thank the goddess. It felt as if I'd taken the poison from our first Trial again, but it was finally dissipating with only the faint headache remaining. Kirsi and Grey had been playing the game of questions back and forth the entire day.

We were barely out of the town, Grey confident Eden would be hiding instead of making herself known. Still, we checked our backs frequently as we moved, if not for the stolen horse's owner, then the dark eyes of the Seeker somehow finding us.

"Thirty-two," Grey answered casually, his voice rumbling down my back from where he sat behind me on the horse.

"You don't even have to stop to count?" she asked from above us.

We'd learned if she stayed out of the horse's peripheral vision, her presence didn't bother him enough to fidget.

"No. Every death is a mark upon me. They may be necessary, but that doesn't mean I've enjoyed them."

"How many deaths do you think the Dark King had?" Kirsi pressed. "Just guess."

I held my breath, waiting for his answer.

"Probably less than me."

She snorted, circling above as the horse weaved around a giant oak tree. "There's no way. Even if he didn't kill all the witches in the Thrashings, he's guilty by proxy for each of the deaths he ordered."

Grey was quiet then, his hands loosening on the leather reins as he sighed. "I know."

"What do you think we should expect from Eden Mossbrook? A warm welcome or instant tension?" I asked, staring ahead at the terrain that would soon turn to rock and a steady incline surrounded by fir trees.

"It's hard to say. If she truly is on this mountain, I have a feeling she'll find us before we find her. Secluded as she is, who knows how the years have changed her? The shifters that come home on rotation have their words bound on arrival, so no information gets out."

"Listen, if I had to run away from home and found myself here, I'd probably hide in a mountain forest, too," Kirsi said. "These humans are delightfully crazy."

"Says the wraith that went back to study the witch hunter."

Kirsi paused. "You knew?"

Even from behind me, I could hear the smile in his voice. "I guessed. You just confirmed."

She vanished for three seconds before Grey flinched, shifting. "If I knew how to fuck with a wraith, I'd do it right now."

She floated in front of us, an invisible leg hanging over each side of the horse as if she rode his neck. "The one and only perk."

"Not true," I said, studying her for genuine feelings. She was hiding behind her sarcasm, and I still couldn't decide if the idea of who she was now was growing on her or not. "You can throat punch people now and not even have to show yourself."

Her brows drew tight, lips pressing into a thin line. "I can barely flick Grey's ear. I shoved a guy off a barstool though, so I guess that's progress. You can stop looking at me like that. I'd still rather be gone completely than… this." She picked at the billowing sleeve of her see-through ivory shirt, her eyes doubling. "Oh fuck."

"What?" Grey snapped, jerking upright.

"I'm going to be wearing this forever, aren't I?"

I looked down at the simple slacks she'd been wearing the day she died. "It could be worse? At least it's not a full ball gown."

She groaned and vanished, content to process her feelings where no one could see her. Some things never changed, I guessed. Glancing around Grey's large form behind me, I peeked in the direction of the town. If someone were to pursue us for stealing a horse, it wouldn't take them long to catch up with such a slow pace.

Grey looked back as well, probably thinking the same thing. "You haven't asked me a single question all day."

I lifted a shoulder. "It's kind of been a horrible day, in case you haven't noticed."

"Not the adventuring type, Moonstone?"

"Not while I'm potentially dying or something."

"I'm hoping for the 'or something,'" he said, pressing his heels into the horse as he scanned the horizon for the millionth time that day.

We picked up speed for no more than two minutes before he pulled back on the reins. He inhaled a sharp breath and held it as he hissed Kirsi's name. She didn't come.

"I'm sorry for this," he whispered before wrapping his arm securely around my stomach and pulling me as close to him as I could possibly get.

I waited for the panic to set in, the dread to overcome me, rising. But there was a preternatural calmness as I realized something was wrong, and the man holding me might be my only safety in a world with no magic.

"Someone's close," he breathed, scanning the space scattered with trees, even searching the thicker band at the base of the snow-capped mountain. "No talking. No arguing. If I tell you to go, you stay on this horse and ride directly west. Keep the setting sun in front of you and the moon at your back. Talk to no one. I'll find you."

"I don't like this plan."

His hand pressed harder against my stomach. "I didn't ask for your approval, Moonstone."

It seemed the slight breeze that had guided us through the chilly autumn day vanished, Grey's warm chest against my back, his massive figure curled around me, an alarming reminder that he also had no magic, only the small knife he carried. He'd have to be a physical barrier, if nothing else. And he didn't owe me that kind of sacrifice.

We slowed to a snail's pace, still moving forward, but only just, as two figures stepped out from behind the trees in front of us. Both men were the size of Grey, which didn't bode well for our odds. My mind worked a million miles an hour, trying to discern which looked the most menacing. The one with white hair and a scar above his eye, or the slightly older looking one with sharp golden eyes and twists of dark hair partially concealed beneath a hood.

Grey pulled back on the reins before squeezing me with his thighs. With trembling hands, I took the leather straps from him as he slid expertly to the ground and took one confident step toward the dangerous men.

They didn't speak as they stared each other down. I closed my eyes, willing my thunderous heart to settle as I considered whether I'd really leave Grey behind and run, or if I'd stay and find a way to help him.

But what could I do? I'd been weakened by headaches and nausea from the day. My injured legs wouldn't carry me for long, and I had no clue where Kirsi had gone. I doubted she'd go far.

Grey took another silent step, and the giant men matched it, sharing a menacing smile. Directly behind the man with the scar, a rock the size of a dinner plate shifted. Had I not been paying attention, I would have missed it. *Kirsi.* I straightened my back on the horse, looking down at Grey and back to the men, weapons drawn.

That rock moved again, only this time, it wasn't an ear flick, not a shove; she'd grabbed a tangible object, lifting it in the air. I watched for any sign that Grey had seen her, but he didn't so much as breathe, taking another step forward.

"What are you doing here?" the black man with golden eyes asked, his voice as smooth as a deep, soulful song.

Grey's swallow was audible. "Just passing through."

Again, the men shared a look. Kirsi's weapon of choice floated higher and higher, though I was clearly the only one that noticed she was about to bash one of their skulls in.

The man with ashy white hair cut a glance to me. "The Dark King's cousin doesn't just pass through the human lands, Grey Firewing."

8
RAVEN

Hearing Grey addressed by his full name, in a land where no one should have known not only what, but who, he was, twisted something deep within me. I believed for a long, long time the human lands, though void of power, were likely safer than our own treacherous home.

Kir hadn't moved at all, not an inch, with that hovering rock. Grey stood as tall as ten men, the tension reaching a level so high I could feel it in my veins. The world silenced as he took another step forward.

"Where you headed, *witch?*"

Grey froze, looking to the sky as if in prayer. I didn't have to hear the words to know what was in his heart. He was going to tell me to run. But how could I leave him to the mercy of these men when he hadn't left me?

My eyes flicked to the suspended boulder above the scarred man's head, casting a slight shadow over his white, shoulder length hair. He was young, maybe only a few years older than me, but his eyes were full of malice. In one motion, Grey yelled and ran forward as Kirsi dropped the rock. Both men sprinted for our companion, the stone missing its target by mere inches.

I squeezed my eyes shut, pulling back on the reins, refusing to watch them shred him to pieces. I couldn't witness another death. Not now, maybe not ever. But as laughter filled the air, I peeled my eyes open to see the three men with their arms around each other, their happy reunion a slap to my face. A cruel joke.

"Do I smell a ghosty?" the beautiful, scarred man asked, looking around. "Best keep hidden, love. It's not safe here."

"Were you followed?" the older, black man asked, his amber eyes flicking to me before assessing the horse.

"I don't think so, but it's possible." Grey clapped the man on his back. "You're looking a bit old there, Tor."

"Blame the pup," he said, jerking his chin toward the scarred man, who was spinning in circles as he surveyed the surrounding area.

"There was a hunter in the last town we were in. He was on our trail, but I think we lost him when we split from our company." Grey swept a hand toward me. "This is Raven Moonstone. She'll be under our protection indefinitely."

I lifted a brow, eyes narrowed on Grey. "And who are your *friends*?"

"The pretty boy there is Atlas," he said, pointing to the one with the scar. "And this is Torryn."

Atlas jerked his head, thick hair falling into his eyes as he smirked. The leather clothing he wore, clean but worn, seemed almost too tight for him.

Torryn placed his large hand onto his chest and dipped his chin respectfully before those stunning eyes met mine. "A pleasure, my lady."

"Always the chivalrous one." Grey pulled the reins from my hands, ignoring my glare as he instructed the others. "Let's go. Before Kirsi grabs any more boulders."

A smile crept across my face as he stumbled to the side unprompted.

"You deserved that," Kirsi said, causing Atlas to whip around in a circle, still trying to find her.

"Tell me about the hunter." Torryn took the lead, winding left and right over a trail easiest for the horse to get up the gradual mountainside. The colorful autumn trees mixed with the firs, reminiscent of home as they grew thicker and thicker.

"Raven overheard a conversation. They referred to him as the Seeker. Black hair and eyes, about this tall," he said, holding out his hand slightly below his shoulder.

A low growl came from Atlas as he listened. Shifter, for sure, I'd decided.

"He's been around these parts. If he caught your trail, you probably didn't lose him as easily as you think. Unless he followed your companions."

I thought of the old couple and what might happen if he captured them. They said they had a place to hide, to start over. But they'd have to get there first. A very small part of me hoped the hunter was chasing us instead. At least then we'd know they were safe.

"Hard to say," Grey said. "As far as I can tell, we didn't have anyone following us, but I'm still not used to the lack of magic here."

"Aw. Our little witch is suffering." Atlas slammed into Grey with his shoulder. "Try being here for five years."

"You've been here for five years?" I asked, unable to help the gasp that slipped from my mouth.

"They're shifters," Grey explained quietly. "On a rotating guard, ordered by the king."

The king. Grey hadn't told them yet of Bastian's fate. How would they react when they found out I killed him? More worry settled in my gut with each step we took. That conversation would have to happen, and I'd have to deal with the fallout. And when we got home, I'd have to do it again.

"Don't make it sound so honorable," Atlas said, sharing a crooked smile with Grey. "Tor and I drew the short sticks."

"That bad?" Grey asked.

"No," Torryn answered. "Aside from the occasional witch hunt we've had to deflect, it's been quite peaceful. Eden doesn't leave the security of the woods, but Atlas and I venture into town. Atlas has taken a liking to a certain tavern. Or rather, the women of the tavern have taken a liking to his pretty face." He chuckled. "They think that scar you gave him is handsome."

"See?" Grey wrapped his arm around Atlas' shoulders, pulling him downward as he ran his knuckles back and forth in the shifter's messy white hair. "I just made you prettier."

"Happy to return the favor." Atlas grunted, crouching low to escape Grey's muscled arms.

"In your dreams, Pup." Grey held him tight for several more steps before finally releasing the shifter, who promptly shoved him with both hands, causing him to trip and fall to the ground.

Torryn shared a half smile with me before grabbing both of the fighting men by the collars and yanking them to their feet, as if he'd done it a thousand times.

A quiet snort brushed my ear before Kirsi whispered, "Who knew Grey was such a man-child?"

"It's nice to see him happy." I smiled. "We rarely get to see that side of the shifters."

"Animals," she added, though I could hear the lightness to her words. The laughter somewhere far away, if only a trace to her haunted tone.

"So?" Atlas asked, tilting his head toward me as he swept the dirt from his black pants.

Grey shook his head. "Better to tell the tale once."

Torryn nodded, reaching up to pat the thick neck of my stolen horse. "I imagine anything that has taken you away from the castle and dropped you here is quite a tale."

They avoided paying much attention to me as we went, laughing like old friends. I didn't miss the way they watched our surroundings, even now, hidden deep within the forest they expertly navigated.

"Tell me Ash has been asking when I'll return," Atlas said, pulling back a branch so I could pass below it.

I felt guilty riding the horse as they walked, but no one seemed bothered. And I knew I couldn't do it. Even now, my energy drained. My eyelids grew heavier, my limbs ached.

"She married Tomas last spring," Grey said, his voice serious.

Atlas jerked to a stop, whipping around, his blue eyes wide. "Tomas? The fucking fox?"

"The one and only," Grey answered, holding his grim face. "Said she couldn't sit around and wait on a guy that wouldn't commit or make her toes curl."

Torryn burst into laughter, the sound deep and smooth through the darkness of the dense forest around us. Grey cracked, his own laughter a sound that twisted my heart, even as Atlas stormed ahead.

"You guys are dicks."

"I take it Ash is a shifter?" I asked quietly, torn on whether I should intrude on their conversation.

"Atty has been friends with Ash since they were pups. She's a wolf, too. The fastest you've ever seen," Grey explained. His eyes flashed to Atlas, a conversation happening without words before the shifter nodded and Grey continued. "After he lost someone he loved, he tried to get over her using Ash."

"But," Torryn jumped in, "Ash wasn't having it. She said she found him... What's the word she used the day we left?"

"Asinine." Grey chuckled, snapping his fingers. "That was it, wasn't it?"

"She meant it in a loving way." Atlas pulled back another branch, letting us all pass him by. "And I don't need or want a partner, especially one that... the fox? Seriously?"

"Is it safe for me to come out yet?" Kir asked, so close to me I jumped at the tone of her voice.

"Only if you're pretty," Atlas joked, releasing the tree limb he held.

In one fell swoop, before he could see it happening, Kir hauled a branch back and whacked him right in the face.

"Okay. Fair. I probably deserved that," he said, rubbing his brow.

Grey clutched his chest in laughter. "Kirsi Moondance, my friends."

She appeared beside Atlas, the ethereal glow lighting the surrounding forest in a soft blue tone. A beacon in the darkness.

"Pleasure," she said with just enough bite, Atlas moved away.

"Since Raven is too polite to ask, what's the story here? Who are you guys?"

"We're guards for Eden," Torryn answered.

The horse, unsettled by her presence, threw his head back, whinnying as he tried to move away from her. I clutched my thighs to hold on as she swooped higher, out of his sight, though I could tell she was annoyed.

"I got that much. But how do you know each other?"

"We were summit mates," Atlas answered.

She sighed. "I died as a witch. I've only been a wraith for about five minutes. I have no idea what that means."

"When a shifter turns eight years old, they have to do a solo run up the peak in the Moss Coven. Once you hit the summit, the trainers are there to begin your education. In order to complete it, you make a final run at seventeen up the highest peak in the Forest Coven with your summit mates. All in. All out."

He paused, and Grey cut in. "When Bastian left to join the shifters, his father was worried he would struggle, being only half, so he arranged it so that I could join them."

Torryn cleared his throat. "Ah. Yes. That's what happened. I'm afraid my memory isn't as good as it used to be."

"You're fifteen years older than we are Tor, stop acting like a grandpa," Atlas said, shoving his arm.

"The Moss Coven summit is just a steep hill compared to the highest mountain in the Forest territory," Grey continued. "Tor was our very unfortunate trainer."

"Eh. He was lucky we broke him in," Atlas said, though the fondness in his words wasn't lost on me.

"So, what? You had summer camping trips to learn how to sleep outside?" Kirsi asked, unimpressed.

"It was more than that, Ghosty. We trained with various weapons. We learned to *become* weapons ourselves. We learned to control the beast through our teen years when all we wanted to do was find women to—"

"I get it," she cut him off.

"Atty and I hated each other at first," Grey said. "We competed at everything. Shifter training is a lot like the Trials, only longer, and far more brutal. Fighting with no rules, pouring rain, and icy weather. Nothing matters besides cold hard soldiers, ready for battle."

"Against the witches?" I whispered.

"Against any enemy of the king," Grey corrected.

I could feel those green eyes on me, even through the darkness. The words he left unspoken circled my tiring mind. I was an enemy to the king. He was warning me to be prepared for the reaction when they learned of … what I'd done. Even in my mind, I couldn't push past the pain that seared my heart like an iron.

They continued their prattling, but I could no longer hear them as my thoughts eddied back and forth between moments of Bastian as the villain of my life and the savior of it. The fine line we'd walked together until the past healed over and we found contentment in each other. In the moments when we shut out the rest of the world, and there was only him and me and a promise of forever that was shattered far too soon.

I tried to swallow the lump in my throat, squeezing my eyes shut as a tear fell free. I wouldn't let them hear me sob. I was not the victim, though my heart protested. The missing piece throbbing within my chest. He'd been a boy once, laughing and playing with these men. Their memories were full of his happiness, a life he lived before I'd been in it. Through my silent tears, I pictured him with us now. Would he laugh as easily as they did? Would he hang his arms over their shoulders and remember his childhood in a happy light?

"Raven?" Kirsi whispered from beside me.

"My heart hurts." I said, because it did. And I just needed someone else to know that I was not okay.

"I know."

I swiped the tears from my cheeks, trying desperately to hide my despair. "I think I would have loved him, Kir. We just didn't get the time."

I felt her then. The cool arm wrapped around me, the head she laid on mine. And for the first time since my world broke into pieces, I felt seen.

"I have to let him go," I whispered. "But I don't think my heart is ready."

"You have a lifetime to let him go. You can hold on a little longer."

I nodded, more tears falling as I remembered all our stolen moments. The rawness he'd shown me in my dreams, when I'd wished for him to be that man so full of light and casual conversation. He'd wanted me to know the real Bastian. The man behind the mask.

The warm glow from a hanging lantern broke through the darkness ahead and, pushing away the last of my tears, I straightened my back, preparing to tell the shifters and Eden Mossbrook my truth. Horrified as they may be, they needed to know the world was changing.

The quaint cottage, built from the trees around us, sat nestled into the mountainside forest. Mostly hidden behind crawling ivy, the arched door was an homage to many of the Moss coven homes I'd seen.

"Can you believe we're about to meet her?" Kirsi asked, still hovering close to me. "Imagine the whole world thinking you were dead for over twenty-five years while you just hid in the human lands. Why do you think she did it?"

"She was running from her mother." I pulled back on the thin leather reins, remembering the harsh tone of Endora Mossbrook's words every time she spoke to me. "Can't say I blame her for that one."

"Indeed." Grey reached up to take my waist, helping me down from the stolen horse. "Are you okay?" he asked, his eyes shifting between mine.

"Fine now," I lied. "Just processing."

"I won't let anything happen to you. They will see reason."

I nodded, backing away from him toward Kir as the door swung open and a witch with no markings stepped out from her home. Sucking in a sharp breath, I changed my mind and shifted toward Grey. She was beautiful, if not brutal. Half of her hair was as white as the moon, falling down her back. The other half, so dark, it seemed to capture the light and devour it. One of her eyes was solid black, a steep contrast to the light hair on that side. The other, so white, she seemed to have no iris. Two halves of a whole; the descriptions I'd heard my whole life hadn't done her justice.

"Eden Mossbrook," Torryn said, a loving twinkle to his eye as he beheld the infamous missing witch. "This is Grey Firewing."

She twisted her face, something strange passing over her eyes as she held a hand out toward him. "I've heard so much about you, Grey. It's nice to meet you in person."

"Likewise." He smiled, dipping his chin before gesturing toward Kirsi and I. "Kirsi Moondance and Raven Moonstone."

Torryn stepped toward me, as if he'd felt my apprehension and deigned to provide an ounce of comfort with his calm presence. If he only knew. A very small part of me felt I should curtsy to the witch who had perplexed the world, but then I remembered that her choice to run from her mother had sent the world into a spiral of torture and heartache. Had she stayed, spoken whatever truth she'd been running from, perhaps our reality would be a different one.

Her strange eyes passed over Kirsi, landing on me before she gasped. "Goddess be damned, you look just like your mother."

9

RAVEN

Grey whipped his head to me as I processed the words she'd just spoken. "You know my mother?"

"Best come inside, dear," Eden said, before looking to the others. "See the horse is taken care of, would you?"

She moved to let us inside her home. The space was small and warm, covered in plants both hanging from the ceiling and in pots along handmade tables, and books stacked everywhere. Something was different, though. Off. Like an anomaly in an unmagical world. I scanned my eyes around the room, wondering why I could feel magic when I shouldn't have. Nothing significant. Like a flicker of light before it turned dark again.

Eden gestured to the cluttered table, and I sat across from her, a million questions swirling through my mind as I tried and failed to build a narrative that made sense. Grey took up so much of the cottage, I wondered what it would feel like with all three men inside. Still, he slid a spindled chair across the floor and sat backward on it, waiting patiently for Eden to speak.

"Me first then, it seems," she said, pouring hot water from an old kettle into three cups. "Where shall I start?"

"How do you know my mother?"

She smiled and, though her eyes were jarring, the juxtaposition of her features and expression made her more of an anomaly than she already was. "Yara Moonstone had just married your father when I left. We were friends. As close as we could be, living in different territories. My mother visited your grandmother's shop often. There was a particular youth elixir she liked, if I'm not mistaken."

She leaned back in her chair, blowing the steam from her delicate teacup, but then her brows furrowed, and she jerked upright, gasping.

"How did you survive the Harrowing?"

I scooted back in my chair. "How could you have known that?"

"The Harrowing is why I left. My father was hardly present, and my mother was a cruel woman."

"Still is," Grey cut in.

She settled again, as if preparing to tell a story she'd waited her whole life to tell, though I suspected she told it each time new guards came. "Many years ago, there was an announcement that peace would be forged between the witches and the shifters, ending our lifelong war. And with that peace, the shifter king would marry a witch of power. Because the Fire Coven ruled over the witches, their royal bloodlines dating back to before the Grimoire was split into seven, it was widely known that they would be the selected coven.

"My mother, and possibly even my father, had other plans. They found records and then met an ancient witch who told them of a dangerous type of magic. One that mixed conjuring and spelling, twisting intention within a seance until it became a curse."

I fidgeted in my wobbly chair, dread rising in my throat with razor sharp talons. She described the type of magic they used to force the death spell upon me, taking away any future magic I'd ever receive. Even now, I struggled to believe their sickening plan had been put in place all those years ago, before I was born. Before Bastian was born. Before there was even a chance to heal our world after the war.

Eden sipped her steaming tea. "I snuck into the gathering of six coven leaders, hiding to listen to my mother spew venom. I'd heard my parents whisper of it before, but this time they declared that the spell they called the Harrowing would be the answer to all their problems. The thirteenth witch born of power in each family line would die. They would consecrate the witches, recycling a full generation of magic, believing it would give them enough of an advantage to overthrow the shifters once and for all. The Harrowing would be our salvation. Sacrifice a few seedlings for the good of the forest."

Kirsi glided across the room until she hovered within an arm's reach of Eden, her slight blue light illuminating the witch's teacup. "Wait. Are you telling us the Harrowing targets specific witches? It's not a random act?"

"Yes. I am telling you that, Wraith. But there is more to this tale. Later, I snuck into my mother's rooms to find that list of witches. I was sick for days as those names swirled through my mind. When I saw your mother's, my oldest friend, beside the number twelve, I knew I had to do something. So, I lied. Stealing the Grimoire the morning I was to be presented to King Dristan as a potential bride, I traveled as fast as I could to warn your mother, to tell her that she could never reveal the truth to anyone or she may die. And then, I fled to the castle.

"Unbeknownst to anyone at that time, King Dristan had already fallen in love with his future wife, the newly appointed Fire Coven leader, Juliette. When I arrived, the coven Grimoire in my arms, I fell upon their mercy. Not as a potential bride, but as a young witch, trying to save the world from the damage my mother would bring upon it. I believed if she didn't have her Grimoire, she would not be able to unleash the Harrowing."

"Well, you were wrong on that account." Kir moved away from the old witch, holding my gaze. "Raven is the only one that's ever survived it."

All eyes fell on me, but Eden's were the most jarring. "How did you manage it?"

"I didn't. Not intentionally anyway. I was only fortunate that the coven leaders and a massive number of witches were nearby. They filled me with power, fighting it. Calling it off."

Eden shook her head, looking at Grey. "Why would they have saved her? They needed her to die."

"I don't think they expected it to work. No one anticipated Bastian to be nearby, to provide magic from the seventh coven. With all the other witches watching them, they couldn't have let her die, not without a show of trying to save her."

Of course. I hadn't considered that every single coven had been represented. And because every Moon Coven witch was there, it more than compensated for Tasa's absence. I'd been accidentally saved, thanks to the king that was no more. And when he'd told me that fact, I hadn't believed him.

"Do you think my mother… did something to try to protect me?"

"Oh, I'm quite sure of that, my dear." Eden reached across the table, taking my reluctant hand in hers. "Your grandmother was a fearsome witch that would have died protecting her family. Your mother was no different."

"My grandmother did die," I said quietly. "Protecting the Grimoire, not her family."

Eden pointed to the spine of a large book stacked below many others on the table. "I gave up my whole life protecting this one."

I wasn't ready. Was wholly unprepared to see that treasured book at the bottom of a casual pile as if it meant nothing. My heart leapt into my throat, Kirsi's audible gasp an echo of my own as we studied the ridges and grooves along the binding. That flicker of power pulsing now.

I pushed a wild curl from my face. "That's why they can't scry for you or the book. The human lands are masking you. But surely Endora has realized that by now."

"I agree. We've had a few run-ins with witches over the years. But the shifters have always—" She jerked her head to Grey before jumping out of her seat. "If you're here, then… who is protecting the other books?"

"Sit down, Eden." Grey kept his voice calm, though her frantic tone scared me.

The other Grimoires were no longer protected beyond the strength of the shifters. With Bastian's death, his magical barrier would die. They had to have known that. Not only had they removed him from power, but they'd also given themselves easier access to their most coveted treasure.

I turned slowly to Grey. "Your aunt. When she cast with two Grimoires..."

Eden nodded, slumping back into her seat. "She took the life and light from the Fire Coven that day with the smallest spell. If they learn... If my mother learns this..."

"That's why we're here. We need to get back as soon as possible."

"But the barrier?" Torryn asked, startling me, as I hadn't heard them return from tending to the horse.

"It's a risk you knew you'd take one day," Grey said, his casual posture a little too relaxed to be believable. He was worried. And I hadn't even considered it, lost in my own grief and guilt.

"You'll find the shipmaster tomorrow," Eden said to Atlas and Torryn. "It looks like we are headed home."

"We?" Kirsi asked.

"The witch hunters are getting closer and closer. The human lands aren't safe for me anymore. I'll either be discovered by my mother or attacked and eventually killed. It's time to face this, come what may."

Kirsi gritted her teeth, moving to the space between Eden and me. "All these years, the royal family has taken the blame for you. They've held your secret no matter the cost to them. And don't be fooled, that cost was great. Stories were spun. King Dristan didn't have a chance in hell of making peace as soon as the witches believed he'd murdered you and hid the Moss Coven Grimoire. And now you just *decide* it's time to go home? To put that thing back on the playing board? This is a mistake, and you know it."

Atlas stepped forward, Torryn just a pace behind him, as Grey rose from his seat.

"Kir," I whispered, standing.

The room swayed with me, rippling like a drop of water in a still pond. The last thing I remembered was Grey, all arms, lunging for me.

10

KIRSI

I swooped low enough to stare into Grey's emerald eyes. "Do you get it now? Something is wrong with her."

Grey laid Raven down on the couch, pressing the backs of his fingers to her brow. He was worried; we both were.

"Could it be the Harrowing?" he asked Eden. "Remnants of the spell?"

She shook her head. "There's no magic here. It cannot be that."

Pulling that fucking Grimoire from the bottom of her discarded pile of books, she slammed it on the table as if it were no more than a journal she'd been dragging around for all these years. I couldn't remember the last time I'd seen one up close. It was smaller than I thought it would be. But the casual way she flicked through the pages of her ancestors' magical knowledge shocked me. The paper was so thin, warm light from the flickering candles in the room shone through them, illuminating the text as she searched.

"You're not going to find an answer in there," Grey said. "The Grimoires are just a record and a collection of first and last power."

"Don't tell me what I'll find in a book I've been protecting longer than you've been alive, boy."

I wasn't sure I was a fan of the witch. Of her cowardice for hiding.

But she'd put Grey in his place, and I liked it, if only for the steel in her veins.

"The Grimoires are a record of life and death, spells, and magic in-between. But there are pages added to this book. Small notes here and there that my parents had etched and added before I took it. If they had any theories about the human lands, they might be here."

Raven stirred again, and I dashed for her, noting the sweat beading on her brow. "She's warm."

Torryn moved into the kitchen for a few minutes, returning with a wet cloth. With a deep sense of kindness radiating from him, he held it out to me. "For her head," he whispered.

I floated backward, hands outstretched, as if he would understand. "I'm not... I can't..."

I wanted to help her. To be the friend I'd been during those scary days after the Harrowing. But I didn't want them to see me struggle to hold simple fabric. So instead, I backed further away. Understanding flashed across his face, but he did not balk, did not smirk, as the other one might have. Instead, he knelt carefully to the floor and placed the cloth over Raven's brow before feeling her cheeks for temperature.

"Only a bit warm," he said. "Likely just the change of weather and altitude. She'll be good as new in the morning."

That confidence in his deep voice was a welcomed relief. Something about the shifter was so soothing, I couldn't help but believe him. Most of the witches I'd met in my life had an agenda, but Torryn's aura was strictly sincerity and loyalty. He nearly reminded me of Scoop. My panther's loyalty had never wavered, no matter my mood, my actions, my attention or any lack thereof. He'd always been there. Fuck, I missed him.

"We should all get some rest," Eden said. "Torryn, see that Grey is settled in. Let's move Raven into my room where the bed may be a bit more comfortable. I'm happy to take the couch."

"You will not be sleeping on the couch, Eden." Atlas' face twisted into something feral as he shut her down. For all his jokes and banter, when the animal within him came out, even in his words, it seemed none would argue. "Grey, Tor, and I can take the living room, the ghosty can keep watch over the girl. You can have my bed."

She shared a look with Torryn, and he closed his eyes, dipping his chin. "Best take my bed instead. I'm not sure when Atty last washed his sheets."

"Hey!" the wolf protested, shoving Torryn with a lopsided smirk.

Within minutes, Raven was carefully placed onto the freshly made bed in a small room on one side of the cottage, and Eden had disappeared into the room opposite. Raven awakened long enough to sip water, those bags under her eyes a deep shade of purple. She'd never been a sickly person, had never had papery skin or a weak demeanor. I hoped getting her home would be the answer, though my gut told me that may not be the case.

The evenings were the longest, I'd learned. With free rein over the world, no one the wiser, I could come and go as I pleased. While the others had bodies that needed rest and nourishment and occasional pleasure, I needed nothing. I wanted to need those things, longed to feel something below my damn fingers, be it the tufts of Scoop's ears, the velvetiness of Nym's skin, the veins in a dried petal... Even a surge of power within me. To stand in a salt circle, to bury my toes within the earth, to feel the cool touch of the moon's purest light kissing my flesh. I would do anything, give anything, to experience those things, if only one last time.

Drifting this way and that, meandering between the randomness with which trees grew on the rocky mountainside, I floated along, content to look up at the scattered stars and wish upon every single one of them to feel my familiar's comfort. To feel anything.

Let there be more than this. Let there be more than this. Let there be more.

Like a chant, a conjuring without power, I prayed to the goddess to relent. But she did not hear me.

A flash of pure white, nearly glowing in the moonlight, slipped below me like a dart. I rotated, staying high above as I breathed in the absolute beast that was below me. Running on padded paws, his fur rippling through a breeze of his own making, *the pup*, I assumed, was anything but in full wolf form. Curious, I followed him, keeping a distance. His long, muscled body pounded the earth, those sharp claws digging into the raw ground, leaving massive wolf's prints behind.

Clouds of air surrounded his maw, his breath showing the chilly night temperature, though otherwise he did not seem to notice the cold. Just as I didn't. Unable to feel anything at all. Atlas knew exactly where he was going as he navigated the incline, pivoting to the right and powering forward until he reached a ledge protruding from the mountainside.

Smooth, black stone met the claws of the magical beast as he stalked forward. All the way to the edge, bathing in the light of the moon, he sat, tucking his long white tail around him as he looked down upon the world. A guardian of the night.

Beneath the starry sky, I wondered if he thought of home in this place. If the feel of the pooling silvery moonlight did something more within him, as it did the witches of the Moon Coven.

I ceased all movement, unabashedly staring, studying the whims of a shifter. They'd always been our enemies. Since the dawn of time, the witches had fought against their rule. Lifetimes and generations of war had forced us all into poverty I hadn't seen yet in the human lands. But what would it be for a shifter to leave this place behind?

Without provocation, the wolf's head whipped toward me, our eyes meeting as the power of that animalistic stare held me in place. I vanished. The wolf did not deserve my awe. But perhaps I did not deserve this view either. Perhaps my bias made me unworthy as he turned and tore off into the night.

By the time I made it back to the cabin, I considered going straight into the room with Raven, but damn, if curiosity didn't get the best of me. Pushing completely through the front door, as if it did not exist at all, I was met with the poignant stare of Atlas, the beautiful wolf shifter, those vulnerable eyes meeting mine as if I'd just learned a secret about him.

"Good night, Ghosty," he said, plopping down on the couch, naked as the day he was born. I knew the shifters didn't lose their clothing when they shifted. I'd seen the change in the past. Arrogant ass. I rolled my eyes and left, content to check on Raven and wait out the final hours of moonlight.

Before the sun rose, Eden woke the two shifters and sent them after the shipmaster. She called him by first name, her eyes twinkling as they left the cottage.

"Feeling better?" I asked Raven as she stepped into the main room of the cottage, the pink returned to her cheeks.

She nodded once, eyeing the Moss Coven Grimoire before taking a reluctant seat at the table and looking over her shoulder at Grey. "Did you ever get a chance to see the Grimoires up close?"

"I don't remember, actually," Grey answered, his eyes shifting around the room. "Why?"

Raven twisted her hair into a braid that fell over a shoulder as she shared a smile with him. Eden brought her a cup of tea, standing with her hands on her hips as she waited for her to sip from the tiny porcelain cup.

"Because this one seems different from the others. May I?" She gestured to the book, but Eden shook her head.

"You drink that tea and have some breakfast. Then we can discuss the wonders of the world."

Raven took a drink before jerking her head back, nearly spitting the concoction over the table. "This is… Is this saffron?"

"For strength," Eden answered. "If you can get past that flavor, you'll also find lavender and cloves."

Raven nodded, dabbing at the tea she'd spilled. "I could have done without the saffron."

Eden shared a knowing smile. "Maybe, but it's going to be a long couple of days, and you're going to need all the help we can get you." She slid a plate in front of her, topped with eggs and toast and something that might have been ham. A generous breakfast. "Grey, I wondered if you could help me with some final preparations outside before we go?"

"What could you possibly have to set in order here? Do you plan to come back?" I asked, the incredulity in my tone as clear as I could muster.

"I do not plan to return, but should a traveler ever wander by and need immediate shelter, this home would be of use. It has served me well, and I hope to leave it behind in such a manner."

Raven shared a look with me, swallowing her bite of egg, and that was all the provocation I needed to secretly follow them. They hadn't gone far, just around the edge of the house where they could not be seen from the few windows along the front of the tiny cottage. I stayed back, listening just in case they could sense my presence.

Grey was carefully explaining that final day at the castle. I wasn't sure if I was happy with his choice to get into this now, but I was glad he'd chosen not to walk Raven through those memories again. Perhaps Eden could serve as a buffer between Raven and the shifters when they found out. There was no way they were going to take the news lightly. Grey continued, explaining how Raven had disappeared through a door and came back a completely different person, me following behind her, the complete chaos as two spells were cast at once.

Eden cleared her throat. "I need to see it. To be sure this is not a trap. You must understand."

I couldn't help my curiosity as they fell quiet, a small gasp the only sound. So, I pushed forward, hoping they wouldn't know I was there.

"Satisfied?"

Ice shot through my limbs as I jerked ramrod straight. That voice. That awful, familiar voice. Trying to put everything together and failing, there was only one thing I could do. I didn't think, didn't stop for a single second as I dashed back to Raven, refusing to consider the ramifications. She needed to know that everything was a fucking lie.

11

RAVEN

I could feel that ancient book as if it were calling to me even now. Words hissing through the timbered walls of the cottage. It wasn't real, only the flash of a memory from the room of Grimoires in the castle. But it wasn't the same. Perhaps it was the lack of magic, but the book was duller, the colors a faint whisper of those I'd seen in the others, as if it too were sick.

Curious, I peeked toward the door to make sure there was no one coming as I reached for the book. It was not mine. I had no business opening it now or ever. But I couldn't help myself. Until Kirsi popped into view just inside the door, scaring me.

"You have got to stop— What's wrong?"

"It's... You need to see it for yourself."

I stood, the stricken look on Kirsi's face scaring me as I ran for the door, trusting her. Within seconds, my entire world changed. I hardly registered Eden there at all.

The world stopped rotating. Time suspended as I stared at the man I thought I'd never see again. A crown of thick, dark hair pulled back from his face, that perfectly trimmed beard a bit more disheveled than normal, but otherwise, everything else was exactly right. The eyes, the perfect pout to his bottom lip even in anger, the casual way he stood. I couldn't move. Couldn't breathe as I stared at him, so real, and yet it couldn't be.

I fell to my knees, all strength whisked away from me. "Bastian? You... You're alive?"

Jaw slackened, he looked at me, then to Kir over my shoulder, his face hardening until only steel filled his silver gaze as he glared at her. "I am."

"How?" I breathed, pushing to stand ... reaching for him.

"Raven, don't," Kirsi demanded. "He's been lying to us. Tell her where Grey is."

That perfectly chiseled jaw ticked. "I can explain."

Stepping backward, I looked at Kirsi. "I don't understand."

"Show her. Show her who you really are."

Nostrils flaring, he clenched his teeth and answered, "This *is* who I really am."

"No. Your other form, shifter."

"Raven, if we could..."

The signs were there. All of them, forever, and yet I'd been too naive to see it all this time. There were no wings, no markings on his body. His face filled with sadness, eyebrows drawn as one moment he stood as Bastian, the dead king, and the next, Grey Firewing.

I stumbled backward, tripping over a rock. I fell, but cool arms caught me as Kirsi swept in. She had my back. Just like she always had.

"But you can't be ... You *lied* to me?"

He blinked slowly, raising his hands. "Let me explain."

"Raven..." Eden whispered.

"No." I shook as fury built. "You lied. And lied. You watched me suffer, cry, mourn you to the point of sickness and exhaustion. And you just..."

I turned my back to him, contemplating my next move as everything we had, every moment we shared, burned to embers as quickly as his favorite magical notes. I stepped once. And then again, wondering where on this forsaken earth I could run. Hide. Have one second alone with my own thoughts. I took several more steps.

"Stop," he demanded. Not the command of a man, the assertion of a king. The desperate need within his voice dancing around the edges of his control. "Raven, don't make me chase you."

Fire erupted within my veins. Hurt and anger and sadness wracked its way through my entire being as I tried to make sense of the world and couldn't.

"You have no right to make demands of me, King. Do not chase me. Stay the hell away from me."

I did not look back as I darted into the forest.

He was Grey. I'd known he was half shifter, half witch. But the wings. We'd flown together that night on the mountain, and he'd been lying to me the entire time. Grey wasn't visiting the witches to stand in for the king, he *was* the king. In a different form. He'd been the one to make my All Hallows Eve mask. But it didn't make sense. I'd seen them together. Both were in the room the day I cast death upon him.

Layers and layers of truths and lies swarmed around as present as any of the saplings as I ran, dodging trees and rocks and low branches. Kirsi's glow had vanished. I didn't know if she followed me now or stayed back to yell at the Dark King. My chest burned harder than it ever had, the illness that plagued me thrumming within my limbs and muscles. I was weak, so fucking weak. But I was also done. With everyone and everything. How could the witches lying for their cause be the end of the world when he was also lying for his?

Down and down and down I ran, occasionally slipping on the loose pebbles below my feet, unable to see beyond one cluster of trees to the next. Utterly defeated, I slid to a stop, bracing my hands on my knees as I bent over, gasping for air. Pushing through the burn in my body until I felt too weak and crashed to the ground, heaving.

"Raven," he yelled from behind me. "There's nowhere you can run that I will not find you. I will chase you all over this world if I have to."

He slid to a stop the second he realized I'd fallen. I tried to stand. Pain shot through my ankle and up my leg and I cried out as he reached for me, shoving him away.

"Don't touch me."

His voice was little more than a whisper as he begged me. "Please don't do this."

"You lied." I tried for more conviction, but failed.

"You tried to kill me."

Narrowing my eyes, I used a tree to brace myself into a standing position, though I still had to look up to glare at him. "We both know I had *no* choice in that. That's the difference here. You had a choice, and you chose to deceive me. All this time. Why? Just tell me why I deserved that when I've been dying inside every day without you. And you've just watched me suffer."

"You may not understand this, but I cannot trust anyone."

I shook my head. "You could have trusted me. How could you stand there and ask for something you weren't willing to give?" Whatever was left of my meek, healing heart was shattered, turned to dust. It was gone, just like every last bit of care I had for anyone and anything. "What was the point of all this? What did you gain in your game?"

"It wasn't a game to me. Every moment you had with Grey was authentically me. The only difference was the mask I wore. Those moments are still ours."

I pressed my back against the knotty tree, folding my arms over my chest. "There is no 'ours'. There is only yours. Your decisions, your lies, your moves."

He stepped close to me, lifting a hand to swipe a wild curl from my face, but I turned away from him. "I needed us to be real, Bastian. When everything else was a lie, when I could trust no one else after Kirsi died, I needed you."

"I was there!" he roared. "I stayed hidden in that room with you when you broke. While you lay on that floor, lost in your own grief, I kept to the shadows, waiting for you to need me. I've never left you. Even here. I left everything behind, left the world to burn to the fucking ground, just to be with you. And maybe I was a coward. Maybe I used Grey to make sure you were who you claimed to be, but can you really blame me? My parents were murdered by the witches. The witches have destroyed everything in my whole life. Every move I make, they are there to wreck me. And I couldn't let that happen with you. I needed you—us—to be real, too."

I stopped. His words were my own poison and antidote. The blade and the binding. My heart beat like an erratic drum in my chest as I stumbled toward him. "You could have told me. I would have understood."

"I tried. When you had your panic attack at Grey's touch, when I saw what that did to you, I knew. But the hunters came. I've wanted to tell you so many times, Raven. All Hallows Eve, I thought I would confess that day, later at the cabin. But by then, you'd already ensnared me, and I couldn't risk losing you if you knew the truth."

He dropped his head, pressing his palm to his temples. "I am not a perfect man. I've made so many mistakes and dragging this out was one of them, but I never did it to hurt you."

"No." I glared. "You did that for your own benefit without a single consideration for me."

Grabbing my hands, he pulled my knuckles to his lips, his eyes shifting between mine. "I know I hurt you, and I'm sorry. Please tell me how to fix this."

"You cannot. We had a plan, Bastian. Our whole lives ahead of us. I thought I knew you. This is not the man I knew. The man I mourn."

"Fine," he relented, moving away as he threw up every wall he'd once had with me, slipping into the role of the Dark King. Back straight, chin high, he looked down upon me as he had the first day in that damn throne room. "You will at least concede to an escort home."

I pushed off the tree, walking past him. "I don't need your fucking escort."

"Wrong," he shouted. "These lands are hurting you. You have to get home."

I hated how right he was. How terrified I was to stay in the human lands. My shoulders dropped. "I have one condition."

"Granted."

"You don't even want to know the condition?"

"As long as you live at the end of this, I don't care what the circumstances are."

"True. I guess it doesn't matter what the rules are. You've never been one to stick to them anyway."

12

RAVEN

It was a cruel thing to look at the man you thought you'd murdered, the man you'd cared so much about, and realize that reality, for all its wonders, would always be a balance of agony and ecstasy. In my heart of hearts, I did not hate Bastian. I did not even condemn him for his decision to keep himself guarded. He'd spent the majority of his life relying on only himself and the small group of people surrounding him. His caution made sense.

I only hated that I hadn't been a safe enough respite for him. Had he told me, rather than let me catch him, the outcome would have been different. I would have known then what I could only question now. His declarations were merely for self-preservation, and that was the only truth I knew. A truth that continued to feed the anger within me.

He commanded the room, sucking the air out of it as he always did, while he sat brooding on Eden Mossbrook's floral printed couch, thumbing through an old book he was not reading. Kirsi swirled along the ceiling, unable to be still as she stared down at Bastian, likely plotting his real death.

"What?" he barked, dropping the old book onto the small, round table beside him.

I'd been staring. Again. I shook my head, looking away to study the only picture on the wall in Eden's home. A massive black ship with matching, billowing sails battling a storm in a tumultuous ocean.

"Ask your questions," he tried again, his voice softer.

"How were you both in the room at the same time?" Kirsi asked, never the timid one.

Resisting the urge to look at him, afraid I'd give away every emotion rattling through me, I stood from the couch, moving to the painting as if the white capped waves were the most interesting thing I'd ever seen.

"The night of the ball, do you remember what the ceiling looked like?"

Kirsi didn't answer, and for good reason. The night before she died, she'd been enraptured by Nym. Distracted in the best way.

"The blood moon sky," I whispered, running my fingers along the painting to feel the rough texture of the artist's work.

"I have a spell that allows me to create illusions."

"He was never really there, then," Kirsi said. "That's why he always seemed so dull and lifeless when you were around. Not because he was afraid of your wrath, but because you simply needed him to be seen and nothing more."

"Correct."

"And everyday you'd go down to the Chosen's hall as Grey?"

"I wanted to get to know the Chosen without fear. I wanted to see who you were when not under the nose of the *evil* king."

"And the day we flew together?" I managed, hardly more than a whisper.

He waited so long to answer, I wasn't sure he heard me at all. The air grew thick, my heart pounding as I felt him before I saw him move. I spun, and he was there, towering over me. My heart stopped. I wanted to reach for him. To end this and feel the comfort his dark strength had always given me. I pushed away that feeling, if only to live in my own fury a little longer.

"I was wrong to lie, but there is nothing about that night I regret. I have a spell that allows me to cast the wings. They are either a conjuring or an illusion. Whatever I choose them to be. When my father and I built the cabin, it was right after I received that spell. He was a lammergeier shifter. That cabin is where he taught me how to fly." He paused for a moment, brushing his thumb across my cheek as I stood frozen. "That cabin will always be the most precious place in the world to me."

Kirsi cleared her throat, breaking the spell between us, and I stepped away, the lack of his warmth notable as I slipped past. Taking my seat on an empty chair, I watched Eden move back and forth through the home, selecting small items to fill the single bag she packed.

"There is a spring with hot water close by. I'm sure a washing will help you feel better," Eden offered. "I've several things you can wear that will otherwise be left behind. Torryn and Atlas will not be back with my—our shipmaster until late into the night, if he hasn't been in his cups."

I thought of the stinging wounds on my thighs and the small bit of attention I'd paid to them as we traveled. "A wash would be amazing," I admitted.

"I have some drying towels there." She pointed. "And I use my own crafted soaps."

"No more saffron?" I asked, an eyebrow raised.

She smiled, so beautifully genuine, the trace of her mother I'd been haunted by in that stare completely vanished. "Just lavender, honey, and sage, my dear."

The small pool of turquoise water was nearly invisible beneath the steam that rolled from the top of it. Hugging all the items Eden sent with me, I carefully slipped out of my boots. The spring hadn't been far from the cottage at all, but Kirsi still insisted on coming.

"I've never been so jealous of you in my whole life," she mused. "Or death, I guess I should say."

"Can you feel nothing at all?" I asked, reaching for the low hem of the stolen gown I'd been wearing for two days.

"It's like my entire being is numb to the— Holy shit."

I lifted the dress over my head, standing freezing and bare in the wild. Slamming my hands over my body, I whipped around, assuming she'd seen something nearby.

"Your legs. Why haven't you said anything?"

The wounds I'd suffered at the final Trial had hardly gotten better. Fire hot and splotchy red skin gave way to the deep gashes upon my thighs. The wound from Willow's magical arrow was smaller, while the other, a gash the length of my palm, looked far worse. Purple veins spider-webbed out from the slice that hadn't begun to scab.

"You need something for those," Kirsi breathed. "No wonder you're so fucking sick."

"When was the last time you got a bloody nose from a stab in your leg? I'm not sick because of these wounds."

"You need to go back and have Eden look at them."

"I'm fine. Really. There are far bigger things to worry about."

"For fuck's sake, Raven. We have to travel again today, and you already move at a slug's pace. They took the horse back to the drunk in town. You're going to have to walk down this mountain. Don't be ridiculous or difficult."

I blew out a breath, trying not to grit my teeth as I stepped into the water, the heat reaching my calves. "I need five minutes of people not telling me what to do. I want to sit here and let my brain stop. Just leave me be."

She flew toward me, the anger on her face clear as she passed. But she'd gone all the same.

Inch by glorious inch, I lowered myself into the steaming hot water, each muscle relaxing, the wounds only stinging a little as I let the water heal my soul. Birds sang a melody of whimsical songs in the forest below, the fresh air a reprieve from the cottage that felt too small. The contrast of the cold temperature above the water and the searing below distracted my mind enough to close my eyes and let the world fall away, if only for a few moments. There were no shifters, no kings, no witches. Just this single escape from everything.

"Get out."

I jerked, covering myself with my arms as I spun to see Bastian staring down at me, his face red, his breaths measured, fists tight at his sides.

"I beg your pardon?"

"Your wounds have worsened, and you've said nothing."

"Can you please flip back to Grey? I think he's a lot nicer than you are." I dragged my hands through the water, letting the steam billow around me.

With little more than a thought from Bastian, Grey stood before me, his green eyes blazing as he glared. "Get the fuck out of the water, Raven. Or I'm coming in after you."

"As Grey or Bastian? Because I'm not sure which I would prefer. I'm honestly shocked I didn't realize who you were sooner. You both have that single vein that pops out on your forehead when you're pissed. Did you know?"

I was pushing, and I knew it. It wasn't like me, but as always, something in Bastian coaxed the anger out as heavily as all the other emotions I'd kept in check my whole life. Apparently, though it felt like everything had changed, nothing had.

"I haven't seen that fire from you in days," he said, turning back into Bastian as he stepped out of a boot. "It's good to see you're still in there somewhere, Miss Moonstone." He pushed out of his other boot, and I swam backward, my body relaxed for the first time since we'd arrived.

There was no denying my immediate attraction to the man that had taught me pleasure in a way I'd never known. As he peeled the black shirt over his head, silver eyes locked on mine, I could hear his voice that first night.

You will look at me when I speak to you, unless I've ordered otherwise.

I melted at the memory. Testing him, I held his gaze, inching backward again. Every groove of his firm chest, a reminder of where my tongue had once been.

"Am I your enemy?" he asked, unfastening his pants.

I didn't answer, moving further back until I was nearly halfway across the small spring.

He flicked his fingers over another brass button, the dare in his gaze sparking everything I'd silenced between us.

"Answer," he commanded.

I could not help the parting of my lips, the wave of desire as my mouth dried. "No."

"Good."

His pants dropped to his ankles. He stood before me, naked, daring me to tell him to stop as he dipped into the water. My eyes plunged below his waist and the dark chuckle that left him sent a shiver down my spine as desire pooled within my belly and between my legs. In one fell swoop, he lunged beneath the surface, disappearing into the darkness of the water and the steam above it. I twirled, searching for him, as a moment passed and he did not resurface. Just as I considered diving underneath, fingers I would know in my sleep swept up the side of my thighs. He emerged from the water inches in front of me, droplets falling down his long lashes.

"I've missed you," I said, moving my fingers into his hair, unable to help my own honesty. "I hate you, but I've missed you."

He grabbed the sides of my face, pulling me closer still until he could rest his forehead on mine. "I would change it all if I could. I just needed to know."

"I think you've always known who I am, Bastian."

"You could have been a million things. And every time I let myself believe that you were truly who you'd shown yourself to be, my mind would rebel. Because how could you be so perfect in the midst of all this chaos? How could you want me? How could I deserve you?" His hands gripped my waist, and I didn't not stop him as he lifted me.

Wrapping my legs around him, I pushed the dripping water from his brow. "I would have understood."

"I'm sorry," he whispered. "I will say it a thousand times if you need me to."

He brushed his lips across mine, an apology, a promise, a reprieve. I leaned forward, needing more. Part or all of him, I wasn't sure. For countless hours, I'd wished for him to kiss me one more time. To hold me and fill me until we were one. Until I didn't know where he ended and I began and nothing but he and I mattered. He was here now, his hands like fire on my skin, hotter than the sweltering water. And I didn't have it in me to push him away. If only to save my heart from loneliness.

The wounds on my thighs ached, but I ignored them as I had been doing, not concerned with my physical being so much as my mental state that had teetered back and forth for hours, days.

Mouths and lips and tongues and teeth, we were frantic, pushing and pulling as the dam of tension between us broke. I could have taken him within me and stayed there forever wrapped in his arms, a world away from everything wrong in our lives, but he stopped. Pushing me away, though he kept his hands on me, his breathing ragged.

"We can't." Water dripped down his face as he leaned his forehead on mine, thumbs caressing my jaw. "As tempting as it is, we can't. Let me wash you, and then we need to wrap those wounds. But I promise I will make up for every lost kiss, every single night without my arms wrapped around you."

I nodded, reluctantly. We were going to travel, and I could not sustain another day like the one before, walking for hours, each step a stabbing pain up my legs, my brain fogging over, the ache within my head. I'm not sure which of those we could help, but any would be a reprieve.

"Okay."

A corner of his mouth lifted. "Was that a concession without a fight, Miss Moonstone?"

"Don't get used to it, shifter."

Bastian was gentle, his fingers tangling into my hair as he poured in Eden's oils, massaging at a leisurely pace. His hands lingering in places that made me squirm as he lathered soap all over my body. By the time the Dark King was done with his ministrations, I felt like a whole new person, inside and out.

He was here, and that was enough for now. A day ago I'd have given anything to bring him back. My pride included.

The scowl on Kirsi's face as we re-entered the cottage melted to shock the second the door clicked shut. Deciding not to dress so we could wrap the wounds, Bastian held me half-covered by my borrowed dress in his arms.

"You okay?" she asked, as if she had all the power in the world to kill the man.

"I'm okay," I answered. "I need some bandages and a few other things."

"I've gathered what I have," Eden said, stepping into the room.

Moving away from them both and into the bedroom, Bastian laid me on the bed. Using the items from the moss witch, he carefully treated the gashes and wrapped them in cloth. But the moment he was done, he crawled over me, closing his mouth over mine as I moaned, now entirely naked.

"I am not broken," I muttered. "Please touch me."

"Touch you where?" he growled into my ear.

Before I could answer, he pressed a thumb over the spot between my legs that belonged solely to him.

"Here?" he whispered. I could only manage a small whimper as he slipped two fingers inside of me. "Or here."

He stroked me relentlessly, holding my gaze. Barely restrained, Bastian leaned over, closing his teeth over the curve of my neck. I groaned, lifting from the bed as those fingers moved with fevered intention. The desire he'd drawn only increased as he pressed his lips to mine again, our tongues dancing as he tested my weakened body. Breasts aching to be touched, body swollen with need, he stroked me until I arched off the bed, discontent with fingers when it could have been so much more.

But then he stopped. Far, far too soon.

"No. Bastian, please."

"I will finish this," he growled into my ear. "When you do not need your strength."

"I will crawl to that damn ship."

He chuckled before lifting himself from the bed. "Later, Miss Moonstone."

Stepping from the room, he left me to dress, though I did not miss the snort from Kirsi. She'd known, of course. I didn't feel ashamed as I stepped out of that bedroom refreshed and more alive than I had been in days.

"I have a theory," Eden said, holding the Moss Coven Grimoire. "What if Raven's afflictions have something to do with the spell she cast? What if she was not powerful enough to cast death? You didn't die, so it must not have worked."

Bastian scratched the back of his head. "Had I not stopped it in the middle, deadening the spell by sending us all here to the land with no magic, I would have died. I tasted death. Seconds more and everything would have been different."

"It's probably just a mixture of exhaustion and dealing with the trauma of the last day at home." I sighed.

"Here." Eden held the book out to me. "You wanted to see this earlier. Help yourself. Just be gentle with the pages."

"You literally had it shoved at the bottom of a book stack three seconds ago," Kirsi said.

"All the same, please be careful."

I swallowed, taking the book from her hands. It was the same size as the Moon Coven Grimoire I remembered. Small enough to blend in with other books, but substantial enough to feel important. The ancient leather was cracked and peeling in places, the emerald stone on the cover dull compared to the others I'd seen. As if this book had aged and the others had magic that preserved them from doing so.

Something strange happened as I opened the cover. It hummed as if it was not an inanimate object, but a sentient being, aware that I sought its secrets. No one else seemed to notice the sound, or rather, not a sound but a subtle vibration as I flipped page after page, reading the witch's names, running my finger down the list of spells they'd created, slipping Endora's scattered notes between my fingers to read them.

There was nothing of significance, it seemed. Only names and spells. Everything from telepathy to necromancy graced the pages of the Moss Coven Grimoire. But Eden was right. For all the power Bastian had been afraid of them having, this was merely a book, a record.

Curiosity satisfied, I passed it back to Eden, and she slipped it into her bag before tying it closed. Only then did I realize that Kir had been peeking over my shoulder.

"Did you see anything?" I asked, shifting to look at her.

"Nothing more than you did."

As Eden and Bastian moved into the kitchen, discussing the plans for our return, Kirsi settled in beside me, her glow beginning to show as the sun faded outside.

"Are you sure we can trust them?"

I nodded. "I'm sure. What use are we to them, honestly?"

"True," she answered. "It's a miracle if I can touch things. But you, you could be valuable."

I nodded. "If I am, then let me be. I'd rather fight whatever is to come with Bastian than against him. I'm hurt he lied, but how long can I blame him for trying to protect himself?"

She rolled her eyes. "Longer than two hours would have done it."

I lifted a shoulder. "When someone you care about deeply dies, Kir, you wish on everything you've ever loved for them to come back to you. If his deception was the cost of his life, of having him here with me, I consider that a wish fulfilled. Besides, I've got enough to deal with without holding a grudge."

"Like them when they find out you nearly killed their king." She jutted her chin toward the door seconds before it swung open and three very large men stepped inside.

13

KIRSI

If I could have smelled anything at all, I was confident it would have been smothered by the stench of the drunken ass captain that stormed into the packed house, crossed the room in three strides, grabbed Eden by the waist and swung her around, before stumbling sideways and crashing into the wall, powerless witch in tow.

A burst of raspy laughter filled the space as the old friends righted themselves, sharing a look that said maybe they were more than that. Eden cleared her throat, adjusting herself before turning to the rest of us, though the captain, with his leather hat and heavy golden sword tied to his waist, had eyes for only her as his steady fingers unscrewed a flask.

"Captain Crowen Gold, these are my friends, King Bastian Firepool and Miss Raven Moonstone."

He turned, tilting to the side only slightly until his eyes landed on me. Looking down to his flask and back to me, he chuckled. "Musta picked up the good stuff this time."

He lifted the drink toward me in a gallant salute before taking a large swig. Then he swept his arm below, bending at the waist. The second he fell forward, Atlas lunged for him, saving him from smashing his face into the aloe plant resting on the cottage floor.

"King," he slurred. "I think there's a wee ghosty behind you."

I twisted my mouth into a grimace. "This is the guy we're trusting to sail through the storms at the border?"

"Don't worry, Ghosty. Crow's been sailing longer than you've been dead," Atlas said, a lopsided smirk on his irritating face.

"I hate to break it to you, dog, but that's not saying much."

"Crow is the only shipmaster I've ever hired." Eden walked forward, lifting her single bag from the couch. "He's only lost one rotation of shifters."

He pulled the hat from his head, revealing a mass of brown hair that fell into long matted twists in front of him as he looked at the floor. "The sea had a lesson to teach me that day."

"And this one?" I asked, an eyebrow raised.

He stumbled forward, stopping before me. Without a second of hesitation, he balled a fist and shoved it through my torso. The tingling sensation of his arm was the only burst of feeling I would ever have. I doubled over, mocking him, and he gasped, stepping away.

"Did I hurt you?"

I rolled my eyes, floating up to the ceiling. "No, you prick, but remind me to return the favor one day."

Torryn snorted, a large hand landing heavily on the captain's shoulder. "Best leave the wraith alone before you're killed where you sleep, Crow."

"Good plan." I glared.

Navigating down the mountain with the drunk shipmaster was, unfortunately, a lot smoother than I'd hoped. Much to my dismay, he only fell once and from that point forward, Torryn and Atlas flanked him while Bastian, in Grey's form, kept to Raven's side. It seemed going down the mountain was a lot faster than hiking up.

"Crow's secured us a covered wagon and driver for the rest of the trip to the coast," Torryn said, glancing toward Raven.

"Didn't want my lady to be seen," the captain declared, sharing a wink with Eden.

Confused at Eden's apparent attraction to the zealous man, I had to remind myself that other than him, she'd probably been locked away in that cottage for years and years with only a rotating guard of shifters. And if all shifters were as obnoxious as Atlas, I could hardly blame her for seeking the attention of a drunkard, who likely had zero boundaries and fewer cares in the world.

The others thanked the driver, and we climbed into the wagon in pitch black, save my subtle blue glow when I was allowed to be visible. I'd forgotten to hide when the human captain had stormed in and, though his reaction was quite surprising, I wished he'd been slightly more sober.

Hunched men smushed together as the wagoner carried his cargo of magical people back toward our home. He was clueless, of course, but I still had to fight a foreign desire to pop up next to him, just to see how he would react.

"A little closer, Atty. You haven't quite taken my virginity yet," Bastian said, in a very Grey sort of way. Though I supposed he was Grey, so it made sense.

"Calm down, Bash. If I wanted to grope you, you'd know."

"I kind of want to grope you, Atty," Crow said, a sloppy smile on his face.

"Nope, nope. Eden, switch places with me. I can't be molested by this guy the night before I die in the ocean."

The wagon swayed as if wild animals had been set loose inside. Eden traded places with Atlas, so he now anchored down next to Raven.

"Do you really think we'll die?" she asked, picking at her nails, her signature move when she was worried.

"Stormy seas make strong sailors, and I've grown up traveling the waters of this world. Be not afraid, lass."

"Who talks like that?" I asked, though I couldn't help my smile at Torryn's wide grin.

He'd been so helpful to Eden, carrying her bag down the mountain, fading into the town with the captain to signal our driver. Unlike the wolf, he hung back, shyer, but always observant. Always roving toward the person he thought needed his help.

"Captain Crowen Gold," the captain said, flinging his hand awkwardly into the middle of the space. "At your service."

"Yes." I nodded, eyes wide as if patronizing a child. "We've met."

"Right." he saluted, unscrewing the cap to his flask.

"Isn't that thing about empty?" Bastian asked, jutting his chin toward the captain's liquor as he rested his head against the canvas covering behind him.

"Let's not speak of sad things," the drunk man answered. He licked his index finger before sticking it straight up in the air. The wagon fell silent as we waited for an explanation. He took a long swig of his drink before pinning Bastian with a serious stare. "She's not going to be an easy sail, King. There's pepper in the air."

"You mean salt?" Atlas asked, wiggling as if it would help him find a bit more room.

"No, laddy. Salt is always in the air. This is the sea."

Eden giggled beside me, still watching the man until he shared a wink with her. Her smile was sweet and genuine, if not odd. I tilted my head this way and that, searching for anything redeeming or attractive about him. If you squinted your eyes until he was blurry and moved your head slightly, the rugged look wasn't too bad. And clearly, he made her laugh. I'd venture to guess his eccentricity was partly for her amusement alone.

Torryn groaned. "Atlas, if you don't stop squirming, I'm going to cut you from nose to navel."

"Let's make it down my back in an intricate pattern. Scars tell stories. I can make something up."

"Like the one on your face?" Raven asked. "How did you get that one?"

The air in the crowded space changed to something like static, and I couldn't help but lean closer, eager to hear his tale.

"The gash in my eyebrow came from a tussle with Bash on the summit run. But this one," he pointed to his mark above, the deeper scar in his forehead. "Witches."

"Tell them the whole story," Eden encouraged, reaching across the wagon to take his hand.

"Laramie Forestbrook." He whispered her name like a conjuring.

As if those words would bring the witch before us now. "She was the most beautiful thing I'd ever seen. Hair as red as the setting sun, eyes like golden honey." He smiled, lost in his memory of the witch that had clearly held his heart. "She was wild and carefree and unlike anything I'd ever seen before. We were forbidden, of course. The witches of her coven had spent her life preaching about the devilish ways of the shifters and why she needed to stay away from us. But her spirit was rebellious, untamed."

He sat forward, his elbows on his knees as he gripped Eden's tiny hand within his own. All traces of teasing had long since left his face as he continued his tale, every bit the wolf I'd seen that night in the forest.

"We stayed closest to the Fire Coven, where we were usually safe. They were the only witches a shifter could truly trust not to turn their backs. We'd usually walk together, and she'd tell me crazy stories as if they were real, making them up as we wandered. Her voice was like a song and her mind, the harmony." He paused, his smile fading, though he sat for several seconds, quietly.

"What happened?" I asked, unable to stop my own curiosity.

"We were walking back over the bridge to the Forest territory, which was where we usually said our goodbyes, when the color faded from her face, the beautiful smile she always wore vanishing. She jerked to a stop, frozen in place." His voice broke. "Blood started pouring from her ears and down her nose, and I panicked. I stood in front of her screaming her name, but she didn't hear me, didn't respond. Just stood there. Even her tears were red as blood."

"The Harrowing," Raven and I whispered at the same time. I'd seen exactly that happen to her. Had felt my own heart break when I thought she'd die. But she'd lived, and I knew Atlas' Laramie had not.

He cleared his throat, but the tension still showed in his voice as he continued. "I didn't know anything about that. She didn't tell me, and I didn't know what to do. I lifted her from the ground and ran. I should have..." He shook his head, refusing to finish his sentence.

"You couldn't have known, Atty. Couldn't have changed it," Torryn said.

"The witches of the Forest Coven attacked Atlas the moment he carried Laramie into the town square, screaming for help." Bastian hunched forward, putting his hand on top of Eden's. "I'm sorry I wasn't there, brother. I'm so sorry."

"They forced me to watch her die," he whispered. "Held me to the ground with magic, the gash from a spell gushing my own blood everywhere. I didn't fight back. I let them destroy me, but they still made me watch. Made me believe that I was the reason she'd died. As if I'd somehow poisoned her. Her chest rose and fell, the blood pouring from her until the light left those beautiful, honeyed eyes and she was gone. No more stories, no more fire. She'd just... gone."

"I'm sorry that happened," I whispered, afraid to break the delicate silence nestled into the limited space between us.

"Thanks, Ghosty," he replied, still haunted by the memory.

The trip remained silent after that. Even the captain fell to snoring as he leaned on Eden and her on him. It was hard not to feel like the villain in Atlas' story, but then I supposed he was just like the other shifters and saw witches as the villains. Though I hated to admit it, they were probably right. The witches of the world believed the lies the coven leaders spun like it was golden truth sent from the goddess herself, and we—they—acted accordingly.

I glanced up to see the Dark King watching me, as if he knew the inner workings of my mind. He'd been the villain many, many times over. Also, based on the lies those witches had preached, it seemed. The shifters had their truth and the witches had theirs, and I was fairly certain the real truth lay somewhere in between.

One by one, the crew within the uncomfortable wagon fell asleep, lulled by the forward motion and rattle of the wooden wheels crunching the gravel below us. Bored, as I usually was at nighttime, I became invisible and swept out of the carriage, sitting next to the human driver. Holding the reins loose in his fingers, his own head bobbed back and forth a few times before the horses whinnied, jerking him awake.

Several minutes passed and again, he drifted off to sleep. I knew I shouldn't. I'd been warned the humans were not used to seeing wraiths, but I couldn't help myself as I floated away from the bench, careful not to spook the horses. I drifted above his hind, facing backward so I could watch the driver's face as he startled awake, reminding me of Scoop. His eyes doubled in size, body shooting upward as I vanished, confident he'd seen me for only a flash of a second. It was enough, though. The smile didn't leave my face for several hours, and the human never fell asleep again.

14

KIRSI

The small town ahead, scattered along the seashore, was barely visible in the early morning, still at least an hour before the sun would rise. The closely placed buildings were the same as those we'd seen in the two other towns, hard to discern from one another and cast in heavy shadow. Occasional lanterns gave the place enough ambiance to feel unsettled as I remembered the hard eyes of the witch hunter. Surely, we were safer here. Though I knew we'd traveled back at least part of the way we'd come before.

Leaving the boring driver, whose hands still shook, I soared toward the town. Curiosity becoming a new part of who I was, I drifted between the strangely similar homes and down the brick laid streets. Rounding a corner, confident the little town would be just as boring as the rest, I nearly swept through the solid body of a guard standing watch. A round hat upon his head, a whistle tucked into his mouth hanging from a silver chain around his neck, he stared forward, unmoving as I circled him to see what or who he watched over.

Though they'd never seen me, my jaw dropped because I knew them. Even beyond the bruising on their faces, hunched over and locked in a pillory, their hands and heads unable to move, I was confident they were the same old people from before. Wasting no time, I flew back to the wagon, burst inside, and punched the captain right in the chest. It wouldn't hurt him of course, but he felt me enough to jerk away.

"Payback, Captain," I hissed before nudging the Dark King.

His eyes flew open, panic on his face as he oriented himself, reaching instantly for Raven. "What is it?"

"The old couple from that first town is locked in the middle of the square, guarded by a man with… well… a whistle. They've got bruises all over their faces, and their clothing is torn to shreds."

"We cannot help them," Bastian said. "We did what we could. But we need to get home. We have no idea the state of the castle, if the barrier of the Grimoires has held, if the coven leaders have taken over and declared war on the shifters. We cannot waste time here."

"Can I talk to Grey? I feel like he would probably join me."

Bastian narrowed his eyes, but Atlas laughed. "That joke never gets old. Remember that time—"

"Save it, Pup," I interrupted. "No one in the town is awake. It's a single man with a whistle. It would take minutes to save two innocent lives."

"She's right," Raven agreed. "We cannot leave them to die."

"Who says they're going to die?" Bastian asked. "We're making an assumption, and I won't take unnecessary risks with you. Not when these lands are causing… episodes."

I saw it then, the gaunt look on her face, the same she had before, the dried blood just below her nose. She'd had yet another episode while I was gone.

"Atty and I can do it," Tor said, his profound voice even deeper in the early morning hours. "We know the way to the docks from here. We can free them and meet you at the ships. If it's as Kirsi says, it won't take long."

"You would do that?" Raven asked, leaning her head on Bastian's shoulder.

He brushed a few wild hairs from her face, the worry in his eyes stirring my own concerns.

"Of course we would. If it means that much to you," Atlas answered.

"I'll come, too. I can show you where they are and grab the key to the lock while you keep the guard from blowing that whistle."

Bastian lowered his chin, raising an eyebrow. "Are you sure you can manage that?"

I wanted to punch him in the face, but I probably couldn't 'manage that' either. "I'll try my fucking best, King."

Torryn made a fist and banged on the backboard of the long wooden bench he sat on. The driver slowed the horses to a stop, and the two giant shifters crawled out of the hole in the back.

Bastian followed, leaving Rave in the back of the wagon to rest, and stretched as he stood in the browning, sandy grass. "Be careful," he commanded. "Do not take risks and don't hesitate. All in. All out. Don't let me hear that fucking whistle."

"We'll be ten minutes behind you," Atlas said, before shifting into the white wolf, his fur shuttering with the effortless change.

The king looked at me one final time before hopping back into the wagon. I saw a bit of Grey in his softening eyes. "You can do this. Just focus."

Faster than I could click my fingers, Torryn shifted, not into a bear, as I'd suspected based on his size, but a giant black and deep blue owl. Only not an owl. A strix. The magical bird of fairytales with a handful of tail feathers trailing behind him freely, as whimsical and free-floating as a curtain caught in a breeze.

Without a thought, the shifters tore off into the night, headed straight for the town as if they'd done this together a thousand times. But there was no plan in place beyond my conviction to grab that fucking key.

The town remained as silent as it was when I'd left it. I stayed above, floating next to Torryn as he called to the white wolf, guiding him between the buildings. I dropped low, disappearing before approaching the man from behind, just as I'd done before. My stomach turned as I watched him, whistle still in his mouth, shaking a palm full of rocks. Pulling his arm back, he threw a tiny stone through the air and pelted the old woman right on her head. She whimpered in pain, her knees buckling.

The old man turned to her. "We are not here, my love. We are a thousand miles away, in another world where hate is not a disease and joy is spread like wildflowers."

"Shut it, you—"

The man stopped mid-sentence as the giant white wolf rounded the corner in front of him, teeth bared as he growled, the sound every bit a promise and a threat. The second the whistle dropped from the man's gaping mouth, I swooped in, swiping at the brass key. But though I'd gotten better at touching objects, I was not perfect. And my fingers moved through the blasted keyring.

The wolf padded forward. I tried again. Fail. I knew the strix remained in the shadows because his form would have been far more alarming than that of the giant white wolf, which might have been seen in the nearby mountains.

But as I struggled with the key, the man threw another jagged rock at Atlas, stepping backward before reaching for that fucking chain around his neck. I needed Scoop. I needed my magic.

In a blink, the man was pinned to the ground, but it was not fast enough as the sound of the whistle pierced the night air. Out of time, Torryn dove with a terrifying caw as he rotated, knife-like talons guiding him straight down toward the man's waist. I reached the pillory, still entirely useless as Torryn pulled on the gold keyring until it broke free from the man's belt loop.

A door slammed open behind us, familiar dark eyes surveying the chaos as the owl-like creature soared high, dropping the keys at my feet. The shifters could not change into human form, which meant they could not unlock the brass padlock trapping the old couple. I cringed as five hunters poured from the house, pulling knives from their belts as they headed toward the wolf.

Torryn swooped again, snagging a long blade from one of their hands before I had to turn away. I could not watch the destruction of Bastian's friends, knowing I'd brought them here.

I had one task only.

Clearing my mind, I remembered how easy these last attempts were if I didn't think about it. If I just intended to touch, I did. So, I let myself, easily lifting the keys from the ground. The old woman whimpered, but there was no time to explain why a key floated mid-air as I popped into view, shoving it into the lock and turning until the click sounded.

The man was freed first, diving just in time to catch his wife from falling.

"There's no time to be afraid. Days ago, you helped a young couple, the night your house burned. Go back to the town they were searching for. Bluestem. Do not stop or talk to anyone. In fact, travel around. Follow the south side of the highest mountain in the distance. If you stick to the trees, you will find a worn path, follow it, and it will guide you to a newly abandoned cottage. Stay there. Live the rest of your lives in peace."

Though stricken, they needed no more provocation as they turned, content to flee. The white wolf's snarl rattled through the town square, and I spun just in time to see the Seeker stalking toward him, knife in hand. Torryn had shifted from beast to man which told me only one thing. Neither of them planned for these humans to live. To ever be able to tell the tale of the night an owl changed into a man before their eyes.

One of the hunters stood completely still, jaw and hands slackened as he stared at a ghost with a blue aura, flying straight for him. A thought occurred to me. A gruesome, terrible thought, but I needed to be useful. As Atlas lunged for the vilest man, Torryn pulled a knife from his own belt, having just slammed his massive fist into the face of another.

The man that stared at me sprang to life, rotating on his heel as he grabbed a blade from his boot. While Atlas was occupied with the Seeker, his back to us, the man closest to me leapt for him, landing on his back as he planted his knife into the shifter's side. I screamed along with Atlas' roar of pain. Frantic to save him, I soared forward, jamming my hand through the back of the man, allowing myself to touch, until I gripped his heart and yanked it out of his back, taking his life as he slumped forward and slid from Atlas' blood-stained back.

A man. I'd killed a man. The bloodied heart slipped through my fingers, plopping to the ground unceremoniously. It'd taken an instant. A single moment to simply … end someone's entire existence. Could I tarnish my own soul after I'd already died? If so, the deed was done.

Torryn, fighting the last man besides the Seeker, roared. Atlas leapt from the ground, knocking down the Seeker, though blood poured from the knife wound in his side, pink flesh showing, even in the moonlight.

"Atlas," Torryn yelled. "Finish this."

Only a whimper came from the wolf. But that single sound was enough to send Torryn into a frenzied rage, tackling the man in front of him to the ground before reaching for his head and snapping it sideways. A simple broken neck by massive bare hands.

Torryn roared, every bit the animal he harbored as he lunged for the final human. Pounding his fist into him as I moved forward to repeat the kill I'd managed. But I was not needed. Not at all as Torryn beat the man to a bloody pulp, then took his knife and sliced open his midsection, ripping the intestines from within and scattering them to the ground.

"Torryn," I whispered, the fear in my voice clear as the night sky. "He's gone. We need to go before more come."

The beast of a man froze, staring down at his bloodied hands and then to the white wolf, still on the ground, far more red than white. He stood, stalking over to his friend, a shifter he'd sworn to protect since he was young, and slid his arms below him. The wolf whimpered again, his breaths a quickened pant as Torryn raised him from the ground and tore off across this seaside town, headed straight for the ocean.

15

KIRSI

Blood dripped onto white sand with each step Torryn took toward the ocean in the distance. More specifically, toward a giant black ship with matching sails. The floating docks were otherwise quiet, the sun barely over the horizon, teeny bits of orange and purple painted leisurely across the morning sky. More than ten thick cables tied the massive ship to the dock, and it swayed heavily, eager to pull out to the ocean.

I wasn't sure if the wolf was still breathing, or if he'd taken his final breath on the run through the small town now full of death at its center. But I hoped it meant the humans would hold a sliver of fear before they chose to condemn another. After what I'd seen, I couldn't say I blamed Eden Mossbrook for being ready to return home. She'd been stuck in a land of hunters, hiding, cut off from any power she might receive. If I were still a witch, I probably wouldn't have managed this long. But my opinion hadn't changed. She could have come home sooner. Spoken her story louder, held the backing of the royals, and prevented a measure of this pent-up animosity we would now be returning to.

"Report," Bastian demanded in Grey's form, his face pale as Torryn hoisted the white wolf, smothered in red blood, up the ramp and onto the deck of the ship.

"The bastard blew the fucking whistle. Hunters swarmed the square, and the wraith and I had to fight them off him. He took several stabs to the side."

"Let me take a look at him," Eden said softly. Stepping around the Dark King, her eerie eyes were full of concern as she ran her slender fingers through Atlas' fur. "Let's get him below."

Torryn carried him across the deck, needing no directions.

"Raven?" I asked, wincing because I was afraid to hear the answer.

Stepping backward on the deck, Bastian clasped his hands behind his back. His throat bobbed, the words fighting their way out. "She can hardly walk. She's fine one minute and completely wiped out the next. I don't understand it, and I've never heard of it. I only hope we can stop it by crossing the barrier."

"You're sure it's not because of that spell she used on you? Because she cast it but it didn't complete?"

"I'm not sure of anything." His jaw clenched. "I don't know the exact words of the command Nikos gave her. It's possible the second we cross the barrier she'll be forced back under his command and recast the spell."

I swayed back and forth as his eyes shifted behind me. Well... through me. I whipped around, realizing there were other humans on board this ship and several of them stood staring, mouths agape.

"Back to work, men," Crow yelled down, breaking the spell as they sprung back to whatever they'd been doing, casting wary glances as often as they could.

Bastian had turned away, looking out over the small town we'd come from.

"You haven't told her, have you?"

His head dropped, a cluster of Grey's blond hair falling. "I will tell her when we get closer. When she can no longer demand to be left behind."

I tapped my fingers along my chin. "You think one of you is going to die, and you're choosing yourself."

"No. I'm giving her the greater chance of survival. Because as she is right now, I don't know if she's strong enough to cast that spell and live through it. But if I have to carry her over that barrier myself, I will."

"She'll never agree to crossing."

"What do you want me to do, Kir? Lie to her? That didn't go over so well last time."

I pretended to lean on the railing beside him, staring at the town in the same way he did. "You cross the border, she casts, she likely dies, and you also die. Or you tell her, and she jumps overboard, giving her life for yours and you live. Still, she dies."

He ran his fingers over his sharp jaw, his face twisted as though thoughts were moving through his mind as recklessly as throwing a giant ship into a storm on the sea. "I'd never let her jump overboard. I'll lock her below if I have to."

"She'd never forgive you."

He tucked his hands into deep pockets with a sigh. "I'm used to being her villain. If she lives, then nothing else matters. I'm asking you now, Kirsi. Leave this with me."

"And if she figures it out?"

He leaned in, narrowing his silver eyes. "Then you keep her from doing anything stupid."

I snorted. "Raven is rational about everything except you. But you have my word. I won't say anything to her until you've had your chance."

I floated up toward the drunk captain, now sober and serious behind the wooden spokes of his ship's wheel. The Dark King followed me, his hands still held behind his back, eyes drawn to the few men below, scurrying about.

"You're sure this is a big enough crew to get us there?"

Crow pulled the leather hat from his head, wiping his brow with the back of his hand. "The last time the sky looked like this, I lost my whole crew. The ship was shredded to pieces, and I woke up marooned on a beach. Sheer luck saved me. See those thunderheads there? I'm not sure a hundred men would be enough to see us through. We'll hope the wind holds steady and do our best. That's all we can do, Your Grace."

Bastian glanced at me and dipped his chin before answering. "We'll have to get her back today. There's no chance of waiting. I'll pay double whatever fee Eden has promised."

A pink blush filled the peculiar man's round cheeks as he put his hat back on. "I, uh..." He cleared his throat. "I'm not sure you want to make that bargain."

The corner of Grey's lip raised, the smirk devilish on his brooding face when understanding settled there. Another peek of Bastian I'd never seen in Grey until now. Though I supposed when one was looking, it was easier to see. Or maybe he'd drawn a clear distinction of the two characters in his own mind.

"What?" he asked, noticing my stare.

"I'm just trying to decide if you're really Grey in the Dark King's body or the Dark King in Grey's body. Which personality is really you?"

His shoulders raised with the deep breath he took. Before answering, he stepped away from the captain, toward the rail on the ship. "In time, you will see that we are one and the same. As Grey, my walls don't have to be quite so high. I can relax and be myself."

I moved left and right, unable to hold still, even in serious moments. "You couldn't be yourself with Raven weeks ago?"

"It's not that I couldn't be myself. I was more myself with her, and also you, than you probably realize. Bastian the king? He lets no one in. Keeps no one close. But Raven has been the exception to every rule since the day she challenged me when the Chosen arrived."

"Fine. But I'm not saying it was okay. I'm not even saying I'm done being pissed at you."

He switched into Bastian, dark hair pulled back, silver eyes similar to mine staring back. "Does this form help with the anger?"

I rolled my eyes. "Pretty sure the only reason Raven forgave you is because she realized she gets to fuck you both now."

He chuckled, wiggling his eyebrows, though it seemed forced, the tension still weighing on him. "Think so?"

"I take it all back. You're such a tool." I half smiled, but it quickly faded as Torryn approached, his face somber, ready to deliver Atlas' update.

The shifter shook his head, the silver in his beard catching the faint sunlight threatening to be swallowed by the clouds pushing in. "Without access to magic, we don't heal as quickly. Eden cleaned the wounds, but they are deep, and he hasn't stirred." He rubbed his hands over his face, reluctant to say the next words. "I'm not sure Atty's going to pull through this one, Bash."

"He will. I'll accept nothing less." He pivoted toward the captain. "How long until we hit the barrier?"

The man studied the sky for several moments before crossing the upper deck, leaning way over the railing to look down at the water, doing the weird finger-in-the-air thing before answering. "Half a day if the weather holds. Up to two if it gets out of hand."

"That's a big variance," Bastian replied. "You're going to have to make that half-day timeline. Once we hit the barrier, you and your men can turn back. I can get us the rest of the way."

Crow wiggled his fingers in the air, whispering, "With your magic?"

"No," Torryn cut in. "With his long swimming arms."

It took Crow longer than it should have to locate the sarcasm in Torryn's words, before his face showed any sign of understanding. If Atlas and Raven weren't in such compromised states of health, I might have laughed.

The second the ship's monstrous iron anchor was raised, and the large cables released from the dock, the behemoth burst to life, gliding along the top of the water, as eager to get to sea as we were. I left the captain's ship several times, circling the surface of the water, avoiding the inevitable. I needed to see Raven, needed to know she was okay, but heavy guilt weighed on me at withholding another large truth from her. Bastian had good intentions, but that didn't make the lie any easier. If it was between him and her, though, I would always choose her life. And not in the haunted form I was in. I wouldn't wish this eternal damnation on my worst enemy. Here, but not alive. No pleasure. Nothing satisfying.

I thought of the way I'd reached through that human's back and ripped his beating heart from his chest. Though my emotions were far more muted than they'd been when I was alive, I could still feel my own remorse. Could empathize with the death that I'd delivered, while harboring hatred for my mysterious murderer.

Moving down into the hull of the ship, I tried not to think of what it meant to go home. I'd been keeping those thoughts from my mind for days. Everything I had with Nym would be over. She was my light and my future, but that was gone. Before it ever really started. Passionate kisses and stolen promises. One night of bliss and then a ball. And that was it for us. A whirlwind of heavy and tragic loss.

Raven would stay with Bastian. The shop… Who knew what would become of it. I didn't need to work, but did I want to? Would I even be able to? And then there was Scoop. But my heart wouldn't let me think about him. About losing my soul partner. The ever present constant in my life, now just… gone.

She lay in a small bed crammed into a tiny room, awake and sipping tea as I crept in. Her dark, thick lashes fell heavy on her paling skin. She looked worse somehow. Gaunt.

"I'm fine. I swear I'm not going to break, no matter what he tells you."

"Men will always think they know better, and half the time, they know nothing."

Raven shared a small smile, sipping again at the herbal tea. "What do you think it's going to be like when we get home?"

"Well, if the shifters have managed to safeguard the Grimoires while we've been away, then I suppose it's going to be pretty similar to how we left it." I settled just above a broken chair propped up in the corner in the teeny room, my knees nearly touching the dark gray sheets on the bed. "There's still Nikos to deal with. Still the coven leaders. And what are we going to do with Eden?"

She shook her head. "I'm not sure. I mean, you heard Bastian say the Moss Coven has been weakening for years because they've been cut off from the power of their Grimoire. Maybe they will feel it when it reenters the realm."

I sat up straighter. "Endora is going to come with a vengeance if she knows that book is back."

Raven placed her teacup on the tray wedged between the chair and the bed, rubbing her hands together before patting her forehead. "I'm not convinced Endora ever cared about Eden's disappearance, to be honest. She was willing to ship her daughter off to a king she hated. And for all these years, Eden has managed to hide from her mother with the book. If anything, I think Endora will be out for blood."

"So, she'll be the same. Headache bothering you?"

Her voice grew quiet as she stared off into space. "I feel like I've been running for days and days and if I could just rest, I would feel better. Sometimes I do, and other times, it's like I can feel myself fading. Like I'm disconnected. I can't make sense of it."

"It's got to have something to do with you being cut off from your magic. Maybe the human lands affect witches differently. We don't have enough information from witches who have left to know if it's something that happens."

"What if casting the death spell is killing me, Kir?" Face full of worry, she blinked several times. "I was never supposed to have it, and maybe Death himself is punishing me, like he said he would."

"I've met Death," I whispered, remembering the hooded figure that pulled my spirit from my body when I'd been murdered. "If he wanted to take you, he would have never sent you back. Whatever is happening, it's not a punishment from him. But we can't rule out the fact that the coven leaders were involved. And they wanted you to die as a thirteenth generational witch. They need you to die to invoke their master plan. They could have done something we don't even know about."

"When it comes to the coven leaders, I'm realizing they've done a lot of things we don't know about and all we can do is hope we discover all the truths before it's too late. But everything starts with getting home. We will figure it out from there, come what may. The coven leaders might be cunning, but so is Bastian."

I threw her a glance, and she giggled softly.

"Fine. You're cunning, too. And we're going to need all that we can get. Eden has the final book with her. And I think we need to convince Bastian to give the books back to the covens."

I drew back, my eyebrows nearly touching. "Have you lost your damn mind? We can't give them those books."

"It's not right for us to keep them from the witches, and you know that. You know what it was like not to have it. To only see it in rare moments."

"If the coven leaders could be trusted, that would be one thing, Rave, but they can't be."

A soft knock on the door was the only warning before Eden swept in with a tray of crackers and more herbal tea. The perfect nursemaid, it seemed.

"I've brought more refreshments. I'll leave you two to chat."

Raven pushed against the mattress, sitting further upright. "No, please join us. I think we need to talk."

"Oh?" Eden sat on the very edge of the bed, leaning in as if she had no clue what we were discussing, though I'd heard her outside the door long before she entered the room. I suspect Raven had as well. It might have been the reason she brought the book up.

"What will you do with the Grimoire when we return?"

"Well." She tucked her hands into her lap. "I suppose whatever the king wants to do with it."

Raven poured from the teapot, the amber liquid steaming as the bits of herbs swirled within her tiny cup. "You've given your whole life to protect that book. Do you believe he should keep them, or should the Grimoires be with the witches?"

She bit her lip, considering the question. Though I appreciated that she didn't take the situation lightly, I wasn't sure which side she would be on, nor which side I *should* be on.

"I think the books are dangerous. I've seen what happens when two books are together and someone casts nearby. We cannot trust the coven leaders with that kind of power."

"But you have to ask yourself ... How did Bastian get them into that magical room if he couldn't cast? And how did anyone use magic at the castle with six of the seven being close by?"

"Or," a deep voice answered as Bastian came around the open doorway to lean against the frame. "We need to ask ourselves what kind of devastation those books can make if someone casts when they are *all* together. As for your first question, I created that barrier before I confiscated the books. When it was only the Fire Coven Grimoire.

They react to *casting* magic, not the presence of it. The barrier kept any casting in the castle protected."

Raven sat her cup down, worrying her hands again as she stared at the end of the bed. "I know you want to keep the Grimoires, but I don't think it's safe. There's peace to be found if the witches are given back those books. If Eden comes forward and tells the story of the Harrowing, the coven leaders can stand trial and new witches can be appointed across the board. We can start over."

The Dark King shook his head, looking up to the ceiling with a sigh. They'd clearly had this conversation earlier and it likely hadn't ended well. "This is a discussion for another time. It doesn't matter what we want for the books right now. Only that we make it home and see what state the Old Barren has managed to hold over these past days while we've been gone."

I studied the permanent long length of my nails, wishing I'd tended to them before I died. "Will we get to look at Bastian or Grey when we go back?"

His eyes flicked to Raven. "Since we don't know what we are walking into, I'll be Grey. As far as everyone knows, Bastian has died. If that's an advantage in any way, we take it. That means I need to trust the three of you to keep the secret."

I left my broken chair to circle the ceiling before landing behind him and flicking his ear. When he flinched, a small wave of satisfaction rippled through me. "Your secret is safe with me, King. I feel like it's only fair now that we're in the inner circle."

He lifted a shoulder, turning to face me. "I'm going to find a way to pick on you, Kirsi Moondance, and you're going to rue the day you—"

"Piece of advice, King. Maybe don't go around making people *rue the day* as Grey. Dead giveaway. Pun intended."

He switched into Grey, moving his fingers through his new blond tresses as he winked at Raven. "Noted."

"I'm going to check on Atty," Eden said, rising from the bed as thunder rolled above us. She pressed her hand into the pocket of the plain apron she was wearing and pulled out a necklace with a charm on the end. "This is going to be a dangerous journey."

When she slipped past Bastian, they shared a quiet smile.

"How dangerous?" Raven asked, pressing her palm into her temple.

"It'll be as smooth as we can manage. Rest. You're going to need your strength."

THE DARK SKY REFLECTED IN THE OCEAN FOR AN ETERNITY. There was nothing but us, and black sails flapping in the growing winds. Just humans running along the deck as the captain yelled at them from his wheel, two shifters, two witches and a wraith prepared to fight nature.

I remained hidden to keep the crew focused, staying near the captain on the highest deck, watching the chaos ensue. Thunder accompanied the day's ambience and as the ocean sprayed the crew, the storms grew. Crow, for all his demanding focus, appeared worried.

The boat rode the top of the tumbling waves without grace or glory. I imagined a canvas of a black ship tempting the goddess as she stirred and stirred the ocean below. The white caps of the ocean, the steep drops of the front of the ship. The silver lightning that webbed across the dangerous black sky. We'd sailed into a melting pot of nature's boundless fury.

I couldn't tell how far away the boundary was. I wasn't even sure if we would see it. But as Bastian held his arms around Raven, the sails rippled in defiance in the wind, and Torryn stood as still as a statue, I began to wonder if we should turn back. I would not die. But I could be condemned to this life alone, forced to watch my best friend perish on a ship intended to save her life.

She'd gotten a fucking nosebleed again. Just moments before Bastian agreed to let her come upstairs and watch. She'd been tossed around below enough that there was no arguing with her. But, in truth, there never was. Not when she put her mind to something. Which I loved her for. Still, to see her pallid face, the rag pressed to her nose, the worry on everyone's expressions, I couldn't help but wonder what the fuck we would get from this dangerous journey.

Crow's triangular hat flew directly through my stomach and

before it could be caught, it was lost to the ocean. He didn't seem to notice though, shouting more orders to his crew as they tugged and tossed the thick ropes below, some wrapping them around their waist and leaping around the deck with haste.

"Someone needs to go get Atlas from below and the rest of you need to tie off," Crow yelled over the pelting rain.

The ship tilted hard to the side before slamming back down into the water. Bastian held on to Raven. Torryn grabbed Eden's arm, her dual toned hair whipping him in the face as he helped her across the ship's upper deck and to a long coil of rope. Once the three of them were tied down, Torryn ran below, appearing moments later with the giant, sleeping wolf.

"How are you going to tie him?" I asked, moving to float beside Torryn.

"You can't," Eden said, brows turned inward. "The ropes will open his wounds."

Tor's lips turned to a hard line. "I will hold him safe."

His words were like a promise between brothers. As if he knew Atlas would have made the same vow had the roles been reversed. Again, the ship rocked and crashed down, jostling everyone on deck but me, of course. There was no threat to me. No fear for my life. The only fear I felt now was for my friends. Old and new. I soared over to Raven and took her hand into mine, even if she couldn't really feel me there, we were in this together.

"I love you, Kir," she yelled over the wind, and I could have sworn when she squeezed, something deep within me felt it.

"No," Bastian growled, tilting her head to him. "Don't you do that. No goodbyes."

She wiped the rain from his face as she smiled. "No goodbyes."

"There," Torryn yelled, jutting his chin forward.

I could hardly see it through the rain that fell in sheets and the wind that tossed the ocean waves as tall as the ship. But in the far distance, barely discernible, was a magical barrier. A massive glimmering wall. A promise of magic and home if only we could reach it. We remained silent for a long time, the others gripping the ropes holding them down as the ship battled the sea in a torrent of fury and chaos.

The humans on the lower deck became sluggish, exhausted. I wondered if they could see the wall and, if so, what they knew of our journey. Though Crow gripped his wheel with confidence, he'd lost his conviction. The finish line was so close, but the sea and sky did not relent. We made no forward motion. Simply battling to stay above the water. The ship's nose rose so high in the air it was nearly perpendicular to the sea. The humans all hung by their ropes, Bastian holding Raven as they smashed into the railing. Torryn gripped Atlas with one arm, the veins in his forearms straining as he held the rest of the weight with the rope coiled around him.

"Come on, you bitch," Crow yelled, eyes wild as he gripped his wheel for dear life, daring the ocean to break him. "I was born to this sea, and I'll fucking die by it."

"Remind me again why we picked this guy," I bellowed into Bastian's ear as the ship came slamming down onto the surface again.

He smiled genuinely. "Only a crazy bastard would ever do this more than once."

"We're not going to make it," Rave called out, the wind whipping her soaked black curls across her face.

"We are," Bastian shouted, determined. "The second we get across that barrier, I'll cast a door. Get through it by whatever means necessary."

"No. The people on deck won't make it back. You have to let me counter the storm with my power. Maybe I can calm the sea," Raven argued.

"You can hardly stand on your own two feet," I shouted at her. "You'll kill yourself trying to do something like that."

Bastian gave me a look that I'd seen before on Grey's face. One that he'd given me just before I was questioned about Breya's death ahead of everyone else. He wanted me to trust him. To let her cross and him die if it meant she lived. And I would, even if she hated me for it.

16

RAVEN

Only the lightning crawling across the black expanse provided enough light to see any part of the war between ocean and sky. We had to be getting close to the barrier, but that would mean nothing if we couldn't pass through. The crew grew tired, Crow soon after, even we, the passengers, were exhausted. Bastian stood tall behind me, arm firmly around my waist as the storm raged on, content to take our ship down. Kirsi was near, though we couldn't see her. Occasionally she would shout above the pouring rain and sharp wind, but for the most part, it was only us in the violent world. Torryn holding Atlas, Eden clutching the Moss Coven Grimoire to her chest, Crow screaming at the sky like a lunatic.

The tip of the enormous ship rose once more toward the sky, forcing everyone to cling to the ropes tied around them for dear life. The creaking and groaning of the vessel held my heart clutched in its foreboding hands as I held Bastian tighter.

"The ship is going to flip," Crow yelled. "That or break in half. You better make a plan, King."

My heart plummeted. "How close are we to the barrier?"

No one answered. He couldn't hear me. But I could feel it. A tiny kernel of power like static I couldn't quite reach.

"How close?" I screamed.

A bolt of lightning struck salty ocean water nearby as the tumbling ship crashed back down to the angry sea. Anything on board had long been tossed over, several of the crew members had also been lost to the gripping fists of the waves thrashing the ship. Feet planted solidly back on the deck, I turned in Bastian's arms to force his attention to me. Cold determination sat in those silver eyes as he stared straight ahead, jaw tight as if he alone could will us closer to our destination. I placed a soaked palm to the coarse hairs on his cheek, shaking him from his own horror-filled imaginings.

"Can you feel it?"

"No. Not yet." He paused, drawing back. "Can you?"

I nodded as the boat tossed to the left, taking on more water before righting itself. "We're nearly there. I just don't know how close."

"Whatever you're thinking, don't do it," he shouted. "You're not strong enough. You'll hurt yourself."

"I have to try. That or we all die. Which is your preference?"

"No!" Kirsi screamed from somewhere nearby. "Listen to him, Rave. If we are as close as you say, he can cast a door. We'll go through."

The ship lifted again, the planks of wood snapping in half directly in the middle. The crew below became a chorus of screams and shouts of chaos.

"She's going to break," Crow yelled. "I hope you really do have those strong swimming arms."

Again, a tiny tug of magic swarmed within me. I stole a glance at Bastian, but no markings appeared, and he hadn't seemed to feel it. Shouting came from behind us as Torryn and Eden frantically untied their ropes.

"What the hell are you doing?" Kirsi shouted, the panic in her voice jarring.

They didn't answer, just took the small window of opportunity to run, sliding across the deck until they were closer to us, Atlas still limp and completely unaware of our plight. There was no questioning the fear in Eden's trembling fingers as she shoved the Grimoire into the ivory satchel that crossed her chest. Perhaps she originally thought it would be safer in her hands. She retied her rope while Bastian helped Torryn with his. They'd made it, but only just as once again, the ship was tossed sideways then tilted to the side so far, I could reach down, dangling from the rope and touch the sea. A surge of power jolted through me. I jerked ramrod straight.

"I have to do it!" I screamed, loosening the cord around my waist.

"Raven, no!" Bastian countered, reaching for me as I pushed from his arms.

"I can't let us die without trying."

Eden flicked a glance toward me, and I knew she was telling me to do it. I saw my mother in that desperate plea. The friendship that they'd had long ago, the life Eden never got to live because she sacrificed everything, believing she was helping the world. She was brave, and so was I. Come what may, I had to do what I could. Drawing the magic from the deepest part of my soul, fighting the restriction of the substantial barrier we still had not passed, knowing the spell would not be as strong as it could be, I cast, turning myself into a conduit as lightning surged for me. Bastian lunged for me, but the rope held him back, drenched in rain, devastated. I flung my arms out, daring that storm as wildly as the ship's captain had to come for me and not the ocean. To provide a reprieve from the relentless battering. I thought I was strong enough to save us all.

I was wrong.

For five long seconds, the storm settled. The world fell silent as the ocean rippled below us, causing the ship to bob but not toss. The barrier was mere feet away, the sheen of a blue light an arm's length from the side of the boat. Blood poured down my face, seeping from my nose. A breeze, a shift in the water, that's all we needed. But as if the goddess knew we'd somehow cheated her magical barrier, the skies erupted and the ocean turned into a giant whirlpool, waiting to devour us all. Bastian lunged for me, Eden screamed, and Crow abandoned his ship's wheel to join us, knowing there was nothing more to be done. The three remaining crew members on deck held onto their ropes as the ship swirled.

Torryn yelled, the velocity of the motion violently pushing him into the slick railing while he held on to Atlas, now slung over his shoulder. The motion of the spin pinned us all back, smashed uncomfortably into the wooden handrails of the deck's perimeter.

"The barrier," Kirsi shouted, popping into view. "It's right there"

For a flash of a second, we'd crossed it. A surge of magic, a breath, and then nothing as we were swept out again.

"Everyone, get ready. Untie the ropes and hold the baluster." Bastian grabbed me by the collar of my dress and yanked me toward him until there was hardly an inch between us. Rain poured down from his lashes, streaking his cheeks. "Don't you fucking let go of me, no matter what happens. Promise me."

There was something he wasn't saying. Even now. Seconds from promised doom, he'd kept something from me. I'd have to process that later because he closed the distance, desperately kissing me until we were both struggling to keep our grip on the slippery rail.

"I'm going to cast the door directly below my feet as soon as we cross that barrier again. Do not hesitate to jump," he yelled to the others as they crowded in.

And then we waited, letting the ship swirl one final rotation. The barrier flashed. Bastian cast. I squeezed my eyes shut, holding only him as the world silenced, and we fell through our miraculous saving grace.

17

RAVEN

I didn't register the fall. Only the onslaught of power coursing through my veins as if I'd been walking in a fog that decisively relented. As if I could finally take a fresh, full breath of icy cool air into my lungs after walking through a fire. Something in the air was off, though. Something heavy and familiar. I couldn't quite place my finger on it. We landed in a heap of tangled limbs on the floor with Kir hovering above us, her eyes glued to me as if watching for my reaction.

"What?" I asked, pushing off the hard ground, only then noticing the terracotta pots toppled over and the broken shelves in Crescent Cottage. The whole shop had been ransacked. I caught her glance at Bastian before she shrugged and moved away as if they'd been anticipating something.

"How do you feel?" Bastian asked, tying his hair back as he scanned me from head to toe with dark eyes, his familiar markings appearing on sun-kissed skin.

Torryn crouched low, placing Atlas gently on the floor and covering him with a blanket that had been tossed to the ground. I cast healing over the injured shifter, noting the sag in his body as the magic caressed him. I'd missed this feeling of power, but I was also immediately struck with unnecessary fear of it, remembering the death spell, remembering the totality of it. Maybe I'd never heal from that trauma.

Torryn's heavy boots thumping across the floor shattered my dismal thoughts. His knuckles brushed my forehead, golden eyes heavy with concern until he was satisfied I wasn't seconds from death. If Atlas was the loyal wolf, Torryn was the wise owl. My heart opened to him a little. As if it recognized the gentle giant for what he truly was. Kind and protective.

Closing my eyes, I felt for the swell of pain within. The pounding on my temple, the weakness in my knees. I took the longest breath I'd been able to in days. "I feel better. Alive. Not on the brink of death. All wins."

"Good god, it smells awful in here." Kirsi moved her hand over her nose though I wasn't sure what that did for her. "What is that? I haven't been able to smell a thing for days."

I lifted a single shoulder, confused. "I don't smell anything."

"That'll probably be your new aversion to sage," Eden said, stepping in a slow circle, drawing all of our attention to Crescent Cottage. This was the first time I'd seen her with markings. Though she looked like she belonged in this world now, it felt strange knowing they'd been hidden for so long. She must have felt the same as she ran her fingers up and down her arms, looking at the small symbols she hadn't seen in more than half her lifetime.

The damage was severe. Though the heavy front door was still intact, almost nothing else was. Whoever had pillaged the shop was clearly looking for something. Crystals scattered the floor like shattered glass, dirt from all the plants covered the floorboards. I only hoped my mother hadn't been in to see it. If she had, I could only imagine the things she'd construed in her mind.

"What happened to this place?" Atlas asked, his voice strong, as if the magic I'd cast had healed him completely. He lived, thank the goddess.

Bastian and Torryn darted for him, one pressing him into a headlock, the other an arm around his waist.

"Still alive, assholes." He shoved an elbow into Torryn's shoulder, holding his side. "Guess I have you to thank for that."

Torryn jutted his chin toward Kir. "Thank the wraith, Atty. She ripped a heart out to save you."

Bastian slipped away from the man-hug to come and stand beside me. One small motion, and his wings appeared. Beautiful, dark and smooth, reflecting the midday sun shining through the dust coated windows.

"Don't get cocky," Kir smirked. "You still smell like a dog, Atlas."

"Pretty sure you already told us you can't smell. But speaking of rancid..." He pinched his nose and stepped away from Torryn. "Try bathing."

"Yeah, I've been attached to you all day, and wet dog doesn't flatter anyone," he answered with a grin.

"Any and all bets are welcome, but I'm guessing this was Nikos," Kir said, eyes pulled together in concentration as she pushed a plant upright. "That aside, what are we going to do about Captain Human over there?"

"I have ears, Ghosty," the captain said sadly, slumped in the corner, his head buried in his hands.

He'd lost his whole crew again. The men on that ship might have been close friends of his, and I hadn't even thought of that loss for him. I'd been so wrapped up in my own feelings, I hadn't truly considered those lives.

Eden crouched to the floor, lifting his chin so he was forced to look into her eyes. "Thank you for your sacrifice, Crowen. You've always done everything you could for me, and I know this loss is devastating."

He forced a smile to his lips. "You're worth every sacrifice, every ship and every drop of water in that sea."

I walked to the back room, giving them their own space. The devil's ivy that normally covered the door from floor to ceiling had been ripped away, the leaves scattering the ground already drying out, and the crunch beneath my shoe was a tiny prick of pain as I considered the state of my livelihood.

I reached for the broom, but Bastian was there first. He snatched it from the hook on the wall and leaned against it as he stared at me as if expecting something.

"What?"

"I thought you would be forced to finish the death spell when we got back. I didn't want to tell you in case it would change your mind about coming, but there it is."

I turned, my heart feeling the betrayal, even if it was only a small thing. "You make it very hard to trust you, Bastian."

He set the broom aside. "When you cast that spell on me the last time, I thought for sure you were going to kill me. The only thing I could think of was what they would do to you if that happened. I didn't consider my own life, of fading away, only the shifters shredding you to pieces. It was a torture I couldn't bear. I sent you to the human lands to save you, only realizing at the last second that I could possibly save myself as well. I wasn't sure if we'd come back. I wasn't willing to risk your life to reverse the decision I'd already made. If it meant I died, I was okay with that."

"You still could have said something." I grabbed a sack from the long wooden countertop below the circular window, noticing the hairline crack in the glass. "My grandmother loved this window."

A heavy hand gripped my arm. He lifted my fingers to his lips before pulling me to him, wrapping me in a hug. I needed those arms around me so badly, nothing else seemed to matter. He was here and alive, and that was a far greater future than I'd thought possible only days ago.

"I need you to stop withholding information from me. It can't be your rules, your world. If we're going to be on the same team, it has to be united. I understand the fear you had, and I'm sorry you didn't think you could trust me, but we're here now. Let's move on and set this right. No more dancing around each other because we think the other is too fragile or volatile."

He pulled away, staring into my eyes with so much relief I thought he'd burst. With a single gesture, his shadows covered the door, giving us privacy. "We're here now," he repeated. "That's enough."

Moving his fingers into my tangled hair, he pressed his lips to mine, and I melted for him. For the wings at his back I thought I'd never see again, the silver that lit differently in his eyes when he had his magic. And for the shadows pooling on the floor and over the door as if his magic yearned for this world. He moved his hands down to my neck, fingers grazing over my collarbone as he devoured me, massaging my tongue with his in a fury of motions that instantly consumed. This was Bastian. In all his glory, just a man, but always a king. Always demanding and always taking me to places I'd never known.

I gripped his damp shirt, pulling him to the back of the small room, pushing aside the debris as I collided with a wall. Shoving his fingers back into my hair, he tugged my head back, pressing heated lips in a trail to the hollow of my neck, letting out a subtle groan. My knees weakened at the sound, his unbridled desire for me as fierce as my own for him. Purposeful hands and tongue and teeth consumed me as his silky, dark wings moved in, cocooning us in a warmth that could have lit the world on fire. Outside this space was chaos and danger, but here, with him? It was only us and the unspoken promises of a future full of these moments.

"Ahem."

"Go away, Moondance," Bastian growled. His fingers gripped mine against the wall.

"Have you kissed Grey yet? I'm not saying I'd judge you, Rave. Just curious."

I couldn't help my smile. The queen of deflection had struck again. Dropping my hands, though reluctantly, I slipped away from our space, leaving the comfort of those wings. "What's wrong?"

"I mean, aside from the obvious state of this place? We've got to do something about the captain. And I'd bet my nonexistent life Endora already knows that Grimoire is back. Plus, the guys are showing off their battle scars and Crow took his shirt off. I'm thoroughly disturbed." She shuddered. "Boys are gross."

"Men," Atlas shouted from the shop front.

She tossed her hands in the air. "I said what I said."

Torryn's low chuckled filled Crescent Cottage and I grabbed the broom and headed back to the front to find him lifting a shelf that had been toppled over, trying not to step on the wares that lay in tatters on the floor. "Tell me again what you think happened here."

"Nikos," Kirsi and Bastian said in unison.

I nodded. "Probably. He's got a key."

"I'm going to need the full story," Torryn said, taking a heavy pot from Eden and setting it on my stone counter.

"Nikos has a spell that allows him to control another person. He's the one that forced Raven to cast the death spell on me."

"He's the one that's been controlling the witches, then?" Torryn asked.

Eden snorted. "If he's anything at all, it's just a pawn in my mother's game."

Gathering the small glass vials still intact from the floor, I simply agreed. "Nikos used to be close friends with Kir and me. Then we tried taking things to a different level and little did I know, he was the literal root of all evil. We have no idea how long he's been controlling things, but that power is dangerous. We know his family went through the bloodletting to leave Moss and join Moon. I don't think Tasa would have agreed to that on her own. I think she was coerced. As far as I'm concerned, Nikos is enemy number one right now, regardless of Endora's plans."

I wanted my sage so badly. Just speaking his name in this place felt wrong. Felt as if we were calling him. My eyes flashed to a smoke stick discarded on the floor.

"Don't even think about it." Kirsi groaned from beside me.

Atlas plucked it from the ground and shoved it in his pocket as he flashed a full-mouthed smile to Kirsi. She rolled her eyes and moved toward the back door of the shop, looking out over the garden.

"Okay, girlie, what's your first magic going to be?" Crow asked, a swagger in his step as he moved toward Eden.

"Do you mind?" she asked me, looking down at the markings on her arms.

"Be my guest," I answered.

The semi-circle on her neck lit green, followed by a double slash on her wrist and then something from below her shirt. She ceremoniously swept her arms through the air as everything scattered about, every broken pot and pile of dirt took on a mind of its own. Her magic raced through Crescent Cottage, returning it to the beauty it had once been. Not a shard of glass was out of place when she was done.

Crow slowly clapped his gloved hands, jaw slackened, as he studied the witch he so clearly adored. "Magnificent."

She whipped around, facing Bastian and me with a gleam in her eye I'd never seen and a smile so radiant, I think we all felt it. Even Kirsi from the back door.

"Another?" she asked, clasping her hands before her as if in prayer.

"You're not a child, Eden. You're a witch. Use your magic as often as you'd like."

Pricking her finger, she let seven drops of blood fall on the ground below her. She spun back to Crow, taking his hand in hers as she flourished an arm in an arch above them, the green glow filling the cottage until the remnants of her barrier slipped over the outside of the shop like a second skin.

"It can't be crossed, and we cannot be heard or seen except by you, whom I've granted exception. It's a very powerful spell."

"A barrier?" Kirsi asked, darting out of the shop directly through the wall and then back inside. "I'm sure it's strong, but I think the scary Dark King should put up his."

I shook my head. "He can't. It's made of shadow, and they think he's dead. That's a lie we should let them believe."

"They've seen Grey cast that spell," Kirsi argued. "At the Trials opening ceremony on Gravana Lake. You said the one over the Grimoire room wasn't visible."

"True," Bastian said, stroking his palm over the stubble on his chin. "But the Grimoire spell only works in the heart of the kingdom, central to all covens. And they think Grey is gone with Raven. As soon as they know we are back from wherever we went, it'll be a witch hunt all over again. So, while I appreciate the vote of confidence, Moondance, I'm sure Eden's barrier is just as powerful."

Eden dipped her chin, her light and dark hair falling over her shoulders. "Thank you, Your Grace."

"We'll stay here for the night," Bastian announced, clasping his hands behind his back as he circled the group of us. "Tomorrow, we'll leave Eden and Crow locked in here and head to the castle."

"Maybe you should test the barrier first," Eden said, sheepishly. "It's been a while. Just in case."

The feeling of something heavy returned to me in that moment. As if there was a presence I wasn't aware of, or something I'd been forgetting sitting right on the tip of my tongue. It wasn't until Eden pulled the Grimoire from her satchel and set it on the counter that I realized the feeling. It was the book, drawing me to it, as if it whispered my name in a foreign language only I could hear.

Bastian eyed the book warily, and I realized he must have felt it, too. A near sentient being finally back to a place of power. Not entirely, but in some ways, reunited with its brethren, the other six Grimoires.

"Best put that away," Torryn said, slipping his hands into his pockets, eyes flashing to me as if he could read my mind. "No good can come from having it out on display."

"What's so special about them books, anyway?" Crow asked, leaning over the counter to get a better look.

"They are the source of our power," Eden answered, drawing a finger down the spine. "The Grimoires used to be a single book, but the witches felt the magic was drawing too thin, so they performed a ritual, The Breaking. Dividing the single book into seven pieces, one for each of our sacred covens." She placed her palm on the light green jewel pressed into the cover. "It contains the first and last drop of blood of every one of my ancestors. Spells one cannot receive but can conjure, dark histories and twisted tales of secrets. Nothing good can come from this damn book, but it is hallowed all the same."

Crow flipped the book open. "Does it have pictures? I like those best."

"Diagrams. It's not a children's book," Bastian answered, slipping a hand around my waist.

I hadn't realized I'd been walking forward until he stopped me. The Grimoire was like a dangerous enticement, calling me. Luring me in as if I had no choice. I hated the way it made me feel as if I'd lost an edge of my own careful control. Turning away, I rubbed my hands down my arms, the hint of a headache on the horizon. I couldn't tell them, though. They'd all worry and hover and get distracted. We didn't need that.

"Are we going to test the barrier?" I asked, changing the attention of the room to something far less sinister.

"Kirsi, Atlas and I will test it tonight after the sun has set. One witch, one shifter, one wraith. That should be enough of an assessment," Bastian said.

"I should go, too," I countered. "Technically, you're only half witch."

"And yet still more powerful than Endora Mossbrook." He lifted an eyebrow, a half-smirk on his face and a challenge in his eyes.

"Fine," I conceded. "But at least go as Grey. The Dark King is dead."

18

RAVEN

The grooves worn into the floorboards of Crescent Cottage from a century of salt circles dripping with various candle waxes were the closest thing to home I'd felt in so long. Sprinkling the black salt into a circle and placing my seven candles around it was mind-numbing and just the thing I needed after the chaos of the day, the long ship ride, and the plethora of emotions my heart still needed to sort out. Eden had cast her barrier spell, but this one was also needed. Protection and blessings in abundance.

Flourishing a hand over the candles, I couldn't help but glance at Kirsi, knowing, though she watched me like a hawk, she was still hurting. Still so far removed from her own magic, she yearned for it, mourned it. She lifted her chin, always willing to show strength rather than sorrow. Our whole lives, she'd been that way. It made sense that, even in death, her nature had not changed.

I stepped over the salt barefoot, letting the familiar boards creak beneath my feet as I felt the power of the circle push over my skin, lifting the small hairs along my arms and down my spine. There was a time when I didn't know if I would ever get to feel this again or want to. But standing here now, the hem of my black skirt grazing the tops of my feet as the candles flickered below me, I couldn't imagine never again feeling the power that rumbled deep within me. It was different now, had been since the Trials. Something had awakened. Something I'd always known was there, but was hidden beneath. Bound.

Eden stepped into my circle next, the candlelight from below illuminating her face and contrasting hair in a way that was equal parts scary and hauntingly beautiful. She was two parts of a whole. Even in her life... exiled and rescued. Living in the human lands, a witch, but not. She slipped one hand into mine as Grey joined us. Truly Bastian in disguise, but it still felt wrong when he took my hand, rubbing his thumb over my knuckles.

"Almost time," Kirsi said, floating up to the uncovered window on the ceiling.

Though many didn't know it existed, my grandmother had praised her moon window, keeping it hidden except for when she spelled in the shop at midnight. She swore the placement of the cottage in the Moon Coven Territory, along with the symmetry of the window's carefully etched glass, held its own sort of power. I prayed she was right.

Using magic to set the intention, I cast healing over myself. It'd never been much of a spell, only something to soothe a headache, or heal a scratch, but with more power behind me now, I wondered if that would change. Pushing my amplification spell, I considered how long it would be until they questioned me. The purpose of the spell circle was to ground ourselves back into the magical world, but I had plans of my own. Far healthier than I had been in the human lands, an ailment still haunted me. It seemed casting death had awoken something within me it shouldn't. Still, the circle, the spells, the moon … they were all I needed to finally feel myself again. Thank the goddess.

"Ready?" Bastian asked, his eyes flicking to my fingers.

He'd seen the motion to cast the spell, likely noticing the way my body finally relaxed, but without the visible markings as the rest of the witches had, he couldn't be sure of anything.

We three bowed our heads, Bastian's shadows swirling below us. Come what may, we needed the goddess' purest blessing to continue this fight. And so, we cast as the others watched from the opposite end of the shop, Crow's jaw slackened, even Atlas' eyes glued to the magic.

Each of us had our own selection of spells, though Eden's were far fewer than Bastian's. She'd spent most of her life cut off from receiving spells and so far, nothing had come to her to make up for lost time. Bastian created his own barrier around us, dark as a starless sky, blocking us off from the room. I pushed the unlock spell, knowing that intention was the derivative of everything and though it worked on doors, it could also work on other things. And then Eden's marking on her arm lit as green as fresh moss, as she waved a hand through the air, humming.

"Sky above, Earth below," I whispered, "Three by three, blessing be." The deep resonance of Grey's voice crept up my spine as he joined me the second time I said the chant, this time louder. Eden joined the third and final time as I lured a candle to us, letting it float in the middle as we chanted much louder.

"Sky above, Earth below. Three by three, blessing be." The hair on my arms stood at attention, a swell of magic swirling as our intention was set. The red candles zapped out, confirming our blessing from the goddess was heard, but none of us moved an inch. No one could see beyond Bastian's barrier. We stood there, steeped in power blessed by the goddess, letting it replenish our spirits and whisper over our bodies like a summer breeze in a wildflower field. This was utter peace. This was magic. *Home.*

Bastian shifted back into his own form, though I wasn't sure he meant to as his eyes glossed over, his wings appearing at his back as the barrier he'd created grew to accommodate his large size. Darkness descended as the candlelight vanished, smothered by the Dark King's shadows, his power growing like a tangible object swirling around and around the circle, drawing me into him as my power coaxed his, stroked it. Alarms bells rang in my head. Something was wrong.

"Eden, leave the circle." My voice rattled, not with fear, but conviction. "Leave now, while you can. Don't touch the salt."

"You need to get away from him too," she hissed back. "He isn't himself right now. The goddess is blessing him."

"Go!" I shouted as the shadows grew denser.

She was gone in a flash, leaving me to the mercy of Bastian's blessing as I stood before him, hand still clasped in his. All of his rage, his passion, his determination radiated through the space, lifting my hair as his power became palpable. As his darkness called to me, drawing my own power. The day I'd seen his barrier the first time, it was a seduction unlike anything I'd ever known. Now, I understood why I'd felt so drawn to it. It was not the man. It was the raw, uninhibited power leashed somewhere within. Not him, but me. And when I cast the spell that took and took and took from me, it renewed everything I thought I'd known of the depths of magic. This blessing was not for Bastian, the Dark King. I dropped his fingers, understanding. He could not protect me from her. Because this blessing was for me.

"Raven." He gritted his teeth.

"Stop fighting her," I coaxed. "I am not afraid."

Hands clasped into fists at his side, he shook his head. "No. It is too much. You are recovering."

"I am many things, but weak is not one of them."

As if a dam broke, he slumped forward, fully spent from trying and failing to protect me from the goddess. Broad shoulders heaved, the muscles in his back rippling as he fell to a knee beside me. The purest white light descended from the sliver of moon peeking through the lunar window in the ceiling. A flash so blinding I had to cover my eyes to stop the searing pain. Though he struggled, I felt Bastian rise to stand beside me.

"You may look," a voice as pure as starlight, as sweet and golden as honey said.

I slowly dropped the arm over my eyes, though the light was still so bright, I could not make out the edges of the face before me. I looked to Bastian, but he hadn't moved a muscle, his head still bowed, suspended in time next to me.

"Fear not," the goddess said. "I have a message for you, Raven Moonstone. Even if your lover wishes to protect you, he cannot."

I could feel the smile in her voice more than see it beyond the powerful starlight. My pulse rattled through my veins in a cadence I didn't recognize as I stood in awe of the powerful being that had gifted our world the Book of Omnia so, so long ago.

She moved toward Bastian, her light casting the most beautiful glow upon his frozen face as she studied him. "I wonder if there is anything he would not do for you. Your Dark King might be fearful, but he is equally fearless. He sent you to the land with no magic, not to save himself, as he would let everyone believe, but to save you. He feared what the others would do to you should he die. He never planned on joining you. Hadn't even thought about it. He simply accepted his death and cast to protect you." Her pause was infinite and nothing at all. "He is worthy, if not broken. Though the broken things we keep tend to be the most extraordinary, do they not?"

I blinked in response, only half aware my jaw hung open.

"Heed my warning and tread lightly, Raven Moonstone. A time will come when you must make a decision that will impact the world. A tiny seed left unplanted will always be only a seed. But change, even if one is content, inspires growth and rebirth. Do not be afraid to sacrifice what others would not." As if the air had been sucked from the room, she reached for me, placing a fiery hot palm against my cheek. "I bless you."

In a blink, the span of one second to the next, she was gone. Bastian gasped beside me, time no longer suspended, our combined power circling the interior of the barrier once more.

He pressed a palm to the cheek the goddess had touched, stroking his thumb back and forth. "She blessed you."

"I think she warned me more than blessed me." I placed my hand on top of his, feeling the texture of his knuckles against my palm as I closed my eyes, reveling in the fact that we were more alone than we'd been in a long time. That the goddess had come to, indeed, bless us. That my power and his power swelled to a suffocating entity within our circle, surging through our veins and bringing us to life in more ways than one.

"Warned you?" His gaze dropped to my lips, and I knew he was thinking the same thing.

"Nothing specific," I whispered. "Just to tread lightly. And we will."

He smiled, sliding his hand up into my hair as he squeezed, tilting my head back. "I've never known you to do anything lightly. You wreck worlds with mere thoughts and call down goddesses with sheer intention. You're unlike anything this world has ever known."

I moved my hands around his waist and up his back, digging in with my nails as I narrowed my gaze upon him. "I'm just a Moon witch with a bad attitude."

He groaned at my touch and the sound went directly to my core, heating me from the inside out. Melting me into a puddle.

"I don't believe a single soul would describe you with the word *just*, Miss Moonstone."

"Then perhaps no one knows me at all," I breathed, moving to my tiptoes to press my lips to his.

He was gentle at first, his massive wings surrounding us as the power swirled and the barrier held. His plump lips brushed along mine. But Bastian had never been the gentle type. He bit down on my lip until I gasped, taking the opportunity to press his tongue to mine, stroking it. With one hand still buried in my hair, he moved the other to my neck, then down to my chest, rubbing the swell of my breast with his thumb as he devoured me.

Every inch ignited. The power pulsating as if it knew my body was already on edge, his shadows moved up my legs like fingers, until every part of me wanted only one thing. The throbbing ache between my thighs, breasts tender, skin alight. He was fire, but I was, too, and I craved the burn.

I pulled away, panting, immediately missing his lips on mine. "We cannot do this here."

"Oh, but we can," he said, stroking a thumb over his swollen bottom lip.

"Can we go to the mountain?"

"No," he answered, taking a dangerous step toward me. "We do not leave the barrier until tomorrow morning."

"But..."

"Call them. Call Kirsi and tell her you're in danger."

I shook my head. "Why?"

Another step. "Because she would burn the world down for you. If she could hear you, she would shift the salt circle and break the barrier."

"Kirsi, help," I whispered.

His dark chuckle at my weakness was nearly my ruination.

"And the barrier will hold?"

A sly smile as his hand wrapped around my waist. "It will hold."

He closed the gap the second I even thought of conceding, pulling my dress over my head in one single motion. Apt fingers removed what was left of my undergarments until I stood before him, bare and wanting. The Dark King was insatiable as he fell to his knees before me, lifting a thigh over his shoulder and pressing his lips over me, stroking with his tongue, hitting that spot in a perfect cadence. I could hardly hold on, my legs falling weak as he devoured me with such delight in his eyes, I thought they alone would be my undoing. If ever I was the strong one, it would never be the case in his presence.

Fingers dug into my thigh as he groaned against me, his shadows tangible, moving over my body until every inch was consumed, every part desperate for more and more of him. He stroked a thumb down my opening. I tossed my head back, the ends of my curls brushing the small of my back. One finger, and then two, filled me. Up and up I went until I stood at the edge of that peak, my breaths growing short before I fell into euphoric oblivion.

He stood, undressing as I watched him with hooded eyes. Within seconds, we were two bodies pressed together. Melting together. Lifting me, he pressed my back against the hard barrier, releasing me slowly down until I took in every solid inch of the Dark King. He growled, nipping at my neck with teeth and tongue, slamming into me, filling me, releasing all of his pent-up tension and longing.

Pressing his forehead to mine, he stared into my face, consuming the pleasure he found there, making sure I felt every single part of him. Digging my nails into his arms, I moaned, feeling myself weaken for him. Every wall rebuilt between us shattered as he reminded me that I was bound to him in a way I could not fight. My power rising to meet his. Those shadows licking my skin, the world coming undone below us as we climbed and climbed.

His swollen lips trailed my jawline as he moved below me. One arm wrapped around me, lifting me up and down, the other hand kneading a breast. Every part of Bastian worshiped my body, calling forth the pool of desire within my belly. The heat between my legs as he thrust.

I moaned again, unable to help the sound escaping my lips. He bit into my earlobe, sending a wave of sweet pain directly to my core. Breaths shortened, bodies slickened, we could have stayed like that forever.

I could see it in his eyes. The way he needed me matched that thrumming of my own heart. There was the world outside, and this one inside. The one we'd begun to build together, the one we'd both die for. Ours.

My breasts grew heavy, the pressure building. I dropped my head to his shoulder, muscles clenched as he tightened beneath me. Legs trembling, we exploded together, his seed filling me as the world disappeared, and, for a moment, it was just his heartbeat and mine. Climbing to the heavens to dance among the stars before falling back to this darkened world.

There was fire in his eyes as we dressed wordlessly. He pressed me back against the barrier time and time again to kiss me. To crush his body to mine as he bowed his head in silent prayer. The barrier was right there, ready to be dropped, but he couldn't find the strength to do it.

He moved his hand down the magical wall. "We could stay, Little Witch. It's safe here."

I wrapped my arms around him, looking up to those beautiful silver eyes. "It's not really safe anywhere, Bastian."

"I know," he whispered. "Not yet."

19

KIRSI

"I know freshly fucked hair when I see it."

Raven, cheeks flushed, huffed as she dug through the packed closet in the back room looking for the cots and bedding.

"It was nothing," she hissed, turning away from me again as she yanked on a blanket and three more toppled out from the small storage space. "Don't you want to hear about the goddess?"

"No. Nope." I floated around her until we were face to face. "I'd much rather hear about Bastian in bed. Oh, or was he Grey? Can we say 'in bed' if you were literally feet from us hidden in a salt circle?"

"Kir!"

"Ugh," I groaned. "Fine. You are such a fun-hater."

She tossed a small blanket at me, but it soared right through my torso and landed on the freshly clean floor in the back of the room.

"What do you think it means?" I asked, all sarcasm gone from my tone. "Cursed by Death, blessed by the goddess."

She finally turned, her face solemn. "I don't know. Truly. But I think I need to go see my mother. I know Bastian wants to get to the castle. We need to know the state of this world, but I need to know what my mother did when I was a baby. She knew I was the thirteenth witch and tried to save me, but what did she do?"

I lifted a shoulder. "I'll go with you, if you want?"

"Are you trying to avoid Nym? Think she will still be at the black castle? And what about Scoop?" She picked at a piece of lint from the pile of old blankets hung over her arm.

With great effort, I lifted the blankets she'd thrown to me. A success, but nothing worthy of celebration.

"I'm not sure what I'm avoiding." If I had a heartbeat, it might have slowed, might have felt heavy. "I think it's Scoop. I can't explain it, but I just miss him. I am so far removed from the witch I once was. It's different."

I couldn't... wouldn't talk about Nym. Wouldn't remind myself that she would always be someone I lost. The witch who'd empowered me to push through the Trials when I'd felt like leaving, who'd been there when Raven was not... The woman that was so easy to love and fear and treasure... I wasn't ready to mourn the loss of us. To see the horror on her face and let it be my final defeat.

But Scoop? The severance of my connection to him, a piece of my soul? No matter how much I might have loved Nym, he would always be my greatest loss.

Raven set her blankets down on the shelf lining the back wall beneath the window. She held her hands out to me, palms up.

"You won't—"

"Take my hands, Kir."

Dropping the blankets onto her pile, I inched forward, sliding my palms over the top of hers, waiting for the chill that was my new curse to make her shudder, to draw back, to run, even.

She held steady, her light blue eyes meeting mine. "I feel you, Kir. And if you cannot, then I will feel for both of us. You are no less than you were a month ago. Changed, but nothing less. If you're hurting, then I'm hurting. If you're celebrating, then I am. You've always been the best part of this friendship. I won't let you falter. Because you would never let me."

A brush, a small inkling of a sensation radiated through my palms. I felt her, too. I moved, resting my forehead on hers as I closed my eyes. "I don't think I want to be here, Raven. I know that must hurt to hear, but this isn't an eternity for me. It's miserable to sit in a room full of people and feel so fucking lonely."

"Then we find a way to send you back."

"Promise?"

Her nod against my forehead gave the same sensation as our joined hands. Whatever I was lacking in this world, the unwavering love of a friend was not one of them. But I didn't know if it was enough. I pulled away, lifting the blankets I dropped.

"You're getting pretty good at that," she said.

I smiled, pushing back the pain as I always did. "Seems silly to even mention it."

"Name one wraith you've ever seen lift a single object." She leaned against the counter, clasping her hands in front of her. "Go ahead. I'll wait."

"I said I didn't want to be here, not that I wasn't a fucking spectacular wraith."

THEY SLEPT. SOLIDLY, BUT NOT SOUNDLESSLY, THANKS TO THE WOLF'S obnoxious snoring. The days were longer now. No rest for the wicked, no rest for the wraiths. Invisible, I'd gathered some of the unspoiled food from our neglected autumn harvest, and Raven had made a squash soup, using her fire magic to sear the fresh vegetables. I wanted to taste that sweetness on my tongue, feel the sensation of being full, but that was no longer possible. I'd hovered in the corner, watching them cast within the salt circle as envy poisoned my mind. The need to feel the power beneath my skin, the sorrow of not having Scoop beside me overwhelmed me. I didn't want to feel this way, but I always came back to it. As if I was supposed to find comfort in that haunting sorrow. I sure as fuck did not.

Leaving Crescent Cottage as they slumbered, I wove invisibly through the town square, noting the groove along the bricks lit by the moonlight. With an eternity of haunting this realm before me, I took my time. Eden's barrier was not the same as Bastian's. It circled the shop solidly but unseen, like a second skin. Luckily, I had Eden's magical permission to cross the barrier. Without it, I'd have never been able to leave. She was powerful in her own way. Lucky witch.

Reaching my hand out, I brushed my ghostly fingers along the familiar buildings packed together in the square. What was I doing? I could absolutely breach any of these walls and explore these witches' domains. Search the shops and snoop through their things. I soared down the road toward Claire Moonfly's bakery, wondering whether I'd be able to see my breath in the late autumn air, if I had any. I didn't even know if it was cold outside. A blessing, I supposed.

Pushing through the door without a thought, I waited for the smell to slam into me as it always did. I remembered hungry days when my father and I would walk by just to smell what we could not have. Disappointment was all that greeted me. Wicker baskets full of breads and muffins and flour and sugar filled one wall. The rest of the store was empty. A sign that winter was coming, and, like it or not, everyone needed to start hoarding their wares in preparation. Most of the witches envied Claire and her family for their endless supply of food when others could only dream of it. I knew better, though. I knew she spent most of the winter months with only bread to keep her belly full, willing to trade with us for seasonal vegetables from our gardens when she became humble enough to ask.

The witches were stupid, I decided. For all their starving, if they would just stop with the animosity and work together, this land would have far less scars. I lifted a long skinny loaf from a basket, the crust crunching and flaking away as I squeezed. I guess that was no longer my problem.

I smirked. I bet the wolf would beg for fresh bread. I shot toward the door. I would bring back one of the pumpkins from the garden and leave it on the counter as payment. However, as I soared through the door, the damn bread couldn't. A solid object. I'd never wanted to punch a window so bad in my life. In my fucking *afterlife*.

I moved back through the door, unlocked the handle and opened it. Like a normal person. After leaving the pumpkin on the countertop minutes later, I relocked the door, hoping the others would be grateful for my single loaf of bread. Still, I would have paid money to see the look on someone's face as a pumpkin floated down the street. Missed opportunity. I'd have to do that again in daylight just for fun. I'm not sure anyone knew the wraiths could just vanish all together, but they certainly couldn't hold things.

"Did you steal this?" Raven asked, slicing the bread I'd acquired.

"No?"

Torryn snorted. "Why answer with a question?"

"I mean ... define stealing. I traded without permission. That's hardly thievery."

Atlas nudged Raven, white hair falling into his eyes "I couldn't care less how she got it. I'm a growing boy. I need food."

"In age or maturity level?" I asked.

He grinned, the scar over his brow lifting. "Definitely both."

"What's the plan, Bash?" Torryn asked from across Crescent Cottage, folding the blanket he'd slept with on the hard floor and tidying what he could. Anything to be helpful.

There were only three small cots in the cottage. Raven, Eden and somehow the drunk captain used them. The rest of the group insisted they were fine without. Raven tried to force Torryn onto one, but I think we all knew there was no way his large frame was going to fit, and he was far too chivalrous, anyway.

Bastian shifted to Grey's form. "Back to the castle. Things seem to be fairly quiet around here. Let's hope it's the same there."

Raven dropped the knife onto the counter, then awkwardly scrambled to pick it up before anyone might notice. Except we all had.

"What?" she asked, pushing a lock of her curly black hair behind her ear. "Just nerves."

I circled above. "Liar, liar, pants on fire."

"Who's a child now?" Atlas teased.

"I think I should maybe go to see my mother before we leave the Moon Coven territory. She knows something about me. She did something." Her voice lowered, but her tone remained severe. "I want to know what it was."

The Dark King cleared his throat. "We can travel back and forth as easily as I can cast a door. We need to know the Grimoires are safe. If we have that, then you can go see your mother, and we can start hunting down Nikos."

Atlas cracked his knuckles. "Ah, yes. Can't wait for a little visit with that fucker."

Raven opened her mouth to protest, but Torryn stepped forward, his heavy boots thunderous on the floor. She stopped instantly. The respect she had for the shifter and his kindness trumping her will to argue.

"Nikos is the problem now, it seems. He's already been here, so we know he's around. He can force anyone into an enemy, even one of us. He's a problem we need to solve immediately. But if we don't know how much power the witches are harboring with those damn books, it makes sense that we check that threat first, then hunt Nikos."

Torryn was loyal, but fair. Offering counsel but not taking charge. I could see that Raven was warming to him quickly. I shared a glance with her, thinking I'd see hesitation there, maybe the empathy she'd always held for Nikos renewed. But there was nothing but fire in her eyes. A woman scorned.

"Fine. Castle first but my mother's second. They might also know something about Nik. Deal?"

"Deal," the king said, kissing her on the head before swiping a piece of fresh bread and popping it into his mouth. "Thanks for stealing the bread, Kir."

"For the last time, I didn't steal it. I left a pumpkin."

The laughter was equal parts bliss and annoyance. Moments later, we gathered in a line facing the blank east wall of the shop.

"We will come back," Raven assured Eden.

"I promise, we are fine. Whoever destroyed this place isn't getting past that barrier. And if they manage it, they won't know what's waiting for them on the other side. Endora Mossbrook may be all shades of evil incarnate, but I am her daughter, and viciousness did not skip a generation."

"Noted," the king said with his chin lowered. "Focus now. Once I cast the door, you'll all walk through so I can close it behind me. If, for some reason, the coven leaders are there, stay close. All in. All out."

He gestured, and a door with shadows as deep as his own appeared before us. Torryn went through first, blade out, body on high alert. Then Atlas and I went. I turned, nearly gesturing for Scoop to follow before I remembered my own plight. Raven followed behind me, sharing a glance before turning away. She'd seen, because of course she had.

At first, I wondered if the Dark King had taken us to the wrong place. But the ground was soot, matching the Fire Coven territory. My stomach rolled as I steadied myself, something foreign thrumming like a heartbeat nearby. No one else noticed and the sensation confused me.

I jerked around to see the king's expression as he moved through his magical door and took in the ruins that were his castle. Not just his castle, but the only home he'd ever known. The sun rose in the distance, the vibrant colors of golden light illuminating the debris in a beautiful, terrible way. Only three partial walls stood. Everything else was rubble. Not a soul in sight. No gates, no guards, not even a whisper of the stable. Everything had been obliterated. Whatever spell had done this took no prisoners.

My heart sank to my stomach as I remembered who had remained in the castle. If Nym had made it back after the Trial, if Scoop had been left behind when she'd gone... were they... killed?

20

RAVEN

I could nearly feel his heart break. As if the shattering of his world had been the decimation of my own. I couldn't look at the remains of his childhood and not feel the tears threaten to come. His face, Grey's beautiful face, was stoic, save the darkness in his green eyes that spoke every trace of emotion he tried to hide.

"The Grimoires." He pointed to the partial walls standing in the distance. "Let's go."

"Bash," Atlas muttered.

But the Dark King was having none of it. He stormed forward, swiping the ash from the air in front of him, the rubble of his castle crunching beneath his boots as he led us. He was hoping for a miracle. But he was denied. The books' pillars stood, some of the walls remained, but all six relics contained in the sacred room were gone. The power they left behind coated my skin in something comforting yet full of sorrow.

"The people?" Kirsi whispered, inches from my side.

I couldn't look into her haunted eyes knowing Scoop had been here. He hadn't joined Nym in the final Trial. I'd left him sleeping on my bed that morning. Curled into the ray of sunlight beaming through the bedroom window.

THE UNBOUND WITCH

"Let's go," Bastian said, casting another door as pure white as freshly fallen snow, a deep and impactful contrast to the rubble surrounding us.

I wondered if he controlled the makeup of his magical doors. If somewhere in the white was a memory of what the castle once was before his mother had turned the Fire Coven territory to ash.

As the others stepped through the door, I grabbed his hand to pull him back. "Are you okay?"

He cut a glance to the castle over my shoulder and back to me. "The only home I need is you."

"Bast—"

He stopped my words with a kiss, gripping my face as he stole my breath. When he finally pulled away, closing his eyes to rest his head on mine, I hugged him tightly.

"I will not mourn bricks and mortar. Only the memories."

"But if you want to talk about it…"

"Don't mistake my silence for sadness, Little Witch. It's simply the foundation of my revenge."

He grabbed my hand and pulled me toward his magical door, saying no more about it.

We stepped into a bustling town of children laughing and playing, and witches hurrying to and fro with loaded carts pulled by steady horses. Taken aback, the clean brick buildings that lined the streets held my gaze. In so many ways, it felt like the Moon Coven from my childhood. Before the poison of the world skewed my view of it. Laughter and chatter and a world of happiness seemed so far away from the reality we knew the world to be.

"The Fire Coven?" Kirsi asked, her voice as awed as I felt.

"Home," Atlas answered, his shoulders slumping.

Torryn clapped a hand over his friend's shoulder. "Home."

"What's the plan, Grey?" I asked, breaking the trance over Bastian, as his mind was no doubt still somewhere in the ruins of that castle, in his decimated legacy.

"You two are free to go," he said, reaching a hand out, in an attempt to shake with Torryn.

The large man looked down, eyes fierce as he refused to take it.

With a lifted chin, he spoke. "I wouldn't abandon you on your best day. I'm sure as hell not leaving you on your worst. I can't speak for the pup, but I'm with you."

"As if I'd miss this," Atlas said.

"If they killed everyone in my castle, there will be no mercy."

Atlas rubbed his hands together, a wicked smile on his handsome face. "Even better."

"We need to meet with the Fire Council. See if they know ..."

A large, burly man rounded a corner, the familiar face needed no time to stroke my memory. He walked with a limp, but the moment his brown eyes landed on Grey, he halted. Then burst into motion as he ran for us. Several members of this coven, and likely most of the shifters, knew Grey and Bastian were the same man. Seeing him stand here in the street after believing he'd died was undoubtedly jarring.

For a moment, just a second, I nearly hid behind Bastian. The Old Barren reminded me of my grandmother's death. From the black uniform he wore, to the hard set on his aged face. He could have been there. Could have been the one that took her life. I had to remind myself that we were now on the same side. Turbulent as that may be.

"You've seen it?" he said by way of greeting.

Grey dipped his chin. "I have. Where can we talk?"

For the first time he looked beyond the Dark King directly at me. In one motion, he'd drawn the sword from his back. Without thinking, on instinct alone, I drew an infinite amount of power, shaking the ground below our feet. He paled, stepping backward.

I relented, closing my eyes to stay the magic. "Sorry. I didn't mean—"

"No." Grey moved in front of me, lifting my chin with his fingers. "Someone pulls a weapon on you, you don't stop to ask questions. You fucking defend yourself. And you never, ever apologize for being the most powerful witch around."

Something in the way he lifted my chin, those fingers pressing into my skin, commanding me as he had that first meeting, twisted my chest. The most formidable man in the world, ordering me to attack his own if it meant my survival.

Torryn took one step until he nearly concealed me with his giant body. He rested his hand on the blade at his back, daring the king's guard to make a single move toward me. My world felt infinitely safer with him in it.

The Old Barren cleared his throat. "It seems we both have some catching up to do."

"Indeed," Atlas said, stepping closer to me. "Barry, good to see you."

"Wolf," the Old Barren sneered, clearly not a fan of Atlas' antics. He dipped a chin to Torryn before turning and walking away.

We followed him through the bustling town of witches—but not just witches. Shifters too, living in harmony, sharing breakfasts at tables outside of small stores. Carrying on as if it made no difference to them that the world had shattered. I couldn't help my envy. Kirsi was not amused, though. She kept visible, eyes lingering on a few wraiths gathered in a narrow alleyway, watching the witches come and go.

We hadn't made it more than thirty paces before an ear-piercing scream broke the joy in the air. The entire town fell silent as a young woman, no older than eighteen, stood in the middle of the street, ears leaking blood. Tears of red pouring down her pale cheeks. Her dark hair fell like a curtain down her back as her head tilted up. I'd know that condition anywhere. Atlas had frozen in his footsteps, staring, unblinking as he watched her lift into the air, her arms outstretched.

"Please," a woman screamed. "Help her."

In a single motion, the witches of the Fire Coven poured into the square. Those with healing magic surrounded the young woman. Atlas remained frozen, eyes locked on the witch, reliving the horror of his lost lover. A memory that seemed to haunt him. Bastian ran for her, and I followed quickly behind. It wouldn't be enough, and I knew it. Even with his power, if we didn't have witches from every coven here to save her, powerful ones... it wouldn't be enough. The Harrowing was absolute.

Still, we tried, pushing magic to the brim toward the young witch, pleading with the goddess to show mercy. But as she dropped to the ground, her lifeless body drained of color and paler than should have ever been possible, the only sounds were the sobs of her mother. Until a static filled the air, nearly suffocating everyone in view. Even the mother paused her mourning to look around, making eye contact with the witches in the gathering. Something was different. And then time stopped. Or so it seemed as every Fire Coven witch froze in place, their eyes glossing over, even Bastian in Grey's form. One second. Two seconds.

"What's happening?" Kirsi asked from beside me.

"I have no idea," I whispered, turning in a slow circle to look at the faces of the crowd. "I don't think it's good, though."

"Could they all be having a receiving at the same time?"

"I don't think so."

As if on cue, the world began to move again, the witches leaving their trance only to stare wordlessly at one another.

"We need to get to someplace safe. The library. Now," Bastian demanded, giving no explanation as he urged the Old Barren onward.

And so we ran. Past flower shops and bakeries, galleries and more storefronts. Until we came to a building taller than most of the others, still brick, but circled with a wrought iron fence.

"This will do," Bastian said, passing our guide to lead us into the Fire Coven library. He knew exactly where he was headed as he surged to the back of the building, past the stacks and cases of old tomes, until he flung an old wooden door open and ushered us inside to be seated at a long table. Once in place, he dipped a chin to his councilman, the Old Barren.

"Wait," Kirsi said before the leather clad soldier could begin. "What just happened in the square? We are not dismissing that."

"The Fire Coven was gifted with more power. Each of us stood together in another realm as the depth of our magic multiplied. That girl was the final victim in our territory. The thirteenth witch born of power in each family line has died. Remember Eden said the Harrowing was to recycle a full generation of power, believing it would give them enough of an advantage to overthrow the shifters once and for all? Well, it fucking worked."

"How much power?" the Old Barren asked.

He placed his hands on the table bowing his head as he shifted back into Bastian. "A third, minimum."

The room collectively gasped.

"Holy fuck." Kirsi said. "How is that even possible?"

"An entire generation of power. Which means two things. I thought maybe the Harrowing had stopped with Raven. But now," his eyes flashed to me. "Either the entire Moon Coven is going to want you dead if word gets out, or maybe the Harrowing isn't done with you. Even if you aren't the last."

I swallowed, remembering the headache I'd suffered until the goddess blessed me. Could it have been the Harrowing lingering?

"No," Kirsi denied. "I won't accept this. There has to be a way to stop it."

"I'm with the ghosty," Atlas agreed. "What do we do?"

"That's not the half of our problems," the Old Barren interjected. "Though I'd feel much safer taking a private counsel, Your Grace. In fact, I quite demand it."

Torryn cleared his throat. "You make demands of your own king?"

"He is aware of how this world is ruled, Strix. Decisions have been shared for a very long time."

"They stay," Bastian said, rising.

"They do not," his councilman argued.

Torryn rose to his feet, ready to face off with the Old Barren, but it was Kirsi that interjected.

"Give your account to our king, and then he will decide who does what. Look around you. The world you're trying to command from the side is fucked up. You've all but ruined it. That castle was full of people and now everyone is gone. We don't know what happened to them and some of us actually give a shit. So, sit down and start talking or you can see yourself out. We'll find someone else with answers. You can't be the only person that knows what happened at that castle."

The man's face turned red, but he did not argue with Kirsi as he slowly sank to his seat. "I will concede if only to save time, Your Grace. Forgive me. Things have been on edge for us as of late."

"It's fine, Barren. Just tell me what happened."

"As soon as you, ah, er... died ... vanished … the magical barrier around the Grimoire room weakened. It held but cracked."

"We went to the human lands. My power was stunted. Continue."

"Within hours of what we thought was your untimely murder…"

His hard eyes flicked to me, but Torryn cleared his throat, demanding he continue without speaking a word.

Torryn had quickly become as protective as Bastian. He checked on me in idle moments, silently watched in others. Concerned but also friendly. Safeguarding the person that mattered to his king. As was his duty, but it seemed to be more as well. Like friendship.

The Old Barren continued. "The witches descended. They somehow knew everything that had happened, though they expected your death, not disappearance. They demanded to speak with Raven Moonstone from the gates. When we denied them any information, they attacked. Taking down the gates, casting on the shifters with no hesitation, even taking out any witches that stood in their way as they stormed the castle. We tried to warn them not to seek the Grimoires, but they were determined. We knew they'd cast their magic and destroy everything, just as we'd discussed, should they ever breach the walls. So, we evacuated immediately, retreating to the township.

"The castle came down in a flash of power. One moment she was standing in all her glory and then next, she was ash. As far as our spies have been able to conclude, none of the coven leaders were killed. Your magic barrier was just enough to save them and parts of the room."

"Unfortunately," Atlas growled.

"How many were killed?" the king asked, his wings appearing behind him as if they were an unconscious thought.

"At least thirty. We've done our best to count the staff and Trial witches. It's been chaos."

"Do you know..." Kirsi's voice faded to a near whisper. "Where are the survivors?"

"Two Moon Coven witches refused to come with us. We sent guards with them as far as the bridge."

"Nym?" she breathed.

He rested his hands on the table. "Miss Moontide is the only one that remains here. She did not trust her coven members."

I snorted, remembering Ophelia's shove in the final trial. "Can't say I blame her for that."

My comment was met with a glare. Cold eyes, wishing my death. A piece of paper landed in my hand beneath the table.
I peeked down without drawing attention to it.

Miss Moonstone,

I don't think he likes you very much. Maybe we should have let you cast on him. Something small. Did I hear you can turn things blue?

Look at me not kicking his ass,
    Bastian Firepool

I COULDN'T SMILE, THOUGH I KNEW HE UNDERSTOOD THAT. I TURNED TO the seething old shifter and wiggled a finger. He didn't notice the hair change. But Atlas did, choking down a laugh as he coughed into his hand. Torryn winked at me but managed to hide his own smirk.
Another note appeared as soon as the first burned away.

Miss Moonstone,
    Should have gone with a different body part.
    All jokes aside, we will need to meet with the Fire Coven elders before we can go back to your mother.

Aim for Atty next,
    Bastian

I NODDED ONCE, LETTING THE EDGES OF THE BLACK PAPER BURN AWAY IN my hand with a smirk.

Bastian pressed his palms into the table, standing once more. "Gather the elders. Have them meet us here as soon as possible."

"If I may, Your Grace." Barren stood. "Perhaps it's better to keep the form of Grey."

"That is my intention," he answered. "But in the privacy of these halls, I am safe."

The old man's eyes flicked to Kirsi. "A wraith may very well haunt this library. If so, do you want them to see you?"

"The wraiths have never been my enemy," the king answered. "But no. For now, everyone must believe Bastian died."

He transformed back into his blond counterpart, sharing a wink with me as the Old Barren left the room, smoothing down his blue hair as if he had an itch.

"Now *that* is a useful spell," Atlas said, clapping his hands.

I forced a smile before bringing the conversation back to the problem now that it was just us. "This is such a mess. The coven leaders are basically explosions waiting to happen if they have those Grimoires together. It's inevitable they are going to cast. It's the nature of who they are."

"We are doing the most we can right now," Torryn said, his voice so smooth as he reassured us. "Whatever the goddess wishes, whether we fight back or not, will be done. Right now, the most we can do is form a plan to get the books back."

I shook my head. "I know the logic behind having the power of the Grimoires contained. But I also know the witches need them. If we give them back, maybe we can end this war."

"Give them back?" Kirsi asked. "They've already got them. They stole them. And they are dangerous. I'm sorry, Rave, but we can't let them have the Grimoires. I'm siding with Bash on this one." She threw him a look. "Can I call you Bash? I feel like we're on that level now, right?"

He smiled, though it didn't light his eyes. "Sure, Kir. You can call me Bash when it's just us. But stick to Grey for now. We have to keep up the façade."

"Okay, Bash," she answered, trying and failing to make light of a heavy situation.

Torryn circled the long table, drawn to the single shelf of books in the room. He studied the spines with his hands clasped behind his back before pulling one from the shelf. He opened the book and blew the dust from the pages, content to read while we waited. He smiled to himself before shoving the book in front of the king, pointing to a line. Bastian chuckled, shaking his head.

"Inside jokes are rude," Atlas said.

Torryn's face lit with delight as he circled the table and placed the book in front of Atlas, pointing at something.

Atlas shoved the book away. "Assholes."

I slid it toward myself, and Kirsi hovered over my shoulder. The top of the flimsy page garnered a drawing of a wolf howling at the moon, accompanied with a bold chapter heading: *How to keep your friendly wolf from shedding, Part One.*

Sharing a laugh, Torryn snatched the book and placed it back onto the shelf. There was something wholesome about this group. Something I'd only had with Kirsi before. As if we'd already been through hell together, and the small jokes among us would always mean a little more.

21

RAVEN

The door swung open, and a little old lady shuffled in, markings covering the majority of the skin that could be seen around her long sleeves and sweeping gown. Bastian, as himself, flew from his chair, circling the table to pull a seat out for the ancient witch. Atlas shifted into his wolf form, taking a corner of the room to guard as more of the elders from the Fire Coven poured in. The first old woman stopped before Bastian, taking his hands in hers.

"We were so worried," she whispered. "My boy, we were so worried."

"I am fine, Nonet. Nothing to be worried about. Please, take a seat."

She smiled once more before dipping a chin to Torryn, now standing behind Bastian's chair. A guard's stance, far more than a friend's. With Kirsi now invisible, and the shifters away from the table, all eyes landed on me. Seven coven elders, all steeped in markings and paper-thin skin full of wrinkles, looking down the table. I wanted to crawl under it and stay there until the meeting was over. No doubt they'd all been told I cast death upon the king. No doubt they'd all decided I was their enemy.

"Miss Raven Moonstone," Bastian said, sweeping a hand toward me. "Please meet the elder members of the Fire Coven."

He went around the room, calling them each by name and sharing a warm smile with everyone before finally taking his seat. These were the witches that had raised him into the king he was now. With his parents' death at such a young age, they had watched him grow. Had likely all felt the searing loss when he'd died.

One of the men from the opposite end of the table stood, casting a spell around the room, a beautiful shade of purple glowing from a marking on the back of his palm.

"A sound barrier," Bastian whispered beside me.

Another stood, a short woman with skin as smooth as a baby's, though her silver hair gave away her old age. She hardly moved her fingers, and the room lit with golden light, pouring over each of us. The warmth of the spell started at the top of my head and inched its way down my body, as if searching for something. Though each of the witches experienced the same thing, all eyes fell to me as the magic ended.

"That one makes sure there are no imposters using magic to deceive us," the older woman that had taken the king's hands said from his other side. "We are so pleased to meet with you now, Miss Moonstone."

"Truly?"

A chuckle from down the table. "Of course. Though, I must admit," another man said, his brown skin identical to Torryn's complexion, though his green eyes were markedly different from Tor's gold, "we did think you were our enemy."

"That is part of the reason we are gathered today." Bastian stood, placing his palms flat on the table as he recanted our story to the elders of the Fire Coven. He spoke of the Trials, hinted at his feelings toward me, then told them of the coven leaders the night of the ball, Nikos' betrayal, everything.

"And now these witches have the Grimoires. And the decimation of the castle has proven they know how deadly those books are when combined," the oldest woman said. She reached a hand over the table, placing it on top of her king's. "Sit, my boy. Let us discuss this."

As if she commanded him and not the other way around, he plopped into his seat, silent as the rest of them.

"Pardon," I said, far quieter than I'd intended to be.

"Speak up, girl," a tall, thin man said. "No need to be shy here."

"I only wondered, that is, I was curious. What do you know of the origin of the Grimoires?" I knew only what my grandmother had shared, and it was possible the story was different.

"Ah," the man answered, standing. "That is a very good question. A long, long time ago, hundreds of years, the Grimoires were not individual books, and there were not seven covens. Only one. It was used to keep record of every spell and every curse, every conjuring and every marking. The original Grimoire, then known as the Book of Omnia, was used to guide the witches. It's said, all those years ago, the book itself spoke to our ancestors as a sentient being. But as the witches became eager for more power, it seemed to elude them. More and more of us were born, and the power of the witches diluted. As if we all shared a single well, and the well was running dry. Our ancestors believed the end to be near. Out of desperation, seven elders gathered in a secret place of power. They spent an entire moon cycle inside a salt circle chanting and casting magic upon the Book of Omnia. Splitting it into the seven Grimoires. They called it The Breaking. Thirteen family lines for every book. And so, the coven's were made."

"Thirteen?" I repeated. "We learned from Eden that the Harrowing targets the thirteenth witch with power down every family line."

"Yes. The Fire Coven's Harrowing is complete," Nonet said.

"What does that mean for the rest of the witches?" Bastian asked. "Do we believe the increase of power will be the change in the world, to take out the shifters once and for all?"

Atlas, who'd been stoic and observant, shifted for the first time, his fur rippling down his back as he snorted.

"Only the goddess knows. But we can be sure of one thing. As long as those witches have the Grimoires, they are hiding, and they are dangerous. After all these years, we've accepted our fate with the Harrowing. But we cannot allow the estranged covens to access that much power," Nonet said.

"Raven is the only witch to survive the Harrowing that we know of, and she's been blessed by the goddess. Is it possible that it will still come back for her?"

The old woman's face fell, grave emerald eyes meeting his. "There is no way to know, my boy. Blessed by the goddess and cursed by Death. Unmarked and very powerful, she is a conundrum."

"What does the elder council advise me to do?" Bastian asked.

"Give us a moment," one of the seven elders said, recasting the sound barrier so that only they were within. We shared a glance as we watched them speak. Some didn't, and some were very animated as they gestured from within their private space.

"Will we do whatever they recommend?" I whispered to Bastian.

He took my hand and brought it to his lips, brushing my knuckles gently before speaking. "We will have our own council after this one has parted and decide together." His eyes narrowed. "'My decisions, my lies, my moves' don't work well, I've learned."

I shook my head, pulling my hand away as I listened to him repeat words I once said to him. "I'm not sure I should be part of this decision, Bastian. I have no training or experience with talks of war, and we both already know how I feel about taking the Grimoires from the witches again."

He opened his mouth to speak, but the barrier popped and was recast around us. All eyes on the king once more.

"We thank you for seeking the advice we would offer." The larger man at the end of the table stood, lifting a golden watch on a long chain from his pocket, studying it for a moment as a marking on his forearm lit a vibrant shade of purple. "Time is not on our side, it seems. Each passing moment leaves us with a bevy of unknown. We cannot assume the witches don't intend mass destruction. In fact, we have to assume the opposite. Which means they must be hunted. Immediately. However, if we send large parties, we could imply war."

"No," Bastian interrupted. "If the coven leaders are to be hunted, it will be only me."

I jerked, spinning toward him. "You cannot mean that. It's dangerous."

He only shared a look with me before instructing the man to continue.

"They could all be together, Your Grace. The girl is right."

Torryn stepped forward, placing a heavy hand on Bastian's shoulder. "Should my king go hunting, I will join him. My life for his, should it be needed."

My heart rattled in my chest, the reality of the situation finally sinking down upon me. This was not a conversation of hypotheticals. Nor a time when others would be the heroes. It was us. And we would likely die.

"Right, then." The elder that resembled the shifter at the king's back stood. "If there's nothing else?"

Bastian shook his head, and the rest of them rose.

"Oh, please do say hello to the wraith on the ceiling for me," Nonet said, sharing a smile before she left the room.

22

KIRSI

"What the hell is the point of being invisible if they know I'm here, anyway?" I asked, popping into view as I watched the old witches hobble out of the library room.

No one answered.

The king shifted to Grey, and Atlas shifted to man. For a moment, the tense room held the silence as if everyone was afraid to shatter something so precious when all that would follow was chaos.

So naturally, I swooped low, laying my back dramatically on top of the table, my hand on my forehead as I sighed. "I guess I'll just have to lie here forever, contemplating the reason for my existence."

"That's pretty dramatic. Even for you, Wraith," Torryn said.

I bolted upright, staring at him with my jaw open. "You're supposed to be the nice one."

He flashed a smile, content to break the tension in the room with me. "I've always been a rule follower. It might be time for a change."

"Oh, shit. What will that make me then?" Atlas asked, moving toward the door.

"Still annoying," I answered.

Our antics didn't matter, though. Raven and Bastian seemed to be in their own silent world. Hands held together; heads bowed as they whispered.

I cleared my throat, grabbing their attention. "What's the plan?"

Grey's green eyes met mine. "I need to check on the castle residents that are now here and make sure they are comfortable for the time being. I also need to see Alexander Firewing about reconstructing my home. Meet back here in an hour. Then back to Crescent Cottage. We will figure it out from there."

I WANDERED AIMLESSLY BEHIND GREY AND RAVEN. HIS BROAD SHOULDERS matched Bastian, but the blond hair still threw me. He walked through the Fire Coven as confidently as anyone that had spent their whole life running the streets and hiding between the brick buildings. I could picture him now, a little dark haired, gray-eyed boy with a silly grin, racing beside a white wolf as they collided with patrons, laughing and stealing loaves of bread simply because they were in too big of a hurry to purchase it. Too distracted by the innocence of a child to care for anything beyond the thrill of one moment to the next. Before his parents were murdered, before the world had shifted into what it was now.

I wasn't ready. Picturing the childhood of the king had kept me so distracted, when the beautiful golden-brown goddess who had captured my heart the first time I'd ever laid eyes on her rounded the corner, my whole world stopped.

I vanished, but not quick enough. She'd seen me. The little black panther on her heels had not. She halted, the easy smile on her soft, gorgeous face fading away as if it had never really been there. Though I remained invisible, her eyes hadn't moved from where I hovered above the ground. She'd seen me, but the look on her face indicated she didn't believe her own eyes.

"Nym?" Raven ran for her, dodging the people in the busy street. "You're here. Oh! Thank the goddess."

She didn't move, didn't respond at all.

"Nym?" Raven asked, looking over her shoulder.

"Is she... did I just see..."

Raven nodded slowly, but my world tilted as a ringing began in my ears. Pure embarrassment rattled through my ghostly form. She saw me, but I was not the same, and she didn't owe me a single thing. What witch could love a wraith? Whatever our future was, it was not together. I moved backward. Panic stroking my urge to flee. Only those beautiful green eyes held me.

"She's here. But she has changed." Raven sounded as if she was speaking with a child on the brink of a meltdown. She could see it on Nym's face as clearly as I could.

Scoop padded forward, weaving between Raven's legs, a yowl coming from him as he rubbed against her. I knew that sound. He was sad. Missing me. Everything hurt. I knew this moment would come, but I wasn't prepared for the rush of emotions. Where everything up until this point had been rimmed in sadness, this was deeper. Devastating.

"Why can't I see her?" Another tear fell. "Is she hiding from me?"

"It's hard," Raven whispered, taking her hand.

Pure green envy shot through me at that connection.

Nym shook her head. "No. It's not hard. Losing her was hard. I've cried every day. I've mourned with her familiar. It took me ages to get him to warm up to me after she'd gone. There were whispers she'd been seen at the castle, and I couldn't let myself believe them. Do you hear that, Kirsi Moondance? You may have died, but you're killing me."

Guilt swirled through me as I watched that golden witch cry. But there was nothing within my sorrow that I could mask with dark humor and sarcasm. The men of our group had been wise to stay away, a small blessing as I let myself be seen, a memory of the person I used to be. Now transparent, glowing and haunted, I was not lovable. And so I stayed there in my shame as her eyes swept over my new form. She took a step forward, as if she could not control her feet. Somewhere in the background, a million miles away, Raven moved back. This was not her moment and, as my sister in all ways that mattered, I knew she only wished for my happiness. If only she knew this was my purgatory.

"I'm sorry," I whispered, my eyes locked on the uneven bricks embedded into the road. I wanted to go back in time. Before it was too late.

Four tiny black paws appeared in my view. Scoop. I sank to the ground, reaching to stroke the softest part of his fur, right below his rounded ears. My hand passed through him, and he darted away, the shock of cold and death scaring him. I hadn't been concentrating enough to touch him. I hadn't been thinking at all, truly. But Nym's gasp as the cat ran away jolted me.

"I didn't mean to scare you." I straightened, finally looking into her eyes.

"Scare me?" she asked, brows furrowed. "I'm not afraid of you. I've dreamed of this moment every night. You're here. And you don't even want to see me. This isn't fear. This is something different. This is... dejection."

I reached for her cheek, focusing, though I was sure she'd turn away from me. She rested her tear-tracked face into my palm, and I thought I felt the warmth of her tears.

"I'm sorry," I whispered, again.

She shook her head, taking a breath so deep her shoulders hiked and fell heavily. As if it were the first full breath she'd taken in a long time. "You weren't supposed to leave me."

I pushed my forehead to hers. "I know. Believe me, I did not want to."

"You're cold."

I jerked myself away. "I know. I can't..."

"It's okay, Kir. I just didn't know. I didn't know what it would feel like."

"Me neither," I replied.

"Are you here for good, then?"

Something in that question gutted me. I knew she was hoping I would say yes, though every part of me wanted to say no. I didn't want to be. Even with her before me, this was still its own version of hell.

"Yes. I was swept away to the human lands with Raven and Grey, but now I'm back, and from what I've gathered, I'm not leaving."

"I'm sorry." She tucked a brown strand of hair behind her ear. "I can't imagine what you've been through. How different things must be." She smiled that half smile that I loved, narrowing her eyes. "Why can you touch my cheek but not Scoop?"

"It's complicated. I have to really concentrate to be able to touch things. It's better now that I've been practicing."

"Come with me?" she asked. "Just for a few moments."

I looked back to Raven, standing with Grey on the street. Nym followed my gaze.

"She's brave. Showing her face around here. Even with Grey, half the witches want to see her hanged."

"No one knows the truth, Nym. And if they come for her, I will personally kill them all. I have nothing left to lose."

Her voice was quiet. The conviction, faint. "You have me."

"I will not hold you to drunken promises we made to each other before ... before I died. You deserve so much better than this," I said, flourishing my hand.

She set her jaw, staring at me. "Your heart may not beat, Kirsi, but your soul is the same."

All the moments we'd stolen in the Chosen's hall in the black castle, the dances the night at the ball, the time we'd shared on All Hallows Eve had played through my mind on repeat during the nights while the others slept. The way her hands felt on my body, her quiet whispers and soft pants as I tasted her. Nym gave me life then, and even now, I could feel a hint of that.

"I'm still an asshole," I promised. "Ask Grey."

She laughed, all traces of sadness gone. "I don't need to ask the king's cousin. I would expect nothing less from you."

"Where did you want to go? I think Raven and Grey have some business to sort. I have an hour."

"Not nearly long enough, but I'll take it."

23

KIRSI

I followed my golden witch through the black stone streets, making eye contact with Raven one final time. She knew. And the eyebrow wiggle from Grey was enough. The Fire Coven's ground was nothing but soot and ash. It'd been that way for as long as I could remember. Unless one was locked in the castle, as the Chosen were, the bottoms of the witches' dresses and soldier's boots were always black. At least it was harder to see the mess in the black castle. A blessing for the workers, I supposed. But here? There was a shared sense of happiness and peace among the witches I'd never seen before. Especially with the shifters intermingling, shopping the surplus of wares and holding casual conversations. Witches and shifters could live in peace. Bastian's dad had ended a war on that principle alone. And I needed to hang onto that as I followed the little witch in front of me, looking back over her slender shoulder from time to time with a smile, just to make sure I was still there.

Eventually, we stopped at a small gathering of crowded thatch roof huts.

"It's not much," Nym said, pulling the door open. "But it's home for now. And it looks like someone decided to join us."

I turned, the faint glow of my ghostly form lighting the black kitten that followed us, his eyes on me, hackles raised.

"Oh, Scoop, stop being a dick," Nym said. "That's your witch."

I snorted. "I wish."

"You are still his, and he is yours. I won't argue with you about that. Your souls are connected, and that's that." She pulled at the strings of the leathery corset around her waist.

My eyes dipped low, the longing I felt suffocating. "You know we can't..."

She moved in so close I ached to kiss her. To actually feel those lips that had been my undoing. "I've loved you and lost you, and missed you more than I could ever find words for. Whatever patience this world demands from me, I will endure. Maybe we just need a little practice." She slid the tips of her fingers over my lips. "Can you feel this?"

I closed my eyes, wishing so badly that I could. "No."

"Pity." A sly tone graced her smoky voice.

She slipped out of her boots and set them at the foot of the makeshift bed, which was really just a pile of blankets thrown on the stacked rugs covering the ground.

"Kiss me, Kirsi. Relieve me of this desolation that has been full of only missing you."

"I can't," I whispered.

"You can."

Her faith had given me more than I could have hoped for. Even when I didn't love myself, she'd been there. Waiting.

I pushed forward, concentrating as I caressed her cheeks, ghostly fingers brushing bare skin. She gasped. I closed the space, pressing my cool lips to her heated ones. Closing my eyes as I focused on touching her. Feeling her. Letting her feel me. Passion erupted. It worked. I don't know what the rules of the wraiths were, but in all these days of no sustenance, no pleasure, mine was here. Before me. Moaning as our tongues caressed each other.

This feeling I'd longed for, the love that pressed through the numbness within my soul encompassed me, putting a small piece of everything I'd lost back into place. And though I wondered how far she would let me go, this was all I needed from my golden witch. This was pure. A love that survived. Though I had not.

"I would die a thousand deaths to have one more real night with you."

She pulled away from me, tilting her head. "This is real."

An ache grew within me. "It was real."

She moved to lie on the bed, looking up at me. "When I was nine years old, I snuck into Amelia Mooncatch's store, determined to steal a pair of socks for my little sister because she'd always gotten everything passed down to her and nothing new. I couldn't bear the holes in her toes that winter."

"I remember this story." I sighed. "You got caught before you could walk out of the store, but I was there delivering a tonic for Raven's grandmother."

"Before I could even try to make up a story, you ran and put every coin you had on the counter, took me by the arm and told Amelia I'd left the money and she must not have seen it because she'd been on the other side of her shop."

I turned, staring down at Scoop. "That was nothing."

The silence of her response was louder than anything she could have said. It grew so loud in the room, I had to turn back to her, just to be sure she was still there. Soft light filled the gaps of her hut, falling along the contours of her face as she stared away, lost in another memory.

"When I was thirteen, Michael Moonfrost shoved me into Gravana Lake on the deep side, near the bushes where the snakes nest. I didn't have my spell to compel the animals yet, and I couldn't swim well enough to make it to the other side. You jumped in fully clothed and helped me." She paused, her eyes finding mine as the severity on her beautiful face softened. "You always jump for me, Kir. Every single time. You have the patience of a saint to give me all the time and space I needed to really see you. To recognize that my heart has and always will need you. And if you think for one second your death took any of that away from us, you're sadly mistaken. If anything, it deepened every single thing that was ever between us. These memories have haunted me, lifted me, and crushed me over and over. I love you. I've loved you since I was a child. It was *never* nothing. You are everything."

I settled down beside her, and as she turned, her stacks of golden bracelets slipped down her arm. We stared at each other, savoring the moment for as long as we could stand the silence.

"I do not deserve your faith in me, Nym."

She huffed a laugh. "No. You deserve so much more. You don't even know the things I wished for while you were gone. Every second I have with you is a blessing from the goddess."

We lay in peace, side by side, sharing memories we had back and forth, getting lost in all that ever was between us and our relationship that spanned a lifetime. My lifetime.

"I can see the hurt in your eyes, Kir. What's wrong?"

I looked away, eyes catching the two cats curled up together across the small space, their breaths easy and slow. "If I hadn't already died, the envy would kill me. I cannot tell you what the void feels like. Missing you and your touch is indescribable. But the loss of my bond with Scoop is the greatest sorrow of my existence. He's right there and won't acknowledge me."

"He just needs time. He'll figure it out."

I shook my head. "It's not just that. I don't eat or sleep. I don't dream or feel. I can't smell or taste anything. I'm living an existence that is hollow."

"You're living an existence that is different," she said, pushing off the bed. "You haven't lost everything. We are here with you. Nothing else matters."

"It's far more complicated than that, and I'm not sure what I'm allowed to tell you right now. You'll just have to trust me, though. Nothing is as easy as it seems."

She twisted the golden bands up her arms and then moved to stand beside me. I lifted myself from the bed.

"Practice," she demanded, her beautiful face fierce as she tugged on the strings at her waist. "Tie my skirt."

"It's not the lack of ability, it's the lack of fulfillment."

She lowered her chin, a familiar fire dancing in her eyes. "I know. Tie the skirt, Kir."

I reached for the silky strands, my fingers passing through the first time. Unwilling to let her see me fail when she'd been so confident, I tried again. Halfway through the knot, I lost focus and dropped them. Frustrated, I turned away.

She moved in front of me once more. "If you can hold your lips to mine, if you can move your fingers up and down my arm, hardly missing a stroke, you can tie my skirt for me. Try again."

"It's not the same."

She crossed slender arms over her chest. "This negativity isn't going to get you anywhere. If you cast that out into the world, that's what you'll get back. If you need hard love, I'll deliver it on a silver platter. I will not let you spiral into the sad existence that consumes the other wraiths. You are Kirsi Moondance. You were a powerful witch, spirit blessed long before your death. I refuse to believe there is nothing in this world that can bring you happiness. Tie the fucking knot, Kir."

It took me three seconds. Three seconds and her conviction and the task was done.

"Look at me," she whispered.

I lifted my gaze to meet her sharp, green eyes.

"You are not alone."

If I could have cried then, I probably would have. I felt so very alone. In the long hours of the nights, but also during the day in a room full of people that didn't understand me. Didn't understand that I'd changed so much. Raven was my rock, and I would die again for her if needed, but it did not mean she understood my sorrow.

"Thank you, Nym."

She held out her hand. "Spin the golden bracelets along my arm. One full circle for each one. I will count. We can practice until touch becomes second nature."

I reached for the first band. "I only had an hour. I'll have to get back soon."

"Then you'd better get started."

One, and two. Three and four. The fifth was hard. The sixth, easier. Up and up I went, spinning her heirloom bands. Eleven and twelve until finally I reached the thirteenth bangle. Thirteen.

THE UNBOUND WITCH

"Thirteen," I said, surging upward. "Nym, tell me the thirteenth band is for your mother and not for you."

She scrunched her nose. "No, it's mine. That's why it has my name etched into it."

I shook my head, confident I'd be sick if I were alive. "We need to go. Right now. Come on."

She yanked on the corset string a final time, securing it to her waist. "Why?"

"Because the Harrowing is not random. And you're a target."

All emotion fell from her face as she looked down to the cats first and then back to me. As if he sensed her shock, Talon leapt from his spot, shifting into a full-grown tiger in a blink. Scoop yawned, ambling over to stand beside Talon, keeping him between Nym and me.

"What can we do?" Nym asked as we rushed through the streets. "How do you even know?"

"I'll explain later," I yelled over my shoulder, heading straight for the library, hoping someone, any one of our crew, would be there. Nym followed behind me with the cats trailing her sprint.

As if the goddess heard me, Torryn and Atlas stepped out of the giant doors as one. It took the wolf one second to see the look on my face until he was running for me. A fierce warrior, ready to attack.

"Are you hurt?" he demanded at once, a growl in his voice.

"No. It's not that."

"What is it?" Torryn asked, the sword at his back already drawn.

"It's Nym. I know you don't know her, but I need to find Grey. She's the thirteenth witch of her family."

The color drained from Atlas' face. "Do you know where the castle staff are?" he asked Nym.

"They're back that way," she answered, pointing down the street. "There's a group of huts if you go around the corner past the flower stand. They would either be there or close to the market square, there's a larger home. They've taken in some of us as well."

"Stay here," Torryn commanded, shifting into his strix form before flying away, his beautiful cerulean tail flowing behind him.

Needing no provocation, the wolf did the same, surging down the street in the opposite direction, toward the huts we'd just come from. There was absolutely nothing any of us could do if the Harrowing struck Nym. I knew that with my whole heart. But it didn't make the truth of it any easier. She could not be saved. Still, if we had a witch we knew would be targeted, perhaps we could shield her with magic. Put her in a barrier similar to something the books were in. If the magic could not get in our way, then maybe there was hope yet. We had to try.

Raven and Grey followed Torryn back, walking briskly but not running. They clearly did not want to alarm anyone, but the panic on Raven's face was clear.

"Are you sure?" she asked before they'd even gotten to us.

"I'm sure," I answered, hovering close to Nym. "She's the thirteenth."

"Grey, could I talk to you in private?" I asked, sharing an apologetic look with Nym. "I have an idea, but it's not one we can speak of out here."

He jutted his chin toward the library and though I knew they wanted to, no one else followed. The second the door clicked shut, he shifted to Bastian, that shadowy look on his face, every bit the Dark King.

"The barrier," I said. "The one you used around the books where no magic can get in. Can we try?"

Scratching the black stubble on his chin, the wheels of his mind turned. He looked away for several moments before making his decision.

"The barrier over the room at the castle was not the same as the one I cast over Gravana Lake. It's partially me and partially a ritual. It must be in the heart of the kingdom to work, but maybe we are close enough. We will need to gather more witches. Which means I'll have to confess that I'm alive. Also, Nym will have to agree to stay within the barrier, no matter what happens."

I could feel the plea on my lips, but he held a hand up before I could fall to ghostly knees and beg him to save her.

"You don't even have to ask, Kir. I will do this for you. If it brings you an ounce of happiness or relief, I will do it."

A dam somewhere deep inside of me broke as I sank to the floor. "Thank you, Your Grace."

He took a knee before me. "A flash of a second before Raven cast the death spell on me, I looked into your eyes and knew something was terribly wrong. That single glance saved me from dying and her from murdering. We will do everything we can to save Nym because it is the right thing to do, but also because you are worthy. And I see you. Your misery is not hidden from me, Kirsi Moondance."

I covered my face with my hands. "I need you to be an asshole, okay? I just can't deal with the mushy shit right now."

He shifted back into Grey. "We were friends first," he smirked, that single dimple flashing on his cheek. "I'll be the asshole to your smartass every day. Now, get up. We have a witch to save."

24

KIRSI

Seven elderly witches stood in a red salt circle in the middle of a sizable room within the home where some of the king's staff were staying. You could have put four of our measly homes inside this one. The furniture was well-polished, the windows covered in drapes from floor to ceiling, richly textured rugs along the floor... You could hardly call it a cottage at all.

It'd been ages since I'd seen anyone use a red salt circle, but even longer since I'd seen magic done with a variance of objects ranging from black tourmaline and rose quartz, to mint and red currant. Chunks of freshly chopped cedar had been placed into a star in the middle.

The house had been emptied, save the owner, the seven elders, and our small group. Torryn and Atlas guarded each of the entrances. Raven moved from piece to piece, casting her amplification spell onto each item before it was placed onto the five points of the star. She let the wax of seven candles drip over the cedar before handing them to the elders. Bastian shifted into his true form, leaving Nym gaping as she finally realized the truth of everything.

"The Dark King is not dead," she whispered to herself.

I huffed a laugh. "He's still an asshole, though, don't worry."

He flashed a grin at me before training his eyes back to Raven, watching her closely as she moved around the elders. Finished, she stepped out of the circle and the king took her place, casting first the black, all-consuming barrier that we'd seen from him so many times. The elders began to chant a medley of a spell I'd never heard before, and I shifted closer to Nym, worried something could strike her at any given second.

Power swelled until it vibrated the very core of who I was. It felt different than it did when I was a witch. Before, it was like a balm, a familiar caress from my ancestors, seeping into me. But now, it was only piercing static. Like a presence that might have grated on my bones, could I feel physical discomfort. I wondered what magic felt like to a shifter. I made a mental note to ask Atlas. Or maybe Torryn. Though he was quieter, I was more likely to get a truthful answer from him.

The darkness of Bastian's magic faded away as a new barrier was formed. Seconds ticked by. The Dark King pulled a knife from his waistband and slid it down his palm, squeezing blood over the flame of each of the candles until smoke lifted from the charred wicks, the flames gone. Each of the candles were put into a basin, and one of the elder witches lit a blue flame below as Raven held it midair with magic. The candles melted down to molten wax.

Each of the seven witches held their palms out to the side, pressing them together, forming a physical barrier. Bastian poured the wax from the basin over each of their paired hands. It must have burned, but none flinched. Soon enough, the swell of magic in the room surged, bursting from the floor as if it were a fountain, dropping into a circular barrier around the room.

"You must each leave a drop of blood in the basin," Bastian instructed. "Only those who have done so may enter or exit the room. With your blood, you promise to protect this witch with your life. This has been attempted in the past and failed. It is not an absolute solution, but it's the only one we have."

He gestured Nym forward, but she shook her head. "No lives should be given in place of mine."

"Don't be foolish, girl," Nonet said, looking pointedly at her. "This is the greatest honor of protection your king could ever give you. But it is also an experiment. If we can save the rest of the witches from the Harrowing ... if we could learn their names or how to stop this curse, then you are only the seed planted. We've yet to see this bloom."

Nym stepped forward, taking the stone basin from Bastian. He squeezed his palm over the white bowl and blood burned at the bottom, letting the deep red liquid coat the surface.

Stepping aside, he held the knife out to Nonet. She didn't bat an eyelash as she sliced into her papery thin skin, letting her blood flow. Raven moved forward then, healing the cut as the next elder took his turn. And so they went, around the five-pointed star, vowing to protect my golden witch. All because a grumpy king decided to befriend a smartass.

Once the spell was done, the elders left, and the shifters returned to the room, a determined look on Atlas' face as he closed the door behind him.

"We have to stop the Harrowing," he said. "How many more must die?"

"We can't commit to that right now," Torryn argued. "The coven leaders could decimate this world, and every second that goes by without us searching, we get closer to that reality. If they are all together somewhere with all but one of the Grimoires, it's a guarantee something bad will follow."

"Then we split up." Atlas shoved his hands into his pockets. "The ghosty and I work on the Harrowing, and you three chase the coven leaders."

Raven crossed the room, peeking out the curtained window. "Before anyone does anything, I need to talk to my mother. It's possible she might have more information about the Harrowing than we do. She's known about it for a long time."

"Back to the shop, then?" I asked. "We can't take these guys to your parents. Your dad will lose it."

Bastian waved a hand and a door appeared outside the magically sealed room. He spoke only to Nym. "This door will vanish as soon as we all step through. If you need anything, Nonet will help you. Should you choose to leave this room, the barrier will fall and right now, we can't promise it's going to save you."

She clutched the ruffled edges of her dress. "Thank you, Your Grace."

"There's something else," he said, eyes locked on my witch. "There will be no magic here once Raven adds the final drop of blood to that basin. It's the only thing we can do to try to save you."

"What?" Nym and I asked at the same time.

"Why me?" Raven asked.

"Because you are the most powerful witch in the room. Your blood will complete the barrier. We take away the magic completely, and hopefully we can stop the Harrowing from striking."

Whatever passed between them in that moment felt intimate and invasive. Even for me. And Raven and I had no secrets, for the most part.

A shade of red raced across her cheeks and down her neck as she cast her eyes away, looking at Nym. "I won't do it if you don't agree. Not having access to magic can be suffocating."

"You will also lose your connection to Talon," I warned, noting the worst part of this.

The spirit blessed marking on her forehead glowed golden, illuminating the dull room. "But I'm not locked in? If I can't handle it, I can just leave. And Talon can be here with me."

As if on cue, the massive white tiger she'd called forward with her magic padded into the room, Scoop on his heels as if he were his shadow.

The Dark King dipped his chin. All royalty and sovereign promises as he let her be the decision maker of her own fate. "It may be painful at first."

I moved to her side, brushing her arm with my own. Hair standing on edge, chills ran over her body as she instinctively shifted toward me. "You do not have to do this. It's possible you still have time. The Harrowing has been running through the covens for many years."

Her eyes lit with solid conviction. "I'm not afraid. I am ready."

I looked over my shoulder to the others. "Give us a moment?"

Atlas wiggled his eyebrows. "Just a moment, eh? You sure it doesn't take longer to—"

Torryn grabbed him by the back of the neck and dragged him through the magical door. Raven promised to return to complete the spell and followed Bastian out, the latter shifting to Grey before they stepped through. And then we were alone again.

I moved my fingers down her arms as I leaned in close. "There's no place I won't search to save you, no one I won't fight."

She smirked. "Just don't go back to the afterlife. Not yet."

"I can't." I leaned my head down, wishing I could feel the pressure of her against me. "I still have to figure out who killed me."

25

RAVEN

The door was the same as it had always been, with a sloping roof overhead nearly touching the ground. I hurried by the small window to my parents' living room, half covered with a bush. Ensuring nobody had seen, I glanced toward my father's hedges by the main street. They were perfectly trimmed, as always, the stack of firewood exactly ten rows high. A lonely spider had spun its web over the far end of the woodpile, but Dein Moonstone would never cast him out. He'd sworn a web was a symbol from the goddess, promising that hard work would always pay off.

"Please?" Kirsi asked for the third time.

She'd left Nym behind, but not easily. And when Kirsi needed a distraction from reality, she put up a thousand walls and focused on nonsense and heavy sarcasm.

"No. You cannot pop in and scare them. You know them. They are already panicking behind that door."

"Then why are we standing here staring at it?" She floated in front of me, giving me a look I'd seen a million times. An eyebrow peaked, and her mouth twisted into a mischievous grin.

I'd finally have to tell my parents my whole story, including falling for The Dark King before killing him. The plan was to lace truth with lies, planting information to get Nik to come to me. Explaining that the king had manipulated me. Just in case Willow or Ophelia had spread information about us. They'd never stand for my relationship with Bastian, but it didn't matter. I needed information, too. Pushing forward, I stepped directly through Kirsi. She gasped.

"Asshole," she hissed in my ear before vanishing. "I'm officially haunting you for the rest of your life."

"Don't threaten me with a good time."

Three solid knocks on the paint chipped door before I turned the brass handle and stepped inside. My mother, stepping into the parlor from the kitchen, dropped the dinner plate she was drying, and it shattered on the wood floor. I lunged to help her pick up the broken shards.

I didn't say hello, jumping straight to the apology. For the broken plate, or worrying them, or disappointing them, I wasn't sure. "I'm so sorry."

"Raven! Good heavens! Where in the world have you been?" She untied the floral apron from her waist to gather the broken pieces. "Your father and I have been worried sick. Nikos stops by every single day. It's as if you vanished. And with the Dark King's murder on your hands ... We thought the shifters had gotten you."

"The shifters? No, Mother. Not yet. Where's Father?"

"Dein? He's been a ghost of himself, Raven."

"Speaking of ghosts ..." I warned, hoping Kirsi had been given enough time.

A moment passed before Kirsi appeared near the kitchen door. "Hey," she said, the sadness in her voice was not lost on me. It must have been so hard to accept her new form in front of witches she'd known for so long.

My mother's voice cracked. "Kirsi?"

"Bless us," my father said from the door, the smooth tones of his aging voice nowhere near as comforting as I thought they'd be. As if the sounds that once soothed me were now betrayed by the lies they'd told.

He came to stand before me, his worn boots scuffed heavily at the toe. I rose to my feet, dumping the ceramic pieces into the apron in my mother's hands. Solid palms landed on my shoulders as he yanked me forward, embracing me. I'd seen my father angry, sad, scared, and determined. I'd never seen him shaken. He pulled away, staring down at me with a gleam in his eye as he wiped away a tear.

"You've really done it. Our daughter has killed the Dark King and escaped our enemies."

I opened my mouth to retort, then snapped it shut, catching myself. If they were proud of this rumor, then undoubtedly, they would take my slip of the tongue to the coven leaders. To Willow, wherever she may be. I couldn't trust them with the bits of truth I'd planned. I wasn't sure I could trust them at all anymore.

Kir cleared her throat, breaking the spell over us.

"How are you here, Kirsi?" my mother asked, dumping the shards into a bowl. She closed her eyes for a second, coaxing her magic forward before casting, a marking on her collarbone glowing orange. The plate, now mended, remained in the bowl as she turned back to Kir. "We went to your funeral."

Kir looked to me for help. "It's a long story."

We'd had a plan, even discussed what we were going to say before Bastian cast a door to send us here. But she must have realized the same thing that I did. We were going to have to wing it. I hoped her part of the plan was already done. She'd remained unseen at first, giving her just enough time to slip away.

"I don't know," she answered. "I was gone, and then, somehow, I came back."

"Nikos will be glad to hear it," my father said.

The adoration mixed with the sound of that name was like talons dragging themselves down my throat, squeezing until I couldn't breathe. Couldn't think. My power boiled in my veins, eager to take revenge, to deal death upon a man that had scorned me so badly his heartbeats were on borrowed time. Something about standing before my parents, remembering everything, all the memories from our childhood since he was twelve and joined the Moon Coven, since we became friends, based solely on the fact that we were the outcast witches. He had been kind and good, and it was all a lie. One my parents had so easily fallen for, but then, so had I.

Kirsi moved closer, brushing a shoulder against me, as if she could see the unbridled rage within me. I let my shoulders sag, unclenched my jaw and fists, and took a deep breath, content to give the biggest show of my life.

Stepping across the room, I sank onto the couch, trying to remind myself that my parents loved me, despite their flaws. They believed they were right, as all the witches did. As we'd been groomed to believe for many, many years. And the truth was, I didn't even know how deep the poisonous roots had grown. Had my grandmother been fooled? Tasa, the former Moon Coven leader? She must have been. But those truths gutted me.

As the others took their seats, eyes glued to me, I began.

"The stories you've heard are true. I did kill the Dark King. I received the power of death and cast it upon him. He sent me to the human lands to try to stop the spell from working. But it didn't work. He is dead." I tried not to think of those silver eyes, of Grey's laughter, of the shadows. Instead, I focused on my feelings before I'd learned the truth. The sorrow and guilt that plagued me shining through my lie. "Nikos tried to warn me, but I didn't listen to him. And now I'm not sure where to find him." Forcing a tremble to my lips, I sold a story of the scared and foolish daughter they thought I still was.

"Right," Kirsi added. "We're hoping he can help hide Raven from the shifters."

I kept my eyes trained to the floor, convinced my father would see anger in the eyes that matched his.

"He will come by," my mother said, sitting to grab my hands. "He will protect you, darling."

I swallowed, keeping my body loose and started on the other reason we came, aside from planting information. "I need to ask you something, Mother. Something that will be difficult to talk about, but I need the answers. Can I trust you?"

"With your life," she said, patting the hand she held. "Always."

I shared a glance with Kirsi before looking straight at my father, still standing, staring at me as if trying to put together a puzzle.

"Why am I unmarked?"

Her eyes doubled in size as she stared at me, gaping. "I don't know what you mean."

And that was it. The proof I needed. She knew, and she easily lied.

"Eden Mossbrook was hiding in the human lands. I found her there, and she told me she warned you that I was the thirteenth witch. You knew the Harrowing would eventually happen." I lifted and dropped my shoulders, mocking a sigh. "What did you do?"

The breath of a moment hung between us like a broken promise. As if she'd never wanted to answer this question, though I had every right to know. When my mother couldn't look me in the eyes, whatever she had to say was difficult for her. Followed by a swallow and a shared glance with my father, I couldn't help the way my heart raced. All my life I'd wondered, and she'd shared in my wonder, or so I thought. Yet here we were. The single question that had tormented me for so long, seconds away.

"What did you do to save me from the Harrowing when Eden warned you that I would be targeted? I need the whole truth."

"It wasn't what *I* did, dear. It was the queen."

If I reacted in any sort of way, she would stop. She would convince herself that I couldn't handle the truth. So, I sat there neutrally. A calm exterior as panic and curiosity ran rampant through my veins. The queen. Bastian's mother. A Fire Coven witch I'd despised, her whole existence wrapped in the lies that were spun for us. Yet she'd saved me.

"What did she do?" I asked, my calmness a farce as I pulled my hand away to clutch the simple, blue cotton dress I'd worn from the few I kept in the shop.

She brushed a black strand of hair from her face, forcing a smile. "When your father and I learned you were on your way, I delivered a letter to the castle. At that time, I had to believe that Eden was alive. I thought maybe the king had protected her from her mother's plan, and, if so, perhaps he could save you as well."

"So, you've known Endora was an enemy this whole time?" Kirsi asked, inching toward my mother.

"No, dear. Endora is not our enemy. Misguided, perhaps, but if you consider her cause, the reason she wanted her plan to work, you can see that she's always wanted to protect the witches."

"Whatever it takes to end the suffering of the witches, we will do it," my father said, his booming voice amplifying the careful tension. "Until it was at the expense of our child. That was the only line we would not cross in support of her."

My mother cleared her throat. "Yes, but when I researched for a way to save you, there was nothing to be done. No one spoke of it beyond terror, and I couldn't find any books that referenced it. We only knew that if the Harrowing was cast, you would be targeted as the thirteenth witch in the Moonstone line. I could only think of one person that could hopefully stop it."

I held up a hand, pausing her to clarify. "You thought if you could show him the innocent life that would be lost, he would be compelled to stop it since Eden's plea hadn't been enough?"

"There was no one else," she whispered. "But I never heard from him. No matter how many letters I sent, as my belly swelled, there was no response. Until one day, when we were sure all hope was lost, the queen sent a messenger. She told me you would be born on the next blood moon. I was to take you directly to the castle that night. My mother hovered nearby, telling everyone that would listen that you'd be the most powerful Moonstone witch."

"You never told her?" I whispered.

Shaking her head, she looked away. "How could I? She and Tasa were so close. Tasa would have had to agree with the Harrowing. We think—"

"The coven leaders were all in on it," my father interrupted, his voice low as he hunched his shoulders, as if he thought they were here, listening through the cottage walls. "Endora couldn't cast that powerful spell alone. It wasn't one she'd received, it was cast in a circle. They had to be involved."

"My mother taught us to trust the coven leaders in all things, and so we did. Apart from this. It's a secret your father and I have kept for all these years."

"What did she actually do?" Kirsi asked. "The night Raven was born?"

"As soon as she arrived, we rushed her to the Fire Coven. The queen was already waiting. She took Raven, wrapped in bundles of blankets, only hours old. I remember sitting in the hall of the black castle, counting every second, thinking I'd made a grave mistake, handing my newborn baby over to our enemy. I wasn't able to go with her, and I don't know what she did. Eventually, she returned, her young son at her side, and handed you back to me. She said that one day, you and Bastian would be linked." She paused, looking away.

I wondered if they could see every hair on my body standing. If they could hear the heart thundering in my chest. If they knew my mind was racing with thoughts of Bastian's mother knowing of our connection. I gulped, hoping I was far more calm on the exterior than I felt on the inside.

My father stood, moving to the window and sliding the simple curtain to the side. "We've done everything we can to keep that from happening, Raven. When you said you wouldn't enter the Trials, we begged the goddess for that to be true. I wanted you to bind your words to me that day because all of this could have been avoided. The moment you entered the Trials, we knew there was no going back, and the queen's words would come to pass." He dropped the curtain and turned to face me, his ice blue eyes full of pride. "Little did she know that link would be the murder of her son."

"All of that, and you have no idea what she did to me? How can that be?"

My parents exchanged another look, and I knew they weren't telling the entire story. I stood, taking careful steps as I paced the floor, agitated that, once again, they were keeping shit to themselves.

"Now is not the time to safeguard your secrets. This is my life, my whole existence we're talking about. I'm not a child anymore." My voice shook with suppressed rage. "Whatever it is, I can handle it, but I can't handle your secrets and your lies under the guise of protecting me. If you don't want me to walk out the door and never come back, you better start talking." I paused, staring my mother down with narrowed eyes. "All my life, you've tried to protect me to an extreme degree, and maybe you thought that was warranted after this initial threat, but it's too much, and it's gone on too long. If you really want to help me, you need to tell me everything."

Kirsi nudged my shoulder, her form of solidarity as I waited.

An unspoken conversation passed between my parents in seconds before my mother took a step back and lowered her gaze. "The queen bound my words, so even your father didn't know the complete truth."

"Didn't, but she died. That spell would have worn off over time," Kirsi said, always in my corner, always ready to fight for me.

My mother raised her head and continued. "When the queen died, your magic returned. Slowly at first, but it grew. The plan was to make you seem like a silenced witch, so absolute that even a spell other witches might cast for detection would never be able to sense your magic. In order to do that, the queen had to give you a portion of her own power. That deep well must still sit within you. I'm sure of it. She only told me she used a place of power beneath the blood moon to perform her strange magic. That is all. And that's all it ever was supposed to be until she died. And then everything was ruined."

It was my turn to step away, nearing the door. "Just because my life didn't go according to your plan doesn't mean it was ruined. I have to go now. When Nikos comes by tomorrow, tell him I'm in trouble and I need him."

My father placed an arm around my mother's shoulder. "We've always done what we thought was best. For you and for the coven, Raven. You cannot fault us for being imperfect. I'm happy to hear you haven't lost faith in Nikos. Someday, you will understand our choices as well."

I nodded. "Maybe someday."

Kirsi looped her arm in mine. It must have taken immense concentration to do as she spun us toward the door, the phantom tendrils of her hair reflecting no light as I swung it open.

The moment we were outside, she whispered, "You should have let me scare them."

"There's still time."

She huffed a laugh and tilted her head toward the back. "I found it. Had to throw it out the window."

"Well, I'm glad it wasn't a waste of time," I muttered, circling my parents' house to collect the little tin box Kirsi helped me steal.

We left the cottage behind, and I wasn't sure if I would ever return.

"Of all the things, they really didn't want to tell you the queen had given you some of her power when she hid your markings and bound your magic. Why would that matter now?"

I pressed my hand to my head, the ever-looming headache swelling, pushing behind my eyes as I ran my fingers over the tin box now tucked in my deep dress pocket. "Bastian's mother was very powerful. That's part of the reason his dad selected her as his bride to end the war. They would never want me to be confident. Confidence is the same as recklessness in their minds. Confidence could lead me to combat the coven leaders, and Goddess knows we can't have that."

"At least not until we get our hands on Nikos to find those bitches." Kir smirked.

I shrugged, grateful she hadn't mentioned my headache. "I'm sorry we didn't really learn anything new about the Harrowing. Such a waste of time."

"Don't kid yourself, Rave. We didn't go there expecting to learn anything. But now, we know the queen bound your power before she died. We know whatever she did was to protect you, and we know she would have given anything for her son. Your power, *her* power, is a gift. Which only tells me you're going to need that. What if going to the human lands unbound the queen's hold on her power within you? We know that hold has been fading for a while, but maybe it's gone now. Permanently. Maybe that's why you were so sick. Because the magic was freed but with nowhere to go it just festered beneath."

"Maybe," I whispered, unwilling to tell her she was wrong.

The magic was deeper, for sure, a sitting storm within me. That swell had been there for a long time, though, since I was given the death spell and forced to use it. I was never chosen by the goddess to be something to change the world. I was selected by a queen with a vision and a heart to protect her son. I was unmarked, but the second that death spell was cast, I was also unbound from whatever spell she'd wrapped around me. The question was, why was I still unmarked?

26

RAVEN

Leaving the small cluster of cottages behind, we stayed off the main cobblestone path, opting to hide within the tree line instead. Evening fell swiftly upon the Moon Coven, bringing a sweep of power through the chilled, late autumn air. Nearby homes nestled in the woods combated the cold with their fireplaces, sending the aroma of softly burning wood into the evening. It would have been nostalgic had I not feared who we might encounter. Fortunately, we hadn't seen a soul since leaving my parents' cottage.

The threat of Nikos was nearly debilitating, considering what happened last time I'd seen him, but now I knew to strike first and ask questions later. A lesson well learned. I no longer lived in a cruel world. I lived amongst cruel people who would spill blood, if only to enrich their own. My perception of everything around me had changed. The sharp points of the rocks lying dormant along a worn path, the poisonous horns of a toad, the thorns of a bush, the whims of a witch... No innocence remained, just the honed weapons crafted by a deadly existence.

A rustling of branches ahead drew me to a quick stop. I exchanged a single glance with Kir before she vanished. Arms raised, I would not be unprepared. The tightly wound coil of magic within me sat taut,

THE UNBOUND WITCH

ready to strike. Catching a glimpse of familiar orange hair, I nearly dropped my hands until a spell whipped passed me.

"Ender, stop. It's me," I hissed, hands still raised.

"Lucky for us," a second voice said from behind me.

I whipped around to see Greer, Ender's older sister, standing with a ball of light suspended between her hands. Without giving her a second to consider throwing that ball at me, I cast, sending her flying backward, crashing into a tree. Her body slumped to the ground as I whirled, facing a pallid Ender.

"We were in the first part of the Trials together. You've known me forever. I am not your enemy." Magic surged through my veins in warning like lightning charging before an electrical storm. "I will not hold back, Ender."

"Too much time with the Dark King," she mocked, hands falling to her side.

"The king is dead. I killed him myself. But he was never the villain. The coven leaders that hide behind their lies and spit venom into vulnerable crowds are the only enemies of this world." I took a step away, hands still raised, wondering where Kir might be. Maybe I'd said too much, had marked myself a traitor by condemning the coven leaders. "Who sent you?"

Her eyes lit with mischief as she looked over my shoulder. Too late, I whipped around to see Greer pulling to her feet, mid-cast. A gust of wind slammed into me. I stumbled backward. Kirsi popped into view between us, her arms crossed over her translucent chest as she stared at a witch that had once been a good friend of hers.

"Boo."

Greer fell again, her spell rebounding off a tree, barely missing me.

"You died," she whispered, her terrified gaze shifting between her sister and Kirsi.

Kirsi studied her nails with a half smirk. "I'd forgotten how astute you were. Thank you for the reminder. Now," she floated closer until Greer was inches from her, twisting her face until it sat at a horrifying angle, her eyes wide and haunted. "I'd suggest you put a damper on that magic before I reveal a really neat trick I learned in the human lands. Turns out, the wraiths have been holding out on us. Also, apparently you haven't heard. She can kill you with a little finger wiggle. I mean, it doesn't sound like fun to me, but by all means, be brave, witch. See what fucking happens."

Greer paled and scrambled back, dirt staining her dress as she moved, jutting her chin out as if it would hide her fear. "There is no *us*, Kirsi Moondance. You are only a memory now. Another unfortunate loss of potential at the Dark King's hands." She met eyes with me. "If you killed him for revenge, then why did you kill Onyx? And Zennik? And Breya? They say you went mad."

I opened my mouth to answer, but a twig snapped behind me. Spinning and casting without thought, I caught Ender with the spell I'd used to throw her sister. But rather than sending her flying, I pushed her up and up and up until a fall would mean certain death. I was confident the only reason she didn't scream was pure shock and fear. A glimpse of white fur beyond made the wheels of my mind turn.

"I will kill you," Greer threatened, standing. "Put her down."

I let the breeze blow through my hair, narrowing my gaze. "Let's not forget you started this fight. Tell me why. You can clearly see I haven't gone mad, as they, whoever they are, have suggested."

"Willow called a gathering of the coven, proclaiming you saved us all, but your mind was poisoned by the man you murdered, and, for everyone's sake, you needed to be found."

"You don't know—"

"It's true," I interrupted Kir. "I killed the Dark King. He was toxic to this land and made me believe things that weren't real. With his death, his spell was broken. But the shifters are after me now as well as the witches, apparently."

She glared. "Why should we care?"

"Because," I said, lowering my voice, though I knew I could still be heard. "There's a shifter they call the White Wolf." I forced fear into my eyes as I continued. "With teeth twice as long as they should be, eyes that glow red in the night, and he stands twice as high as any other wolf in this world. I came to warn my parents, but I'm afraid it's too late for all of us." I looked over her shoulder, studying the shadows within the trees. "He's here."

"I don't trust you, Raven Moonstone."

A low growl from within the woods was all the sign she needed as the last bit of color drained from her face. "Please, let my sister down. This is your battle, not ours."

"Scared of a little wolf?" Kirsi asked, the cold, hard tone in her voice a shadow of what it once was.

"Four witches against one shifter? We could take him," I said, looking over her shoulder as I raised my arms, slowly bringing her sister down.

"N-no. I want no part of your troubles. Willow and Nikos charged the Moon Coven with your capture, but you're not worth it."

"Nikos? Do you know where he is? He's the only one that can help me now."

"Let us go, and I will tell you."

Another ferocious growl sounded from within the trees.

I released the final hold on Ender, and she darted for Greer, though she kept her eyes on the forest.

"She's right here," Ender yelled. "Raven Moonstone is right here."

"Traitors," Kirsi hissed as the witches ran the opposite direction of the threatening growl.

One second passed. Then another as the chirps and bird songs of the forest filled the air. I breathed a sigh of relief at their silent retreat, exhaustion tugging on my limbs.

Kir circled me, a wicked smile on her face. "You don't think they went to get help, do you?"

"Nah. You know them. They'll spread gossip, but they aren't going to do much beyond that. They're probably too scared the big bad wolf will hunt them down."

"True. You can come out now, oh fearsome puppy."

Atlas, in his human form, stepped from behind a tree, his arms folded over his broad chest. "Red glowing eyes? Really?"

I shrugged. "You'll haunt their nightmares now."

"At least you got the size right," he countered.

Kirsi snorted. "How long until Nikos shows up?"

"If we have any chance at all of catching the coven leaders, it better be soon," Atlas said, turning to lead us deeper into the forest toward a tall, hulking figure leaning against a magical door.

"Oh, Grey, so lovely to see you," Kirsi said before vanishing over the threshold.

"Don't mind my glowing red eyes," Atlas said to Bastian before following.

I paused, kicking at the dirt with my boot. He raised an eyebrow, but I shook my head. "It wasn't great. My parents were less than helpful. Your mother, however, is the reason my power was bound. And apparently, all the witches think I've gone mad."

He wrapped a strong hand around my waist, pulling me toward him. A golden lock falling into his eyes. I didn't have to remind myself this was Bastian anymore. I moved the stray hair and stood to my tiptoes to press my nose to his. A welcome moment in the tumultuous night I had. His solid form grounded me, and I may have even felt the headache lessen slightly at his touch. His longing.

"It's taking everything in my power not to chase those witches down," he confessed, the hardness of his tone, the force behind his words proof of his true nature.

"They are not our enemies."

He pressed a thumb under my chin, forcing my eyes up to his. "Anyone that casts a spell toward you is my enemy. Anyone that has a single cruel thought about you is my enemy. Anyone that stands between you and whatever it is you want in this world is my enemy."

"Even if it's me?" I sighed. "I'm not sure bringing the Moss Coven Grimoire here was a great idea. I know Eden wanted to come home, but surely, Endora feels that magic. She might be on her way to us right now."

Fire lit his eyes. "Good. Saves me the trouble of having to hunt that bitch down."

We walked through the magical door to Crescent Cottage seconds before it disappeared. Torryn stood at the window, hands clasped firmly behind his back, watching the quiet, moonlit street. The back-door creaked open, and Kirsi, Torryn and I all spun in surprise. The strain in the room budding as we prepared for the next part of our plan. But it was only the captain, standing with dirt-covered hands, holding onto three squash and a small pumpkin.

"You should consider bathing once in a while," Kirsi said, moving away from him.

I rushed forward to take the pumpkin, noting the soft side.

"If we don't get these out of the garden soon, they will go to waste." Eden reached for the squash. "I'll make soup for supper."

Crow's stomach growled as if on cue.

I turned to Bastian, leaning into his ear. "Is there a bath I can't remember in the mountain cabin?"

"There could be," he growled back.

My body jerked in response to his answer, a blush creeping across my cheeks. I tucked a curl behind my ear, smiling. "I meant for the captain. We have to leave soon if tonight is the night, and I hate to leave him without the option."

Bastian turned his back to me, gesturing with his hands to conjure a door, this one made of pure black stone, refusing to acknowledge the plan he completely disagreed with and happy to delay it.

"Aw, come on," Crow whined. "It's not that bad."

"Yes, it is," we said in unison as Bastian pushed him toward the door.

The second they stepped through, a tiny black note drifted down from the ceiling. I snatched it from the air with a half-smile, remembering our days in the castle that was now rubble.

Ms. Moonstone,

What favors might a king tally for helping a stinky old captain bathe?

Suffering silently,
   Bastian, more handsome than Grey, Firepool

I stifled my giggle as the edges of the note ignited, the embers burning away the evidence.

"Debatable," Kirsi whispered over my shoulder.

I turned, wondering what she meant, but she just pointed to my hand. "Grey is definitely more handsome."

"Nah. Bash has that whole dark and moody thing going for him. Plus, have you seen that jawline?" Atlas asked over the top of a book he'd picked up from a shelf.

"I had no idea you were so interested," Kir answered.

"Handsome recognizes handsome. It's a curse, really."

Moving away from their teasing, I crossed the store, studying the back door. Eden came to my side, looping her arm with mine. I stared out over the half-harvested garden, hardly believing all the changes since the seeds were planted. It seemed a lifetime and yet only a second ago.

"Are we sure no one can see Crow out in the garden? Not only is this place supposed to be locked down, but he's human and a big liability."

She patted my hand. "I've cast a darkness spell over him. As long as he's only out under the moonlight, no one will see him. And I've been teaching him our ways. In a few days, he'll be able to pass as a silent witch who grew up as an outcast. If anyone ever questions him, they'll never know the truth."

I gave her a pointed look. "Let's just hope no one questions him."

"Indeed," she smiled. "But we can't stay locked in this shop forever. Eventually, I'd like to return to my home. I know that won't be anytime soon, but someday."

"Do you think she'll come?" I whispered, though I was sure I already knew the answer.

Torryn moved to my side, providing that easy comfort he always did. Squeezing my shoulder, he smiled down at me, his long, twisted hair falling forward. "Have faith, Little Witch. If she comes, we will be ready."

"Oh, she'll come. Not for me, but for her Grimoire, she'll bring the world down."

"That's exactly what I'm afraid of."

27

RAVEN

The rich smell of roasted squash permeated Crescent Cottage so thoroughly, I was certain if there were any witches anywhere near the square, they would end up on the outside of the barrier to the shop, staring in the empty windows with total confusion. To them, they would see the battered store we'd found the day we arrived, broken glass and not a sign of life within. But I didn't know if that would hold true for the aroma.

Torryn wrapped his massive brown hands around his bowl, grinning from ear to ear as he stared down at Eden. "The goddess blessed me the day our paths crossed."

"Oh, stop." She swatted his arm. "I am no longer your charge. Your flattery is wholly unnecessary."

His face fell. "Every word I've ever spoken to you was with full sincerity. It was never about watching over you or gaining your trust."

A blush crossed her pale cheeks. "I didn't mean—"

A swirling mass of red magic appeared in the shop, and without thinking, I raised my hand to cast as Atlas shifted into his wolf form. My first thought was the Grimoire. Though I hadn't seen her put it away, I knew without a doubt it was sandwiched between two stacked pots under the oak counter in the backroom. A decent hiding spot, but still one that called to me. The magic thinned for a moment before Bastian and Crow fell from the half-cast door in a heap of soaking clothes and red faces.

"What the hell?" Kirsi surged forward. She swooped low to help Bastian to his feet, but he managed on his own.

"Blame him," he said, pointing at the captain. "Absolutely refused to bathe without clothes on and then wouldn't let me help him out of the water."

"Bloody witches and your magics. Can't let a man wash his ass in peace."

"No one's washing their ass through their britches, Crow," Torryn said, biting back his giant smile.

He moved to his feet, dripping water all over the shop floor. "I wasn't going to give him a show."

Laughter filled the air, each of us with smiles on our faces, the heavy mood shifting into something lighter, easier. And he knew it. Crow smiled, winking at Eden. Embracing the character just to make her smile. I thought he probably loved her, even if she didn't know it yet.

Relishing the relaxed camaraderie between the witches and the shifters twisted something in my heart. It could have been like this. From the dawn of our days, had there not been so much abhorrence bred into our minds. Had our ancestors not steeped our world in ruination by drawing that line between us. I wanted this. And I'd fight for it. Smelly captain and sopping wet king included.

"For the thousandth time, I wasn't looking."

"Mhmm. That's what they all say… right before they get handsy."

"Always a valid threat with this one," Atlas said, clapping Bastian on the back, water spraying from his dark, damp shirt.

"You all make me want to murder someone," Bastian said, storming off to the back room while everyone else continued to howl with laughter.

I used the opportunity to sneak a moment alone with him, slipping through the repaired vines hanging from the door frame. Silhouetted in moonlight, taking his true form with his back to me, every heaving breath, every ounce of heated power rolling off his body in cascading shadows drew me nearer. I knew what happened inside wasn't the reason for this angry reaction, something else was bothering him. I'd forgotten how dangerous and angry he could be. As if he'd been holding himself back and composed since we've returned and every part of him was near breaking.

"The shadows serve a purpose," he whispered.

"And that is?" I asked, stepping forward to run my hands down the hard muscles of his back, surprised he hadn't conjured his wings.

"They tell me things. Like when pretty, little witches approach quietly."

I moved my fingers along his side as I circled him, staring up at searing silver eyes. "Do you want to talk about it?"

"Talk about what?" He gripped my neck, his thumb stroking softly.

"You're not really mad at Crow."

"No. I'm mad at the world. At my total loss of control. At the witches who have us cornered. Of sitting here like a fucking target, waiting for them to make a move. Your new plan can't be the only answer. Waiting for some prick to show up and give us information he might not even have. The Harrowing is out there, still taking its course." He gripped tighter around my neck, pulling me in as he whispered. "We tried to save Nym, but have done nothing for you."

"You've done everything for me."

"Grab your head one more time, Raven. Keep pretending that you are well and not suffering."

I couldn't help but flinch at the power lining the edge of his voice. The growl and desperation competing, even as I could see the longing on his face. I should have known that I wasn't fooling him. I tried to pull away, but he held me firm.

"Fear is power," I whispered, reminding him of words he once spoke to me. "I am not afraid, and I will not give them that power."

"I am not afraid of them," he said, equally quiet. "I am afraid of me. Of what I will do when I get my hands on them."

"You'll have to beat me to it."

I closed the space between us, pressing my lips to his so fiercely and for so long, I thought we'd faint from lack of breath. He moved his hands into my curls as he held me. Seconds ticked by, each one relaxing those broad shoulders more and more as we lost ourselves in one another. A kiss that was far more than a kiss. It was a bonding. A promise to each other that we would not fall victim to cruel witches in a struggling world. A tear fell down my cheek as I felt every emotion he poured into the heated moment. Where we'd both reached the cliff of our wit's end and now, we jumped.

"How confident are you in the plan?" he asked, moments later.

I pursed my lips. "The one you refused?"

He took a step backward, sliding his hands into his pockets. "It's dangerous and reckless, and you're the one at risk."

I shook my head. "That's exactly why it's going to work. He's overly confident when it comes to me."

"Fool," Bastian said, a forced smile on his face.

"I know you don't like it, but he hasn't come here yet, and we don't have time to sit around. If he doesn't show up, then fine. But I think he will."

"We put it to a vote, Bash," Kirsi said from the door.

"Kings don't care for votes much, Kir," he said, his voice hollow as he lowered his head.

She swooped around, moving between us. "I won't leave her. I won't let him hurt her. I promise."

"Promises are only good until they are broken."

"How poetic," she said, turning to face me. "You need to eat something, and then we go."

I nodded, slipping my hand into Bastian's and pulling him out of the room. The others sat on the floor, Crow with a small puddle around him, eating squash soup from mortar bowls in silence.

Atlas looked up from his dinner, made eye contact with Bastian, and shook his head. "Looks like you've lost the battle, friend."

"It's not a battle," Eden countered. "It's a good plan, and it's going to work. You just need to leave first. So, eat up."

Torryn stood, setting his bowl on the counter in the back of the room. "Ready when you are, Pup."

Atlas tipped the stone bowl to the ceiling, licking every last drop before springing to his feet. "We'll be back before you know it."

Bastian waved an arm in the air, conjuring a door, a mark on his arm glowing. "If Clariss refuses, we think of something else."

"So, don't let her refuse," Kirsi added from behind us, arms crossed over her chest. "We don't have time to fuck around, and we need her to gag Nikos."

"Such foul language," Atlas said with a wink, shifting and bounding through the door.

Torryn's exit was far less dramatic as he shook his head and followed. Eden gathered Crow's bowl and used magic to clean and put them away.

"Honestly, that's probably the most useful spell I've ever seen," Kirsi said, moving up and along the ceiling. "Makes me miss Scoop, though."

Bastian filled two bowls with the thick, orange soup, passing one to me. "I'm sure he's content with Nym's tiger for now."

She shook her head, looking toward the door he'd cast. "I don't want him to be content. I want him to want me back."

It was the most honest thing I'd heard her say in a long time, and something about those words hanging in the room held everyone else silent as we finished eating and watched that door to the Fire Coven, waiting and waiting. Each moment passing feeling a little heavier.

When Atlas' black nose pierced the threshold, the white wolf leading a familiar face through the entry, I couldn't help jumping to my feet, wondering how she would react to seeing me. If Atlas had told her the whole truth, or if she'd come in blind.

"Your Grace," Clariss said, bowing low before she stood and crossed the room, pulling him into a hug. I hadn't seen my appointed castle maid since I'd left that fated morning to complete the final Trial.

"I'd heard the rumors that you were alive, but I had to see for myself." She turned to me, her lips in a hard line as she studied my face, and then the worn black dress. "You look as frumpy as I found you that first day, girl."

I forced a smile. "Thank you for coming."

Clariss crossed the room, taking both of my hands. "I wouldn't have come for you had I not learned the truth from Atty. I'm sorry I didn't have more faith, Miss Moonstone. But also, I swore I'd kill you if I ever saw you again. I thought you should know."

I smiled. A real, genuine, ear-to-ear smile. "I missed you."

She pulled me into a hug, and I sat in those warm arms for a moment longer than was probably necessary, grateful to have a sliver of vulnerability before the real work started.

"Shall we go?" Torryn asked, rubbing his hands together.

I looked at Bastian, recognizing the fact that he absolutely didn't want to follow the plan, but was doing it anyway. A win. Small, but something. My eyes circled the faces in the room until I landed on Eden.

"Go. I'll be fine. I'll look after the place for you."

I dipped my chin before slipping my hand into Bastian's. "Let's get this over with."

"Famous last words," Atlas said as we stepped through a new door rimmed with old, rotten wood, a clear picture of how Bastian felt. But who could blame him, really, when I was insisting on being the bait?

28

RAVEN

"Is the door open?" Kirsi whispered from beside me, though I couldn't see her, could hardly see anything through the night.

"Looks like it," I answered. "Stay close."

It was only a crack, really, as if someone had left in a hurry and didn't bother looking over their shoulder as they tugged on the heavy wooden door. The markings on the chipped wood from our selection into the Trials had been carefully washed away. While dirt still stained the outer parts, the center was cleaner than it had been in years.

With one decisive look over my shoulder, staring into the darkness where I knew he stood, waiting with baited breath, I pushed inside the home Kirsi and I had shared for so long. It smelled of dust and abandonment. Of stale crumbs and unwashed bedding. Maybe even a little hope and unanswered prayers.

With the bank of clouds that had moved in blocking most of the moonlight, I could hardly see the outline of our dilapidated furniture.

"Hello?" I whispered. Not only to Nikos, should he be hiding within, but anyone or thing that might have sought sanctuary in our home.

The silence was so loud it crept along my skin, causing a ringing in my ears. As if I were seeking noise so desperately, my mind conjured what was not there. I twisted my wrist, lighting the red candle in the window, as I promised Bastian I would do. Wandering our home, I lit the others, one by one, remembering the last time I was here. The day of Kirsi's funeral.

"It's empty," she whispered, clicking the door shut. "But he's been here. There's a note."

Stepping toward the door, I snagged the piece of paper nailed into the frame.

The only safe place for you now is behind me. I hope you've learned your lesson.

ANGER BILLOWING, I RIPPED THE NOTE TO SHREDS, LIGHTING EACH individual piece in a lone candle as I pictured his imminent demise. The single look on his face the instant before death snatched him away forever.

I blew out the red candle and lit it three times. The signal to take cover and wait. And so we did. After moving the couch toward the window, I sat on it to watch for movement and time to pass. I didn't know if he'd even try to go back to the shop after destroying it. I knew it was him, though. He'd taken extra care to avoid the small things that he knew were most precious to me. My grandmother's apron. The small line of glass vials along the shelf closest to the door with the last bit of herbs she'd ever gathered. The blanket over the cot in the back I'd wrapped myself in the night she died. No one else would have known what those things meant to me. No one else would have taken such care.

He'd been to my parents' house every day, though. He was still searching. And if not at Crescent Cottage and not at my first home, this was the only logical place he might find me. A place where we had memories together.

My eyelids drew heavier and heavier as I waited. But the moment I slipped into sleep, Bastian was there on the threshold of my mind.

"Wake up, Little Witch. You cannot sleep."

"He's been here," I answered with a yawn in my dream.

Bastian closed the blank space between us, gripping my arms. "Do not hesitate. If you feel threatened at all, kill him. No information is worth your life. You have that spell for a reason."

"I can hold him off until Clariss comes. Have faith in me."

"I have all the faith in the world in you. It's him I have a problem with."

He jerked away from me in my dream, vanishing without another word.

"Raven," Kirsi hissed in my ear, yanking me from my sleep. "I think he's here."

The sharp snap of rocks beneath the hoof of a horse whipped through the room. I leapt to my feet, heart instantly racing as I realized I didn't know what I'd do to start this. I gripped the tin box in my pocket as I slipped to the bedroom in the back, holding my breath as the door crept open and heavy footfalls broke the tension-filled silence.

"Raven?"

I gasped, stepping into the hall as I heard my father's voice.

"Raven, your mother is worried and sent me to check after you. Are you here?"

Seconds became minutes in my mind as I weighed the option of answering or not. Bastian was going to come flying through that door if I didn't give him the signal soon. Which meant I really had no choice.

"I'm here," I said calmly, walking out from the back room, rubbing my eyes as if I'd been completely asleep.

"You didn't lock the door?" my father asked, but there was something different in his eyes, some kind of spark I'd witnessed when he was full of fight, but yet his body, his posture, were all calm, apart from the hand resting on the knife in his belt, the milky white moonstone, our namesake, practically glowing in the faint light.

I'd seen preternatural calm before, felt it. Like being trapped in one's own body. My heart sank to my toes as I realized what was happening.

"I'd hoped Nikos would come for me. I'm waiting for him."

Then there was sadness. A swell of it as his eyebrows turned in. Nikos had forced him to come first. To be the sacrificial pig before he would enter. And my father was only a victim. Perhaps they both always were. My heart ached at that thought. A truth I'd never considered.

"Would you like to take a look around? Make sure everything looks okay?"

That must have been what he was ordered to do. I let the flame flicker in the candle. A signal to Bastian and company to hold back.

Walking behind my father, I wondered if he was scared of what might lurk in the shadows behind me. If he thought for sure he would meet his maker here and now, forced to face whatever it was in this world that might protect me from Nikos. Because he was only the bait. Just as I was. But I could see him through this. Make sure he got out and gave whatever sign was needed.

"Where is Kirsi?" my father asked, his tone suspicious, the words hardly his own.

"She has her own path to follow, Father. She cannot be tangled in mine. These are dangerous times."

He planted a heavy hand on my shoulder as he checked the small corner room Kirsi slept in. Moving like a snail, as if he fought the demands of the witch, just as I had. "They are, my girl. More so now than ever. You will do well to remember that."

I dipped my chin, a tear sliding down my cheek. My father, the victim. "I'm safe. I promise."

His eyes said everything his mouth could not as he nodded and walked out of the door. It would be only moments before Nikos followed, I was sure of it.

Turning to Kirsi as my hands shook, I placed the kettle atop the stove. "Go to Bastian, tell him my father is under Nikos' spell, and if I had to guess, he will be here any minute."

Casting, I lit the wood within the oven and straightened my back.

"No," Kirsi answered.

"Kirsi, you have to make sure they don't come rushing in here. It'll ruin everything."

"Flicker your candle or do whatever you're doing, but there's no way in hell I'm leaving you alone right now. You wanted Bastian to stick to the plan, you have to do the same."

A low bird call sounded from the back of our old home. We locked eyes before hustling to the window. A magical owl with a billowing tail glowed within the tree line behind the house. Kirsi shot through the wall, dashing toward Torryn's shifter form.

The front door creaked open.

"Raven?"

His voice was like the hiss of poison dripping into freshly ground salt. Like the stink of rotting fish lying on the riverbank in the summer sun. A weapon steeped in lies and power. I let steel move through my veins as I walked down the hall, facing the man I'd sworn to murder.

"Thank the goddess you're here, Nikos. I thought you'd never come."

He looked around me before shutting the door. I circled, placing my back to the candle as I extinguished the flame for one second and lit it once more. Ten minutes. That's all I had before Bastian came barreling through that front door. I just had to stay alive, alert and in full control until then.

"Are you alone?" he asked, though he certainly knew the answer.

A brush of cool pressed into my neck. Kirsi. I was not, but he would never need to know that.

Making my voice shake with what seemed like fear while truly it was suppressed rage, I answered. "Unfortunately. I've been hiding for days and days. I managed to see my parents today, but that was all."

He shoved the dark blond hair from his face as he sat on the couch, eyeing me carefully. "You killed the Dark King."

"Just as you asked me to."

"No!" he shouted. "If you had done it like I'd asked, it would have happened the night of the ball beneath the blood moon. When I was there to get you out."

I moved to the stove, pulling the kettle away before the whistle blew, hands shaking, the quiver in my voice wasn't entirely for show. "A lot of things happened all at once, Nikos. We were together, and then we weren't. You were so demanding, and then you were so kind. And then you helped the coven leaders force the death spell on me, and I didn't understand. But I do now."

I poured the hot water into two cups, lifting the tin box from my pocket with trembling fingers. My mother's herbs. Strong enough to put a horse to sleep, gentle enough to leave the victim unharmed. Though I could make no promises once that door flew open.

I let the fear of Bastian's next kill sink into my voice as I whispered. "They're after me, and I have nowhere to hide." Cool magic fell over my skin as he tried to calm my nerves. I jerked away, nearly spilling the tea, lit only by candlelight in our old home. "Please," I whispered. "Don't use your magic on me. You know how it makes me feel." I shoved the tea toward him before taking a swig of my own hot water.

He looked down at the cup in his hands, shaking his head. He knew. I wasn't sure how, but certainly he did.

"Sit down, Raven."

"I don't want—

"I said sit down!" he shouted. "You like your men controlling, do you not? Isn't that what you found so irresistible about the Dark King?" His green eyes glimmered with hatred. "Why should I believe that suddenly you want my help when the last time I tried to help you, you ran off with *him*?"

I brought the teacup to my lips, hoping he might follow out of sheer habit. "He twisted my mind, Nikos. He spent hours showing me things that were not real until I couldn't determine what was true and what wasn't. He was the devil in disguise, and I fell victim to his lies. You cannot fault me for that. I know you don't. You wouldn't be here if you did."

"No," he said, falling back until he sunk in the couch. "I cannot fault you for being an imbecile. You come by it naturally, it seems."

He didn't even glance up to see the reaction I swallowed with the hot water. But as if the goddess heard my plea, my cheek warming where she'd touched me, he brought his cup to his lips and drank as

THE UNBOUND WITCH

well. I had no idea what my mother used for such a small cup, but I'd wager to bet, I overcompensated.

"What is this?" He pulled the cup from his mouth with a sour expression. "It has no smell and no taste. It's just hot."

I shrugged, turning to glance out of the window. "It's dried lavender. I found it in the windowsill when I got here. I'm afraid the sun dried it too quickly, and it lost its flavor."

"Might as well have handed me pond water," he said, holding the cup out. "Take this away."

"You don't have to be so rude to me," I snapped, something I would have always done.

"Let's not pretend anymore, Raven."

Chills ran down my spine as I felt the power he called forth. If I played too far one way, he would get suspicious. If I got feisty, he would fight back. Somewhere in-between was a fine line I needed to walk for only a few more minutes. And then, come what may, the circumstances would change.

"What exactly are we pretending?"

"This isn't a passing conversation between friends. You are mine now. You'll do what I say when I say it without question. In exchange, I'll keep you alive. Don't fool yourself into thinking you're anything but a tool for my cause. You had your chance. We could have been great, you and I." He stepped forward, a marking on his neck glowing as he ran his index finger down my cheek. "But you had to go and fuck it all up with that monster."

My heart stopped. I remembered Bastian's words. *If you feel threatened at all, kill him. No information is worth your life.* Kirsi's cold, invisible hand wrapped around my arm. Either she was going to rip his heart out, or I was going to cast the spell swelling inside me, begging to be released. The pressure of my own magic became overwhelming as the headache I'd been running from resurfaced.

"Don't even think about it," he whispered, his lips so close to mine I could vomit.

I couldn't see his eyes in the dark, but I felt him falter as the door slammed open, and Bastian stood in his true form, staring, heaving, seething as the world fell deathly silent. Two great forms filled the door frame as Bastian stepped into the room. It didn't matter, though. Nikos hit the floor with a thud, sealing his fate.

I barely registered his movement as the Dark King crossed the room, rolling Nikos with his foot to confirm he was out before crushing me to his chest. "If you ever consider making yourself bait again, you might as well kill me first. I'll never do that again."

"Noted," I said with a relieved smile, holding him as tightly as he held me.

"It's clear," Atlas said out the door, welcoming Clariss into the fold.

"One more second, King. That's all you were getting before I ripped his fucking heart out. You have no idea how close I was." Kirsi floated back and forth across the ceiling as if she'd prepared for battle and had to work the nerves out.

"It's not over yet." Torryn grabbed Nikos from the floor and plopped him onto the single spindle-backed chair we kept near the stove.

His head rolled forward, and rather than catching him, the shifter stepped to the side, letting him crash face first into the old, dusty floor before picking him up and repeating the process. This time, his head fell backward. I cast, pulling vines from between the floorboards, watching them wrap around the chair so tightly they marked his skin, thorns digging in, drawing deep red blood.

Bastian hadn't moved a muscle. Staring down at Nikos, jaw clenched, fists balled like hammers at his sides. It took me two seconds to realize what he was doing. What nightmares might he conjure for a man he wanted to skin alive? Based on the sly smile that inched across his face, I didn't want to know.

29

KIRSI

Sweeping back and forth through the cottage, casting a blue glow about the dark room, I stared down at the man I'd thought was our friend. A lifetime of lies had spilled from those lips, an entire existence that was a farce. The questions I had were countless. But I wasn't sure if I'd even get my turn based on the glare full of fire coming from the Dark King.

We'd agreed he would take Grey's form. Keep the charade as long as possible, but when he crashed through that door as broad and dangerous as I'd always pictured him before I ever met him, I understood it. There would be no need for disguises. It would take an insurmountable effort for Nikos to live past these next few hours. Though if the king himself did not wrench the life from the prick tied to the chair, the wolf, pacing the threadbare rug near the door in human form, surely would.

In three passes, Atlas had learned where each creak and groan of the old floor was. He avoided those spots, striding in silence as we stared, waiting for the monster to awaken.

"Are you ready?" Bash asked, looking at Clariss, who stood with her chest up and chin high. Her hands wrapped around Torryn's, and if I stared hard enough, I could see the bead of sweat cascading down her temple, although the room was likely cold.

"As I'll ever be." Her voice was solid. Determined. That of an old maid that took no shit, and though she may have been shaken on the inside, outside, she was hard as nails.

Atlas and Tor moved like they could read each other's minds. Shifting the small bits of furniture to the outskirts of the tiny room, giving just enough space for Raven to pour a black salt circle with a star in the middle. She cast like it was a dance, moving lit candles and creating a space seeping with magic and power. Keeping her eyes closed, she moved her hands, tidying up the scattered grounds of salt, leaving no space for errors. With the candles in place, she finally finished, giving the Dark King a slight nod.

He stepped aside as she swiped her hand through the air, releasing the thorny vines and using magic to move Nikos' slumped body into the middle of the circle. A marking with two opposing half arcs intersected by a jagged line lit on Bash's neck. His eyes bore into the crumpled man as he began to twitch and whimper. The Dark King stepped forward, pulling out his knife to slice away Nikos' clothing, exposing all of his hidden markings. He snorted once before covering Nik's little dick with his shadows.

Clariss stepped to the edge of the circle, never crossing a single grain of salt as she cast and all sound vanished from his trembling lips. I moved higher, getting a different vantage point, swallowing down my jealousy. Knowing these gathered witches were pulsating with a power I'd never feel again. The moment Scoop entered my mind, I shut it down. Shut down all thoughts and feelings and simply became an empty vessel. Insubstantial and haunted, nothing more.

"How much did you give him?" Bastian pulled his gaze away from his victim to lift an eyebrow to Raven.

She shook her head. "It was dark. I couldn't see very well. Just a pinch or two of the powder."

"And this leaf," Atlas said, studying the bottom of the cup.

"He could sleep for days with that amount of venica root mixed with a gurriand leaf if the power was spelled properly," Clariss said.

"It was," Raven and I answered in unison.

THE UNBOUND WITCH

"Moonstone witches are born herbalists," I continued. "And if not born, then taught before they can walk. There's a reason Crescent Cottage is worth traveling to."

Clariss shook her head. "Better get comfortable. It seems we'll be here for a long time."

"No. He will be drowsy, but that will only make this easier. Atlas, shift. You're going to become his nightmare."

A wide grin spread across the pup's face before he melted into the beautiful white beast and stepped to the edge of the circle. A low growl rumbling from behind his teeth as he crouched down. The king cast once more, penetrating the dreams of his victim until he was thrashing on the cottage floor. Nikos' eyes flew open, his mouth carrying a soundless scream as he came face to face with the beast. Though sluggish, he scrambled backward, slamming into the edge of the salt circle that held him in place.

Bastian's inky shadows seeped along the floorboards, begging to break the barrier and smother Nikos. As if they had a mind of their own, they inched forward, pulling back at the last minute and trying again. A physical embodiment of what the king wished to do, it seemed.

I moved closer, unable to help my curiosity as I took in the terrified face of a man I once thought a friend. His eyes were wild, frenzied. His dark blond hair tousled in all directions, even his clothes, now discarded in a corner, were more crumpled than usual. But there was something else. Something I wasn't sure the others noticed, or would have, aside from Raven. The crow's feet around his eyes. The withered look growing along his hands. These weeks must have aged him, and something told me Nikos had more of a story to tell than we could ever guess. A marking glowed on his arm, and he twisted a hand, but his mouth could not form the words for his command.

Raven cast upon him, pinning his bare arms to the ground beside him, holding him there. I locked eyes with Bastian, and he dipped his chin. I wanted one single question answered, and he'd grant me that favor as an answer to a promise he'd made when I died. Nikos thrashed about, drool falling from his mouth as he fought against the magic. A prickle of sunlight gathered in the far corner, and I wondered how much of this day Nikos would see.

"Cat got your tongue?" Bastian asked, sliding his hands into his pockets.

Nikos' eyes doubled in size as he huffed a breath, looking between Raven and Bastian, questioning what he was seeing.

"I believe the word you're searching for is 'how.'" Bastian answered as Atlas released another growl, following the circle until he was sure he'd be seen. "We won't be answering your questions today."

The king whipped his hand through the air, and a tendril of his dark shadows surged forward, crossing the barrier and plummeting into Nikos' chest. He writhed. Lifting from the ground, still silent, as pain wracked his body and sweat beaded on his forehead. The shadows retreated, hovering in a ball as Nikos fell limp, his eyes rolling into the back of his head.

One second passed. Two. And then the ball of shadows struck again, disappearing until all of Nikos' veins turned black, creeping over his skin like a spider's web. His back arched as much as he could with his hands pinned to the floor.

"Bastian," Raven whispered.

But the king did not relent. Did not look up. Simply pulled his magic away and struck again like a serpent. There had been rumors of the king's shadows, but no one truly knew their purpose. And though I didn't fully believe this was the extent of that magic he wielded, I was confident he'd trained long and hard for this moment.

"Your Grace." Torryn's low, firm voice was like a tidal wave in the room, shaking everyone from staring at the spectacle.

The shadows lifted from Nikos' body, hovering like a ball of smoke above his chest. Bash knelt to the floor, whispering, though he remained deadly calm. "If you so much as think of casting a spell in this room, hell will descend upon you in ways your mind could never imagine. I will pull your bowels from your body inch by inch, keeping you lucid and alive as you watch me turn you inside out. Do you understand me?"

I heard Raven swallow and swooped closer to her. This would not be an easy day, no matter what the man on the floor revealed. Nikos nodded frantically, eyes locked on that ball of pain. Bastian bowed to Clariss, and she stepped slightly behind Torryn before removing her magic.

The scream that ripped from Nikos' mouth was one of agony and irritation and ire. I could have bathed in it. The satisfaction of hearing him suffer. To watch a man struggle is to stand on the outside of his thoughts. But to *hear* it ... The vibrato in his voice, the string of pain... Maybe I was sick and twisted, but then maybe I'd lived and died for this moment of salvation. Nikos may not have killed me himself, but he'd certainly been responsible. I only needed to know by whose hand.

"Where are the coven leaders?" Bastian asked, squatting on the floor near Nikos' head, staring at nothing.

"My words are bound," Nikos spat.

The king shook his head. "No. Wrong answer."

The ball of shadows fell, colliding with Nikos' chest. Again, that song of pain ripped through the room, mixed with gasps as a pool of crimson seeped from below him. Atlas inched forward, nearly touching the circle as he snarled. Nikos flinched and turned his head away, his eyes locking with mine as a single tear slipped down his cheek. My answering dark smile must have shocked him because he closed his eyes in defeat.

"Okay," he rattled. "Stop... and I will tell you."

Bastian pulled the magic away, and a marking on Nikos' forearm lit, he opened his mouth to scream but didn't get a single syllable out before Clariss stepped forward, casting the silencing spell she'd once used on Raven. Bastian rose to his feet, shouting with fury as he swung his hands forward and let all of the shadows cascade around the room into the barrier, smothering Nikos until we could not see him.

The moment they pulled away, Nikos' pale face turned to look at the king, and he nodded frantically.

"That was your one and only pass to test me, asshole. Now give me a reason to let you walk out of this house. And don't tell me your words are bound. You're too smart to agree to that, so let's skip the bullshit and get to the point."

Raven flinched, likely remembering when she had bound her words to the coven leaders. Again, Nikos nodded. As Clariss withdrew her spell, he rolled to his side and vomited.

"Gross," I hissed, swooping down. "Hey, Nik. How's it going?"

He peered up at me and then finally to Raven. His voice was like stone against stone. Aged and haggard as his words raced for her. "You were supposed to die. I watched you for years, and the moment my Harrowing finally struck, you still lived."

"*Your* Harrowing? That's not even possible. We know more than you think we do, Nik, so cut the lies. The Harrowing was discovered by Endora Mossbrook before we were even born. Eden overheard, stole the Grimoire, and took off for the castle to try to save the witches," she said.

"No," he rasped, a shadow circling his neck. "I discovered the Harrowing in records buried in the Moss Coven mountains."

"That's not possible."

His devilish eyes flicked to Raven. "In this world, there are few things that are not possible, should your will be greater than your obstacle. Age is fluid if you know how to bend it."

I snapped my fingers in front of his face, trying to peel back his attention. Seconds ticked by as he held that ugly grin on his face, waiting and watching for her to put meanings behind his words.

"But you... It can't be... M-my grandmother's Fountain of Youth elixir?" Raven stumbled backward. "That's why you ransacked the shop? How old are you?"

"More than twice your age, girl. Your grandmother held my youth in her hands until she was killed."

"But we've known each other since we were twelve."

"Start at the beginning," Bastian demanded, the calmness in his voice a clear threat.

Nikos tugged, trying to free his arms but could not, and his words didn't come easily. "I would have never come to this disgusting coven had it not been for my inability to compel anyone but witches or Tasa's open defiance. She wouldn't let me get close enough to control her for many years. She refused the Harrowing. Refused to do what must be done to overtake the shifters. The

Harrowing is our salvation. Sacrifice a few seedlings for the good of the forest."

My brows lifted. "How much elixir did you take to go from old as dirt to twelve?"

"Viana Moonstone kept me well stocked, though she did not know it."

"But why?" Raven asked, her face still twisted into confusion.

His eyes began to bulge as he became more maniacal, even in pitch. "It was a disguise, you senseless hag."

Bastian struck hard and fast, his shadow magic completely severing a finger from Nikos' hand. He screamed, this time something far more delirious.

"Call me another name, and it won't be the king you have to fear," Raven said, wind that no one else felt whipping through her hair as power oozed from her.

Nikos whispered, his resolve falling. "I can only compel a witch within my own coven. And only one at a time. Control Tasa, control the whole Moon Coven. I killed an entire family line, performed a bloodletting, and joined this coven for one single purpose. To see the Harrowing set into motion. To help the witches out-power the shifters and set the world straight. A cause every witch born to this world should have stood behind. Sacrifices be damned. I could have done so much more, but my conscience is clean. I did only what *had* to be done. Even with the mind of every witch in my coven at my fingertips, I still only did the bare minimum. I am not the evil in this room."

"And what did you do after my grandmother died?"

"You've been making the elixir for me for ten years," he confessed with a demon's smirk. "I had others gather the ingredients, but I needed you, Moon Witch."

"That spell has to be stirred for a month straight," she argued, refusing to believe him.

"Magic, Raven. Use your brain."

She shook her head, her jaw slackened as the truth of the violation came over her. "You cannot affect the memory."

"I can tell your mind to forget, and you will obey." Sweat dripped down his forehead as blood poured from his hand. "You only did things in small moments when no one would notice. I did not steal months or weeks from your mind. Only minutes when you would work late in your little shop. I'd keep you there until the time was necessary, and you were too gullible to know the difference."

A silence unlike any this world had seen crept through the room like a serpent weaving its way around Raven's stilled and stunned body.

"Tell us how to stop the Harrowing," I said, pulling the attention from her. She needed a moment, and he'd never give that to her, relishing in her shock.

He laughed. A full belly laugh, as if he weren't the naked victim on the floor of my old home. "Wouldn't you like to know?"

Atlas' jaw snapped as he snarled. Nikos flinched but did not crack. Spell circle be damned, the wolf stepped over the line, trapping himself in with our prisoner. He stepped over Nikos, drool dripping from his fangs as he bit into his neck, growling.

"You will answer," Bastian said.

Another tear tracked down his cheek as slowly as the blood down his neck. Atlas pulled away but remained over the top of him.

"I will... I will die in glory... knowing it took so many of you to hold me."

"Answer."

"I cannot. I have never discovered a way to stop it."

"You've never tried," I growled.

"Why would I?"

"Tell us where the coven leaders are," Raven said, lightning forming in her hands.

He turned his face into the bright sunlight, maybe wishing they would come to his rescue. "We stormed the castle moments after word spread of the king's murder. We knew exactly where the Grimoires would be. Breya had been the final test. Her death was all the confirmation we needed. For years, we've been accumulating information on the layout of the black castle."

"Accumulating?" Clariss shrieked. "You've been torturing witches. One of your own pinned me down in a hallway after breaching the walls. You are not the savior of witches. You're just like the others. You have one person in mind only, and that's your damn self."

He groaned, another trickle of blood falling as each word became a chore, a rasp. "Endora waited for the king's barrier to weaken and took the books. We met at the castle door, but Storm and River got into a fight, claiming they couldn't trust the others not to come for their Grimoires, so they agreed to separate in pairs. Half of them believed that the king had spread a rumor about casting near the books when they were together, and the others didn't. When only Endora and Circe were left standing outside the castle with me, Endora cast. Her magic is so weak, no one died, but the castle was obliterated."

"So where are they?" Bastian asked again.

He shook his head, refusing to answer. The wolf stepped back as the shadows descended again, seeping into his mind this time. He writhed on the floor, the lower half of his body twisted back and forth as foam poured from his mouth, followed by another trace of blood.

"You cannot kill him," Raven said, leaving her spot in the circle to take Bastian's side. "Not yet. If you want this kill, then it's yours. But not yet."

He turned, brushing his thumb across Raven's cheek. "He is not dying. Death would be too easy for him. I'm just showing him what it feels like to die. My shadows are forcing him to believe it is happening. That is all."

"It better hurt," Clariss said, her cheeks more flush in the early morning light. "It better hurt like hell."

"It does," he whispered, pulling the shadows away once more.

Several moments passed as we all waited for Nikos to gather his senses. He looked terrified. Lost in a room he didn't recognize as he managed to speak. "The only location I know for sure is the Storm Coven. Widower's Grove. There are two witches there."

"Good boy," I hissed into his ear. "Now, if you don't tell me who killed me, I will take your life."

A smile spread across his face, gruesome and terrifying as I watched him age before my eyes. Bastian's magic must have been stripping the elixir from his very bones.

"Have they not confessed?" he whispered, age marks scaring his skin.

I pulled away, all the possibilities wracking my brain. It might as well have been a confession that he'd coerced someone... But whom? I glanced at Raven, but she had turned away. Whether disgusted by the sight of torture or the truth of it, I wasn't sure.

"No," I muttered.

Atty growled, a warning likely stirred by the desperation I couldn't hide.

Nikos flinched, rushing his answer. "I cannot answer because I don't know. I ran into someone hidden in the castle shadows. In the shrouded hall, I simply compelled the hidden witch to find the king's blade notably missing from his side that night and kill you at the first opportunity." He coughed. "It wasn't personal. But Raven, here, needed a little encouragement."

"Not personal? Not fucking personal?" It took every ounce of self-control not to rip his damn heart out. Atlas moved in front of me. He knew what I could do. What I would do. And he'd never be able to stop me if I couldn't control myself. But then Torryn was there too, building a wall so I could not see the asshole on the floor. I turned, seething, eyes locked with Raven. Her anger and shock was as evident on her reddening face as it was mine. She nodded once, and I knew she wouldn't hold back anymore.

"Will Raven die?" Bastian asked. "Will the Harrowing come back for her?"

He laughed again, blood spattering the floor. "She will die, and that's all that matters for the curse. Be it from the Harrowing or justice, I cannot say."

"Justice?" Raven whipped around, slamming her hands forward.

Nikos slid across the floor, crashing into the wall, Raven's power throwing him out of the salt circle. Thunder cracked outside as clouds appeared from nowhere, covering the morning sun. There was no concealing the rage in her, the storm, the power she'd been holding back, as she held him pinned to the wall.

"Raven," I whispered in a half-hearted attempt to stop her, but she could not hear me, could not hear anything as the wind whipped through our home, destroying the last of our belongings in her fury.

"I've lived ten years of your lies. So did Kirsi. I've bent to your will for longer than I ever knew. You needed me to make that elixir for you, didn't you? You needed my grandmother until she died, and then you realized you weren't powerful enough to make it yourself. Then, when you thought I was gone, you broke into Crescent Cottage and ransacked the place. Tell me you manipulated her with magic!" She screamed. "Tell me you cast your filth on my grandmother!"

She didn't give him a moment to answer before crossing the room and planting a closed fist across his face. She used her magic to throw him into the opposite wall, and then bring him back. "You've always played the victim," she seethed. "Let me show you what being a victim fucking looks like."

He shook his head frantically, for the first time ever, finally seeing Raven for the witch she was. She'd always been kind, but the fire within her had also always been there. I'd never been so proud.

"Look at my face," she demanded. When he would not, she shrieked, "Look at me!"

His head turned slowly, showcasing his defeat. "Is she still beautiful? My daughter?"

She didn't acknowledge his words. "You will forget everything. Every face in this room, every person you've ever known. Every single discovery of your entire life will be gone after I cast this spell. A real victim is someone that is innocent. Let me show you what that fucking feels like."

She waved her hand through the air, the fear on Nikos' face fading into confusion and then nothing. His mind was blank as he rediscovered himself bleeding and pinned to the wall, a furious witch staring him down, a storm brewing within the cottage and outside of it. I didn't miss the look Torryn and Bastian exchanged as Raven continued.

She flicked her wrist once more and fire ignited below him. We all stood silent as it licked up his legs. Another cast and lightning struck him in the chest. Bastian stepped forward, placing a careful hand on

Raven's shoulder. Tears streamed down her face as she dropped her arms, and Nikos sank to the floor.

"Holy shit," Atlas murmured, returning to his human form.

"Definitely," Torryn added.

Clariss pointed to Nikos. "Look."

His skin began to peel. Flaying first from around his mouth and ears. His eyes jerked open, a new expression of dread on his face until he died, melting onto the floor, the skin severed from his bones.

Raven raced out the door and vomited. The entire group followed.

"What was that?" Atlas asked, staring at Raven.

She wiped her mouth, shaking her head. "It wasn't me. I swear."

"*Plurgis Anun,*" Clariss said, handing Raven a handkerchief from her pocket. "The coven leaders must have cast on him. They couldn't stop him from speaking, but they could detect it with the right spell. When he gave away their location, it activated the spell and killed him. Though he wasn't much longer for this world anyway."

"I'm sorry," Raven muttered.

"Sorry?" Atlas said, hanging his arm around her shoulder. "That was the coolest thing I've ever seen. Remind me not to get on your bad side, Little Witch."

"It could have been so much worse," she whispered.

30

KIRSI

"Where are we?" Standing before a wall of windows, I stared down over a stretch of mountains capped with snow sparkling like glitter in the fresh sunlight.

"The Forest Coven," Raven whispered, a blush of pink creeping over her skin. "At Bastian's secret cabin."

We'd just split ways with Atlas and Clariss. They'd gone back to the Fire Coven, and we'd taken a different door. I'd expected the same familiar walls of Crescent Cottage. Clearly, so had Torryn as he huffed a breath of air into his palms, trying to warm them while looking around the mountaintop cabin. I'd nearly forgotten what it felt like to be cold. Or warm. Or tired. Or hungry. I just was. And each day that passed, I forgot a little more.

"Why are we here?" I asked, shaking off the realization of my existence, convinced that if I didn't think about it, it wouldn't matter.

Bastian slipped behind a long counter in the open space near what looked to be a small kitchen. He leaned over the slab of stone, holding his hands in a fist as he took time staring each of us in the eyes before speaking. "Eden Mossbrook is Nikos' daughter, and we need to decide what to do with that information."

Raven gasped. "How do you know?"

"How many times in your life have you heard anyone speak of Endora's husband or lover?"

The world stopped. "Literally never."

He nodded. "Did anyone else notice he was aging? As the magic stripped away from him? He wasn't lying about that. I could see it in his first dream before I manipulated it. But Nikos worked in the record hall for the Moon Coven, and Eden told us her father did as well in Moss. More than that… the words he spoke were verbatim to hers. 'The Harrowing would be our salvation. Sacrifice a few seedlings for the good of the forest'."

Raven gave a small cry, stumbling backward until she collided with a chair and plopped down. She buried her face into her hands. I was sure this wasn't the time to tease her for making out with someone that could have easily been her grandfather, but I absolutely wanted to.

"Sorry, Little Witch," Bastian whispered, crossing the small cottage to kneel beside her, placing a large hand on her thigh and one on the back of the chair.

"How could my mother have been friends with their daughter and not realize who he was?"

I took the other side of the chair, not kneeling but matching the king's height. "In their defense, how could they have ever guessed it? It's probably why Nikos knew so much about your family. How he eased himself in with your parents so effortlessly. How he knew exactly where to get that elixir. You have to remember, he appeared to be twelve. They would have never suspected him, and even if they did, he's definitely been controlling them since we were kids."

"I wish I could have killed him myself," Raven whispered.

"It wouldn't have changed anything. That betrayal you feel? The urge for revenge? It'll never be satisfied," Torryn said from the window. "Let your heart find peace knowing the weight of his life is not on your hands."

"Or maybe he'll come back as a wraith, and I can spend eternity fucking with him," I added, not entirely joking.

Bastian rose, pulling Raven to her feet. He walked her to a

different chair, casting toward the fireplace until it was roaring and crackling and heating the frozen room.

The door clicked open, and Atlas stepped in, rubbing his hands together as he stared at the king. "You just had to put the door outside, didn't you, Bash?"

"For old time's sake." He flashed a smile that didn't reach his eyes, and then filled Atlas in on his revelation.

"I don't know. We've been with Eden for years. And she did come to the castle, sacrificing her entire life and all her magic to save the witches."

I looped around the room, weighing all the truths. "At this point, I trust no one."

Bastian's silver eyes tracked me. "We know her father's magic wouldn't have held sway over her in the human lands. Even if he'd commanded her to take the Grimoire for some other unknown purpose, once she got there, she would have known."

"Did you see his eyes?" Raven asked. "He might not have genuinely cared about anyone else in this world, but when he asked about her… before I…"

"He loved her," Torryn finished. "He might have damned the world, but he loved his daughter."

I shook my head, my hair billowing around me in slow motion. "If he loved her, he would have tried to find her."

"I don't think so," Atlas said. "If he really loved her, he would have wished her to be as far away from this bullshit as possible. And he left the Moss Coven behind over a decade after she disappeared. He didn't care about their power. Or maybe he did and recognized it fading, so he got out when he could, hoping he could give Eden a boost in power when he shifted covens."

"She was his blood as well. A half Moon power, half Moss power witch," I agreed. "I guess business as usual until all hell breaks loose?"

"Anyone have a better plan?" Bastian asked, his wings appearing behind him, stretching from one side of the cabin to the other before he tucked them in.

"I do," I answered, coming to a halt near Atlas at the door. "You want to know if Raven's still being chased by the Harrowing. I have to find the answers to save Nym, and we have six witches to hunt down. It's time for me and Atlas to split from the group. We'll find the answers we need while you three try not to let the world explode."

"Crescent Cottage is still centric to this plan," Bastian said. "Before we go back, does everyone agree that Eden can be trusted?"

"No," I said.

"Yes," everyone else answered.

"I trust no one. Not even the pup."

"Smart lady." Atlas grinned.

Bastian arched an arm, and a clear glass door appeared. Rather than step through it, we looked on to see Eden and Crow sitting behind the workbench. They didn't notice the door. Nothing had changed. There hadn't been a great revelation, no big surprise, they simply sat, talking as if we hadn't left at all.

The king was the first through the wide opening, and though he remained calm, he still tried to hold everyone behind him. I wasn't the only one with trust issues. The witch and the captain looked up from their conversation, smiles melting as they took in the crowd of somber faces.

"What happened?" Eden asked, jumping from her seat.

"What can you tell us about your father?" Bastian asked, giving no warning at all.

She shook her head. "Not a lot. I always knew he loved me, but my mother hated when he would try to get close to me. He was around sporadically when I was young, less so as I moved into my teens. He and my mother discovered the Harrowing together, and, shortly after, I left. Why?"

Raven sighed. "Do you know any spells that your father had? Any markings that would identify him? His name? Anything?"

"Is he dead?" she whispered.

"I think so."

"His name was Nicholas. I know he had a marking on his hand that had a bottomless triangle, like a mountain."

Raven moved her fingers through the ends of her black hair, her eyes cast to the floor as she sighed. "Your father moved to the Moon Coven after you left. He took copious amounts of elixir to conceal his age and real identity. Without going into details, he's dead."

"Nikos?" she asked quietly, jaw slackened, looking up to Torryn.

"Nikos," he confirmed.

"I'm so sorry," she said, moving closer to the captain. "You must know this changes nothing. I had no idea."

"We know," Bastian said.

"Well, most of us do," I corrected.

"That's why it feels different, though," she said, looking out the window, though the sun shone through. "He converted to the Moon Coven, and I feel... different here. I thought it was just me trying to get used to my magic again, but I think it's the moon."

"Standing beneath the moon as a member of this coven is like soaking in a milk bath," Raven whispered. "There's nothing more rejuvenating."

"Half black, half white hair and eyes, life split between magic and non-magic lands, it's only fitting I'm also split between two covens," she rationalized, still looking out the window.

Moments slipped by as we waited for her to say anything else. For Raven to, but the awkward silence grew.

"We going to sit around here or get shit done?" I asked.

In minutes, the men had shifted the shelving along the west wall as Raven and I cleared the terra-cotta pots and bags of soil out of the way, moving everything to the opposite side of the room. The king cast six identical doors, each with a different emblem atop them, but nothing intricate beyond that. Pacing the floor, hands clasped behind his back, I finally realized his resolve was fading. Bastian, used to commanding his own world, was struggling with the upheaval of his life and security. I couldn't say I felt sorry for him. As much as I respected him and the truth of who he was, this terror and madness, mixed with a little starvation, was daily life for a Moon witch.

"Atlas, you know the drill," the king said finally.

"I do."

Sweeping forward, I stopped beside him. "I don't."

"Their group won't need the doors, but we will if we want to be able to travel quickly. So you and I will be able to use these. We can come and go from here as we want, but the back side to each door is hidden in the covens," the pup said.

"Should we get separated, Raven and Torryn can also use them," the king added.

"And us?" Crow asked.

"It's best for us to stay here, hidden and behind my barrier," Eden said, taking his hand. She then looked to Bastian. "He's not used to being stuck on land. It'll pass."

I moved to the River Coven door. "No time for small talk. Let's go."

Atlas glanced up to the emblem, twisted his brows and shrugged, following me. Torryn muttered something about being safe, but we'd already passed through the king's magic.

"Why here?" the wolf asked, spinning in a circle to take in the mass of water surrounding the riverbank we emerged on. "It smells like fish. Dead fish."

"I don't know. I just picked one to get out of that fucking shop. I'm open to suggestions."

He grinned, wide and proud. "You're not going to like my suggestion, Ghosty."

"Don't be dramatic. What have you got?"

"The wraiths are nosy bitches."

Rolling my eyes, I moved past him, avoiding the water. Avoiding the reminder that I'd never feel it again. Not a single drop. "What do you possibly know about wraiths?"

"You... er... I mean, no. They... them. They hang out in the Fire Coven because no one gives them grief."

He wasn't wrong. I'd seen several wraiths in the Fire Coven. I didn't know if he was teasing about the gossiping or not, but it was more of a plan than I had. It also possibly explained my growing curiosity about every little thing. I turned back to the door without a word and surged through. The others stopped mid-conversation to stare.

Torryn lifted a brow, and Atlas shrugged. "Nothing to see here. Carry on."

The snort of laughter from the captain was not lost on me as we slipped out of the shop again.

"Well, that was awkward," Atlas said.

"Don't care."

We stood on the ground of what I'd known the Fire Coven to be. Ash and rock. The ground was pure black as far as the eye could see, with scattered dead trees on the horizon. The door we'd arrived through became a mirror, hardly visible to the naked eye if you weren't looking for it. Everything about the Fire Coven felt sinister. Even the clouds carried a hue of gray. As if standing in a place marked with such undesirable history would somehow stain you, turn you against the world if you let it. And I wanted to let it, until I remembered that beautiful black witch with arms ringed in gold, waiting for me to save her. Somehow.

Atlas spun in a circle one way and then the opposite, bringing his hands to block the sun that was already hidden behind the clouds. "We're not far away from the main village."

"Which of these dead trees gave that away?"

He smirked. "That one."

Before I could even pinpoint which tree he was talking about, he shifted and began running. The pads of his paws, the fur rimming his claws, stained black from the barren lands of the Fire Coven. I soared ahead of him, turning back to wave delicate fingers. The long neck of the wolf extended as he pushed himself harder and harder. The glint of humor and challenge in his eyes was enough to really start the race.

The ground flew beneath us. I'd never pushed myself to see how fast I could soar. I felt like a bird. Like I was flying inches above the ground, the beauty of a giant wolf pounding the ground beside me as we moved. We were on the outskirts of the village in minutes. Atlas shifted back to his normal form, winded, but exhilarated.

"Needed that," he panted. "Same time tomorrow. Got to keep my slim figure."

"I was hardly trying," I lied.

"Me... too."

I couldn't help my laugh, but when he stopped short, his head whipping toward me with large eyes, dread fell over me.

"What?"

"I've never heard you laugh before. Not like that."

My shoulders sank with relief. "Don't get used to it, Pup. There's no place for happiness in my world anymore."

"Well, that's not true, is it? You're not alone and suffering. You've got Nym... and the rest of us." He turned, leading the way toward the town square.

I slowed, watching him walk away as I thought about what he said. I did have them. But only until they died. And I'd have to suffer the death of each of them before I was left behind. I caught back up, trying and failing to brush away those horrid thoughts.

"Do you want to stop and see her? Before we find a wraith to ask?"

Every single part of my soul wanted to. But I was afraid I wouldn't be able to leave her and Scoop behind again. Even if the creature didn't feel our bond, I did. And I missed him desperately. I wondered what that said about me. I mostly felt sorrow and sadness, a bit of pride and a dash of anger. But as I slowly became more, beyond what we knew the wraiths to feel, I realized that the rift between the shifters and witches wasn't the only problem in our world. We'd closed ourselves off to everyone.

"No. I don't think so."

Atlas came to a full stop at the edge of the cobblestone path, rounding on me. All sense of his usual light humor gone from his piercing blue eyes. "I know what it's like to watch someone die. I know what it means to feel a loss so strongly you want to give up on this world. She felt that. But now she has more time with you. I'd give anything to have Laramie back, no matter what she looked like. I'd be willing to bet your witch feels the same."

"You don't know anything about me." I moved away from him as if I could put a wall between us.

"Wrong. I watch. I listen. You're afraid. You're so afraid of your own future, you're hiding from it. You want to save her, but that doesn't mean you've let yourself believe you can actually be with her. You'd rather run. You'd rather use insults and anger to reinforce those barriers you've built between yourself and the world. You're mad. You're so fucking mad, you can't stand being around anyone most of the time. I see you, Kirsi. You suffer. But you are not alone."

I sank a little closer to the ground, stripped bare. "I hate me."

He put a hand between us, his palm facing me. I stared at those callused fingers for several seconds before I pressed my own palm to his and looked up into his eyes as I made sure he could feel me.

"Then I guess I will love you enough for the both of us."

"Don't look at me like I'm some damsel in distress, needing to be saved from the dragon. I've got news for you. I am the dragon." I dropped my hand, confident I could feel a heart thrumming within my chest, though I knew it was impossible. "And don't get any kinky ideas, Wolf," I joked, though half-heartedly.

"Don't worry, Lizard Ghosty. You're not my type."

We started moving again. "Too translucent?"

"Nah. Too nice."

The laughter was pure and genuine, and when he caught my eye, listening to the sound, I didn't turn away. Instead, I slipped my hand into his. "Thanks."

"See what I mean?" he joked.

It didn't take long until we were back into the market square full of witches and shifters mingling. When Atlas yawned beside me, I realized how tired he must have been. How tired everyone must have been. They'd been up all night and half the day, and I'd guess he was also hungry. If I took the time to go see Nym, he could rest and eat. And I could just be with her.

"Hellooooo," Atlas said, waving a hand in front of my face. "Are you in there?"

"Sorry. I got distracted by your stench. You need a bath."

He winked at a witch passing by, eyes glued to her as he answered. "Yeah. Bath sounds good."

"Wraith first." I snapped my fingers in his face.

"Don't worry. I'm eternally single and focused."

"Eternally single?"

He flashed a cooked grin. "Personal preference. What about them over there?"

Following his line of sight, I spotted the cluster of three hovering near a cart, eyes distant as they merely floated with blank faces.

"Perfect." I surged forward.

"You can't just march up and talk to them," he said, following behind me.

I looked over my shoulder, confused. "Don't be ridiculous. Of course I can."

"Suit yourself." The smile should have been a warning.

I soared around the crowd of witches, approaching the wraiths huddled together. They didn't bother looking at me nor at each other.

"Excuse me," I began.

Atlas called over the top of several patrons. "You're going to have to—"

"I can manage a simple conversation." I turned back to the wraiths, the ethereal tendrils of their lower halves wafting in a breeze that didn't exist on this plane. "I wondered if—"

They screamed, jaws dislocating in a horrifying manner, demanding the attention of every single person nearby as they scattered, winding themselves in circles around carts and darting into and out of the alleys like a bunch of scared kittens. Only they weren't scared. Their faces remained as blank and dull as they were when we'd spotted them.

I soared after the one closest to me, diving right through the middle of a fruit cart, my body preparing for impact before remembering that if I didn't try, I wouldn't touch it at all. The wraith I chased was far more used to her intangible body, diving as she moved. She was faster than I was. Never leaving the square, commotion rose as we went. If she really didn't want me to chase her, she would have just become invisible, but she didn't. A tower of squash balancing on a table in front of a tiny store toppled over as a heavier set woman backed into it, trying to avoid the feel of a wraith touching her.

Keeping an eye on the ghostly figure, I peeked around for the wolf. Catching a glimpse of him with his hand over his mouth as he tried to suppress his smile. I'm sure I verbally growled as I pressed onward, more determined than ever to catch the fucking wraith. But how would I catch her? I couldn't just reach out and grab her, could I? Did the rules work differently than with humans?

With renewed determination, we rounded a corner. Stretching forward to snag the bottom of the gown that flowed behind her, I groaned as she slipped my grasp. Nothing tangible to hang on to. Again, we circled the square where she darted into an alley and slammed to halt, screaming again before she surged toward me, her face haunted, eyes gaunt.

Atlas stood at the other end of the narrow alleyway, hands in his pockets as he leaned against the building.

I lifted my chin. "See? I handled it."

"Oh, yes, you did, all mighty wraith. It couldn't possibly have anything to do with that salt circle I just poured on the ground. Which, by the way, I wouldn't recommend crossing unless you want to be stuck in there with her. Lavender, salt and wraiths don't play nicely together."

"I hate you," I scowled, peering down at the grains on the dark alleyway.

"You do not. We're best friends now, Ghosty. Partners in crime."

A deep and hollowed voice cut in. "Why have you captured me, Kirsi Moondance?"

I drew back. "You know my name?"

The wraith moved to the edge of the circle, an eerie smile crossing her features as she twisted her head. "The vines of stories and secrets wrap around this world through the whispers and curiosities of wraiths. We hear much and speak little."

"Yeah, I heard you were nosy. Anyway, I need to know what you might have heard about the Harrowing. And also, could you stop doing the twisty head thing? Because it's creepy as fuck."

She whisked around the circle, her arms outstretched as she let out a moan. Atlas rolled his eyes and sighed as we waited for her. Had my growl earlier actually come out as a moan?

"Creepy…" she sang, circling once more.

"Any day now." I crossed my arms.

"It is not the nature of wraiths to care enough to save the witches. Day, week, year … I have all the time in this world and the next."

I whipped around the outside of the salt barrier to hover next to the wolf. "If you weren't dead, I'd kill you for sport."

"Certainly, you would, *witch*."

31

KIRSI

Being referred to as a witch felt like a slap in the face. Either because I wished I was one, or because she'd spat it like a curse word. I wasn't sure. Either way, I was not fucking impressed.

"I know it might be hard to connect the pieces here, but I'm not a witch."

The wraith with sunken eyes and a smile too wide for her face laughed. The sound wasn't of this world, but something far more dark and sinister. I'd experienced death, but she seemed to have experienced hell. Or came from it. Maybe she wasn't wrong because we weren't the same.

"Why have you trapped me, Kirsi, not-a-witch?"

"Again. What do you know of the Harrowing? Is there anything you've heard, or do you know of anyone we can ask to learn more about it?"

"The witches aren't inclined to listen to the wraiths." She moaned, circling the bottom of her prison, trying and failing to blow away the salt that held her. "Had the witches listened to the wraiths… had even one of you asked… you would have known the secrets of your precious coven leaders; the truths of your handsome Dark King."

THE UNBOUND WITCH

"I mean... handsome is debatable, really. Have you seen his cousin?"

"Yes," she whispered, a corner of her mouth lifting. "It's too bad the king is dead."

"It's all so sad. Anyway, the Harrowing?"

She giggled, a tiny light in her eyes as she looked at me, and I knew without asking that she was already aware that Bash was not actually dead. She did hold secrets, dark and dangerous ones.

"The witches consider no one, and don't fool yourself, they do not consider you, either. They will grow old and die, and you'll watch and then continue on, anchored to haunt this land for all eternity. There is nothing but time. I will gather information, out of respect for a 'not witch', but in return, you must release me from this existence."

I shook my head. "I don't understand. How am I supposed to do that?"

"Gather a fireseed, a whispering pearl, an agate stone stolen from the swamp witches falls and everything else you'd use for a purging circle. Create a seance of three behind the veil atop the world, and I will be there to report what I have found."

"But if you can leave this world and want to, why wouldn't you have done it yourself?"

She swirled around the circle, taking her sweet time to answer my simple question. "You haven't been listening, not a common trait found amongst us. Do better. The witches will not help the wraiths. I require a seance to leave. And besides, how would I hold the stones?"

I glanced toward Atlas and back to the ghost. "You truly cannot touch physical items? At all?"

Her eyes narrowed on me as her somber face returned. "A lesson you will sadly learn since you have clearly not yet."

"That's all the questions for today," Atlas said, swiping his foot over the circle. "We'll collect your items and be in touch."

"I look forward to it, white wolf."

We stood in silence for several minutes before turning toward one another, the ghost long gone. "Did she—"

"Best not speak of it here," he cut in. "Let's go find your witch."

The fucking door was hanging off a hinge. How many witches had passed by this house and not noticed it? I surged forward, Atlas shifting to match my pace as we raced for the elder's home we'd essentially locked Nym in. One second he was beside me, and the next he slammed into an invisible barrier, unable to cross.

"Go!" He growled. "Be careful."

I hadn't felt the barrier, hardly heard the crackle as I passed through the witch's spell meant to keep others out. Thank the goddess it was a weak spell compared to what I'd witnessed from Eden and the Dark King. Effective on shifters, but it wasn't enough.

The old wooden door creaked open on a single bolt. I didn't stop. Navigating the place I'd only seen full of old witches, finding two withered bodies on the floor, I cringed. For a heartbeat, the whole world was silent, as if I was passing over a graveyard. The spell the Dark King cast forced them to protect Nym with their lives. And so they had… in vain.

A crash of what could only have been furniture in the room beyond yanked me forward. Rounding the final corner of the home, I took in a scene I couldn't have fathomed. Nym, standing on a desk in the back corner, arms outstretched in a defensive stance with Talon roaring as loud as he could toward the door where a woman with long gray hair stood between us, her back to me.

Nym's green eyes met mine in sheer dread. She moved her hands as if to cast, to control the white tiger at her feet, but nothing happened. Not until the witch I couldn't identify lifted a blood-stained hand and ran it down the king's invisible barrier. It cracked like glass before shattering the magic into pieces.

Nym's head fell backward, her arms open as magic she'd been cut off from poured into her. When she righted herself, she didn't pause for a second, casting to take over the tiger that bound across the room. I turned invisible, sneaking past the witch that held lightning in her bloody hands. Ophelia. The old, determined witch from the Trials.

"This has gone on long enough." Her haggard, old voice walked down my spine in a way that would have given me goosebumps, could I have them.

Talon took one step as Nym's spirit blessed marking glowed, but Ophelia cast and sent him flying into the wall. I wanted to do something, anything, but as I surged into the room, I slammed into a magical wall. She'd put a fucking salt circle down to trap me, and I'd floated right into it, entirely unaware. I wondered how she'd known I would come. But of course I would. For Nym. I could only stand and watch as baby Scoop arched his back and hissed. If she cast upon him, she would likely kill him.

Nym didn't waste a second, leaping down from the desk and surging forward. Magic spells sprang around the room, cracking into the walls, destroying the furniture, sending books flying. A snake Nym had thrown got past Ophelia's spell, and it hissed at her feet. She paused for a second, and that's all Nym needed to send Talon forward once more, pinning her to the floor.

"Why?" Nym asked, needing none of my help as she looked down at the old crone.

"Thirteenth witch," she croaked. "I'm tired of waiting for you to die. No one would have questioned your death in the Trial when you fell over that cliff."

Nym cast another serpent, letting it coil around Ophelia's body as her familiar backed away. "You pushed me. I didn't fall."

"Did I?" She grunted. "The old memory is failing."

I made myself visible, and Nym immediately swiped the circle of salt trapping me. Freed, I hovered a bit too close to the witch. "What do you know about the Harrowing?"

Her body turned purple as the snake coiled tighter and tighter, though when her eyes landed on me, I still shared a sharp smile.

"A shame..." she managed.

Nym moved her fingers, and the snake relented, if only enough for her to take a breath with compressed lungs.

"You were saying?"

"A shame you died. That mouth of yours was so entertaining."

"I can assure you, it still is," Nym said. "What do you know about the Harrowing?"

"Only that..." She gulped. "Only that the Moon Coven has a chance to be stronger now with Willow in charge. Once you and Raven die. We thought the Harrowing was a curse, but it turns out, it's the goddess' blessing for us all. She wants you to die."

"Funny. If the goddess wanted me to die, why did she send you?"

Nym twisted her wrist and the snake coiled once more. She stared through gritted teeth as bones snapped, cracked. As Ophelia's eyes bulged, her face swelled, and she was crushed to death, the light leaving her eyes.

I could not look away. Death. A sweet escape. Venom. A moment of bliss. A dagger of deliverance. That single second between this world and the next hovered in the room, and I could nearly feel it, taste its bitterness on my tongue. And then it was gone. As completely as the old witch dead on the floor.

"Kir?" Atlas yelled from the hall. "Are you alive? I mean, still dead?"

"Yes, asshole, I'm still dead."

He filled the frame of the door with his broad shoulders, the scar on his face seemed redder, as if colliding with the barrier of witch magic irritated it somehow. He swept his hand through his thick, white hair, forcing a smile. "Do you guys ever notice death literally follows you?"

"More like chases," Nym said quietly, still staring down at Ophelia, the snake gone.

"I REALLY DON'T MIND," ATTY SAID, STANDING OUTSIDE NYM'S HUT. "Take the time you need with her. I've got plenty of ... friends around here to keep myself busy."

"You don't have to lie, Pup," I said, biting back my smile. "Only a mother could love that scraggly face."

He stroked the stubble along his jaw and grinned. "Only someone that hasn't had a beard brush the inside of her thighs would say that."

"Ignoring half the shit you say brings me far more pleasure, I can promise you that. Asinine comments aside, since the barrier was a failure, we don't really have time for leisure. Every second Nym is not protected, she's in immediate danger. One night only. And then back to work. You're sure you know where to find the fireseed?"

"Relax, Ghosty. I've got this."

Nym stepped behind me, the gold bracelets on her arms jingling. "Meet here in the morning, then? We'll have a check in with the king and then head to the River Coven."

He wiggled his eyebrows. "Don't stay up too late."

"Fuck off, Pup."

For years, when I'd seen Nym in a group of people, when she'd stopped by the shop for crystals or herbs, or when she'd occasionally met us for moondancing, I'd had to control my glances. I'd had to hold myself back from making a damn fool of myself for her. I never shied away from anyone. I never backed down from a dare. I'd punch anyone in the face that deserved it, but she was always my single allowance for vulnerability.

As we watched Atty saunter down the road, calling out a name and waving, Nym moved closer to me, staring. All the nerves I'd ever had with her returned.

"Do you remember that time when we were thirteen, and we snuck into the bakery on All Hallows Eve?" she asked.

I nodded, shifting backward.

"You convinced me we'd never get caught stealing those three loaves of bread because you'd gone in and watched. Sure the baker would never miss them because he'd forgotten to write down his daily baking that day. You knew my mother was sick, and we hadn't eaten in days."

I nodded slowly. "I remember."

She took a step closer. "And when we were sixteen, Onyx shoved me down into the river, and I cut my foot. You ran and got Raven, convinced I was dying, though it was only a cut."

Again, I nodded.

"Our story," she gestured between us, "didn't start when we entered that castle. Our story started ages ago. When we were kids and didn't even really know what love was. What it meant to be dedicated to someone changed on a whim back in those days. But not for you, Kirsi. You never wavered."

"Not once," I whispered. "I had a reckless crush on someone I didn't have a chance with."

A breeze picked up, lifting her dark hair from her neck. She closed her eyes, turning away from the chill. "The chance was always there, waiting for you to get the nerve to take it. I thought about that a lot after... you died. How losing you wasn't like losing someone I'd just fallen for. I'd been falling, inch by inch, my whole life."

"I'm so sorry this happened to you, Nym. This isn't the future you dreamed, nor the one you should have."

She balked. "I'm not sorry, Kir. Not for a single second of time I get with you. I'll take it in whatever form I can."

The gold marking on her forehead flashed, and Talon stepped from the hut, Scoop at his heels. She moved toward me, holding a hand out. I took it, focusing on the sensation of holding her hand, of feeling her.

"I have an idea."

I could hardly think beyond the way our fingers fit so perfectly together. As if my life as a wraith were penance for something so flawless. A cost I'd pay over and over as this golden witch led me confidently through the Fire Coven village, never once dropping my hand or acknowledging the people that glanced our way.

She picked up several items from the cart vendors along the main street, stopping to share kind words, or let the children pet our familiars. She fit right in, and they'd welcomed her openly.

Eventually, we made it to the end of the street, turning to wind through a few others with scattered homes built on charred ground. The Fire Coven territory wasn't beautiful unless one had an eye for it. It was, instead, a bit haunting and dark. Dead trees where there might have been groves before. But several of the homes had gardening beds raised from the ground, covered in fresh soil with watering pails and tools stacked nicely in corners against their homes. They'd traded for coins or goods in the market and most seemed genuinely happy, which was honestly pretty strange.

I drew up short when I saw a large man sitting on a bench outside of one of the homes polishing a pair of giant boots. Nym had slipped from my hand, but when her eyes met mine, I could tell she knew exactly who we'd stumbled across.

"Kirsi," she whispered. "Don't."

"As if I can resist this perfect opportunity. Go hide behind that tree."

The mischievous smile on her face as she pointed to the sandwich on the plate beside him was why I'd fallen for her. She was always a team player. No matter the task. She put the kittens in her large side satchel and snuck away.

I vanished, floating toward the man. He took a large bite of his simple dinner and sat it back on a plate beside him, humming as he chewed and worked circles into his boot. I waited a few moments, watching his casual routine of taking a bite, setting down the sandwich, picking up his cloth and dipping it in the small black tin, working his way down his shoe.

I swiped the polished rag first. He set the food down, turning to look for the cloth. Assuming he'd dropped it, he bent to look beneath the bench. I quickly dragged the rag through his sandwich and as soon as he sat up, dropped it on the bench.

A snicker from the tree behind me nearly gave us away as the Old Barren whipped around to search for the sound. But Nym held her breath, and he turned back, lifting the rag and going back to work. I hung back, waiting. The second he bit into that sandwich and his face turned sour, I yanked the boot from his hand, whacked him across the face with it and tore off toward Nym, afraid my laughter would get her caught.

When the Old Barren jumped out of his seat, whirling around in confusion, the sound of Nym's giggle soothed something within me. I didn't think we'd ever have moments like this again. Her laughing at ridiculous shit I did. But here we were. She'd claimed I never wavered. But neither had she.

When the beastly old man disappeared into his house, we soared down the street, laughing, as the most beautiful golden witch led us out of the village and down into a valley, a small pond of water the final destination.

She reached into the satchel and set the two kittens on the ground before taking out the small bag she'd gotten from the market. Setting the satchel on the ground first, she sat, so as not to cover herself in ash.

With a smile still plastered on her face, she gestured to the ground beside her. "Come here. I want to try something."

I lowered myself, confident something in my chest fluttered, though it couldn't have. Not really.

"Close your eyes, beautiful."

I pictured the lashes I might have felt against my cheeks, the blush that might have come before. Saddened a little, noticing all the small things I'd never have again, my grin faltered.

"I'm not sure how you are able to manipulate things with your hands, but I wondered if we could try something different. Open your mouth."

I opened my eyes and pulled away from her. "You're not sticking some foreign object in my mouth out of sheer curiosity."

She laughed, the sound like the twinkling of a thousand stars, and I couldn't help my own.

Rolling my eyes, I moved back in. "Fine."

"Close 'em," she ordered.

I did as she said.

"I'm going to stick something you like in your mouth, and you're going to try to guess what it is."

"Okay, I like this game. It better be a body part."

"It's not." She snorted. "Just concentrate on feeling with your tongue."

"Licking you to make you scream is far more enticing."

"Kirsi Moondance, you focus."

"Fine, fine." I opened my mouth like a good little girl, waiting.

"You have to try to hold it in your mouth first. Just concentrate on that."

I could feel the weight of something small on my tongue, but nothing more than that.

"Your only hint is that it's red. You guess what it is based on the taste or texture, and I'll let you undress me in that water. Show me what it's like to be a wraith."

I jerked upright at that sinful promise. Not that I'd ever be able to feel the stroke of pleasure again, but to hear it on her lips, to see her legs tremble for me, I'd gladly guess every object in the world. Still, I tried to play her game.

Rolling the item around in my mouth, I found it to be soft but firm. Not smooth, but a dimpled texture. I moved the object to one side of my mouth and then the other until a juice leaked free. Fruit maybe. Red fruit.

A strawberry, I was sure. The moment I thought the word, perhaps by memory alone, the most subtle hint of sweetness exploded on my tongue. Drawing the fruit out, keeping my eyes closed, I whispered, "Strawberry."

"And this one?" she asked.

I didn't have time to pull away before she popped something else into my mouth. The sweetness I'd tasted before, swept away by something tart. It wasn't a memory then. I'd really tasted that strawberry. And this. The blueberry.

Opening my eyes, I pulled the fruit from my mouth, leaning forward to lick the juice of another strawberry from Nym's chin. She giggled as I crawled on top of her, laying her back, pressing my lips to hers until her giggles turned to laughter that melted away as the kiss deepened.

She was it for me. She'd always been it. I lifted the edge of her dress as her breaths shortened. She arched. Needing to feel me against her. But when I pressed further, she pulled away, standing to lead me into the water while she remained clothed.

The dress she wore clung to her skin, revealing every shapely curve of her body. Her stare held mine as she dipped below the crystal-clear water and swam backward. Resurfacing, droplets falling from her lashes and dripping from her hair, I let my eyes fall to her hardened nipples.

"Can you concentrate enough to undress me?" she asked, her tone smoky.

I could have melted into a puddle at those words.

"Probably fucking not, but I'll give it one hell of a try."

She threw her head back and laughed again as I dipped into the water, moving toward her. The second I got my hands on the ties at her waist, she dipped below the water, kicking, swimming away. The dress flourishing behind her as my legs did for eternity.

If I wanted to undress her, I was going to have to catch her. This was a game I could play. I surged forward, snatching the loose strings again and focused as I ripped my finger through the laces, forcing them loose. She swam to the surface to catch her breath, and I held the bottom of her skirt, watching as she whirled out of it, her long, brown legs moving gracefully through the sun-kissed water.

I dropped her skirt near the bank as she waded, watching me with those green eyes. I approached like a predator. She darted to the right, but I caught her. In my full arms. Not just a brush of skin or a hand held. I wrapped her in my arms.

Caught by surprise, she gasped, her eyes lit with desire. I ripped the top over her head, exposing only her cream-colored wet chemise that left absolutely nothing to the imagination.

She stopped the game, letting me pull her to the shore. Stepping out with her hand in mine, the final piece of clothing clinging like a second skin. She shivered as I reached for the bottom of the fabric and lifted, exposing her naked flesh.

Focusing on touch alone, on solely her pleasure, as mine would be found wrapped in hers only, I brushed a hand down her stomach, smiling deviously as she clenched those muscles.

Pulling the chemise from my fingers, she laid it upon the ground, using it as a blanket. The desire in her eyes, the way she reached, weakened me. She sighed as I spread her legs, eyes fluttering shut.

On a prayer, I closed my mouth over her core, concentrating until I could taste her. She moaned at the sensation, lifting her hips, undulating as she begged me for more. I took my time, though, tasting, massaging, sliding my tongue between her folds as I devoured her slowly.

Labored gasps and desperate moans escaped as I moved. Sliding up her body, taking the swell of a breast into my mouth as I let my fingers swirl over the hard bud between her trembling legs.

I wanted to tell her everything I was feeling. The weight on my chest when she was near. The way her laughter made me weak. The depth of my dreams of a future that began and ended with her alone. But I couldn't manage a single word as I watched her twist her face into absolute pleasure, the fading sun lighting her golden brown breasts with a warmth and glow that only lent to the blissful moment.

"Kirsi," she gasped.

My name on those plump lips sent a shockwave of pride through me. Sliding up her body, I licked the crook of her neck, relishing the salty taste of her skin. She whimpered. Down and down I went, leaving a trail of small kisses over her navel, dipping lower, over the mound and closing my mouth over her core, the sweetness coating my tongue.

Thighs quivering, she called my name again. And again. Until she was screaming with pleasure, her shouts likely reaching the village as I moved relentlessly. Stealing every second of euphoria until she could take no more. Until she twisted away, needing to catch her breath.

We let her clothes dry off on the dead branch of a nearby tree and lay beneath the stars forming in the sky. Taking this moment for just ourselves when the rest of the world was pure chaos and destruction, urgency and desperation... I hadn't known I'd needed it.

Later, familiars in tow, we wove ourselves back through the village and to Nym's thatch roofed hut. The moment the door shut and the felines settled, padded paws sounded outside the door.

I turned to Nym and she smiled, nodding. "You might as well let him in."

Swinging the door open, the white wolf laying in front of the door started.

"Eternally single, huh?"

I stepped aside, and he dragged himself to standing, swayed to the left a bit, crashed into the door frame with a yelp and then flopped on the floor inside the door. Within seconds, the pup was snoring. Scoop lifted his head to investigate, jumped over Talon, and pounced on the wolf. Atlas didn't move an inch as Scoop kneaded his kitten paws into his side, spun three times on top of him, and curled into a ball. The sheer black fur, a beautiful contrast to the wolf's white.

"I don't even want to know why your familiar just snuggled a drunk wolf," Nym whispered, her smile radiating through the room.

"Atty is harmless," I answered. "Scoop only sees the goodness in him... But don't fucking tell him that. He'll brag for days."

32

RAVEN

"Hesitation is a breeding ground for disaster."

I threw a hand on my hip. "And what, may I ask, Your Grace, is *distraction* a breeding ground for?"

Lifting an eyebrow, I smirked as his smug grin melted. Shadows cascaded along the ground below him, as if he floated on air rather than stood on the snow-covered earth outside his favorite mountainside cabin. Then I blinked, and he was gone, swallowed whole by the shadows. Firm fingers crossed my belly before I even registered the movement.

He pulled, jerking my back against his chest as he spoke into the crook of my neck. "Endless heaps of pleasure."

Bringing my arm up, I turned into him, only giving myself a second to let his body heat mine before casting. Bastian let out a sharp hiss on impact as he was thrown over the side of the mountain. I waited a beat. And then another. Until wings flapped, and he surged back over the top landing before me with predatory grace.

"You're getting predictable, Miss Moonstone."

I kicked at the hard crust of snow on the ground. "I could turn your dick blue for fun?"

He brushed a thumb across his lips, eyes darkening. "Does magical color accompany a flavor?"

I wiggled my fingers in the air. "Only one way to find out."

Jerking the band of his pants open, he looked down, wide eyed. I used the opportunity to strike him with real magic, lighting his pants on fire from behind. He yelped and dashed for me with a playful growl. I turned to run, feigned an injury to my ankle, and fell into the snow.

Bastian drew short, instantly concerned. He stepped close, and I cast again, corded vines wrapping around his ankles and dragging him backward.

"Hesitation is a breeding ground for disaster, Your Grace."

He countered, smothering me in inky shadows until I couldn't see a thing. I cast blindly, sending forward frost in abundance. The shadows dropped just in time for me to see a blue-lipped king, all color gone from his face, breaths visible in the air, be dragged over the edge of the mountain by the vines.

I peeked over as he fell. "Truce?"

Knife in hand and wings combating the wind, he didn't say a word as he tackled me to the ground. He wrapped his wings around us then heated the area until his face softened.

"This is supposed to be a training lesson," he rumbled into my ear.

"Then why are you getting your ass kicked?"

"Because, Little Witch, you are a delicious distraction."

THE MOST BEAUTIFUL MAN I'D EVER LAID EYES ON LEANED OVER THE long counter separating the living area and kitchen of the hidden mountain cabin, perusing an ancient map as I studied him. The sun pouring in through the windows fell on his long, dark lashes; the beard he kept groomed, slightly unkempt from these last chaotic days. With the sleeves of his black shirt rolled up, showing the corded muscles of his arms, he could have been a daydream. Or a nightmare, depending on who stood before him.

THE UNBOUND WITCH

I stared, remembering the first time we'd come to this cabin. What he'd done with hot wax and ice, commanding my body. Shocking me. Taking me to places I never knew existed without ever leaving this room.

A piece of fiery black paper fluttered from the ceiling, landing in my outstretched palm.

I believe you're staring, Miss Moonstone.

"I MIGHT BE," I WHISPERED.

"You need to rest. That was the deal. We leave first thing in the morning for the Storm Coven."

"It's daylight, Your Grace."

He finally glanced up, a devilish smile on his face as he held my gaze. His infamous shadows, full of danger and secrets, crept along the ground, pouring over the mismatched furniture and up the cabin walls, smothering the glass windows until there was no more light in the room. Not a single flicker. I swallowed my gasp as I fell backward onto the chair.

"Shall we play a game?" he asked, inches from my ear, though I hadn't heard him move. "Do you need a distraction, Miss Moonstone?"

"Desperately," I answered, reaching for him.

"Undress." Though his voice was a whisper, it wasn't Bastian, but Grey instead.

I paused. Listening. What was he thinking?

"Problem?" he whispered, still Grey, breath brushing my shoulder.

"N—no." I slipped out of my clothing. Each touch of my own fingers against my skin calling it to life in a way that only happened in his presence.

"The most important part of a relationship with a shifter is embracing all versions of him."

A candle lit in the far corner of the room, and although it was still dark, the light gave a glimpse of the sharp edges of Grey's face and a flicker of green eyes staring into mine. I took a deep breath, reminding myself that this beautiful face belonged to Bastian, too. Grey was mine, as much as the king.

He held a hand out to me as another candle lit, showing more of Bastian's shifted form. He spun me, moving his knuckles down my bare stomach as he pressed my naked back to his clothed chest. I pressed my eyes shut, picturing Bastian.

"No." The low rumble of the king's voice went straight through me. "This is your distraction."

"Grey?"

"Not really. I am still Bastian. Grey is just a name."

I spun in his arms, reaching for the face of a man I'd come to cherish. He was right, of course. The divide between them in my mind had never completely gone, though I'd known the truth.

He lowered his lips to mine, and I buried my hand into his sandy blond hair, willing my mind to see the man behind the fingers burning down my back. I gasped when Grey's hands, Bastian's hands, roamed my body, eliciting a stroke of pleasure as his fingertips brushed over my breasts.

I arched against him, pressing myself hard enough to feel his desire growing firm for me. Tilting my head, I moaned as his teeth gripped the skin on my neck.

But he pulled away, whispering into my ear. "Say my name."

"Bastian," I whimpered, closing my eyes as I rested against him, strong hands lowering.

"Tsk, tsk, Little Witch," he teased like Grey, and I could nearly picture the crooked grin. "If I were your king right now, I might punish you for a wrong answer."

"Grey," I managed as I writhed against the fingers circling between my legs.

"And will you let me feast upon you?"

Something within this moment felt wrong but wholly right. He'd done such an exquisite job convincing me of his relation to the king, a deep dark part of my soul felt like I was betraying Bastian for feeling so attracted and tempted by Grey. But as the seconds ticked by, as his question hung between us, we both knew I would not deny him. My arousal, the heat between my legs, had already betrayed me.

"I am yours, Grey Firewing."

He chuckled and moved away, back into the shadows as one of the candles went out. "Follow my voice."

I stepped toward him, the cool floor causing my flesh to raise, my thighs to brush against each other. He moved, the candlelight exposing the profile of the king. I bit my lip, holding back the smile as I realized his game. One man. Two faces.

Stepping close to my Dark King, I raked my nails down his bare chest, the familiarity of this naked body comforting. But when he shifted below my touch, I did not move away from Grey.

A thud filled the silence as he fell to his knees before me, brushing his mouth over my navel. I whimpered at the soft sensation of his tongue, and he chuckled, moving upward at a snail's pace. With weakened knees, my breath hitched as he circled my breasts. Emerald eyes practically glowed in the shadowed room as he lowered his head, feasting as he'd asked permission to do. Not as a king, but a man.

Grey savored me as he moved along my body, taking his time, pulling the swell of my breast into his mouth and moaning. The vibration went directly to the base of my spine, dipping lower and pooling in my belly. An ache built as I pictured him pressed inside me. He reached my neck before I dared breathe again, grazing his teeth up and up along my jawline, until finally, he touched his soft lips to mine.

There was no space between us, not an inch of give as he moved to his feet and lifted me from the ground, wrapping my legs around his waist, his hard length pushed against me. Setting me on the cold counter, he placed a hand around the back of my neck and the other between my legs, pressing firmly against the bud. I gasped at the sensation, instantly wanting more. Lost in the darkness with every other sense heightened.

"Grey or Bastian. Your choice."

"If this is some wicked Trial of yours, I'm going to fail," I answered.

He huffed a laugh. "Choose."

"Grey," I breathed.

He brought a hand to my collarbone, urging me backward until I lay on the counter, the cool stone slab like ice against the heat of my body.

"Don't move," he whispered.

Trailing tiny kisses up the inside of my thigh and down the other, he skipped the only place I needed to feel him. Throbbing with desire and waves of heat cascading over me, my hips lifted from the counter. But then he pulled away, vanishing into the darkness. Just when I thought to sit up, he pressed his lips to my earlobe, sliding down until he could sink his teeth into my neck. A blissful bite of pleasure as Grey's fingers trailed over my stomach. I squirmed, and he disappeared again, taking my breath with him.

"Do. Not. Move."

I smiled at the tone of his voice. The need for absolute control as he teased me.

"I want to feel you."

"Do you?"

A single finger brushed my rib cage. I reached for him, but he was gone. Seconds passed before his hot mouth closed over a hard nipple and slipped away again. In and out he moved, taunting me, bringing my body to life in a way I didn't know possible as I anticipated his single touch upon my sensitive skin. The light caught Grey's face again, his softer features filled with adoration as he looked at me in a way I'd never seen from him. I wasn't sure how long I'd been attracted to him, but whatever he was doing was breathing fire and life to that thought.

As if he could read my mind, feeling accomplished in his task, Grey kissed me with so much passion, I thought I'd stop breathing. Stop thinking. Stop everything just to hold this moment for as long as I could. I melted for him, for Bastian. One man.

His hands became fire once more, brushing my skin, bringing me back to life. His mouth left my lips to close over my core, a single

THE UNBOUND WITCH

grazing of the sensitive bud and I lifted my hips from the counter, desperate for more of him. All of him.

Again, he pulled away.

"I don't think I like this game, King," I managed.

He laughed from across the room and, within a second, his fingers pressed into my thighs, pushing my legs apart once more. Grey's tongue slipped over me. The heat and pressure grew within as he worked relentlessly. Back and forth he stroked until both of us were breathless and could handle it no more. He paused to trail kisses up my body, grabbing me and lifting with hardly any effort.

We moved from the counter to the bed in the middle of the living area. He pressed himself against my opening, pushing forward until I could feel the ache from his size. Pulling back, he thrust again, going just beyond that point, preparing my body to feel every solid inch of him.

I moved my hands down his back as Grey drove all the way forward, pushing himself to the hilt. My nails dug in, feeling the pleasure as thoroughly as he did. Until it was only pleasure, only him and me, and nothing else in the world mattered. In and out he moved, gracefully and in a perfect cadence as I lifted my hips, taking all of him, needing all of him. Minutes turned to eternity as his breathing grew ragged, the summit of desire growing between us. I squeezed, preparing to fall, to burst. He groaned, throwing his head back in a roar that was all beast and no man as he pulsed, the shadows falling from the paned windows as he lost all control over them, taking us both to a place of immeasurable pleasure.

I didn't blink, didn't breathe, as he fell beside me. I studied the look on his face seconds after euphoria. He was everything. Darkness and light. Eternity and never. Grey and Bastian. He was the beginning and the end and all the space in-between. The moon's kiss and the sun's heat. He was fire, and he was mine.

"Come with me," he said, standing, still naked as the day he was born, though he'd taken his true form once more.

I slipped my sweaty hand into his, leaving my clothing behind as well. He cast a new door in the middle of the room and pulled me through the warm water that fell from the threshold as we crossed. I ducked my head and giggled as droplets of fresh water fell down my body. The space was mostly dark, though light shone through the waterfall we hid behind, lighting the smooth stone interior of the magical cave.

Bastian took both of my hands, raising them above my head as he backed me against the slick slab of a rock wall. I thought he would kiss me. Spread my legs and take me again right there. But instead, he leaned his head against mine, closing his eyes as he drew a calming breath.

"Do you want to know why you drive me mad, Miss Moonstone?"

"Maybe."

"You are my only weakness," he breathed into my ear. "My only equal. My only future. A year ago, I would have given my life to keep this world from burning. And now, I'd sooner light the world on fire and watch it burn than see you suffer its wrath. You've changed everything. I think I've fallen in love with you, Little Witch. In fact, I don't think I'll ever stop falling."

The world went completely still. The mist from the waterfall, disappearing. The air, gone. The weight of his words hung between us as I let them wash over me. For a second, he was vulnerable. For a second, he was just a man. Naked and glorious and in love with me. Me. What had I ever done to steal the heart of a villain king and see it for what it truly was? Not dark at all, but pure and light.

I slipped my hand out of his to place it on his heart. "I think I have loved you since the moment we met."

He threw his head back and laughed so hard I thought he'd cry. I saw him fully at that moment. All of Grey and all of Bastian. All of the shifter and all of the witch.

He yanked me forward, still laughing until he could manage words. "You are such a terrible liar."

I could have corrected him. Could have told him how his power enraptured me even before we met. How touching that powerful, black barrier on the day the Trials were announced changed everything for me. But I didn't. Because I fell in love with Bastian in all the little moments along the way, too. The rose petals falling from the ceiling. The fiery notes full of humor. The night he stayed with me, hidden in shadows, after Kirsi died. The day of her funeral when he took every step he could to comfort me. Standing beside me as Grey, no matter the looks, because I needed him. I loved him then and now, and I knew the second I thought he had died, I would love him always.

"How does a bath sound, love?"

The word would never hold the same meaning for me again. Not when it was used as a measurement of my feelings for him. I scanned my eyes up and down his backside before answering.

"Like heaven."

He moved to the side, showing off a pool of dark blue water, clearer than any I'd ever seen.

"A gift, then," he said, holding a hand out so I could sink into the steaming bliss while silver eyes devoured me.

"Rule one: trust no one. When we step through the door, Widower's Grove is a field, and it's about as dangerous as it gets. The Storm Coven has placed rods as beacons for the lightning, but they are only a margin of help. The witches are hiding there for a reason." Bastian stepped around me, tightening the black cloak and lifting my hood before doing the same for his own. "In and out. We find the Grimoires and separate them. That's our only goal right now, witches be damned. If you get in trouble, abandon everything and run for the door."

"What if they trap me?"

He grabbed me, yanking until our noses were touching. "Then you fight like a goddamn warrior until I can get to you."

"Helpful." I shook my head, noting the headache back in full swing. A single throb turned into several as tracers followed movement within my vision. They were getting worse. But I couldn't say a thing if I didn't want to be strapped to a bed somewhere. So, I forced a smile. "I'm not afraid. Let's go."

"You should be," he said over his shoulder, walking through the door.

The last time I'd been to the Storm Coven, constant claps of lightning and pouring sheets of rain had mixed with the heavy scent of sulfur and fire, creating an ambiance of terror. The witches that lived here didn't stay above ground because of the danger. I'd prepared my heart for what it meant to stand in the middle of a field in this coven. Prepared for the thrashing of rain and ground-rumbling thunder.

But the sun shone.

There was no flooding rain. No crack of lightning. Only a wide expanse of hills covered in an endless golden field, the tips of grass blowing gently in a cold breeze. Everything was dead or dying, but this couldn't have been the right place.

"Was that a test of some sort? Before we go to the Storm Coven?"

Bastian in Grey's form turned to me, the color drained from his face as he pointed to the ground. "This is the Storm Coven, or so it was."

The outline of a person scorched into a burnt section of the earth laid a few paces down the hill from us. I stumbled forward, tasting the charred ash on the breeze. Something within me jolted. Looking back as Bastian who spun as he studied the horizon, I realized he hadn't felt it.

Trusting my instincts, I followed an invisible pull. As if the goddess nudged me forward. I kicked through the long grass, quickening my pace down the hill we entered on and up another until a glistening caught my eye.

"Raven," Bastian warned.

But I didn't listen, carrying onward, curious and determined. It hadn't been a glisten, but a tiny stroke of lightning, and then another. Not cracking across the sky or dropping to the Earth, but rather an orb of storm magic, swirling and crackling. As I grew closer, I could make out the leather spine of a book. The Storm Coven Grimoire was trapped within, whispering something I couldn't quite understand. I reached my hand forward, no longer able to fight the pull to touch it.

"Raven, don't!" Bastian barked from directly behind me, grabbing my wrist.

Time slowed. I couldn't pull my hand away. It was as if magic itself had forced me into this moment. I looked back to the king. To the fear and desperation in Grey's green eyes. Then back to the orb, drawing me as if there were a cord attached. When time commenced, I did something I'd never meant to do. Something I'd never forget from this day until my last. I cast upon Bastian, hitting him square in the chest with a bolt of lightning before turning to close the distance between myself and the book suspended in air.

33

RAVEN

I waited, stunned. My fingers dug into the aged leather of the magical book as Bastian slowly rose to his feet, pinning me with a dark stare that said far more than any words might.

Letting the book drop to the ground, the whispers it hurled quieting as he stomped toward me.

"I'm sorry. I didn't mean to do that. I don't know what happened. It was like I couldn't control it."

The fire didn't leave his eyes as his head snapped up, catching something behind me. I lunged for the book and whipped around as Bastian raised his hands to cast.

"No!" I jerked. "I know them."

"Knowing someone and trusting someone is completely different," he growled.

"I said I was sorry."

He didn't take his eyes from the silenced witches, making their way toward us as he whispered, "New plan. Rule one: don't touch magical shit floating in the air. Rule two: trust no one. Hide that book."

I wrapped the book into the folds of my black cloak, and it hummed against my body. Once they were close enough, we could see the fear on their faces, even as they looked into the face of Grey. He waved an arm in an arc, enclosing the group of us in a dome of fire. The witches huddled closer together, moving slower.

"Nobody likes a showoff," I whispered.

"Actually, most people do when it involves fire," he said in a very Grey sort of way before approaching the others.

"You ... you're..." the one I'd known to be Margreet stammered.

"Alive?" I asked, quirking a brow.

"And with the king's man?" She whispered the words as if saying them louder would reveal a scandal.

"What can you tell us about what happened here?" I asked, confident they'd be leery to speak to Grey.

The silent witch chanced a glance at Grey before studying the ground. "Isolde Stormburn and Xena Foresthale forced all of the witches down into the pods, claiming a mighty storm was brewing, and they had a plan to harness its power. Everyone gathered in the same hall where we met you for your Trial, and waited. And waited. But they never came back down."

"They stopped the storms," the man beside her whispered, his mousy brown hair tied up in a bun the way Bastian liked to keep his. "When the elders came up to check, it was quiet. Xena was gone, and Isolde was dead. Burned into the ground as if she'd been struck by the lightning she commanded with her magic. I don't understand."

The third witch spun in a circle as she looked over the horizon, before turning back again. "Where is it?" she asked, her high-pitched voice panicked as the flames grew around us, never expanding outward, but crackling and snapping as the heat pushed in on us.

"Margreet, it's not even out here anymore," the mousey one said.

"The Grimoire is untouchable now, we think. It's floating in an electrical orb somewhere in this field. The elder witches voted us responsible for its return."

I glanced at Grey, who would not meet my eye. "Can I speak to you for a moment?"

He flicked his hand, and the fire vanished.

"Stay here," he ordered the silent witches as we stepped away.

Placing us in his own barrier so we would not be overheard, he crossed his thick arms over his chest, waiting. Clearly, he was still upset about the whole... blasting him through a field thing.

"We have to leave the book with them."

He went deathly still. "That isn't an option, and you know it."

"It is the only option. You know what happened here. Xena had the Forest Coven Grimoire, and Isolde had Storm's. One of them cast and not only did the storms stop all together, but Isolde died. Xena got spooked and ran off. We can't possibly hunt down the books and keep them. It's not safe for us to travel."

He shook his head, rubbing his jaw. "Raven, be reasonable. It's too dangerous, and I know you can see that."

"What was the plan here? To come in and steal the Grimoire, but then what? It's more dangerous to take that thing to the next coven, where there could be two more Grimoires and risk both our lives and half the world. We can leave the Grimoire with the silent witches. You can bind their words if you must."

"This can't be the long-term solution."

I pushed my fingers through my hair, looking up at the eerily still sky. The Grimoire hiding beneath my cloak continued to whisper. Louder and louder, like a nest of cicadas in the summer. Bash didn't seem to notice at all. I placed my hand on the book as if to soothe it, feeling another jolt of electricity before an absolute truth struck me so completely, I stumbled backward. I was connected to this book. Not just physically, but something more. All the books.

"What is it?" All hints of annoyance and frustration left his face as he reached for me in concern.

"I, uhm. It's the book. It's... I know where the others are."

"Just like that? You know?" He clenched his fist at his side as he looked up with a sigh. "I'm telling you that book is as dangerous as they come. We need a long-term plan."

"We will make those decisions when we have to. But we must leave this Grimoire here. No one is going to let that book go. It's too precious to them."

Bastian stepped closer to me, remembered he was actually Grey, and moved away, aware that we could be seen if not heard. "That's exactly the problem. We'll never get it back."

I looked over my shoulder at the three awkward witches staring at us, though they could hear nothing. "Bind their words."

"You make them agree to it, and I will let this go for now."

"Deal."

He dropped the barrier, and I crossed the long, golden grass back to the others. Pulling out the Grimoire, I noted the crackling purple stone embedded into the old leather. Though it was a solid object, I could nearly see the storm raging within it. Every part of me wanted to open the book, get lost in the pages of power and history and magic.

"I'm not sure if you would have been able to pull this from the orb it had locked itself into, but we will consider letting you hold onto it. However, there may come a time when we need this book back, and you must bind your words. If we need it, it will be returned to us. Peacefully and without incident."

The two men shook their heads. "That isn't our promise to make. Our families need this book to keep their power strong."

I pulled the book to my chest, letting the talons of its grip on me seep into my skin, though no one else noticed. Nor did they hear the incomprehensible whispers it hissed into my mind like a snake. Pulsing as it lured me, I had to force the temptation away, to concentrate on anything else. "Your families sent you out here to see if you would die trying to collect this book. You owe them nothing."

"She's not wrong," Grey said, stepping forward. "The coven leaders have kept many, many secrets from you. Starting with the origination of the Harrowing, the lies of the Thrashings, starving you to keep you angry at the king and thus the shifters. The story of our world is not as it seems and, though I've told Raven we can trust no one, she assures me we can trust you." He called magic to his palms, letting the shadows dance between his fingers. "Can we?"

They shared haggard looks, and I understood their hesitation. They'd spent their lives seeking the approval of witches who looked down on them, classifying them as nothing more than burdens in their lives. A waste because they had no magic. Though I'd been granted magic, was born with it, then bound by Bastian's mother, I'd been an outcast just like them. Still, I hoped they could see the desperation on my face. Because if they didn't comply, we would simply leave with the book and even more animosity in our world.

The second that thought crossed my mind, the book's magic gripped me once more. Begging me not to leave it behind.

"Yes," Margreet whispered, picking at her fingers. "You can trust us fully. I will return the book if she says it is needed. I don't trust you, but I do trust Raven, and that's as much as you will get from any of us."

"Will you bind your words?" Grey asked.

"To her. If it is what must be done," she said, lifting her chin.

"Margreet," one of the others interjected.

But she raised a hand to stop them. "You know as well as I do that there is no choice here. Even if we take this book back to the others, supposing the king's messenger lets us take it, what will happen in our coven? Who will take ownership of the book? Everything is dangerous right now." She locked her green eyes to mine. "Moon above, earth below, I bind my will to thee."

Bastian pulled a knife from below his cloak and handed it, hilt first, to the witch. Her resolve was more powerful than some of the magic I'd seen from her coven. She may have been silenced, but it made her no less fierce.

She sliced the blade across her palm, touched the blood to her lips and handed the knife to the others. They looked at her as if she'd grown a third head, but with one pointed look they both backed down, repeating the process.

The power of blood magic sat in the air as Margreet took the Grimoire from my hands, running her fingers over the top of it. I wondered if she could hear it like I could. Could feel its power vibrating through her body just by being near it now that she held it. I searched her eyes for a trace of that feeling, finding nothing, though I could feel the void from where the book had sat in my hands.

The second the others dropped over the hill in the distance, the migraine pierced through my skull, taking me to my knees. I hadn't even realized it'd subsided until it came back with a vengeance. But this time, there was no hiding it from Bastian. He scooped me off the ground, cast a door, and took me straight back to Crescent Cottage.

When Eden and Torryn jumped for us, Bastian's resolve was gone as I pushed from his arms. He looked down at me with a myriad of emotions and when I gave no explanation or excuse, he turned away.

"I know I said you could stay here and help guard," he said, looking at Torryn. "But I think we're going to need you to come hunt with us."

"Gladly. I found Alexander like you asked. He's headed to the castle today," the large man said, looking down at me. "Now, what happened?"

I rolled my eyes. "The king is dramatic. And who is Alexander?"

"He is reconstructing the castle with his magic," Bastian said. "Hopefully. We need a place to store the Grimoires. We can't chase the witches with them, we can't trust the witches to keep them. I need to rebuild the barrier I had at the castle. I can't do it here, either. It needs to be in the center of our world."

"You're still sick." Eden pressed her palm over my forehead. "And warm."

"It's just a headache. It's nothing like it was in the human lands."

Torryn whipped a handkerchief from his pocket and held it toward me. "Your nose is bleeding."

"I'll pass on the used hanky. I just need a minute to myself." I stormed into the back room, leaning on the counter as I pinched my nose, reaching for a clean cloth, my mind pulsing with pain. I tried to cast the wound away, but it didn't work because I didn't know what I was casting against.

The wheels of my mind turned as I thought about the unbinding of my power when the death spell was forced upon me. Maybe this was death's curse. It would be the easy answer. But I didn't think that was it.

Six witches cast upon me that night under the power of the blood moon, covering all seven covens. When I was saved from the Harrowing, all covens were present, including Bastian in the shadows, holding the Moon Coven Grimoire. There was a connection there, I knew it.

Peeking over my shoulder, I heard the hushed voices of the group outside arguing over what to do with me. As if they had a choice over my fate. While they were distracted, I dropped to my knees, studying the towers of terracotta pots below. I didn't need to guess. I knew exactly where the Moss Coven Grimoire was. Setting the top pot to the side, I reached in and pulled out the relic. The magic pulsing from this book was far more subtle than the Storm Coven. Which made sense. It'd been without magic for a very long time. The real question was, why was I tied to it?

Moving my hand down the grooves of the spine, I checked over my shoulder one final time before opening the fragile pages of the Grimoire and thumbing through. Right now, it wasn't about the sheets filled with family trees, dates of births and deaths, records of spells and markings. It wasn't about the added pages and notes in the spine drafted with ink that was now fading; it was about the power, the words that seeped into the air like a whisper.

"We are," it seemed to say, so faintly I wasn't sure those were the correct words.

"We are what?" I whispered back, flipping another page.

A commotion in the front of the shop pulled me from the conundrum of the Grimoires. I stashed the book back into the pot and covered it, dabbing the cloth to my nose again to make sure the bleeding had stopped before I stepped out.

Bastian had taken his true form and, though he locked eyes with me, he did not push or shove himself into the space he knew I needed. The tension was already tough and, as Crow picked up the pieces of broken glass from the floor, apologizing for his clumsiness, I forced myself to remember that everyone here was fighting their own battle, and, though it felt like it, I was not alone.

I didn't need to tell them about my theory of being connected to the Grimoires yet. Not until I was absolutely sure. Adding more to the pile of shit we were in was exactly the opposite of what everyone needed.

"Okay?" Torryn asked, sidling up next to me, his giant presence calming.

"Okay," I whispered, sharing a smile.

"I think giving up the alcohol may be better than trying to make your own," Eden said, pinching her nose as she used a cloth to soak up whatever Crow had spilled.

THE UNBOUND WITCH

"I'm a human stuck in a world of magical creatures. I can't sail home without a ship and crew, and I can't stay here without my rum. What would you have me do?"

The old captain's usual smile was gone as the stress and strain in his voice shone through.

"It won't be this way forever," Bastian said, leaning down to help pick up the glass. "I'll see what I can do about getting you some wine."

"It's for the nerves," the captain answered. "I don't want to leave. I just want to feel something normal."

"Fair enough," the Dark King answered.

"I'll be back in twenty minutes," Torryn said, slipping into the Fire Coven's door.

Eden sat heavily on a wooden stool near the counter, swirling a spoon in her tea. "I wish I knew what normal felt like."

Her dark and light hair caught in the sunlight pouring into the window as a shadow passed over her face. I hadn't taken the time to wonder how she must feel. Every moment of her life had revolved around sacrifice and small pleasures. I wondered what her life would look like in a year. In five. Once we hunted the coven leaders and forced them to see reason or resign their positions.

"Oh good, you're here." Kirsi's voice was like home to me.

Seeing her, even in wraith form, slip into the cottage with Atlas directly behind her, brought me a comfort I didn't know I needed. Bastian was everything in the world, but that didn't take away from my friendship with Kir and how selfishly I coveted our bond.

It wasn't until Nym stepped through, two familiar kittens on her heels, that I realized something had gone wrong.

"Explain," Bastian said, staring down at the witch. His anger was not with her, but she couldn't have known that.

Nym lowered her chin before curtsying. "I'm sorry to say that Nonet has died, Your Grace."

The fury in his voice faltered. "What happened?"

"Ophelia killed Nonet and used her blood to break the barrier. The man that was there with her died as well, but I didn't know his name."

"Alec," Torryn said quietly. "His name was Alec."

Eden gasped, crossing the room to wrap her arm around him in a hug. "I'm so sorry, Tor. I know how much he meant to you."

Torryn turned, facing away from the group of us for a moment as he collected himself. My heart broke for him. When would the dying stop?

"We have to go to the River Coven," Atlas said, pulling the eyes away from his friend, so Torryn could have his moment. "We've heard from a wraith that might be able to get us some answers on the Harrowing, but she's requested... some things. There's a waterfall we need to get to."

"I can move the door if you know where it is," Bastian offered.

"It's just past Cauldron's Bluff."

"That's too close to the swamps. They'll see you."

Kirsi moved forward. "I'll go in alone. Invisible."

"Not a chance, Ghosty. You don't know where you're going, and those swamp witches have all kinds of spells and traps. It's not safe."

"We also have to go to River." I moved to Bastian's side, pressing a hand to his forearm, hoping he'd feel my apology in the gesture. I wasn't making this process easy on him. "Can I see your map?"

Bastian cast a door to the cabin, left, and returned within a minute. He slid the long canvas along the counter. We all circled around, even the familiars. Scoop remained glued to Talon's feet, and Kirsi watched him sadly as he chose another witch.

As everyone else looked over the map, focusing on the River Coven, I leaned down, picked up the tiny black panther and walked around the counter, stroking him behind the ear. I'd asked for the map for their sake, not my own.

I knew exactly where we needed to go, able to feel the pull to the seven Grimoires like a thrum of tightly woven string in my mind. Each book had a different pluck, a different pitch of the same thread. There were not only seven Grimoires calling me, though. There were eight notes of temptation and importance. The eighth being the most curious and most continuous pulsing. Like a heartbeat in the middle of our kingdom. The black castle ruins.

"I could drop you here," Bastian said, pointing. "You'd have to cross over this river, but you could get in the back way and have less trouble."

"No. Then we'd have to climb the bluff straight on."

"Not if I float up to the top, get the stone and come meet you."

Atlas narrowed his eyes at Kirsi, dropping his chin. "I'm telling you it's not safe for anyone to be in the swamp alone at any time. We have to go together. We have to *stay* together." He turned back to the map, tracing careful details as I leaned over, watching him. "We need to be right here. It's the only way we avoid most of the swamp but circle around and drop down the waterfall."

"That's near the gathering place for the River witches," Bastian warned. "You'll have to be careful."

"Got it. Reckless all other times, careful this one. Piece of cake."

Bastian punched him in the arm. "Don't be a smart ass. All in. All out."

"I think we should leave Scoop here," Nym said quietly.

"Agreed," Kirsi said, moving toward the feline in my arms. "He's not going to be safe out there."

"I'll look after the little guy," Crow offered, reaching his hands toward me with the brightest eyes I'd ever seen from him. "Come to old pappy now."

"Old pappy?" I asked, handing Scoop over.

"He's not a fan of strangers," Kirsi and I said at the same time.

But Scoop curled himself into a ball, right in the captain's arms, rubbed his ear against the leather vest he wore and promptly fell asleep.

"He knows his pappy," Crow whispered, turning to snuggle the cat.

"If we're not back in an hour, come after us," Atlas said, face solemn as he stared at Tor.

"I'd already planned on it," the shifter answered.

I hadn't realized how dangerous the River Coven was. The threat of the swamp witches hadn't reached the Moon Coven in ages, but then the witches were never their targets. Always the shifters. Their coven leader, Circe, was the youngest of the leaders, and I would have bet the shop six months ago that she was well and truly good. Even when we were selected for the Trials, she was the kindest to me. And now, we were hunting her.

The second they left, my stomach began to churn. They'd gone straight into the lion's den, it seemed. Bastian bumped me with a shoulder and held out a fist. He dropped a handful of various crystals into my palm and jutted his chin toward the map.

"Distract yourself. Where are the other Grimoires?"

The stones clicked together in the most satisfying sound as I shook them, working out my nerves. Closing my eyes, I focused on those individual thrums in my mind. Eight beautiful notes, each one pulling on me, willing me to step toward them. One would be manageable, but instead, they felt neurotic. A chasm of pandemonium, willing me to split myself apart to appease them equally. I pulled the green agate from the selection and placed it near Crescent Cottage.

"Moss is easy. It's in the back room." Shaking the stones again, I selected the purple, moving counterclockwise over the map. "Storm has moved. It's no longer in Widower's Grove. It's somewhere close to here."

"Good. They didn't take it back to the group. Keep going."

I pulled the sodalite from my palm and moved toward the River Coven, avoiding that foreign heartbeat in the castle. "Oh, shit."

Wide eyes met mine as I placed the next directly in the center of the swamp, then pulled the milky white moonstone and placed it on top of the other. "Willow is with Circe in the River Coven, and they are close to Kirsi's waterfall. There are going to be eyes all over the place."

34

KIRSI

Swamps were like the goddess' angry curse upon the world, unless you were a wraith. Nym swatted the bugs that bit at her skin, she and Atlas trudging through the muck, side by side, as they tried and failed to be quiet. The wooden huts were like nothing I'd ever seen. A network of rope bridges connected all of the elevated homes several feet above the dangerous waters. Iron lanterns hung, lit, though I knew it to be daytime. You couldn't tell, though, surrounded by a thick canopy of trees that blocked every inch of the sky. The only peace was the sound of water falling somewhere in the distance.

The swamp witches were still members of the River Coven. They attended their gatherings and partook in their celebrations, but rumor said they were of a different breed of river witch. Far more feral and hot tempered, but equally less civilized.

"We'll have to circle around," Atlas muttered. "If any of them come out, we'll be caught. It's too deep to take my wolf form."

"Thank the goddess. I didn't want to have to smell wet dog all day," I whispered.

"Again, Ghosty... you can't smell. Stop pretending like you hate me. We're best friends."

Nym huffed a laugh. "She wouldn't tease you if you weren't."

A splash in the water halted us. Atlas turned back, yelped, and quickened his pace.

Glancing back at a haggard old witch, I pushed Nym forward. "We can't stop. Hurry."

She hustled, lifting her skirts higher. I was torn, though I knew what we'd agreed upon. Stay together. But I could go on ahead, grab the waterfall crystal and be back before they even made it halfway at this pace.

"It's too dangerous," Nym said, as if she could read my mind. "They could—"

"Run! Run! Run!" Atlas yelled from behind us.

We whipped around to find four witches above us with arms raised, their faces full of eerie delight.

"Go, Kir. Get the stone. We can hold them off," Atlas said, running for us.

I didn't hesitate, turning invisible and rushing forward. Seconds. I only needed seconds to get over the waterfall and swoop down. But I couldn't leave them behind. No matter the cost, I knew they weren't going to be able to win, being so heavily outnumbered. I circled back, hating myself. Hating everything about all of this.

Nym cast. A flock of birds descended upon the witches, diving in talons first. Momentarily stunned, the old crones got caught in the shuffle of trying to fight off the birds.

My team could have run then. Could have saved themselves. But they didn't. They fought on, trying to give me as much time as they could, and they didn't know I'd turned back. I raced toward the witches on the rope bridge above as Atlas said something to Nym under his breath. She shook her head, and his growl was loud enough to hear beyond the caw of the diving birds. We were doing all of this to save her. To stop death's clock on her and she was risking everything anyway. Because she thought of the other victims when I thought only of her.

He wanted her to go, to save herself, and she wouldn't. I knew her. She'd fight with her last breath if she thought it was for a greater purpose. She threw her hands in the air, power buzzing as she faced the witches. The earth seemed to tumble below us, the sky beyond the trees rumbling.

A witch on the swaying bridge cackled as she cast, her spell landing right on Nym's chest before she could manage whatever she'd been conjuring. Only a few more seconds and I'd be on them. A few seconds was a lifetime in the middle of a witch fight, though. Crossing behind them, I surged forward, jamming my hand into the witch that had struck Nym, gripping her warm beating heart and ripping it from her chest.

The crone beside her, long nose and all, screamed in outrage as she turned to see her twin collapse to the ground. As if she'd gone mad, she gripped the corded railing of the bridge and sprang over it, her magic carrying her forward as she surged for Atlas, totally unaware that I was to blame. I made to grip the next witch's heart, but she turned and stared right into my eyes, as if she could see me.

"Wraith," she said, before jamming her hand forward.

A blow struck me so solidly I flew backward, head over heels through a door of a swamp witch's hut. Hardly having time to register that I'd actually felt something, no time for thoughts of the death that coated the hut in every corner, the skin on the walls, the bones for furniture, I soared away, wishing an hour had passed.

The witches had vanished, save the body of the fallen. I rushed forward. Nym was on the ground, unmoving. The water level wasn't high enough to drown her, though her arms lay to her sides, her feet nearly submerged.

Atlas, though? He'd taken higher ground in wolf form, no longer caring who might catch him. As if they'd dropped from the sky, the crones circled, their thin, bony legs and bare feet splashing through the water as they closed in. The wolf bared his teeth, snapping his jaws as he lowered himself, growling.

Another cackle from the collective hags was the final sound as they descended. I needed my fucking magic. I needed Scoop. I needed to be alive again. I could do very, very little, and as defeat wrapped itself tightly around my throat, I watched as they dragged that white wolf through the swamp, body limp, all fight gone. Looking back at Nym, still on the ground, I warred with myself over leaving her or following the pup. In the end, I'd need her. And no part of my soul could leave her behind.

35

RAVEN

"Five minutes, half an hour, I don't care," I fumed. "They're not going to be safe in there. We have to go after them right now."

"Atlas is smart. He can manage this. It's better for us to go in here if we can." Torryn pointed to a more southern spot on the map, while Bash remained silent, watching the door. "If we can get there without having to go through the majority of the swamplands, it's a better strategy. If we follow Atlas, we land all the way over here and have to sneak through."

"We'll use two doors," Bash answered. "It's still going to be dangerous, and we have to stay very close together, but we can check on Atty, then leave as long as they are good."

"If we were going to do that, we should have just gone with them," I said.

"It's easier to hide a wolf and a witch than all of us, and you know that."

"Are you sure you should go?" Eden asked. "If you're not feeling well, you can stay."

"I'm not going to break," I snarled.

And that was it. No push back from Bastian, no need to treat me like something fragile. If I wanted to go, he wasn't going to try to stop me. Torryn's wink solidified my decision.

"Rule one?" Bastian whispered into my ear as he shifted into Grey.

"Don't touch magical shit floating in the air."

"Rule two?"

"Trust no one."

"Atta girl," Torryn said, flinging his heavy cloak around his broad shoulders. "You'll have to tell me about the floating stuff later, though."

Grey's dimple was the last thing I noticed before standing ankle deep in sour water beneath a heavy covering of willow trees and giant oaks with low hanging moss. It felt like standing between freshly hung sheets drying on a line. Moving the moss to the side, a swarm of bugs flew out, buzzing and stinging my skin.

"Shh," Torryn said, bringing his finger to his lips.

Without another thought, I cast the spell over us that would silence our footfalls. At least we wouldn't be heard splashing in the water. But Torryn shifted beside me, his beautiful flowing tail a near mockery of the gorgeous wings spread above me as he lifted from the ground and soared forward.

Bastian placed a hand on my shoulder and pulled me down to a crouch in the putrid water. We waited as the strix went on toward the rushing sound of the waterfall. A whistle. The great scream of a magical bird pierced the air and Bastian was up and on his feet in seconds. He wouldn't be able to fly fast with me, and we'd sworn to stay together, so we ran.

My heart raced, matching the falls of my feet, the warm water splashing until I was nearly drenched, panting as we approached Torryn, standing next to Kirsi, who cradled Nym in her lap.

"They took Atlas," Kirsi said. "I tried to stop them, but I couldn't help both of them."

"Which way?" Bastian snapped.

Nym shuffled in her arms, coming to, and Kirsi sagged in relief, pointing to where Atlas had been taken.

Torryn leaned down, scooping the golden witch into his arms. "She's waking, but we need to go. He won't last long."

"Take her satchel," Kir said, holding the bag with a baby white tiger inside. "He won't grow larger without her magic, don't worry."

Bastian cast a door and we raced for it, skidding to a halt as another appeared beside it.

"Take her to Crescent Cottage," he told Torryn. "When you step back through, be ready for anything."

"Yes, sir." He turned to Kir. "She'll be fine, I promise."

"Okay," she whispered, watching him cross through the magic door.

"You can't let yourself be distracted," he said to Kir. "Either go with him or be fully here."

She straightened, the fire in her eyes lighting. "I'm here. Let's go."

"Invisible," he commanded, and she listened as we stepped through the second door.

It was weird, crossing one plane and appearing in the next in an instant, but it was stranger in the same lands, only the space of a short jog ahead of where we were. We could only go small spaces at a time, searching for the witches. Faster than running but still unsettling.

"We're closing in on the books," I panted as we ran. "They're probably the length of Gravana Lake from us right now."

"Do I want to know how you know that?" Kirsi asked, slowly.

"No."

When Bash cast the next door, it took us further ahead. So far, in fact, we landed beneath a group of huts, hoisted on stilts. Torryn stepped out right behind us, having left Nym to Eden's magic, looking around wildly with a curved dagger in his hand.

"Good for now," Bastian whispered. "But at the end of this bridge above us is a larger building. Circe Rivervale's home. I'm guessing she's in there with the Grimoires."

"And Willow," I said, eyeing the place I thought Kirsi to be as she brushed my arm.

"I can pop up there and take a look," she offered.

"That place has probably got barriers to the gills, and wraiths are no exception to them."

"Oh, that's what she did to me." Kir nodded. "One of the swamp witches cast and it threw me backward. She must have cast a barrier outward, and it struck me."

"I'm sure you're right. And that hut over there," Bastian pointed to the one left of where we were, "has got a spirit blessed witch inside with an alligator familiar. Sometimes she lets him loose in the swamp, so keep your heads up."

"Imagine snuggling that at night," Kirsi answered, still invisible.

"There aren't any barriers," I said, straightening myself up. "They've got both the books, and everything is normal here right now. They haven't cast."

"They could have had the barriers up and placed the books inside like I did," Bastian countered.

"I don't think they would have taken that risk."

"Well, I'm not willing to find out unless we have to," Bash answered. "Are you?"

I shook my head.

Moments passed as we listened to the footsteps move back and forth over the bridge, saw the shapes of people moving about through the cracks and gaps in the wood. No one spoke above, though. Whatever they were doing, it was silent.

"Hey," Kir whispered. "They've got Atlas in the hut with the red lantern by the door, and the witches are evacuating this area on Circe's command. No one is allowed to speak or cast magic anywhere near this place."

I threw my hands on my hips. "You went up there?"

"You said you weren't willing to take the risk, so I did."

"How did you find out if they aren't talking?"

"Oh, no. They've been told not to speak, but whoever the two in that hut over there are, they're quite chatty."

"You're going to get yourself in a world of trouble one day," Torryn said with a smile.

"You're right. I could die. I'd better stop."

The smile on Grey's face took me back for a moment. Before he was Bastian. When he was just the king's messenger riding in a carriage. For all the heavy happening right now, there was such a playful side to him that really spoke to Kir. They could have been the best of friends. Before the world broke and we were tasked to fix it.

"Thanks for going, Kir."

Tor moved in. "I'll go after Atty. You see if you can get to the coven leaders."

He crawled to the edge of the bridge, shifted, and lifted himself off the ground, diving unseen into the line of trees on the backside of the huts.

"There's not going to be a stealthy way to do this. We have to go in, hope they are smart enough to keep their magic at bay, and overpower them. If anyone casts, we could all die."

Kirsi cleared her throat. "Wouldn't want that now, would we?"

36

RAVEN

I clutched the edges of my cloak, squeezing my eyes shut. This could all go horribly wrong, and odds were, it would. I sent a prayer up to the goddess and pretended I could feel her ethereal warmth against my cheek where she had touched me. We inched forward under the cluster of huts and wooden bridge, through the sludge of shallow water and putrid weeds, toward a set of stairs near the farthest building. Moss hung low from the musty planks, tangling us in foliage as we passed.

A sharp hiss from Kirsi was all the warning we had before the alligator's eyes popped up above the water, directly in front of us. My heart froze. I held my breath. No longer concerned about being seen, we turned and ran. But also very well aware that we could not outrun the alligator in the water. He was too fast. His body, twisting and thrashing, causing more of a commotion than anything else around. We were steps from a separate set of stairs. The beast's long giant mouth opened directly on my heel and snapped shut, barely missing me.

Kirsi turned feral, diving for the beast. I looked over my shoulder just in time to see her riding on top of the alligator and shoving her hand into his eye socket to rip out his eye.

"I don't know where his fucking heart is," she screamed, though it was still hardly audible over the splashing of the water.

"Go!" Bastian ordered, shoving me up the stairs while the animal turned, trying to find his assailant. "Remind me to tell you how much I love you later, Kir."

We ran up the stairs, diving behind a hut. The beast didn't follow.

"Okay, but maybe tell me what to do with this thing first?" She shoved her hand forward, displaying the bloody eyeball.

"They make for a nice stew," an old, croaky voice said from behind us.

Spinning, I took in every disgusting feature of an old, spirit blessed swamp witch. Cavernous wrinkles covered her, rimming her mouth and enhancing her paper-thin skin. I expected markings on most of her body, but they were sparse, or lost within the crevices of the wrinkles and hiding beneath the age marks.

She lifted the edge of her thin black dress, showing off long yellow toenails, and bony, little legs. "You will return that eye, girl. Or I'll trap you in a salt circle and have your little friends here for dinner."

Kirsi dropped the eye. It plopped on the ground in front of us, rolling slightly. My stomach rolled more than it did. I glanced up to Bastian, whose eyes hadn't left the witch, fists heavy at his side. Unable to cast, I'm sure he felt as restricted as I did.

"Where is your coven leader?" he asked through gritted teeth.

"She'll be along," she answered.

I swallowed, wracking my brain for a way out of this. But it wouldn't be me that saved us, nor Bastian or Kirsi. Instead, Willow Moonhollow stepped around the corner, bashed the old witch over the head with a dampened log, and looked over her shoulder to make sure no one had seen her. The wound she'd gotten from the final Trial had nearly healed, leaving its permanent mark across her face in an angry red scar. Her eyes were distant now. Complacent even.

"There isn't time for explanations. Follow me."

I stepped backward, hiding my bark of laughter. "You want us to trust you?"

She swatted her chestnut hair over her shoulder as she looked at Grey. "I just saved your asses, didn't I? I'll take you to the Grimoires.

Isn't that what you've come for? I've been sitting in the miserable swap waiting for my chance to leave, but I'm stuck until something happens. Strict orders from Endora Mossbrook. You have to take them and go quickly. Before Circe gets back."

"What choice do we have?" Grey asked, stepping away from me. "Come on, witch."

The words were meant to drive a bit of doubt into her mind about everything the world might have assumed happened after the death of the Dark King. Perhaps I was his prisoner, just as we'd planted back in the Moon Coven. The delight in her eyes at his command spoke volumes. Still, why had she saved us? I turned over my shoulder, but Kir was nowhere to be seen.

Willow led us directly to the main walkway, the small village of huts stemming off from it. I thought her foolish to show us off, to not hide in any capacity, especially after she'd just attacked a swamp witch. But there was no one out, no sounds. As if all the witches hid in their huts or had managed to leave the area as they'd been commanded to do.

The two Grimoires thrummed louder in my mind, their pull gripping my throat from the hut we were being led to. I braced myself for the whispers to begin. Like the buzzing of bees, audible but hard to understand beyond the 'we are' I'd maybe heard before. Each step we took seemed to be a pluck of that tight string between us. The one no one else seemed to have but me.

I dragged a ragged breath into my lungs, trying to prepare myself for the next several minutes. Casting when in danger was an instinct. Even I couldn't say I would remember in a moment of weakness and refrain from using my power. Still, whatever Willow's game, I was glad to be rid of the swamp witch.

Approaching the leaning cabin at the end of the bridge, Willow halted, dropping her head for just a moment before pushing open the door. She moved to the side, letting us go first with her head down, as if ashamed to show the scar upon her beautiful face. Stepping into the darkness, I had no doubt Bash would have preferred to send his shadows in first, but since he could not use magic, we had to simply trust the witch I would have killed in the final trial, given the chance.

THE UNBOUND WITCH

Entering the room with two Grimoires nearly took me to my knees. I could hear them, feel them, nearly taste them, as the potency of their power seeped into my veins. I wanted them in my hands. Needed them.

Bastian's hand clapped around my wrist, stopping me from my slow progression forward. I had no idea I was moving, but when it came to the Grimoires' steep magic, it seemed I couldn't control myself.

A match and then a candle lit in the back of the room, illuminating Circe's round face. Heart dropping into my stomach, I cringed as Willow laughed behind me. She'd betrayed us. And we'd known it was going to happen. We knew we needed to get to this hut, regardless of the circumstances, but the fact that she thought she'd won, outsmarted us somehow, irritated me.

"Will you fight me for them?" Circe asked, as more candles lit around the dark room, revealing the faces of several old swamp witches.

"I'm honestly surprised you know how to light those candles without magic," I said, taunting, though I had no right.

"There are many things about the swamp witches that might surprise you, Raven Moonstone," Circe said. "Did you know they found a way around starving by eating the creatures of the swamp? And when those ran out, they turned on each other."

One of the witches ran her tongue over her yellow teeth as she peered into my very soul with sharp black eyes. I stumbled backward, disgusted and terrified in equal measure. But Willow planted both of her hands on my back and shoved me forward so hard I fell to my knees. Grey flinched, but otherwise did not move to help me. In fact, he let loose a small laugh. I turned to glare at him.

One of the others, a man, tilted his head to an eerie angle as he looked at Grey. "Why do you laugh?"

"I prefer to see the murderer of my king on her knees." He smirked.

Circe slid forward, setting her candle on the table, the orange glow lighting the leather books that called to my heart. "You're a good liar, but a liar all the same."

I tried to stand, but the River Coven leader lunged for me. Fighting every instinct to cast her away, I let her come. Let her wrap her arm around mine, haul me to my feet and place a dagger to my neck.

"We'll have to kill you the old-fashioned way, I'm afraid."

"Why?" I asked, buying time, hoping Kirsi would be able to free Atlas.

"The moment you fought the death spell, I knew you were not the savior we hoped you were. Given every chance in the world to see our cause through, you failed. You failed when you looked at the Dark King during your mind Trial without an ounce of hatred. You failed when you refused to kill him. You failed when you killed him and didn't—"

The door slammed open, and a giant white wolf surged into the room, soaring over me as he landed on a swamp witch and ripped into her throat with a ferocious growl. Atlas was a god damned beast. A glorious specimen of heart and loyalty. He'd been scratched deep on his face, but he seemed no worse for the wear as he snarled.

Chaos ensued. Grabbing the boned hilt of the knife at my throat, I planted my elbow into the gut of the River Coven leader. Willow screamed, but I knew one absolute truth. Those swamp witches wouldn't have a clue what to do without the use of their own magic.

Circe may have ordered them not to cast, knowing what would happen, but the odds of them listening when threatened were not good. As soon as a witch's life was at stake, she wouldn't hesitate. We needed to separate the books quickly. I dove for the Grimoires, snatching them from the table and inching my way toward the door.

"Give me a book, Rave," Kirsi said, popping into view. "Give me one and let me get it the fuck out of here."

"How fast can you go?" I asked, a prickling, greedy part of my mind wanting to refuse.

"Faster than anyone else," she promised. "Trust me."

I nodded, pushing a book toward her. She soared out the door with the Moon Coven Grimoire and all I could do was pray she was faster than these witches were desperate. She'd always made a point to show me she was near when she was invisible, and times were dangerous. This time she hadn't. She'd gone for backup and delivered. As she always, always did.

Torryn blocked the door, grabbing one of the witches by the throat and throwing her across the small hut. Circe had clambered away from me, attempting to hide behind the remaining swamp witches. No one had noticed the books were gone.

Bastian pulled me from the floor in one motion, pushing me behind him. "Stay back," he commanded, pulling a knife from his belt.

I stared into Willow's face for a split second, my eyes cutting to the scar. I raised my hands. "Don't even think about it," I warned. I wouldn't have used magic, but she didn't need to know that.

Jerking left and then right, Willow soared around me, hoping to take cover with Circe, but she didn't give a shit about her. She shoved the moon witch toward Torryn with a grunt.

The inside of the cabin burst into a hue of orange and yellow, the sound of rushing fire filling the tiny war zone. A surge of flames licked up a dusty old curtain in the back of the cottage. One of the swamp witches must have started the place on fire in an attempt to escape. Smart really.

Smoke filled the space, ripping into my lungs as I twisted for the door. And then it happened. Someone in the swarm of the room cast water to put the fire out. It might have been instinct, it might have been suicidal, but as we all braced ourselves for impact, the explosion of magic didn't come. Whatever happened, however far Kirsi had made it, was just enough.

In one fell swoop, everyone stopped. Realizing they had magic, the swamp witches closed in. Atlas was slammed against a wall and pinned there. Tor roared, his great form running full speed until he slammed into an old hag, having just enough time to pull his blade before someone cast a sphere of water around him. He struggled, gripping his throat. Drowning. Heart racing, I searched the faces of the four remaining witches.

A blast of magic struck me, yanking me forward, toward one of the swamp witches. Her eyes were wild as more and more of her markings began to glow green. I didn't hesitate. Didn't stop to think about the ramifications as I cast death upon her. The spell ripping from me as if it sucked my own life from my body as well as hers.

The world pulsed with a full charge of energy, the swell of power deafening the room as one moment the witch was standing and the next, she crumbled to the ground. I winced, waiting for the headache, the drip of blood from my nose, the raging sickness to take over, as if that had been what ailed me, but it didn't. Whatever it was that was making me so sick, it wasn't that spell. I felt more alive than I ever had. Invigorated and finally free of the bonds that held me, even if they were only loosened. The earth rumbled as I gathered my power again, the sky from beyond the window darkening. Anger and a demand for control took over as I ripped away the magical bonds that pinned Atlas to the wall in a fury I'd never known.

Circe made a move to cast upon Willow. "You brought them into my home."

I should have let her cast. Let them settle their own battle, but I couldn't. In one move, a simple flick of my wrist, Circe was dead as well.

Willow's eyes bulged as she whipped around, mouth gaping.

"You're a moon witch. It's time you start acting like one," I said.

The rest of the witches cowered away from me as I strode toward the small group of heroes that had my back and raced into danger to save me. "We are going to leave this coven behind and not look back." I stared at the terrified witches still standing. "I suggest you honor your dead and go about your lives. If I ever see a swamp witch again, I'll kill them on sight."

Willow walked out first and ran off, her boots fading down the wooden walkway. Before I could pull the door shut, a single spell whipped passed my head. I didn't know what it was, but it barely missed. Bastian spun on a heel, heading straight back into the hut, the door slamming behind him. I tried to follow, but the door was sealed shut with Bastian's power.

Torryn grabbed my shoulder. "Let him go. You don't want to see this."

And so, we waited. Through the screams of torture and the crash of magic as the Dark King did what he did best. It was not in his nature to leave crimes unpunished. I no longer faulted him for that fury.

When the door opened once more and he stalked outside, rage melted into something on his face that was broken as he fell to his knees before me, wrapped his arms tightly around me and hung his head.

He whispered. "I'm sorry. I'm sorry you had to cast that spell again. I'm sorry for losing it. I'm sorry this is what our lives have come to and being with me has made it so much harder on you."

"I'm not sure that's true at all," I confessed, running my fingers into his disheveled blond hair before brushing my lips along his.

Atlas limped across the deck, placing a heavy hand on Bastian's slumped shoulder. "Let's get the fuck out of here."

37

KIRSI

The phantom heartbeat I wasn't supposed to feel stopped in my chest as I approached Crescent Cottage. To anyone else, the windows provided a dark glimpse into a ransacked store, but to me, given immunity to the barrier cast like a second skin over the building, there was a beautiful woman standing inside that I seemed to always be leaving behind. Since the moment we decided to be together on All Hallows Eve, our world had been turned upside down, and no matter how hard I endeavored to right it for her, I failed.

Each moment that passed without answers to end the Harrowing was another step closer to death for Nym. I didn't want to picture Death's cold hands wrapped around her throat. The forlorn look on her face the second before she was ripped from this world. The twist in her gut as she realized what was happening and could do nothing to stop it. But those were the images and thoughts that plagued me each second the deadly curse ripped through our lands.

Circling the back of the store so no one would see the front door open, I slipped through the gate and knocked quietly. Nym was there to greet me, beautiful green eyes falling on the River Coven book in my hand before moving to the side so I could enter.

"Don't cast," I warned her and Eden.

"I hardly remember I can," the older witch answered.

After placing the newest Grimoire on the table, I realized it meant nothing to me anymore. Beyond the fact that it was dangerous, I didn't feel a connection to it. Didn't mourn its loss or celebrate its return. It was just another item in the world. But Nym eyed it carefully, looking at me with a question in her eyes.

"We need to wait for the others to get back before you can touch it. It's not safe right now. But I did get this." I held out my palm to show her the stone from the waterfall.

Nym peeked over her shoulder, her brown hair falling forward before leaning into me.

I concentrated on touching her with my forehead instead of my fingers and when we connected, a small gasp left her lips as that beautiful smile spread across her golden brown face. I needed her desperately. Wanted her when I didn't think I would ever want for anything again. Beyond the sensations and rewards of life, beyond the afterlife even, she was all I wanted. And I feared I'd never truly have her. And that was so unfair to her.

She closed her eyes, sighing, and I knew she needed this moment as much as I did. It wasn't until Scoop walked toward us that I lost all sense of self, faltered, and floated backward.

"Don't move away from him," the drunken captain said. "Just give him a minute to reacquaint himself with you."

I rolled my eyes, but did as he suggested. I'd seen the panther nestled in his arms and honestly, I would have tried anything. Pushing all my focus forward, as he neared me, I brushed a finger through the thick, black hair behind his oversized ears. I prepared myself for him to cower away, to hiss at my closeness, but instead, he took another small step forward, tilting that adorable head into my hand.

"Told ye so." Crow laughed. "He knows who he belongs to."

"Used to," I whispered, afraid to scare him off.

Nym knelt down, her skirt pooling on the floor, scaring him enough that he took a step away from us. "Try lifting him."

"I can't. What if I drop him?"

She rolled her eyes. "You carried that book all the way here from the River Coven. I'm certain you can lift a cat for a few minutes."

I reached under his belly, waiting for him to arch his back and scramble away. But he did none of those things. Instead, he simply paused for me to bring him to my chest. And so I did, forcing the physical touch there as well, more for him than me.

When Raven, Torryn, Bastian and the wolf came through the River Coven door, I dared not move. I didn't want to scare him. But as Atlas came close, kneeling with a giant smile on his face to see the connection we'd made, Scoop hissed and scrambled away.

"I just want to pet you, buddy," he said as Scoop stopped at Crow's feet, clawing at his pants until he lifted him.

I pushed away the ache in my soul at the blatant rejection.

"You saved our butts, Kir," Bash said, walking over to look at the book. "But we've got to get this thing out of here. Tor and Atty, with me to the castle."

I swooped in front of the king, halting him before he went through the door. "I know it's getting late, but we need to keep going if we are going to get answers. Can we bring Atlas with us, or do you need him?"

Bastian, in Grey's form, bit his lip to hide his smile. "Are you telling me you *want* little Atty to go with you?"

"Excuse me, Bash... I'm a fucking blast."

"Whatever helps you sleep at night, wolf. Your choice?"

"Obviously, I'd rather go with the pretty girls than stare at those mugs all night. You'll be fine without me?"

"Yes. We should be back by morning."

THEY SLEPT IN A PILE OF OLD BLANKETS ON THE FLOOR WITH FULL bellies. Atlas had run off to the Fire Coven, snagged some stew meat and breads and cheese, claiming he'd put it on Torryn's tab, and the moment everyone was stuffed, their eyelids grew heavy and one by one, they fell asleep, listening to the captain blow on some strange instrument he kept in his pocket.

I spent the night below the moon, stroking the fur of my familiar and wishing we had the bond we once did. They didn't know. None of them did. We could complete the seance for the wraith, get the information to stop the Harrowing and save the remaining witches, but then where would I be? The wraith's heavy words sat like an anchor on top of my chest. The witches didn't care about the wraiths. But even the wraith had called me a witch. So what was I? I could touch things, though she could not. I could feel. Could even hear a heartbeat, somewhere. Was it Scoop's? Being spirit blessed had to mean something when you were a spirit, didn't it? Did I break the rules because of it? Even still, would they perform the same ceremony for me when this nightmare was over? I stared up at the stars, repeating the recipe over and over in my mind. It could be my deliverance.

The chatter of voices outside the cottage woke Atlas early. We'd shaken Nym awake, grabbed the seance items we needed from the shop, and headed toward the floating isles of the Whisper Coven before anyone else stirred. Time was ticking, and we only had so long until another of the coven leaders got too brave and tried to bring down the world.

38

RAVEN

I jerked awake, shoving the blanket off me with my heart racing. The world tipped to the side as I sat up too fast and nearly lost my vision. That single stroke of disorientation sent a wave of pain directly to my brain. Instinctively, I reached for my nose and, when my fingers came away red yet again, I looked around the room, locking eyes with Eden who'd jumped from her place on the floor to get me a hand towel.

When she knelt beside me, she reached for my head, but I knew what she'd find. Tiny beads of sweat covered my neck, cooling the fever. She'd find them on my head as well.

I grabbed her wrist as she tried to pull away. "You cannot tell him. Not yet. Not until I figure it out."

"And how are you going to do that? A stroke of luck? This is reckless. And dangerous and he needs to know. If something happens to you..."

Her voice trailed off, but the implication was there. He'd never recover. And I knew it. With every part of my soul. We were bonded. Our destinies entwined since the moment his mother had that vision. And as the window of time began to close on us, I wondered if I'd ever be able to tell him. To watch him mourn me before I left this world.

I held the cloth to my nose until it stopped bleeding and cast to send it away, refusing to get up for just a few more moments as I considered my next words carefully. "I need you to promise me you'll give me more time. Once this stuff with the Grimoires and the Harrowing is handled, I'll tell him everything. I don't want him to worry more than he already is. He doesn't need another distraction."

"If it worsens, I will not keep this from him."

I closed my eyes, taking a deep breath as I wiped away any evidence of sweat with the sleeve of the shirt I wore. "Thank you. I know what I'm asking isn't easy."

"No," she snapped. "It's foolish."

"What's foolish?"

Torryn's deep, timbered voice caused us both to jump. We hadn't heard them enter and I was glad they hadn't heard more.

"Chasing dangerous witches hoarding explosives," Eden answered with ease. "But here we are, all the same."

She kneeled down to wake Crow, swiping his hair from his brow so gently, the captain hardly stirred.

Bastian didn't feed into the conversation at all, moving directly to the map still laid across the counter. "Where to this morning, Little Witch?"

"Did you even sleep?" I asked, rising from the blankets, slowly this time.

"We did. Caught a few hours after we got the new barrier in place. It took a bit longer than I remember from last time, but the Moon and River Coven Grimoires are safe for now. We can worry about getting the other books there later."

His voice was more jovial than I'd heard him in a long time. Securing a couple of the Grimoires and taking a night away must have eased his mind.

I leaned over the counter, looking down at the swirls of lines and intricate borders. "Here."

"The isles?"

"I know they hate you," I said, "but I've come to learn they all do, so let's just get this shit over with."

He raised an eyebrow. "Well, aren't you a peach this morning?"

"Something like that." I moved the stones on the map accordingly. "Moon and River are in the Fire Coven now." My heart skipped a beat. "At the castle?"

He nodded, a pure boyish smile on his face. "Wait until you see how it's coming along."

I shared in his joy as if it were my own. "I can't wait."

A twinkle in his eye gave me so much more hope than I'd had in days. "So, where are the others?"

"Well, Moss is still here. Cut off from Endora, we hope. Storm hasn't moved. That's four. Xena is …" I paused, moving a jade crystal. "She's hiding in the Forest Coven. But she doesn't have another book nearby, so at least she's somewhat safe. And the last two are in Whisper together."

He moved, wrapping his arms around me. "So, two more stops and this nightmare is over. Then we can go home. For good."

I snuggled into his arms, stealing a moment of strength from his solid body. Dipping his head, he pressed his lips to my neck.

Lifting a shoulder to push away the tickle, I continued. "We still have to figure out how to announce you're actually alive. And we have to figure out what we're going to do with these witches that want to ruin the world, but other than that, we're golden."

"Piece of cake," he whispered, squeezing tighter, as if he'd never let go.

"As soon as the others figure out the Harrowing."

A low growl escaped his lips as I listed our compounding problems. Something negative sat upon my heart today and I couldn't shake it.

"I'm sorry."

"Don't be. You're right, and it's foolish to let our guard down for even a second." Giant, black wings circled us as he kissed my head and then tilted my head back to kiss my lips.

Finally, my shoulders sank. My heart slowed. The tension building around me faded away. He spun me to his chest, and I stood there for several seconds, listening to his steady heartbeat.

"Everything is going to be okay, Little Witch. I promise."

A hysterical laugh burst from my throat. "Don't make promises to me you cannot keep, King. I may be losing it over here, but I'm still very aware that everything will likely go to shit."

"Give me back your fire. Give me the witch that stood toe to toe with the Dark King and dared him to see her for anything less than the fierce woman that she was. Give me back the warrior that stormed through my castle, sending my men flying as she tried to get to me, to rip my throat out."

"Don't be silly. I wasn't going to rip your throat out. I was going to rip you to shreds. Big difference."

He chuckled and I savored the sound before stepping away. "Let's see this done."

"Any idea which coven the others are in?" Torryn asked, standing near the edge of a small, floating isle in the Whisper Coven.

"No clue. They were gathering pieces for that wraith's spell, last I knew. What's our plan here?"

Grey shoved his hands in his pockets, and I couldn't help missing Bastian's form. I'd seen so much of Grey lately, I'd begun to miss the silver eyes and dark hair. He'd cast the wings in the shop, but it wasn't the same. Not really. And though he could have taken his true form in there, he hadn't stayed long enough to bother.

"I forgot how windy this place is." Bastian blocked his eyes with his hand. "We're going to need you to guide us as close to the Grimoires as you can. Remember that Endora and Dasha are both here with books. Do not cast unless your life depends on it. We'll blend into the crowds and try to listen to the whispers. See if we hear anything about no casting, or the two witches we need."

I crossed my arms over my chest. "You two aren't going anywhere without being recognized. It's a good thing we're on the outskirts as it is."

They shared an incredulous look and I couldn't help my short laugh as I gestured to them with a single hand. "You're literal giants. Practically baby trolls. They *are* going to notice you. It's ingrained in our minds as children that shifters are larger. Plus, they've seen you, Bash. You're not blending in. And I don't need to follow the whispers, I can follow the Grimoires. I know they are in that direction."

Bastian slumped his shoulders. "I can be a little smaller."

"No, sir. You can't." I laughed again.

"What do you suggest, then?" Tor asked, lowering himself to the ground, so as not to be seen.

Bastian and I joined him and I wracked my brain for an idea. But there was only one and they weren't going to like it.

"I'm going to have to go by myself. The Whisper witches keep their cloaks on all the time because of the wind. I can blend easily enough."

"No. Absolutely not. Not with Endora nearby."

"I'll just go investigate. See what I can learn, where everything is, what people are saying. I'll report back and we can make a plan from there."

"Still a no," he said, eyes narrowed. "I will not lose you to something so foolish."

"She's right and you know it, Bash."

Tor's agreement shocked and settled my resolve at the same time. I'd seen Bastian listen and take his advice on several occasions already. But the shifter had never balked at my ideas. Had never turned me down because Bastian was king. He was kind, fair, and brilliant. Level-headed when the rest of us were not. He'd grown on me so much, his presence always inspiring something within me to ground myself. To be calm. There were times when I found myself moving toward him in a room, just to feel that profound sense of tranquility.

I took a deep breath. "This is easy and something I can do. I've been mingling with them my whole life. I've basically trained myself to blend in when I don't. They won't be able to see that I'm missing markings. Any trouble and I'll double back. I promise."

Bastian's teeth ground together as he covered his head with his arms and planted his face to the ground with a growl.

"I know where Dasha lives. I know where they gather. Why can't we just go in hot and fast, grab the books and get out?"

"Bash ..." Tor said, quietly. "You saw what happened with just a few swamp witches."

Seconds ticked by. He knew he wasn't going to win the argument, but he was desperate.

I scooted closer to him and lifted his chin until he was forced to look at me with those green eyes of Grey's. "You wanted the witch with the fire to come back to you. I'm here now. And I'm ready to go. I won't, if you don't want me to, but I'm sure I can do this."

"We have no other choice," he ground out.

I blinked several times, letting those words settle in. He'd conceded. The all-mighty Dark King was letting a little Moon Coven witch go in by herself. Maybe he was a fool. But then I was too, so at least he was in great company.

"Just need to figure out how I'm going to get over there," I said, pointing to the biggest island I could see. Though it wasn't higher than the others, it was bordered with tall trees. There were several bulky isles, which I was sure held the vineyards and the homes of the witches. These small outlying ones probably saw few visitors.

"I can send you to a place closer in. One that's got a bridge. You'll have to follow it around several isles before you make it to the backside where there's a path to get up. They sometimes have guards though, so you're going to have to be careful."

"How good is that lifting spell you have?" Torryn asked, studying the ground we lay upon. "The one that moves things."

"It's as strong as she is," Bastian answered without pulling his eyes from me. "Flawless."

Even full of nerves, even fighting for my safety, he still never wavered in his solid belief in me. If I could have crawled into his arms, I might have.

"Do you think you could move that boulder?" He pointed behind us, near a few trees.

"Sure. Do you want to use it to hide?"

"No. I think you should ride it over there. Get yourself up the wall and into the mass of people with magic instead of the bridge. It'll draw less attention."

I wouldn't be the only one. Though we were far out from the main isles, we could see the small specs of witches, using whatever magic they had to move between the closer isles. Hardly anyone had taken the scattered bridges we could see.

"That'll work for me," I said, moving to my feet.

Bastian stood as well, pulling me behind a tree so we wouldn't be spotted from the direction of the other land masses. "How long should I give you?"

"I don't know. I think you're going to have to wait it out. If I'm not back by nightfall, then there's a big problem."

"I'm not laying on a floating rock all day while you risk your life for a goddamn book."

I pressed my hand to his chest, feeling his racing heart below my palm. Closing my eyes, I took a few long breaths, willing him to calm. It wasn't magic of any kind, only the love between us as our souls recognized each other.

"You have to let me do this. Give me until sunset. If anything happens, I'll come right back. Can you watch me? Like you could in the castle?"

He shook his head. "I only watched you through the shadows. I won't be able to cast them that far away."

"Then I guess you're going to have to have an ounce of faith and a heaping pile of self-control, King."

He moved his hands up my neck, stopping to lift my chin until our eyes met. "If you die, I'll shred this world to pieces. I'll burn it. I'll dig a fucking grave and send it straight to hell."

"That sounds like a lot of work," I teased.

His face fell. "I'm serious, Raven. You die, I die. That's it."

Pressing my lips to his, I grabbed his buttoned shirt, closing the final few inches between us. "I will come back to you. I swear it."

"Don't make promises you can't keep, Little Witch,"

Casting, I pulled the boulder to me, stepping away to lift my hood. "I'll see you before the sun touches the horizon."

He held a hand out to help me onto the boulder. "You'd better see me long before that."

I looked over at Torryn, who lay on the ground staring at the comings and goings of the other witches. "Don't let him come after me until sunset."

"You have my word," he said, dipping his chin. And I knew I did.

39

RAVEN

Steadying myself on a boulder as I pushed it across the open expanse of floating isles with vicious drafts of wind and dirt wafting from the bottom of them was less than ideal. I'd learned quickly not to get too close to the underbelly nor to look down at the angry ocean below. They looked as if they'd been dug from the ground with a spade, the cone shape of the bottom full of long growing roots from the trees that pressed through the upper side. The dangling roots were treacherous, and they would reach for anything that got too close.

I wondered if they would save someone if they fell off the edge of the isle. But then I remembered all the horror stories my grandmother had told me as a child, warning me to never wander the isles. If only she could see me now. She was probably cursing my name from the heavens.

I couldn't grip the edge of the stone to hold on because it was too smooth, too worn down by years and years of ferocious wind. Instead, I had to do my best to hold the boulder steady while still being quick about it. I could feel Bastian's eyes on me, and I didn't want to give him cause for concern. He would have preferred to fly me himself, I'm sure. But that would have lasted two seconds until every witch from here to the farthest isle was on top of us.

Pinching the edge of my cloak to hold the hood up, I approached the first large isle and crested the line of trees. My heart dropped into my belly as I accidentally looked down and realized just how high I was. Any higher and I could have disappeared into the cloud bank.

Lowering myself to the ground, I stepped off the boulder, leaving it buried in the line of trees along the edge of the isle. Standing here felt a lot like how I'd imagine standing in a frying pan must feel. The walls were too high to escape by normal means, and each second that passed pulled me closer to my own demise.

I wasn't sure what I expected the homes to look like. The witches here were ruthless, but the dwellings were simple cottages placed on a grid-like structure with rock paths between them. Nothing seemed sinister or menacing, even as I peered out over the small vineyard, picked clean for the winter. The tangle of gnarled branches placed in clean rows, the trees nearly bare of leaves, the grass mostly dead ... The Whisper Coven wasn't a mystery. It was beautiful.

I could feel the proximity of two Grimoires as if they called to me. But I also needed to know exactly where the coven leaders were and what was happening here before I went back for Bash and Tor. Knowing where the books were didn't mean a thing if they were surrounded by three hundred witches.

I walked with purpose toward the center of the isle, my black cloak billowing behind me as I stepped closer to three witches moving in the same direction. It felt so strange to be alone, surrounded by people. I wasn't sure if any witches hid in their homes. Instead, they gathered in clusters, moving this way and that. I wondered what all the commotion was about and hoped it had something to do with Endora's presence.

"Clara had her baby two Saturdays ago and she says he's already sleeping through the night," the witch closest to me whispered.

"He'll be a lazy bum, just like his father," another answered, waving to someone across the row with a smile that didn't look genuine.

She peered over her shoulder in my direction, and I quickly turned, stepping easily to the side as if I'd not been eavesdropping. I waited a second to see if she would call out to me, but they were too submerged in their own gossip to give a damn about that.

"Hurry! There's bread at Neena's."

The witch that had spoken dragged a small child behind her. With arms covered in markings, one hardly noticed how bone thin she was. How hungry and gaunt her child was. They were starving. Bastian had donated a crate of food and they'd dropped it over the edge of the isle, preferring to die rather than take his offering. Sad really.

The rose-colored glasses at the change in scenery faded as I watched the people passing by me. All were thin, everyone's eyes a bit wild, and none of them traveled alone. Apart from me. I pushed myself into another group of whispering witches, realizing their coven's name was incredibly appropriate.

"Wings and all," the youngest next to me hissed. "Flying through the Forest Coven."

"That can't be true. She killed him. I heard the shifters have all evacuated to the Fire Coven to hunt her down."

I fell back a few paces, enough to hear them, but far enough to keep the attention from falling on me as I listened to the gossiping men with a lump in my throat. Bastian couldn't have been seen in the Forest Coven. The cabin was in the mountains there, but he hadn't gone flying beyond our training session ... Gossip was like poisoning the water and feeding it to your friends. Eventually, someone was going to be hurt by it. It was just a question of who. Bastian wouldn't care if they spoke of his resurrection in secret. No one could confirm it and, when he was ready to reveal himself to the world, he would do it with a reckoning.

The part about the shifters, though? That was proof of how fast the whispers could spread. Having dropped that thought in the Moon Coven only days ago, I couldn't help but wonder who'd carried it all the way here. And if it were here, it'd likely gone further.

As I walked, face cloaked in the shadow of my hood, I wondered what Endora thought. Did she think Bastian was dead? Did she care that the shifters were hunting me? Did she want me for herself now that she knew without a doubt I carried the death spell? She'd killed her own lover, cursing him should he speak of her. She cared for nothing.

"Yes, the Moss book."

I nearly stumbled. Walking past another cluster of homes up a hill toward what must have been a very small market, inching closer to the next group. A blonde, with her hair down to her waist in braids and no cloak, took the arm of her companion. A man with a long, black beard and sunken eyes.

"She must be mistaken," he grumbled. "That book's long gone and anyone that says otherwise is a downright fool."

"I thought the same, but Endora confirmed it to Beatrice. Their power hasn't returned, but they believe it is no longer fading."

I had to keep myself steady when every ounce of me wanted to jerk to a stop, grab her, and force her to tell me more. But that wasn't the plan here.

"I'll believe it when I see it," the man said.

The blonde patted his arm. "Later, then."

He harrumphed an agreement and said no more. As we approached the few stands at the top of the hill, I stopped to see what they had. Some simple crystals, a few decks of cards, twine, fabric in many colors… No food. Not an ounce of the wine they were known for. Each of the items were priced for trade though. Instead of coin, I could get a jar of dried mint for an apple. A new cloak for any meat.

"Quick, grab her," a man shouted above the swarm of people, pointing directly toward me.

I took a giant step to the side, looking over my shoulder behind me as my heart raced, boomed even. There was no way they could have recognized me, but I was in trouble all the same. Four witches with arms outstretched marched in my direction. I searched the crowd, wondering if I could take them all on, if I should let them take me somewhere more private. All the scenarios raced through my head in seconds as I thought of the king on the isle, likely pacing while Tor tried to calm his unbridled rage.

I needed to get close to Endora though, and if this was the way to do it, then so be it. With one goal in mind, I kept my hands to my side as they rushed toward me, but when they raced passed, I spun, nearly taking a relieved breath, until I observed them grab another woman.

"I watched you take it," one of the men said. "Give it back."

"I didn't," she cried, clutching something wrapped in cloth to her chest. "Look around. There's no food to steal here."

The man took the cloth, revealing a slab of cooked roast and lifting it above his head to the crowd. "This was taken from my cart. This woman is a thief."

A small child clutched the ends of his mother's skirt, wailing as the man showed off her meat. I didn't miss the wink he shared with the man next to him as they dragged the lady through the tiny market. I wanted to save her. To protest the unfairness. But they'd discover my true identity if I did that. Sadly, I kept quiet, knowing they were likely taking her to Dasha and I needed to follow. The prisoner didn't risk casting, likely in fear of the whole mob turning on her. For that, I couldn't blame her.

Perhaps that was why these witches traveled in pairs. A friend could vouch for you, a child was far less reputable. Who knows how much she'd worked to gain that meat? What she'd meant to trade it for. The crowd began to throw stones at the woman as they dragged her on. Eventually, the child let loose and ran backward, as fast as his legs would carry him down the hill. Hopefully to get help for the woman whose screams still filled the air.

Shoulders pushed into me as the crowd grew more intense, growing as we passed more and more witches. A lynch mob, before the woman had a chance at a defense. The stones grew bigger as she thrashed back and forth, trying to rip free of the man's grip on her brown hair.

"A shifter and a wraith, working together, I swear," a man with red hair said, trying to weave his way in the opposite direction of the crowd.

I paused, people slamming into me as the words swirled through my mind. It couldn't have been. But then what were the odds he spoke of anyone else? I needed to follow the woman to see if they were taking her to the coven leaders, which oddly enough, was not the direction of the Grimoires. But if these other witches were going after Kir, Nym and Atlas and I could warn them, or save them somehow…

I shifted back and forth, watching the man with red hair slip through the crowd. I'd lose him in seconds at this rate. I looked back toward the woman being dragged, torn. With a heavy sigh, I turned, following the red-headed man back down the hill. Bastian was going to kill me.

40

RAVEN

Coppery hair was my only target as I tried to push through, curious if he would say anything else. Anything that might mean I didn't need to continue following them.

"You're on your own, Theodore. I'm not messing with a spirit blessed witch today," the short woman beside him said. "Last time we went poking around Emeril's cottage, that fucking bear came out."

"She hasn't got a familiar with her. Just the wraith. She hit the detection barrier."

"And the shifter," another said. "Probably a Fire Coven bitch."

Giving up all hope of finding the coven leaders, I followed them closely enough to see which direction they were headed. My heart raced as I avoided all eyes and hustled along, confident everyone was looking at me. They missed *nothing* here and everyone was an enemy. Even their own.

As the line of trees loomed closer, I realized I couldn't follow them over the edge of the wall without them noticing. Panic set in. I wished I could make myself invisible, like Kir.

They turned though, following a different path away from the edge, but the swarm of witches had also grown thinner. In another fifty paces, it would be obvious I was following them. A thrum of power pulsed through me as I realized they were moving directly toward the Grimoires. Wondering if the others had already been captured, I raced forward, passing the copper haired man as I surged toward the books.

A low, continuous whistle rang through the air as I approached a building unlike any I'd ever seen. Not a cottage, but something made of stone. The doors were merely open archways behind a magical barrier. A circular tube of stone surrounded the building. As the wind filled the holes at the top of the tube, it pushed through, creating the sound I'd heard.

This wasn't a store or a home. It wasn't a gathering place or a place of power. It was a temple. A place to guard the Grimoires. I paused, wondering how strong the barricade might be. Mirroring a few of the crowd passing by, I blocked my hand from the sun rising in the sky and peeked inside, searching for my friends. The inside of the stone building was cloaked in shadow.

I gazed over the scattered crowd, eyes landing on the copper hair I'd followed across the isle. He had turned and was nearly out of sight. I made a mental note of exactly where the Grimoires were and continued on, confident he would lead me to Kirsi. Until I rounded the corner of the temple and realized no one here had been instructed not to cast. No one whispered of it, no one so much as hinted there were books here.

Alarms rang in my head as I started to back away, realizing just how dangerous this place truly was right now. I should scream. I should warn everyone. But I couldn't manage a single sound as two familiar witches came around the backside of that stone building. Endora's long, silver hair swept to her knees as she used her cane to strike Dasha across the face. Dasha fell to the ground, holding a hand out, trying to block Endora's ruthless attack.

"Oh fuck," I whispered, backing into someone by accident.

I pulled my hood up, hiding my face as I apologized and tried to move backward. But I couldn't concentrate on anything. Not as Endora threw a knife and Dasha cast to block it.

A ripple of pure, raw magic exploded through the air in a tidal wave of destruction. It had only been a small spell, something to push the knife away, but it didn't matter. The second that wave of power billowed out, throwing every witch within the vicinity away, I jolted. Realizing I had been the only one not affected.

But then the ground rumbled, the world tilted to the side, witches began screaming and I realized... the fucking isle was falling out of the sky. Not a racing plummet, but we'd hit the ocean soon enough.

Chaos ensued. Witches poured from everywhere. The only thing I could think of as I stared down at Dasha's dead body was the Grimoires. Endora must have had the same thought as she scrambled to her feet, caught my eye, stumbled back for a second and then ran.

The surge of power had shattered the barrier surrounding the stone building. I shoved past the old witch, confident she wouldn't catch up, praying she wouldn't be foolish enough to cast again. Something about my connection to the books had saved me once, but I doubt it would again.

As I ran into the building, my eyes adjusting to the darkness, two witches lay dead on the floor. They'd been too close. Endora screamed behind me; her arms outstretched as if she meant to cast.

"Do it and you'll die," I warned.

"Are you so familiar with death that you can predict it? Have you taken it as a lover now that your precious king is gone?"

"I'm not playing this game with you." I raced for the closest book and snatched it from the golden pillar it sat upon.

"Games, Trials, balls, funerals ... Nothing matters without magic, but then ... my sweet daughter has returned, hasn't she? So will my depth of power."

I lunged for the other book, but again the isle swayed, and I crashed to the ground, sliding across the floor. Endora screamed behind me, the maniacal sound raking down my senses as I turned to see her bony, old fingers close around the second Grimoire and run for the door. The Fire Coven book.

I crawled toward the other side, eager to get out the door, to save myself from crashing into the ocean. Again, the isle tilted and a loud crack shook through me. I looked up, saw the ceiling crumbling, and my heart stopped. A rush of absolute adrenaline poured over me as I fought like hell to scramble over the broken stone floor and surge out the door.

I fell just outside the building, the Whisper Coven book clutched in my arms as the world tilted again. Witches fell over the edge of the isle, sliding down pathways, as houses crumbled. A large isle above me dropped several feet in the air, eliciting a chorus of screaming. The entire coven territory was falling. Magic could be seen in the distance, and I was so grateful the original blast of power had pushed most of the witches far away from me. Especially when Endora's bony fingers wrapped around my wrist, digging in, nails breaking the skin as she scrambled for the second book.

I fought back, pushing to my feet, and leaning as far forward as I could to stay upright. But Endora had another knife in her hands. Knowing she couldn't cast, she still intended to kill me, just as she had Dasha. She held that blade to my throat, smiling as if she'd just won her own freedom.

"The book for your life, girl. Choose wisely."

The ground fractured below me as two towering figures dropped from the sky behind her. My saving grace. Bastian. Not Grey, but my Dark King stood with his expansive raven wings as far as they would reach, shoulders heaving, eyes locked on the knife.

But Tor? His face was no less menacing. No less a promise of death as he stormed forward and yanked the knife out of Endora's withered hand before she could even consider using it. A marking on her collarbone ignited.

I sucked in a breath and yelled. "Run!"

Bastian grabbed me in less than a second and took off for the edge of isle, Tor right behind us, shifting mid-flight as we lifted into the air, leaving that old witch behind, though we hadn't managed to get the Fire Coven Grimoire. The sound of wings beating against the pull of the isle falling at an increasing rate was the most horrifying sound of my life. I didn't dare look down as we got as far away as possible. I simply clutched the book to my chest and buried my face into Bastian's.

"Thank you for coming after me."

"I never was good with following orders, Miss Moonstone."
I swallowed my laugh as I froze. "Oh no! Kirsi!"

41

KIRSI

The low whistle that Atlas let out as he leaned over the edge of the floating isle made Nym take an extra step back. Wind whipped over the top of the small outlying land as much as it had the day we'd come for our Trial initiation. The sparse land provided little shelter from the gusts as the ocean spray, even this high up, still found its way to us, leaving droplets on Nym's cheeks.

"How are we supposed to get to wherever we're going?" Atlas asked.

"How are we supposed to find it?" Nym followed, tying her hair back and patting the satchel along her side. She'd kept Talon close, always. But I'm sure the heights were unsettling to him. They were to me, and I had no chance of falling, or being blown by the gusts.

"Well, I guess I'm going to have to carry you, unless either of you have any other bright ideas?"

Atlas huffed a laugh. And then continued laughing. And laughing. Until tears ran down his cheeks and, if I were human, mine would have been red from anger.

I crossed ethereal arms over my chest as I swooped close to him, the blue from my haunted glow casting onto his pretty, scarred face. "Well then, if you have a better idea, let's hear it."

He stopped laughing and scratched his head, pinching his lips together so another sound wouldn't escape. "We could try a running leap? Might make it in my wolf form."

"I'm not interested in might," Nym said. "I'll go with you Kir."

I hadn't thought it through really. I'd carried a book for ages, but could I lift and carry something, someone, so large? I could carry Nym if I'd had to when I was alive. The pup though, he was a damn giant. I wasn't even sure he was lighter in wolf form.

"Don't look down," I whispered as I scooped Nym into my arms.

"No shit," she returned, clenching her eyes closed.

It took so much of my concentration to lift her off the ground, I'd begun to doubt the plan before I even moved. "Maybe once around this isle first, just to be safe."

She nodded, but didn't say a word as I lifted off. There was no weight. No muscles to strain, no problem lifting or carrying. It was simply the contact. Concentrating on feeling where our bodies connected as solidly as those tiny grains of sand I'd practiced moving on the human lands. I could do this. Easily, as long as I didn't get distracted.

I soared over the edge of the isle before she could open her eyes. Thankfully, the sun hadn't risen, so we didn't have to worry about being seen as we glided between the gaps of the isles, searching. I'd considered the closest large one, but as I circled and found no waterfall, I had to move to the second. Slightly smaller and a bit higher, the pouring water on the back side was a sight for sore eyes as I pressed through it. Nym gasped at the chill.

"You okay?"

"I'm fine," she said, clutching her stomach as she placed a hand against the wall and dropped her head. "Just need to get my body oriented and dry."

"I'm going back for the pup. Don't go up without us."

"I won't." She lifted Talon from her satchel and raced away as I headed for Atlas.

He grinned as I approached, holding his arms out, as if I should just lift him to my hip like a child. I couldn't help my giggle as I shook my head. "I don't think so, Pup. You get carried the same way."

"You're going to cradle me like a baby? What's the difference?"

"Less awkward if we get spotted." I said, holding my arms out.

He looked down and back up to me. "You want me to just jump in?"

"It's no less humiliating for me, wolf. Nym's waiting."

He shook his head and raised a leg. I reached below him and lifted him off the ground.

Hanging an arm over my shoulder, he got awkwardly close to my face and made that stupid grin he loved so much. "If we weren't best friends before, we definitely are now."

I made myself invisible and laughed and laughed at his quiet, high-pitched squeal the entire way to the waterfall isle, stopping under the water to drop him. He stepped away completely soaked, and Nym covered her nose.

"You smell like a wet dog."

He shook his hair wildly, still smiling. "Compliment taken."

I moved past them toward the back of the cave. Just as I'd hoped, there was an access point to climb up and out. I had no idea where it led, but we needed to get up there regardless.

"Is this where we're supposed to do it?" Nym asked, staring at the hard stone surface.

"Behind the veil atop the world ... Any other ideas?"

"Our ghosty is a smart cookie," Atlas said, moving to climb up the rocks.

"Wait!" I yelled a little too loud. "You can't go up there like that."

He looked down at his soaking wet shirt, soothing a hand down his chest. "Afraid they'll throw themselves at me? Good point. I seemed to have left my change of clothes back at the shop."

"No, mutt. You're a shifter. They'll sniff you out a thousand miles away. You're a giant."

"Ah... right."

"What if you go as the wolf and we pretend you're my familiar?" Nym asked. "Kir can be invisible and then it's just you and I."

"I think that's still risky."

"This whole damn thing is a risk," Atlas said, before shifting into the wolf.

"I guess that's our answer, then."

Nym kept Talon secured at her side and lifted the deep hood over her head as she broke the surface and climbed out of the hole in the ground, hiding among a line of dead trees on the edge of this isle. We looked down over the other isle, but could hardly see anything in the budding dawn.

The sun seemed to rise faster this high up, though. One moment the world was dull and gray, and the next, a peach hue cast over the ocean below and the Fire Coven's ashen ground in the distance. Even the clouds took on the fresh morning color. I wondered if that wraith was watching her final sunrise this morning, knowing we were hopefully hours away from getting our answers about the Harrowing and releasing her.

The isle seemed to come alive with the rise of the sun. Maybe it was the smaller size, but it seemed the population was denser than the Moon Coven. I supposed when we held a gathering on Gravana Lake, we did fill the docks all the way around it.

"Any guesses where to?" Nym asked, trying not to be conspicuous, talking to her familiar as a man yawning so loud, he likely woke the neighbors passed by.

"Just go forward and keep your head down," I whispered. "Try to get into a group of people. We need to find a whispering pearl and I have no fucking clue what that is."

Nym answered with a nod, and we moved toward a small cluster of cottages surrounded by trees that would have been hard to see through, had they been full of leaves. A yelp from Atlas was the only warning before I slammed into a barrier. Nym passed right through, but the two of us did not, and the magic laced in the barrier had revealed us both.

It was only a single second, but as I caught the eye of a copperhead man watching us, just before I vanished and Atlas shifted back, I knew we'd been caught.

"Nym," I hissed.

She looked over her shoulder only then realizing the pup hadn't followed her. Making an awkward long circle, she hustled back to us.

"There's a barrier. I think we were seen and we can't get through.

We're going to have to follow along the outside, away from these homes."

"I think we have to send Atlas back," she said under her breath. "They're staring."

She was right, of course. If they had a spirit blessed witch in the Whisper Coven with a giant white wolf as a familiar, they would all know it. None of us had expected the isles to be quite so... open. Watching our back as we vanished into the tree line, we dropped down as quickly as we could.

"This isn't going to work," Atlas said as he shifted.

"It will." Nym's enthusiasm had faded, her words lacking conviction.

"You're going to have to stay behind and probably keep Talon also. We can't hide that marking, but as long as no beast is with you and your hood is up, it'll be easier."

Atlas ran a hand down his face. "I can't let you guys go alone."

"We are full grown women, Pup. We'll be fine."

"So I'm just supposed to sit here?"

"How great are your drawing skills?" I asked, reaching for Nym's satchel.

"You want me to doodle and watch a baby tiger while I sit here?"

I held out two pieces of chalk, one white and one black. "I need two circles drawn on this floor side by side with about an arm's length of overlapping. They need to be as close to perfect circles as you can get them."

He drew in a deep breath, his shoulders slumping. "How big of a circle?"

"Atta boy." I smiled. "Spread your feet apart. A little more. A little more. There. That size oughta do."

"I'm going to make the best damn circles you've ever seen, Wraith. You aren't even ready for this kind of perfection." He squatted on the floor, holding the white chalk as far away from him as he could, and rotated.

"That's quite possibly the worst circle I've ever seen. And it's getting wet because of the waterfall. Try again. We'll be back as soon as possible."

"I hate this job," he grumbled, picking up Talon and sitting on a rock closer to the back of the cave. "There's no such thing as a perfect circle," he called after us.

Nym laughed as she climbed out, swearing he was a full-grown child. I would have agreed, but I knew him. Knew he teased, putting on a show to draw the tension away from the final day. From the truth of sending a wraith into the afterlife. A fate I may have one day. As long as we were successful. But there was another question swirling in my mind. One I dared not ask aloud, only let it sit on the heart I no longer had.

The Whisper witches rose with the sun, worked and spent their entire days outside, and retreated to their cottages at night. They listened to the ocean roar, the wind blow, and felt every ray of the sun. Though I'd loved being a Moon Witch when I was one, I think I could have loved this world, too. Until the screaming on another isle started. Witches moved to peer over the edge, some taking off in flight, some vanishing.

If Nym didn't blend in, she'd be seen, so she followed along with the witches and we watched as a woman was dragged up a hill toward a pillory while a mob threw rocks at her. Maybe the wraiths were nosey bitches, as Atlas had said, but based on the gawking, the Whisper witches were no better. The crowd at the edge of the isle worked their way back to whatever they were doing, clearly not surprised by the attack on the woman on the lower isle.

"Their disinterest is how you know that is not rare," Nym breathed, the tips of her fingers fighting the wind to keep her hood up. "We should hurry."

She walked toward a woman carrying an empty woven basket on her shoulder with a stained apron around her waist and her hair tied up with cloth.

"I'm sorry to bother you, but I'm trying to find a whispering pearl and I wondered if you could tell me where to find one?"

The woman's chocolate eyes moved slowly up and down Nym's cloaked body as she grimaced.

Not friendly either. Noted.

Tilting her head toward a small cluster of carts, she grumbled something unintelligible and continued on. Nym thanked her, though the woman didn't acknowledge it, and moved toward the carts. When I slammed into another barrier, flashing to visibility for a second, I hissed a curse and whispered to Nym to go on without me. Moving carefully around the barrier, the only thing I could do was watch and wait and pray like hell the goddess was on my side today.

She spoke to several of the small cart owners, all shaking their heads or pointing without any sort of exchange happening. After she'd made her rounds, she hustled back to me, brushing past without even realizing I was there.

"Nothing?"

She jumped at my voice but kept moving toward the waterfall. "No. Well, yes. But they won't trade anything but food. I've got a small bit of dried beef for Talon."

"You should have just taken it," I said.

"They're starving, Kir. Look at their bones. Their eyes. These people are suffering. There's too many of them to keep fed. They can hardly keep gardens in this wind, there's no hunting on the isles except birds and fish when they can get them. I'd no sooner steal from my own mother."

She slipped into the trees, lowering herself down once more. When she returned with a small bit of brown paper, I moved backward, really seeing her. She could have taken it. I've seen her swipe things many times over the years. I think we all had when we got a little too hungry or desperate. She was like a phantom. The day we'd arrived at the castle, she'd stolen a pair of my gloves. I hadn't noticed until she was wearing them two days later with that sly little smile on her face. That time wasn't desperation. That was something more. Something fierce and playful. Something daring I'd found so attractive. But she also had a heart. A giant one. And maybe I found that attractive, too.

Before I knew it, she was up the small hill toward the market and back again, a tiny bag in her hand. Her shoulder passed through mine as her back went rigid and she stumbled a step. With a small gasp, she walked up the path in a different direction than the waterfall.

"Where are we going?"

"They're watching me," she said, her voice shaken. "The man said the pearl was basically useless and asked where I'd gotten the meat and when I lied, he flagged down another. They couldn't understand why I'd traded something of such value for something worth nothing. I stepped away before he could get there, thanking him."

I glanced over my shoulder. They could have snagged her and there was nothing I could have done about it.

"Jump over the edge of the isle. Now."

"What?"

"Run and jump. I'll catch you, I swear."

"I can do many things, Moondance, but that's not one of them."

"Thief!" someone boomed from behind us.

"If you trust me at all, you have to run."

And so she did. Spinning on a heel, she dashed for the tree line as a mob of witches moved toward her. I rushed past her, trying not to notice the tear that slipped down her cheek as she took that final step and leaped over the edge, a trail of dirt falling below her as she held back her scream with her eyes shut. She landed with a plop and I dashed to the left, toward the waterfall before the growing crowd made it to the edge and saw her.

Pushing through the water, Atlas stopped us with a panicked yelp. "Don't drip. Stay back."

"Shh!" I warned, gesturing above us as angry voices yelled from a distance, pouring down the opening.

Setting Talon on a small ledge, he pointed toward the ground where two nearly perfect circles had been drawn in black and white chalk. Leaving Nym near the entrance to pull off her dripping cloak, I moved into the cave, gathering the items from the satchel.

"Let's get this done and get the fuck out of here. If I never come back, it'll be a day too soon."

"Agreed," Nym said, slipping off her boots to move without dripping water.

She held her hand out to Atlas and when a tiny, pearlescent gem dropped into his palm, his eyes doubled.

"We did all this shit for a regular ass pearl? The shop had a jar of these on the bottom row shelf by the door."

"Okay, first, creepy you know that and second, it's called a whispering pearl, so it must be different. They didn't think it was useful, but that doesn't mean it isn't. This spell is rare."

He sniffed the pearl and shrugged. "Looks the same, smells the same. It's the same. That wraith was fucking with you."

"Was she?" The haunted voice from the Fire Coven echoed off the walls as the wraith surged out of the flowing water, studying the spell circle.

"Have you been following us this entire time, just waiting to pop in and say hello?"

"The wraiths are a network of watchers and whispers, Wolf. There was no need."

One moment they were standing there, the next, the isle jerked sideways and Nym slipped, her feet still wet, sliding toward the gaping hole the waterfall covered. She screamed just as Atlas lunged, snatching nothing more than her fingers. He held tightly, trying to pull her back in, but Talon was not so lucky. He slid with tiny claws digging and scratching the stone, desperate to get a hold of something. Watching that white tiger fly past Nym and tumble down wrenched something inside me I shouldn't have felt.

It happened in slow motion. She looked at me, horror stricken, then down over her shoulder toward the falling feline, then to her fingers barely holding Atlas. In one movement, one single second, she let go.

42

KIRSI

The vibrating scream of the wraith from within the cave hidden behind the waterfall was nothing compared to the sounds outside of it as the isles all around us began to sway and drop. Witches everywhere were tumbling, falling off the isles. Not just ours, all of them. Something had happened, but I couldn't focus on that, couldn't think, as I dashed for the ocean, flying past Nym.

When she landed in my arms, having caught Talon in her fall, her fear was my fear, her heart was my heart. The life she'd nearly given to the ocean was my life. I'd almost lost her and, as she trembled in my arms, not crying, but wracked with fear, I knew the question I was going to ask the wraith had changed. I no longer wanted to leave this world with the ghost, I wanted something more. And I think I always had.

The axis of the isle had shifted. I floated around the waterfall, and reentered the cave, flying all the way to the back before setting them down.

"We must hurry," the wraith demanded. "The isles are falling."

"Fuck the spell. We have to get out of here," Atlas said, gathering the items he'd laid along the floor.

"No!" the wraith screamed, surging forward to steal the pearl. But her hand passed through it. She could not touch it. She whirled to me. "Do you see? This is what I said would happen. No one cares about the wraiths enough to set them free. No one will save you from this misery of an existence. You are doomed for eternity, just like we all are."

I paused. Frozen entirely for one second. Two seconds. Nym moved to my side, reaching for my hand. "We will do the spell."

"No," Atlas raged. "We'll die in this hole."

"We have to try to save her," I said, my eyes pleading with him.

We couldn't do it without him. The spell required one shifter, one wraith, one witch. If he crawled up that hole and left us behind, we couldn't go on.

"I'll release you, Kir. I swear to you. If this is what you want, I will find a way," he said, sadness in his voice. "You won't be left alone here. I know that's what you're worried about, but I won't let it happen. And we can find another way to get the answers for Nym. I'll search the entire world for answers. I swear it."

"Atlas," I whispered, moving toward him. "We have to do this. We don't have time to wait, and you know it."

His massive shoulders rose and fell as he clenched his jaw. "Fine. But do it quickly. And you have to answer the Harrowing questions first," he said, turning toward the wraith.

Her eyes glowed from within. "No. You must place the items first. I will not be fooled."

"Then we aren't helping you," Nym said, casting until Talon was full sized. "You can take your answers and be damned to haunt this world forever."

I moved my fingers into phantom hair, frustrated. "No. This is exactly what is wrong with our world. No one can trust each other. I'm not going to be part of that anymore." I turned to Atlas. "You know how much you mean to me now. I hate you, but I love you. And every witch that condemns you for who you are is missing out on loving you, too." I turned to Nym. "I've loved you since we were seven and you cast a snake, sending it up Zennik's pant leg and forcing him to his knees. You are fierce and loyal, but you are also loving and would never see someone suffer if you can save them. We can save her."

The isle jerked to the side and the two corporeal beings jerked their hands out to steady themselves as the sound of Talon's claws scratching the rocky surface made me shudder.

"Make the circle," Atlas whispered.

I could feel a steady heartbeat now. Not a phantom feeling, nor an echoed sound. It was there, truly. And those quiet words from Atlas nearly broke me.

Nym took two steps forward, placing the seed first at the northern point of the circles. The pyrophytic plant seed would only activate once covered in flame. She lifted her hand to cast, but the isle shifted again, sending the three of them tumbling.

"Damnit," Atlas yelled. "Faster."

He grabbed the waterfall stone and placed it closest to the waterfall. "This isle is falling. If it goes again, this is going out the fucking entrance. And then we move, spell be damned."

"Agreed," I yelled over the commotion outside, grabbing the whispering pearl and screaming as it seared my palm.

"Oh, you can't touch that," the wraith said as she watched us scramble. "It's for the living only."

The isle dropped several feet this time and with it, my composure. "Thanks for the fucking warning, asshole. If they drown in here, no one is going to be left to save you. Do you want to be freed or not?"

She swept around the room, looking out the cave entrance, the waterfall now completely gone. "Desperately."

Nym grabbed the pearl and held it in her hands. "Move into the center, where the circles intersect, and I'll begin."

The wraith did as she was told. Atlas took his spot on the floor next to the fireseed and Nym cast once more, a golden hue of her magic filling the room as she placed the whispering pearl below the wraith. Reaching into her satchel, she pulled out the dried fig, moon water, and earthworms. Each item was rushed into place and, as if the world felt the seance initiate, the screams from beyond silenced. The room sealed with magic. The world outside dropped again, but this heavy spell felt immune, though I knew it was not. Nothing moved. Nothing shifted. The power of the spell circle was electric.

"Answer the question," Nym demanded, her eyes beginning to glow with power.

"Say the spell first," the wraith countered.

"No." I shifted toward the ethereal being. "You will answer. We're all here, risking our lives and to help you. It's time to follow through with your part of our bargain."

The ghost looked down to the pearl and back to Nym before she turned to me. "The Harrowing can be stopped. Though several more innocents will likely die before you can manage and there's no way to save your friend other than to hurry. Those that cast the spell must *all* be killed. Their blood gives life to the curse. Take away their lives, take away the curse. That is the answer you seek."

Dread fell over me as I realized what she was saying. Endora would have to die and there was a good chance Nym would go before her.

The isle fell into complete free fall and Talon hunkered down at Nym's feet. Within seconds, we crashed into the ocean.

"A spirit held and thrice released behind the veil atop the world. Unbound of spirit. Unbound of heart. Unbound of mind."

Water seeped into the room, locked beyond the barrier of the spell, but rapidly growing. The wraith spread her hands, waiting for the spell to ooze over her, a smile on her lips. I wanted to be strong, to push away my desperate curiosity, but as half of the ghost vanished, knowing she'd be completely gone in less than a minute, I surged forward, into the circle.

Nym screamed and Atlas growled in frustration.

"Can I become a witch again? Please, if you know, you must tell me."

The pull at the bottom of my form was immense. A sliver of blissful peace crept upward. I pushed away the desire as I reached for the wraith, failing to grip her ghostly hair, wishing she would look me in the eyes.

"Answer me!"

"You'll need a much older wraith for that answer, witch. Seek Meliora within the cliffs of Fiannah."

"Why do you call me a witch?" I asked as I realized I couldn't hear Nym's scream.

"Not a *witch*, girl."

"I don't understand."

She laughed, pushing me out of the circle, that pull on my lower half being sucked away. "You have never been a wraith. You are simply a wish."

43

KIRSI

All this time. All this time, I'd thought I was just like them. I'd seen the differences and not seen them at all. I refused. In many ways, appearance mostly, I was absolutely a wraith. But I also wasn't. I was a wish. Raven's wish. Somehow that made being here less like a jagged knife in the heart. Whatever the rules were for me, I *could* feel things. I *did* care when it was so obvious the wraiths were lacking such a depth of emotion. Their only solace in this world was gossip. We were not the same.

The spell circle dropped, and water rushed over us, bringing me back to the present disaster. The isle was sinking.

"I'm going to bring you back to life just to kill you myself, Kirsi Moondance," Nym shouted, wading in water that rose to her chin. "If you want to leave so badly, then you should have just gone."

The hurt in her voice was devastating. She hadn't heard what I'd asked the wraith. Hadn't heard the answer I was given. She thought I wanted to leave her, and I didn't have time to correct her as she moved toward the upper hole to leave the cave.

"No time for threats," Atlas roared, swimming in the rising water that sat nestled under his chin. "Up. Get up and out of here, now."

I shot straight through the ground, circling to help them out of the hole. Talon went first, his great claws digging deep valleys in the dirt as he pulled his soaked body from the cave ceiling. Nym came next, struggling as she fumed, but managing as Atlas pushed her from behind. By the time the pup got himself free, the top of the island was sopping wet. It was sinking into the ocean, and we were the only ones left. The waves crested, shoving into their legs as we raced for higher ground.

"Take Nym and get the fuck out of here," Atlas yelled as they ran.

Nym cast, leaning down to scoop up tiny Talon.

"I can take you both," I shouted over the crash of waves.

"No," Atlas yelled. "This isn't just a few hops from isle to isle, Kir. It's too dangerous and you have no idea how much you can handle."

"I can do this," I insisted, stopping in front of him.

He shook his head, ashy white hair falling across his scarred brow. "No, Kirsi. I won't negotiate. Take Nym and go."

"Atlas," I began.

But instead of listening, he shifted into that beautiful white wolf and darted away, leaping into the tumultuous ocean. The pull of the isle sinking to the bottom of the sea would drown him. But I couldn't leave Nym behind to save him, either. My newly discovered heart shattered into a million pieces as I surged forward, scooped that angry witch into my arms, and lifted her off the isle.

She tried to push at me, to scream for Atlas, but I hardened my resolve and raced for land.

"You were going to leave. You don't get to save me after you were going to leave me again, Kirsi Moondance," she bellowed.

I looked down, trying to see the snowy fur somewhere below as we moved. "I wasn't trying to leave you. I was trying to stay."

"What?"

"I'll tell you about it later. Help me look for Atlas."

We screamed his name over and over as we moved across the top of the sea filled with debris and drowning witches, swimming for their lives, though the sinking masses of land sucked them below like a wicked undertow. The dirt from the isle churned in the water, turning everything brown.

With our heads down, eyes squinting as the sun reflected off the water, we almost missed the black wings that soared in our direction. Cradling Raven in his arms, Bastian coasted beside us, his wings stretched so wide, I could hardly hear him over the sounds of the flapping. He'd revealed himself, then. As alive as he ever was.

"Tor's missing," he shouted. "Where's Atlas?"

I couldn't help the way my voice cracked when I spoke his name. "Atlas... is in the water somewhere."

A woman directly below me screamed as the roof of a home pushed over the top of her. She tried to hang on, to climb on top of it, but she wasn't strong enough and was gone within seconds.

"We have to send these two back to Crescent Cottage. I can cast a door, but you'll have to jump," he told Nym.

A flush of green crossed her face, but she nodded subtly, blocking her eyes to see over the unforgiving sun. Trying to find a white wolf in a raging ocean filled with debris while staring at the glaring sunlight's reflection would be our downfall.

"Wait! Raven, can you calm the wind?" I yelled. "Or bring in clouds to block the sun so we can search the water?"

Bastian beat his wings several times, lifting them higher. I hadn't heard her reply, couldn't feel the wind to know if it had slowed. Only by the calmness over the sea did I notice the change. The witches in the water, crying out in relief, with one less battle to fight. Gray, billowing clouds moved in, covering the brightest light.

"They won't hold," Raven yelled. "It will either start to rain or they will dissipate, but that's the best I can do."

Bastian cast a door below us. Peering down, I could see the wooden plank floor of Crescent Cottage. I swooped.

Before Nym leapt, she reached for my face. "Find him. Whatever it takes."

"I will," I promised as she dropped into the shop.

Raven followed, her black cloak billowing as her arms stayed clutched around another Grimoire. Two books were in our store. I hated the thought of anyone being there with them after seeing what had happened with the isles. Someone had cast and decimated the land. It was the only explanation. But it was not just the land that had suffered. The death count only continued to grow. And while most

Whisper Coven witches could use magic to move between their scattered islands in the sky, that didn't mean many of them had the power to see them safely across the ocean.

"We should separate. Cover—"

Bastian jerked to the right, pulling in a wing to dodge a spell cast in his direction.

"You did this," someone shouted. "You have always condemned us and now you've come back to see us—"

I snatched the fucker from the water, giving him a moment's reprieve from swimming before racing toward the sky.

"Kirsi," Bash yelled, soaring after me.

But I would not be deterred.

"If after all of this bullshit you're still too blind to see the truth of your fucking coven leader, then you can go directly to hell."

I released, watching that asshole fall and fall until he was seconds from crashing into the ocean. A door appeared below him and he vanished into some other world. Saved by the king he so quickly attacked.

"Now is *not* the time," Bash said, before going completely still. So still, in fact, he dropped nearly into the water before opening his wings.

"Someone cast on Tor. That's the only reason he could be missing when he could have flown out of danger. His feathers will look black in the water. You go that way and I'll go this way. Meet me in the middle," he said, dividing the debris in half with his hands.

There wasn't an option for them to be gone. There just wasn't. We'd find them both and get back to safety, and that's all there was.

They're alive. They're alive.

Repeating the words in my mind, I scoured the clusters of things floating and moving, thinking of the gentle giant, Torryn. Of his deep voice and soft smile. The way he held onto Atlas on a raging ship caught in a storm and never faltered.

If Torryn saw Atlas in the water, he would have gone after him. It would absolutely be another reason why he was missing. I whipped around, searching the sky for Bastian, hoping he hadn't put himself at the mercy of the witches floating on top of the debris. A small fleck of black wings swooped low. Sparks of magic flew through the air toward him. The Dark King, as I knew him, had to be using all forms of self restraint not to fight back. Too worried for his friends, he cast his shadows below him, sending them surging over the water to blind the witches.

I turned again, diving into the water, but I couldn't see through it with all the dirt from the isles. Resurfacing, convinced it was too late, I almost didn't hear the whimper. The slight sound of a pup, running out of steam.

"Atlas," I screamed.

I couldn't see him. He was there, right there, somewhere, and I couldn't see him.

Surging high above the water again, I did another sweep, listening. Not a sound this time, but two stunning light blue eyes met mine. He was vertical and sinking, already beneath the surface, arm reaching for me, his beautiful face disappearing as the fight began to leave him.

I dove.

Never in my life had I prayed to the goddess as hard as I did in that moment, wishing for time to slow, for the fucking ocean to recede. Something, anything, to save him. Slipping into the water, I concentrated as hard as I could as I wrapped my arms around his, our chests pressed together as I pulled against the drag of the isle below us, begging and pleading to get him a breath.

He wiggled. Just enough for me to know there was still life within him as I hauled him upright out of the water, his long body covered in mud. But it was not the wolf that terrified me in that split second. Not his lack of fight. He'd be okay. He had to be okay. Instead, it was Torryn. The strix looked like he'd been half beaten to death, feathers missing, his beautiful tail half gone, with a single talon wrapped around the muddy tail of the wolf.

He slipped. Only inches, but enough to know I could not haul them both to shore, still miles away. Atlas' whimper in my ear spoke more than words. He feared the same. The life of his friend was slipping away. A spell struck Atlas in the stomach. He flinched as I moved and Tor fell several more inches, mostly limp and hanging upside down, but still holding on.

Another spell. A yelp. And then he was gone. Falling and falling back into the ocean.

"Torryn," I yelled, diving, though I knew I couldn't catch him. Not without dropping Atlas.

These witches deserved to die. Every last one of them that had somehow managed to survive the fall. They were not the saviors of our future. They were not going to be swayed to peace. They were simply the ruination of it all.

I couldn't look down. Couldn't see that powerful man hit the water and leave this world behind. Couldn't look into Atlas' face and see the strike of pain as his friend was lost to us all. But black wings descended. Bash dove, flying through the air faster than I'd ever known possible, crashing into Torryn with outstretched arms, the billowing of shadows below. And then he climbed and climbed until we were side by side. He didn't say a word. Didn't look down to the limp birdlike body in his arms. He simply tore off toward the horizon on a prayer.

44

RAVEN

They didn't use the magical doors. Too afraid to have power anywhere near the books, Bastian and Kirsi dropped out of the sky, landed in the back garden, and kicked the door down in a fury. Kir dropped Atlas onto the blankets laid out on the floor. Though not wet, he was completely covered in dirt.

Bastian, though? He stormed across the shop, sweeping a hand over the counter to throw the dishes to the floor before laying a beautiful limp bird upon the stone. The sound of the glass clattering to the floor, some breaking, some not, shot a pain through my mind. I spun, grabbing my temple as if it would save me. Thankfully, my nose did not bleed this time.

"What happened?" Eden swiped a hand over Tor's face.

Bastian brought a fist to his mouth as he took two steps backward, shaking his head. "We have no idea. Witches were casting, they were drowning, he was attacked by someone… it's hard to say."

"Magic," Atlas said, limping toward us, holding his side. Blood seeped through his fingers, mud caked his hair, and the scar on his face could hardly be discerned through the other scratches on him. "A fuck ton of magic all at once. I jumped in the water, saw all the witches attacking him. I tried to get him, Bash. I swear I did."

Eden reached her hand forward, hesitated for a second, and pulled it away. "Get the Whisper Coven Grimoire out of here, right now." She crossed the room, snatching the book I'd left on the counter, and placed it into Bastian's arms. "Take it to wherever you've taken the other books."

He barely registered her words. Had hardly moved, unable to take his eyes from Tor.

"What is it?" I asked.

"Feel him," she said, jutting her chin toward the shifter. "He's got so many spells cast over him they're fighting to complete. One goes off, this whole place is dust."

The moment sank into my bones like an anvil. Glancing over the back wall of the shop, I gulped down my fear as I turned to the Dark King.

"Bastian," I said, bringing a palm to his cheek to turn him toward me. "Please. Take the Grimoire to the castle. We can help him, but you need to go. Right now. We can't have it near the Moss Grimoire."

He clutched the book in his hand and stumbled backward in shock. But absolute rage would follow and Goddess help whoever crossed paths with him when that happened. He stepped numbly toward the door with the flame on top.

"He better be alive when I get back," he whispered, then tore off through the door.

It was not a threat. Not a command from a king. Simply a prayer.

"Atlas?" Eden looked down at his wound with an eyebrow raised.

He nodded and she cast, stopping the bleeding from the gash in his head as well as his side. He didn't slump in relief though, only inched his way toward Torryn.

"What's the plan?" Eden asked, running her fingers over several glass vials on the back shelf. "Seeds of life won't do a thing for him. Black tourmaline might help ground him if the magic—"

"Eden," I whispered, taking her hand, though my heart was breaking. "None of these things are going to save him."

Atlas, who'd bent over Torryn's body, jerked upright, eyes pinned on me.

Kir moved in. "Don't say that, Rave. There must be something. We're in a room full of shit. Think."

"I didn't say I couldn't help him. I meant she's not going to find it on the back wall." I swallowed, stepping away so everyone could see me fully. The captain, the golden witch, the missing witch, the wolf and the wraith. "I've seen this before, when I was just a child. There's only one elixir that might save him, and there's a good chance it won't."

"There's no way to get him to the human lands and even then, we'd be leaving him to die," Atlas said, trying to predict my thoughts.

I kept my voice low and calm as I waved a hand, casting. "That's not it."

The entire wall of shelves behind the counter slid to the right, revealing a tiny hidden room. "The reason Nikos came here and destroyed the shop was because he was looking for my grandmother's spells. The ones that had secret family recipes and used magic only a few could wield."

I swiped my hand again and waited as a small glass vial floated across the room, landing in my waiting palm. The wall slid shut and I locked eyes with Kirsi. We'd sworn we'd never tell anyone of these spells. She nodded, hope rimming her eyes as she inched closer to Atlas. None of them had a clue what was coming. Neither did I.

"We will not do this unless it's unanimous. Right now, Torryn's been blasted with so many spells at once, none of them can fire. If we leave him like this, he will die. His body isn't built to hold magic. This bottle has an old spell locked inside. It looks like a seed, but it will draw magic like a sieve, straining it through his body one at a time. Each spell cast upon him will still strike. If we're lucky, he will remain unconscious. If we're not, he will wake and the shock alone, whatever they did to him, will kill his weakened body. Anything and everything in between can happen."

Atlas shook his head. "He's too ... he can't ..."

"He is strong," Nym said, slipping her hand into Atlas'.

"There's no other way, then?" Kir asked, staring at Torryn.

"I vote no," Eden said, crossing her arms over her chest. "He'll just suffer and then die. There's no peace in that."

"Then we make our own peace with his death," I said, setting the jar on the table.

"I'd take the pill," Crow said, lifting the bottle to shake the seed within. "If given the choice, that is. Wouldn't want to waste my last shot at life on a fear of the inevitable."

"I'm not voting for his death, so I say we give it to him," Nym said.

"Atty?" Kirsi whispered. "He's like your brother. What do you think? I'll vote however you do."

He glanced over at the Fire Coven door and back to the lifeless shifter. Rising in stature, he closed his eyes. "We save him. By whatever means necessary. He can kick my ass later and I'll thank him for it. As long as he lives through whatever happens."

I took the jar from Crow and placed it into Eden's hands. "It's the only chance he has."

She sank back into a chair with the jar like it weighed a thousand pounds. Her hesitation was warranted. She loved Torryn. Had spent so many years with him in the human lands. If he didn't live, we'd watch him suffer his final moments of life.

Seconds turned into minutes, the focus of the room shifting from Eden back to Torryn. Atlas fell over him, sobbing, while Kirsi and Nym tried to console him. It might as well have been his funeral.

I spent those moments remembering all the things that made Torryn who he was. He was the voice of reason, a guiding father figure to Bastian after his own father had died. He was their family. But then, looking around the room, to the way my best friend clung to the wolf, I realized *our* family had shifted.

It wasn't just the two of us against the world anymore. Our family was what we made it. Who we chose to let in and love and protect us. And that included the drunken captain who'd fought his way through a storm because he loved a woman enough to see it through. A golden witch who'd fallen in love with another and, though she'd changed, their hearts had not. A clan of three shifters who were fierce and loyal to a fault. And a witch who'd sacrificed her own freedom to try to make the world a better place. We were a broken, ramshackle, pieced together group, but we had each other and every day our bonds were tightening.

Eden rose, setting the bottle on the table. "Okay. But I won't be able to watch it."

"Watch what?" Bastian's dangerous voice rolled up my back as he entered the shop, shadows billowing below him as if he needed them to take the edge off or he'd lose it all together.

I explained the spell to him and watched as hopeful eyes turned dark and doubtful.

"Do it," he commanded. "He'd save each of our lives every single day if he had to. We will do the same."

I took the jar and closed my eyes, using my amplification spell to activate the magic trapped within the outer shell of the seed.

"The spells will strike one by one, and I have no idea how many. This won't take long, but it'll be hard to watch."

Bastian cast a new door in the back. "Everyone goes. I'll stay with him."

"I'm not fucking leaving," Atlas growled.

Kirsi didn't budge. "I'm staying with the wolf."

Eden, Crow and Nym stepped through the door and into the mountain side cottage. When Bastian lifted an eyebrow to me, I simply moved to his side and took his hand. "Not on your life, King."

Several seconds later, Tor's strix form began to glow bright gold, lifting from the table on its own.

Kirsi pinched her face in disgust. "Someone cast that to show everyone else where he was."

Torryn shifted into his human form, still glowing, still floating above the counter. Then back to the strix and back to the giant man again, his layers of clothing slashed as much as his body in bird form. My stomach turned as something snapped. And then something crunched. His fucking bones. Tor wailed and dropped from above as a man, slamming hard onto the counter.

"Fuck," Atlas said, willing himself to breathe.

I buried myself in Bastian's chest and he held me, though he trembled. Torryn was suffering, the moans coming from him were something from nightmares. I should've never opened that wall. Should have never suggested this form of torture. I couldn't even think of what must have been going through the others' minds as they watched his bones break, reform, and break again and again.

"How much longer?" Bastian asked, his voice cracking. "It's hurting him, Raven. It's hurting him."

"I don't know," I whispered, though I wasn't sure he could hear it over the deafening snap of Torryn's spine.

Atlas roared, hopping onto the counter and throwing his arm over the shifter's broken body, apologizing through his sobs. Kirsi flew to the ceiling and floated back and forth as if she were pacing in her own way, those eyes never leaving Torryn. I stepped to the side so Bastian could join them, taking Torryn's hand as he gripped Atlas.

I cast, doing what I could to help mend his bones or ease the pain. With power unbound, I was stronger than I once was. Maybe something would help. Though it was hard to tell beyond the screaming and the disgusting sound of a body literally breaking. Spell after spell wracked through him and we took turns trying to comfort him, and each other, as we waited.

Torryn began coughing violently.

"Turn him over," Bastian demanded.

They rolled him on his side just as an immeasurable amount of water poured from his mouth. It flowed as the spell ran its course, until it turned to a thick, black tar. He coughed until his eyes opened, tears falling.

Atlas swiped his hair back. "You're fine, Tor. It's all okay now."

"Alec?" His voice was little more than a croak, throat raw.

"No, buddy. It's Atty. And Bash is here."

"Right here, Tor," Bastian said, kneeling to look into his face.

But Torryn couldn't see them. Couldn't see the shop or any of the chaos. His eyes were lost in another world, another time, an illusion that would cause him more emotional pain than the physical damage as he once again called his dead lover's name.

"Alec, please. Don't be mad."

"Nobody's mad, Tor," the wolf said, laying his palm on his brother's face. Because maybe they hadn't really been brothers, but they'd earned that title.

Kirsi drifted down from the ceiling to rest her head on Atlas' shoulder. "He isn't here, Pup. He's a million miles away. It's another spell. I'd guess one that takes him back to one of his most painful memories."

Atlas shook his head. "No. They wouldn't do this to him. Not this one."

"Please. I love you." Torryn shook. "I'll make it right. It was an accident."

Atlas' dark eyes met mine. "It was a training camp accident. Tor was assigned to Alec's little brother. There was an accident and he died. Torryn never forgave himself."

"Damnit." Bastian fell all the way to his knees, leaning in until his nose was on Torryn. "I forgive you, Tor. Do you hear me? It's Alec and I forgive you."

"I didn't mean to," Torryn whispered, tears pooling on the counter as he lay on his side. "I tried to save him."

"I know you did," Bastian said slowly. "Everyone knows you did."

Tor's eyes fell closed, but sobs wracked his ruined body. Bastian cast over him, his shadows doing a full sweep as the shifter relaxed, taking several slow breaths. Another marking glowed on the king's neck, and he too left this room, diving straight into Torryn's mind. If not to bring him peace, then to make him severe promises of revenge.

But those seconds would be short lived as the shifter arched his back off the table, screaming as Bastian stumbled backward.

"What happened?" I asked.

"Something woke him up. Another spell."

Kirsi moved away from Atlas, sweeping back and forth. "Pain."

Torryn's body arched, his shoulders pressing into the counter as the rest of his body contorted to an unnatural angle.

Atlas circled, moving to Tor's head. He stroked his fingers in Torryn's twists of hair as he whispered words we could not hear. He never stopped. Hardly took a breath as he spoke. And all anyone else could do was stand and watch and wait. I prayed the goddess would see this through. Would acknowledge the suffering on his weakened body and grant him the life he fought for. But only time would tell.

When the room fell silent, we held our breath.

"Is it over?" Bastian dared to ask.

I lifted a shoulder, shaking my head, afraid to make any promises. Because even if the magic had been drained, he'd still have to fight for his life. We waited. And waited. And waited. Atlas lay his head on Tor's chest, eyes closed with tears dropping as he listened for a heartbeat. But when his face twisted and he sobbed, Bastian rushed forward, pushing him away so he could listen. Atlas turned away, finding comfort in Kirsi's arms.

"He's not dead," she promised. "He's not gone yet. I would have felt it. I would have known."

"He's barely there," he answered. "How can he fight? How can he come back after all of that?"

Bastian turned, grabbing Atlas by the collar and hauling him forward until they were nose to nose. "You do not mourn him. Do you hear me, Atty? He is not dead and you do not mourn him. You send that energy out into this world and it will harness it and see it through. Don't make me kick you out of here. One mind, one goal."

Atlas nodded with hardened eyes. "One mind. One goal."

45

RAVEN

After hours of sitting with the guys, Kirsi and I moved away to give them space. I would have loved nothing more than to sage the shop. But we'd taken all of it out back so Kirsi didn't suffer during our time here.

We moved like we were numb. Like the world had not betrayed us once again. Torryn's breaths became steadier, no longer shallow and ragged. We ate together, Bastian, Atty and I. We sat a little closer together on the floor than we needed to. Letting the somberness in the air settle over our hearts and into our minds, though we probably shouldn't have.

"Kir," Bastian said, breaking the endless silence.

She jumped at the sound of her name. "What, King?"

"Did the wraith have answers?"

My heart sank at his question. His mind was wrapped in death. He would live through this hell again if the Harrowing returned for me. And though he could do nothing for Torryn now, he'd need a distraction. Two books remained out in the wild. Three if you counted the one the Storm Coven silent witches were holding. But for now, the three books were separated by territories.

"Each of the witches that were part of casting the Harrowing curse has to die."

"Done," he said with finality. "Every damn one of them."

I left, digging the Moss Grimoire out of the back room and setting it on my lap as I settled back in beside the Dark King, his mind in murderous places. We'd kept this book away from the castle, knowing that if Endora would come for any of them, it would be this one first. Opening the fragile pages of the book, I studied the lists of ancient witches, reading through the notes of nonsense and speculations down the side. Suspected affairs and murders. Unrecorded spells and traitors. Not much of note, but history all the same. A distraction. An ambiance of whispers from a sentient book that only I could hear but could not understand.

It'd become abundantly clear that I was connected to these books in a way no one else was. And though I didn't know why, thumbing through the book, I thought maybe I'd finally figured out why I was so sick. Why the human lands were killing me. Coming back to the land with power hadn't saved me. Because I was still dying. Just as the Moss Coven book was dying. It'd been left disconnected from magic for too long. When I touched the other books, they practically hummed with power, their whispers strong. This book though, I could hardly feel anything at all.

Atlas stood from the floor, placing his hands in his pockets. "Who do we have left? I'm over this shit."

I answered quietly. "It was cast by the coven leaders, I believe; one from each coven."

Bastian shook his head. "That can't be the case. The Harrowing began under my rule and I sure as hell didn't take part."

"Then the only witches left are Endora and Xena. Tasa died first, thanks to Nikos. Willow wasn't a coven leader then. We've taken everyone else out just trying to get the books," Kir said.

"There's a piece missing, I know it. It had to have been all seven covens," I said, peeking down at the notes in the margins again. "I can't find it in here, but it has to be."

Kirsi moved toward the door leading to the cabin in the mountains. "Guess we'd better call them back. Check with the only person who might know."

Eden.

Bastian nodded, and she was back within minutes, the rest of our crew in tow. They entered the cabin quietly, all eyes falling to Torryn, who we'd moved to the floor and covered with blankets.

"He will live," Bastian announced. "We don't know the extent of his injuries just yet."

Eden fell to her knees beside him, running her fingers through his long locks of hair and as if trying to find solace for her own heart. She dipped her head and cast, placing her hands over his body. She nodded, lowering her eyes as she rocked back and forth.

I'd understood Eden in the small moments. When she'd prepared tea in her cabin like my mother had. And when she nursed Atlas on the ship. When she'd used her magic to put Crescent Cottage back together because she knew how much it bothered me. When she'd attached herself to an old captain because he had no one else. I hadn't given her enough credit. Hadn't taken a step back and looked upon the witch that always *only* gave to others. She'd given her whole life to try to stop the Harrowing. She was a healer. In her spirit, as much as her magic. She'd saved me with a warning to my mother before I was ever born.

I knelt beside her, placing my hand on her arm. I didn't know if she knew I was dying. She'd seen the illness when no one else had. But she'd also kept her promise and not said a word. And for that, I would always be grateful.

She pulled away from Tor as a tear fell, forcing a smile. "He's going to be just fine."

"You are the bravest witch I've ever known."

She bowed her head again, placing her hand over mine, understanding melting over her. She leaned into my ear so only I could hear the next words she spoke. "We'll find a way to save you, Raven Moonstone. I promise."

My heart cracked. She knew. All this time, I'd kept a careful distance between us, unsure of her and her loyalty, and she'd known. Had kept my secret, even when I didn't deserve that loyalty. I owed her my life, but I also felt like I owed her so much more. I owed her the chance at a life she'd given up all those years ago.

"We need to ask you about the Harrowing. Is it possible it was cast with only six coven leaders and not seven?"

She rocked back onto her feet, standing as she stared off into space, those opposite colored eyes of her focusing on nothing. When Bastian stepped toward us, his face full of questions, I looked away, unable to answer a single one of them. Not yet. Not when he was already in such a fragile state of mind.

"No," Eden answered finally. "It would have had to be all seven."

"But who would have cast for the Fire Coven?" Atlas asked, still standing with his hands in his pockets, eyes watching Torryn.

When Eden shook her head, Kirsi moved forward. "I know someone we can ask."

46

KIRSI

"Who are we asking what?"

That deep, soulful voice of the man lying on the floor was music to my ears. I whipped around, unwilling to miss the look on Atty's face when Torryn spoke. Full of relief, Atlas dropped to the floor, scrambled over the blankets and grabbed hold of him.

When the shifter hissed in pain, Atlas shot away, horrified. "Sorry. Fuck. Sorry."

"Never thought I'd be so happy to see that ugly ass mug again," Tor said with a half-hearted smile.

"Took you long enough," Bash said, his shadows finally lifting from the ground.

Torryn slowly sat up. "I'll try to be faster next time. Do we have anything to drink?"

Eden let out a hysterical laugh as she grabbed a cup of water and handed it to him. "Music to my ears."

After several gulps, he lifted himself from the floor, slowly and with a grunt, but at least he was standing. "Stop staring at me. It's unnerving. Who are we asking and what are we asking them, Wraith?"

"First of all, I'm not a wraith, as it turns out. I'm a wish, and apparently it's different."

"A wish, huh?" Atlas smirked, his scar wrinkling over his forehead. "You look like a wraith, smell like a wraith and definitely have the attitude of one. I'd say you're a wraith."

"Go jump in the ocean again, dog," I growled.

When he winked at me, grinning from ear to ear, I knew the pain he'd just gone through had eased. And though he may never fully recover from the horror, he hadn't lost his spark. Or his joy.

"Remember when Atlas said the wraiths were nosey bitches? Well, as it turns out, he was right. They live for it ... or die? I don't know. But anyway, there's one named Meliora and we're going to have to go to the Fiannah Cliffs to find her."

Bastian rubbed his hand down his face. "Does this just never end?"

"I'm going," Raven said. "I've got some questions of my own to ask, if they are so knowledgeable."

She was hiding something. Behind her forced smiles and overly calm demeanor. She wouldn't make eye contact with me and that was always a clear sign of something wrong. I'd pester if I needed to, but not in a room full of people. She might have been able to keep it from them, but not from me.

"I'm going too," Torryn added.

"You can barely walk," Atlas bit out, all teasing gone.

The shifters faced off, both serious.

"You're not my keeper, little pup. I said I'm going and that's that."

Atlas lifted an eyebrow to Bastian.

The king only shook his head, raising a shoulder. "I don't give a shit who's going where, but it's not happening tonight. We hunker down, get some rest, eat a real meal and start tomorrow fresh. Apparently, it's going to be another full day of murder. I can't handle those days on an empty stomach."

He grabbed Raven's hand and pulled her through the Fire Coven door without another word.

"I bet they're going to—"

Nym slapped her hand over Atlas' mouth and he licked it. Twisting her face in disgust, she pretended to gag and wiped her hand down his chest.

"Keep your slobber to yourself, wolf," she teased.

He wiggled his eyebrows, looking at me. "No wonder you like her so much. She's delicious."

I smirked. "You have no idea, Atty."

"Spare us all the details, Kir." Tor chuckled, leaning over the counter to shift his body weight.

"Still got that salt, Pup?" I asked, inching closer to Atlas as we waited some distance away from the edge of the Cliffs of Fiannah.

Located at the very southern tip of the Moon Coven, I'd never been here. In fact, I didn't know many witches who had ever ventured this far south. There may have been whispers of wraiths, but that was never the problem. The cliffs were dangerous. So high in the air, and a straight shot down to the tumbling ocean where white capped waves crashed into the crags.

Atlas patted his chest, indicating a pocket somewhere beneath his jacket. "Never leave home without it, Ghosty."

Wraiths swarmed the cliffs, darting into a small cove and back out, some coming to float near us, though none of them spoke, only watched. Bastian stepped forward, breaking himself from Raven long enough to request an audience with Meliora.

"You will wait, Dark King," one of the ghosts answered, flying away and vanishing over the edge.

We inched closer to the edge of the high cliffs, looking down over the water as we waited for the wraith to return. It seemed to take hours. In fact, it probably did. The wraiths had eternity to suffer this life, a few hours were nothing to them. Especially to someone as old as they claimed this Meliora to be.

The moans of the wraiths filled the sea salt air as we stared at the ocean. Torryn shifted back and forth on his feet several times. He'd insisted he come and, though no one thought he should, no one argued against it either.

Eventually, the wraith with long, flowing hair returned, a mischievous smile on her face, as several others joined her. "Meliora will see you," she said, looking only at me.

"And my friends?" I asked, crossing my arms over my chest.

She shook her head. "Only you. And the death witch. No one else may enter. Including you, King."

Bastian's dark, silvery eyes found Raven's as he bit back his immediate anger. "This is my kingdom. I will go wherever I please."

The wraith tilted her head slowly, the long tendrils of her hair moving as if they floated in water. "You may, in fact, enter. But if you want the answers you seek, you will not. Only the wish and the death witch."

He took a step forward, but Atlas stopped him. "Let them go. There's no sense in drawing it out."

"Every single time we leave them, all hell breaks loose."

"Yet we're all still standing here," Atty said, staring into Bastian's hard face. "Let them go."

Raven turned to a seething Bastian. "It's just a conversation. We'll be back before you know it."

"If you aren't back in one hour..."

She shook her head. "We're not doing that again either."

Turning on a heel, she stepped forward. "How does a person that cannot fly enter your cave?"

The wraith giggled, it was haunted and dreary and echoed off of nothing at all. "She finds a way."

The beings all vanished at once, the haunted moaning ceasing.

I grabbed Raven's hand. "I'll take you."

We landed inside the dark and dank cave, only able to see what the glow of my body would illuminate. Raven cast a floating flame, but it hardly showed more than black walls, dripping with sea spray and a slippery stone floor.

"Come," a wraith whispered beside us, guiding us forward.

That heart I wasn't supposed to feel beat wildly as the whispers of the wraiths grew to a deafening level. So many chattered at one time, echoing off the tunnel walls, I couldn't follow a single chain of gossiping conversation. They spoke of all the covens, of witches and shifters. Of affairs and old secrets. It was absolute chaos. Clearly the central location of all the wraiths' whispering.

The one we followed stopped short, taking a side tunnel without warning. She raced forward and Raven struggled to keep up, running as fast as she could. It was like the blind maze Trial, which felt like millennia ago. I held the middle ground, making sure Rave could see me while I kept eyes on the wraith, who flew about with haunted laughter. I could always escape. I could simply move through the ground, but Raven would be trapped, should they intend it.

The narrow tunnel grew darker as we weaved through. No amount of growth on Raven's flame made a difference. I missed my connection with Scoop in that moment. He would have navigated flawlessly, and I could trust him. Eventually, Raven gave up and extinguished the magic. Somehow, the lack of magical light made the tunnel a bit brighter, as if the glow from the wraiths was something far more natural here.

"Do you know why you were allowed to come, witch?"

Raven shivered at the words from a being that appeared from nowhere, likely coming straight through the wall. "No. But I'm grateful all the same."

She'd put her shop owner's smile on, used the voice she'd taken with every patron that walked into the store. Though Raven was always kind, very few saw her true self. She never wore her struggles on her skin and confided in almost no one. Still, I could see something was stewing below the surface.

"As you should be." The wraith surged around her, twirling and twirling as if she meant to intimidate the witch.

But she'd gone toe to toe with the Dark King and won. Raven had faced the swamp witches with absolute rage. She'd taken Nikos to the brink of death. She wasn't afraid. In fact, she was more. More than she'd ever been.

"You will come forward and see Meliora, witch. And then we will see how confident you are."

"Lead the way," she said with quiet conviction.

I tried to follow, but another surged forward. "The *wish* isn't invited."

"The thing about me is, I've never taken orders well. In life or death. So, unless you plan to send me back to the afterlife, you can fuck right off."

As Raven disappeared down the tunnel, the wraith's only reaction was a sly smile as he tilted his head. "Follow me, then,"

"I don't think so."

He flew in closer. "I can show you how to listen if you wish to hear your friend's questions."

"Try any funny shit and I'll spend eternity figuring out to pin you to this Earth in an endless cycle of torture."

His eyes lit with mischievous delight. "Consider me intrigued."

"I seriously hate wraiths," I said, rolling my eyes as he turned and led me in a different direction than Raven had gone.

But true to his word, we entered a cavernous room above a cyclone of wraiths circling the high ceiling, looking down on a curly haired, unmarked witch holding her hands clasped behind her back as I'd seen her king do a hundred times. An ordinary wraith, no more significant looking than those surrounding me hovered above a throne she couldn't sit on, looking entirely amused by whatever they were discussing.

"But have you tried? Perhaps it is different on a wish."

"No." Raven shook her head.

"Evangeline, come forward."

A haunted face moved casually through a wall, entering the room as if she'd been waiting for her name to be called. With sunken eyes and a face boasting a permanent frown, the girl inched forward. The lower half of her body in tattered skirts and bone thin legs flowing beneath her in a perfect rhythm as she waited.

"Cast death upon her. See if you can end her misery."

"I will not perform for you or any of your nosey following. I'm not here for placating curiosity."

"I wish it," the wraith whispered, moving toward Raven. "Please."

"What if I cast on you and you have to relive your death over and over because the spell cannot complete on a wraith? What if you're stuck in an eternity of misery because you agreed to be a pawn?"

The wraith moved closer. Afraid I wouldn't be able to hear her, I lowered myself to listen. I wasn't sure if Raven's questions were private or not. She hadn't asked for me to come along, hadn't protested when we were separated. I didn't want her to know I was eavesdropping. Perhaps I shouldn't have been doing it at all, but I needed to know if she was in danger, and hiding it because if she was somehow trying to pacify the rest of us, I wouldn't stand for it. Not after watching her suffer in the human lands.

"I already live an eternity of misery and I am not a pawn. I was selected from a pool of wraiths that were willing to try this. To leave this world and—"

"Are you afraid to cast upon this wraith because if it works and your friend, the wish, finds out she would demand the same?"

Raven stepped backward. "I... no."

Another wraith flew forward, whispering in Meliora's ear. She smiled and continued as if she hadn't heard a thing.

"If you could send your friend back to the afterlife, would you?"

I dropped lower. We hadn't thought about using the death spell to send me back. But if she could... I supposed there was a time I would have agreed. I would have coveted it. Thinking of Nym, though. And Raven. And Tor and the pup... I don't know what I would choose now. I'd lose them eventually. They'd all die and I'd be stuck here. I knew I didn't want that.

"Kirsi is like my sister. If we shared the same blood, we couldn't be closer. I would give her my own life, if it meant she could have hers back." She lifted her shoulder, blocking her ear as if something had tickled her. "You can bring her here right now and I would cast upon her if she asked for it."

"I have other plans for your wish, girl. You will cast death upon this wraith, or I will not answer the questions you have asked."

There was no warning as Raven turned to the wraith and struck her with the death spell. It surged through the room like an arrow and landed right in her chest. Everyone stopped. Even the ancient ghost on the dusty throne inched forward, eyes wide as she stared and waited. You could have heard a spell drop in the static of silence.

The wraith held her hand to her chest and for a second, one tiny fraction of a moment, I envied her. But I was not as trapped as these other wraiths were. I could find another whispering pearl. Wondering if they'd been destroyed in the crash of the floating isles, I looked around, watching the faces of the other wraiths. Hungry and desperate as they stared at my sister. And then I knew. If she could send this wraith to the afterlife, they'd never let her escape this maze. They'd fight the Dark King with everything they had to hold her as a weapon. And then another war would rage. As above, so below, quite literally.

Raven must have realized the same, moments too late as she stepped toward the door, eyes still glued to the wraith. But nothing happened. She'd felt the spell strike her, but hadn't changed otherwise.

"Pity," the old ghost said, sliding backward. "We could have had so much fun together."

The rest of the beings circled the room at a new pace, more determined than ever to unsettle the witch left to the whims of an ancient ghost.

"You will answer all of my questions now," Raven said. "That was our deal."

"Indeed it was, Witch."

"How old are you?"

"That is not the question you truly came here to ask, is it?"

She twisted her hands through her curls. Showing her first sign of nerves, I couldn't help but pity her. Something was wrong and, whatever the burden, she didn't want to share.

Still, she raised her head and dropped her hands. "I'm going to die. I'm connected to the Grimoires and they are dying. The Moss Coven Grimoire is nearly there already. Is there any way to save them, or me?"

I froze. The wraiths circling me, passing through me, concealing me as something within me seized. I wondered how long she'd known, but mostly I was hurt she hadn't confided in me. Maybe Bastian wouldn't have been able to handle the truth, but I could have. And still, she hadn't trusted me.

But how could I be selfish when she was dying? At least for me, there was no time to fear Death. But Raven had taken from him. And when she met him a second time, he likely wouldn't show her mercy.

He'd take her with a fierceness he thought owed and she would have no defense. She was right to fear him. Just as the world should have feared her more than it did.

"Do you know why the witches severed the original Grimoire?"

"Because the witches became so plentiful, the power was diluted, and they thought that splitting the book into seven parts would consecrate the power and replenish it."

Meliora smiled, leaning forward as if she had the juiciest secret to tell and the most captivating audience. "Or so they would have had the world believe."

"Go on." Raven moved forward, playing the role the wraith expected of her.

"Power, girl. It always comes down to wanting more power. Not because the original source was weakening, but simply because there could never be enough. The Harrowing is a curse cast for the same reason. A group of witches eager for more. They did not learn from the mistakes of the past.

"Long ago, a single witch was sacrificed in a spell to split this world. Of mind and body, spirit and sound, of heart and voice and power, the original Grimoire was always seven points of magic. When those foolish witches placed the Book of Omnia on a pedestal directly in the center of this world, they poured the blood of that poor witch over the book as if it were a poison and cursed it seven times until the Grimoire was thoroughly broken.

"Born of deadly curses, how could they have ever expected the power to remain, the books to be safe? That is why they cannot be near each other and the origination of a spell. They are as alive as you know them to be, and they despise the magic that severed them. They are a danger to this world, in their current form."

"How can you know that, if no one else does?"

Meliora lifted herself from the dais, floating over the few steps, moving until she was so close to Raven, had it been me, I'd have moved away. "Because I was the sacrificial witch. I have watched the world fall to pieces every single day since and I have enjoyed every last second of it. I'm done answering questions for the day."

47

RAVEN

My mind raced with a thousand emotions as the wraith had relived her story. I wanted to believe she was lying. That the truth I'd heard my entire life wasn't a falsehood, but the witches were not to be trusted, not even with our own sordid history. Still, I had more questions, and I couldn't let her go just yet. I walked a fine line, pushing her.

"I am sorry that happened to you. I know it changes nothing, but if you want to be released from this world, we can repeat the spell that was cast over the wraith before the isles fell. If you wish it."

The room filled with haunted echoes of laughter. Confused, I searched the dim light for something I didn't see, but there was nothing beyond black cave walls and the racing of wraiths high, high above us, eavesdropping.

"Do you know what a whispering pearl is, Miss Moonstone?"

I shook my head slowly.

"A beautiful product of the isles that no one but the wraiths cared about. Laced with magic of the earth and not from the hands of a witch. They were special to us. Unique in that, they could only be found within the heart of the islands that never truly touched the Earth."

I sucked in a sharp breath, understanding dawning on me. "The isles fell ... the pearls are gone."

"Indeed, they are." The ancient wraith floated backward. "So, you see, the witches disregarded the wraiths for so long, your ignorance has become our eternity. We have no other way to leave this world."

"Unless I can find a way to restore it."

The whispers began again. As if the books finally found a way to solidify their words, though none were near. Creeping up my spine and over my ears. Speaking over the ancient wraith with murmurs that felt like poison. Louder and louder they grew, filling my mind with urgency.

They won't like it.
They won't let you do it.
You mustn't tell them.

Shaking away the thoughts that were mostly within my mind, I lifted my shoulder again, wishing I could block them out. Wishing I didn't know that I'd die soon.

"Something wrong?" the wraith said, mocking me as she mimicked my movement.

I tried to stoop to the level of the wraiths, adding inflection into my voice that imitated that of a gossiping old crone. "I've heard a story that I think even you won't have. I'd love to share it with you, if you have the time."

She rested her hand below her chin, leaning in as another wraith appeared from the wall and whispered in her ear.

"Not now. I'm busy," she said, trying to swat them away.

But when the messenger completed his secret, her face lit with delight as she gestured for me to continue.

"They say the former queen was a clairvoyant."

She waved a hand, disappointed. "Everyone knows that."

"Yes, but did you know she used that skill to bind my power? She'd heard the Harrowing would strike me and tried to save me."

"Yes. Yes. She took you to the pedestal used to split the Grimoires, the one in the heart of the castle, and cast upon you, splitting her own power in the process and binding you to the Grimoires because she'd had a vision. This isn't news."

"Yes," I said, trying to keep my face from reacting to that last piece of information, should she detect the trap and stop answering questions. "She lied to my mother. Told her she was simply hiding my spells so I would resemble a silenced witch. But as you and I know, she had much bigger plans for me. It's interesting though, don't you think? The final piece of the puzzle?"

"Mmmm quite so. But do tell me what your thoughts are first."

I smiled, stepping forward as I lowered my voice. "The seven that cast the Harrowing... ghastly."

"Six and a half, if you ask me. A shame the way it all worked out, honestly. To think she knew and still didn't save herself."

"I know," I said, shaking my head. "I just don't understand why she would have done it."

"I wondered the same, for a while. Witches aren't known for their generous hearts. But the queen was a different kind of witch. Like you in many ways."

My heart dropped into my stomach as she spoke. Concealing my surprise, I agreed. "I believe she knew of my connection to her son, and that's why she agreed to save me. And when she died, so unfortunately, the magic she'd used to bind our power slowly began to fade."

"Fortunately for you, the Grimoire's collective power is concealing those markings. The death spell is a hideous mark on the skin."

"So, I've heard." Using the careful clues throughout our conversation, I decided to throw myself to the wolves and make a guess about the final piece of information I'd needed. If I was wrong, Meliora would know I'd baited her, but if I was right, we could end the Harrowing. "I also heard when the witches killed the queen, they had to cast the Harrowing curse with her blood *before* she drew her final breath. Imagine if Bastian had seen that. Did you know he was supposed to be riding with his parents on the road that day?"

"Of course. His own stubborn will saved his life as he insisted on riding behind them. Was that your story?"

"I didn't think anyone knew that Bastian had seen his parents murdered by the coven leaders. You really do know everything."

She rested her head on her palm. "It's a curse in its own way. Tell the wish she may come forward now."

You mustn't tell them.

Pushing away the voices in my mind, the voices that sounded more and more like those foreign sounds of the Grimoires than my own thoughts, I waited as Kirsi floated into the room behind the wraith that hadn't let her come before.

She avoided eye contact as she came to my side, and I wondered if she'd heard any of it. If she knew I was destined to die. If she'd heard the answer we needed to save the witch she loved.

"Tell me who killed me," Kirsi blurted out, no pretenses or attitude.

"It is time for you to leave this room, Raven Moonstone. I do hope you mind the voices and not your conscience."

48

KIRSI

The door behind me clicked shut and I wondered how often it had been opened, if ever. The wraiths on the ceiling of the cave descended, as I'd expected them to. Moving like a school of fish, they circled the room, far more curious about me than they were of a witch.

"Do you see the stone on the ground below you?"

I crossed my arms over my chest. "Yes. And no. I'm not going to perform for you either, so you can get that thought out of your head. I look like you. I thought I felt like you. I'm told I ... smell like you. But the wraith I released was right. I'm not like you. I am different. I can lift that stone and throw it across this room. I can hold a beautiful witch in my arms and whisper promises at night. I can feel more than sorrow, curiosity, and anger. I can feel my heartbeat. I can feel happiness."

"It is impossible," she said, surging forward to circle me like a hawk. Without warning, she pushed herself through my body, wracking me with a thousand years of sadness and anger before she moved away, eyes wide with wonder and intrigue. "You are different. Only just. But different all the same. Can you smell? Or sleep? Can you taste the delights of this world?"

"I'll answer your questions if you answer mine. And if you ever do that again, I'll spend an eternity trapping every fucking wraith I find in a salt circle for amusement."

"Ah. I spent about ten years of my youth convincing witches to do the same. It gets boring. As all things do."

I couldn't help the twitch in my mouth. She'd been stuck as a ghost since dirt was discovered. Her twisted mind could probably have conjured a better threat than mine, damnit.

"Who killed me?"

Long fingers thrummed together. "It was your lover, of course. She was caught whispering with Nikos the night of the ball. After you'd had your... passionate moment in the hallway and said goodnight."

The heart I didn't have? Shattered.

Nym.

The golden witch that had snatched my heart had pierced it with a stolen blade and never found the courage to tell me. I wanted to crumple. To dive into the floor and never come up again. To let this pain consume me. Tears pooled in my eyes. Real tears.

Meliora moved toward me again, studying my face as I willed those fucking tears not to fall. To let my weakness be my own and not a strain of gossip around the world. But that fiery tear slipped down my face and landed on the floor in a splash, stripping me bare before a room full of beings I would never be like. Exposing the difference between us... that tear was my damnation. I didn't belong here. Or anywhere.

I wanted out. I needed to soar. To move away from the walls that crept in on me, threatening to swallow me whole. To hide from the hundreds of eyes that watched me. But I couldn't move. I was frozen in place and horrified. The spectacle. Always the spectacle.

The old wraith lifted her hands into the air. "Everyone out."

On that single command, the rest of the beings left through the walls of the room, but I didn't trust they were truly gone. The emptiness was a reprieve, though. If not from my own mind, at least the judgment of others. The knowledge that I'd come before them as a fool and they'd all known it when I hadn't.

"Sometimes the most painful stories are the truthful ones. Gossip can be full of lies and twisted tales, but those that shock us the most are the ones of fact. You've come here to ask a different question, haven't you?"

"No," I lied, holding back every ounce of emotion I could muster. But I needed to know. If not for her, then for myself. "Yes."

She simply stared at me with blank eyes, uninterested in my feelings.

"Can I become a witch again?"

She shook her head, something that could have been regret filling her face. "For years, I tried. Confident there would be a way. But there is no path that moves backward in this life or the next."

"Then I am stuck here, like this... forever?" I could hardly manage the words as I begged her for a different answer than I knew she'd have.

"I wouldn't think so. You are a wish. A wish fulfilled should be all that is needed for you to leave this plane behind and go on to the next."

"But we tried." Another tear fell and I raged inside at the betrayal of my own emotions. "I answered the question that brought me here and nothing happened."

She lowered her head as well as her ethereal voice. "Then I am afraid that is your answer."

"That's no answer at all," I whispered as I turned to leave the room, devastated beyond measure.

"One more thing," the being said to me as I pushed the door open and glanced at Raven who'd been standing there waiting. "The Moss Coven leader is pacing outside of your little store."

Her final words were simply a match to the pyre.

The race back to the entrance was winding, dark, and filled with more emotion than either of us wanted to process. Running, Raven looked over her shoulder to me several times before mustering the courage to pry.

"Everything okay?"

"Yes," I lied. "It seems my killer will never be discovered. You?"

"All great. We got the answers we needed. They used Bastian's mother's blood. That's likely why they killed her."

"And you? Are *you* okay?"

"Never better," she lied, facing forward to follow our leading ghost back out of the tunnel.

It seemed we both needed time to process the truths we'd learned. She was destined to die. Soon. And I was destined to stay here for eternity, alone.

49

RAVEN

I wanted to tell her. Should have, even. But I couldn't speak the words aloud, and I couldn't be sure she wouldn't try to stop me. Kirsi could be trusted beyond anyone I'd ever known in my life, but because she loved me so fiercely, she would try to save me. And as the whispers in my mind grew, I knew without a doubt what needed to be done and she would never allow the sacrifice.

I couldn't look into Bastian's eyes and say confidently, when the moment came, I'd make the final move his mother seemed to have donated her power for. Maybe that was the key. Maybe she'd given me her own power to help save me. Maybe I needed to trust her vision.

There was really no time for heart-to-hearts lately. Nor would there be in the foreseeable future. Not with Endora standing outside the barrier of the shop, finally coming for her sickly Grimoire. We could only hope the magic would hold for the moments it would take us to deliver the news and get there. It would only be a matter of time now before she personally went after the remaining books. I could feel them. The thrums of power. I knew they hadn't moved from where we'd left them, but when she was ready, she'd only need to scry to find those outside of Bastian's barrier at the castle.

Four powerful figures stood, waiting for us in a single line with hardened faces as we neared them. I'd have to find the time to tell Bastian that his mother's death was to initiate the Harrowing. But right now, that wasn't the most important thing we'd learned. Kirsi dropped me to the ground and instead of flying to meet Nym, she stayed at my side as I raced, hardly stopping to greet them.

"Endora is at the shop. We have to go."

Bastian slowed down to cast the door as we ran. When it appeared, we fell into a single file line to get to Eden and Crow as fast as possible, ready to attack from the inside. Either way, Endora had to die in order to save every remaining target of the Harrowing. But, with no warning, a searing pain ripped into my head, causing me to fly forward, nearly falling. When we passed the threshold, the world didn't change around us. We stepped through the door as if it were an empty frame dropped into the center of our world.

Absolute horror fell over me as I turned just in time to see my beautiful Dark King clutch his chest and fall heavily to the ground.

"Bastian!" I screamed, shoving the others out of the way as I tried to fight through my own pain and reach him.

Torryn and Atlas were faster, throwing themselves to their knees to get to him. They rolled him to his side as he groaned, shoving them away. I landed seconds later, nearly losing my vision as the world spun.

Bastian reached for me, pulling me on top of him as he rasped. "My magic ... gone."

"Raven?" Kirsi whispered, lifting me from Bastian's arms to look into my eyes. "Are you okay?"

I nodded, pulling my hair from my eyes to look into my oldest friend's face. She knew, too. Maybe not everything, but enough to be worried.

"I'm okay. I can only feel them. That's all."

Her face hardened at my easy lie. She knew the truth and the only thing I could do was look at each of the others and press my lips together, hoping she would understand. But instead, her eyes flicked to Nym and then back to me before moving to Atlas' side.

"Run," Bastian said, gripping Atlas by the collar of his shirt. "Save them."

Shifting, he turned to Kir. "Race you there, Ghosty."

And they were gone. Nym followed, riding on the back of her giant white tiger, barely able to keep up.

"Let me help you." Torryn groaned, hardly in shape to lift himself, let alone someone else.

Bash pushed him away, standing on his own as he shifted to Grey and then back to himself. Most of the time, I was used to either one of them, but seeing the kind face of an old friend in this moment was jarring when I wasn't ready for it.

"Just checking," he said, limping forward. "It's going to be a slow jog the whole way. Endora must have found someone with the power to mute magic."

"I'm getting too old for this shit." Tor shifted and, though he struggled to lift off the ground at first, he managed, still moving faster than we were.

It took Bastian less than five minutes to recover from the loss of his magic. As if it were only an adjustment, like stepping into the human world before he was oriented, though still powerless. But this was a scar far deeper. Something that stripped away the person he was in a land he was meant to rule over.

The pain throbbing through my mind was so debilitating, and by the time we stepped on desecrated ground, I hardly even noticed it. I could feel the loss of my own color as much as I could see it in my palms. Bastian cast worried glances my way, but ultimately stayed the course, sheer determination of a scorned king driving us all the way across the Moon Coven.

But we were not prepared for what we saw. I knew it would be brutal, the loss devastating. But there was not a building untouched. The damage started long before we neared the shop. Most of the aged cobblestones were dislodged from the ground as if an earthquake had loosened them. The entire square had taken damage. Not just the square but everything as far as I could see... If not gone, destroyed. Kirsi floated over the top of the space where Crescent Cottage should have been. Where the floor my grandmother had died upon used to be. The cot I'd slept on as a child, only a memory. The damn doorknob we'd never had fixed... Gone.

She swooped low, grabbing me by shoulders and crushing me to her as I began to cry. The itchiness in my throat turned to a sharp pain I could not swallow as tears raced down my cheeks. The weight of the world fell on me, crushing me. I cried. For Bastian, for myself, for the Moon Coven witches. For the lives that were undoubtedly lost in this devastation. For Eden Mossbrook, the witch I'd never even given a chance to, keeping walls up when I should have let her all the way in and embraced her when I could have; the healer that saved me. For the drunken captain who'd given his final days to a witch locked in a store and had only complained when his drink ran dry. For a tiny black panther who'd been my only solace as we mourned the loss of his witch together.

"I'm so sorry, Kir."

She cried. Real tears fell from her eyes as she held onto me, holding herself in corporeal form, only to provide comfort. Strong arms wrapped around us. I didn't need to look to know whose they belong to. A king of witches, who held no magic. And then the shifter who'd nearly died and the friend that'd saved him first. I waited a beat, pausing for Nym before I realized... she may have suffered her own losses this day, separate from these. She was likely gone already, searching for her family. Looking to see how far this devastation reached within our coven.

"There's no way she caused this much destruction and lived through it," Bastian said, pulling away from the group as he kicked at the ground.

"Help!" Someone screamed, somewhere down the road.

It wasn't even a consideration in our minds. One distress signal and we were running. Racing for the voice. We'd all suffered enough. If we could save one single person from despair at this point, we would. Especially someone who so easily asked for it.

"Where are you?" Torryn growled, pulling at fallen debris near where the baker's shop used to stand.

"Bit further," the man yelled.

Before we could dig him out, another voice cried for help. And then another. We spread out, lending hands to our neighbors. Listening to their stories of what they'd witnessed. As each was so greatly affected, they began to pool their remaining resources. Each witch contributing to the greater good of the community, wracked with destruction.

Endora had come at last, warning all of the witches into the stores as she claimed to be destroying a great evil I'd hidden in mine. And maybe I would have been their enemy, had I not been there to help dig most of them out. To show them I was just as sane as I ever was and whatever stories were being spun, it was none other than the Dark King, tunneling into the ground to help rescue the children and find food for the families.

"Your Grace," Torryn barked from the far end of the square. "Come quick."

Bastian ran for the shifter, myself and several others hastily following, stripped of their prejudices, if only for these moments where who you were didn't matter as much as whether you could help the injured, locate a missing person, or find an extra set of hands.

As we approached, Bastian held a hand up, signaling for the rest of us to stay back. He knelt in the dirt where Torryn pointed, and lifted a large, red stone, brushing it across his chest to clear it of dirt and debris. Having only glanced that stone one time, I still knew exactly what it was.

Endora hadn't found a witch to mute Bastian's powers. She'd destroyed the Fire Coven Grimoire and Bastian held the only piece left of it in his palm.

50

RAVEN

By destroying the Grimoire, she'd annihilated all of the Fire Coven's magic. Each witch living there would now be at the mercy of those with power. Their only safety, found behind the shifters they lived and worked side by side with. It would be enough, for now, but only just.

Bastian, though? Still shifter, but never again able to conjure his wings. Never again able to feel the cool relief of those shadows or the simple means of travel. He may have seemed fine, but I would bet my last crystal the outside was only a hard façade for the fury within. And the absolute devastation as his identity was stripped away.

"Nothing important," he forced out, slipping the stone from his coven's Grimoire into his pocket. "You should all go to your homes. Find your neighbors, offer helping hands and save what you can of yours. When something like this happened in the Fire Coven, it devastated the entirety of our territory."

The witches we'd helped turned away. Likely, we'd never see that level of kindness from them ever again. But people tended to bond over shared misery. Once they became desperate, realizing exactly what they'd lost, this world would be turned upside down. Endora had made the grandest mistake by obliterating all the covens. The shifters were no longer our greatest enemy. Starvation was. And we'd already been so close before.

"What's the plan?" Atlas wiped his hand across his forehead, smearing more dirt.

Bastian slid his hands into his deep pockets. "I don't even know where to start."

"Start?" Kirsi forced a laugh. "This battle has already begun, King. It doesn't matter where we start, we're going straight for the finish. Endora Mossbrook is as good as dead and you all can join me, or you can sit here and mope, but I'm ending this."

The Dark King contained his tremble, eyes glancing to the ground before twisting his neck in anger. "Endora Mossbrook has every advantage."

"She killed your mother," I whispered.

He pinned me with an angry stare. "I know. I was there."

I shook my head. "She killed your mother so that she could use her blood to enact the Harrowing. Juliette Firepool was the seventh witch. If we can take out Xena Foresthale and Endora, that's it. The spell is over. No more witches die by that curse. Nym and I are saved."

"Are you though?" Kirsi snapped. "You're only getting worse. I know you felt the Grimoire die."

I rubbed my hand over the back of my neck, pinching to ease the tension. "Leave it alone, Kir."

She moved behind Bastian. "No. You're not taking care of yourself. What difference does it make if the Harrowing is stopped if you're going to die anyway, Rave?"

"Kirsi, stop this. I'm ... I'm not dying. And this isn't just about me. You're supposed to be saving Nym, too."

Her eyes lit with flames as she glared at me and then vanished.

Atlas sighed. "I'm with Kir. We need a plan. But sitting around here fighting with each other isn't the way forward."

"I have to go check on my parents. Why don't you guys just decide what we're doing and let me know."

"Raven," Bastian said, his voice low and threatening.

"I don't need your Dark King shit right now."

Spinning on a heel, I stomped away, more frustrated with myself than anyone. I could feel those eyes on me, though. Even now, when I spoke to him like that, he was not used to it. He'd commanded his world for so long, to give up control was a physical blow to him. But I'd never played by his rules, and he knew that.

I'd lost everything I'd ever worked for in one afternoon, and I needed time and space to process everything. I thought of the shop, of the home we'd shared as sisters, now tainted with murder. Of the night we'd dropped our blood into the cauldron, nearly too drunk to remember. Of dancing below the full moon half naked and lying in the warm grass summer after summer staring at the stars with hungry stomachs and happy hearts. Of the way she'd always defended me so recklessly, just because she fucking loved me. I should have just told her. I'd been holding so many things from her since the moment we entered the damn Trials. She didn't deserve it. I didn't deserve her.

Bastian hadn't even tried to follow me. I knew he wanted to. Knew the moment I'd spoken those words to him, he'd like to command me to stop and speak to him. To run his fingers down my throat and remind me that he was the one in charge.

My mind became lost in thoughts of him as I approached a half-standing building that used to be my parents' home. My heart dropped into my stomach as I inched forward, then stumbled back. I'd been so unfair to them as well. Hadn't considered Nikos' persuasion would be the reason they'd been so pushy these last years. I feared now it would be too late.

"I'll go with you," Kirsi whispered, appearing beside me.

I would have thrown myself around her had I known she would be able to catch me without warning. "I'm so sorry, Kir. I should have told you everything as soon as I figured it out. I just ... I don't know what I'm doing. And everyone needs to know everything about me, and I can't even find two minutes to myself to just figure this all out. And everything keeps falling to pieces."

"You're rambling." Her voice was calm. Steady.

I paused, taking a breath. "Are you okay? I have no idea what the old wraith told you."

"It was Nym," she whispered. "Nym killed me."

I gasped, stepping toward her. "I'm so sorry. I hate this. All of it. I hate the space between us now. I hate that I can see you hurting and can't fix it. I hate that it was her, of all the people in the world. He had to choose her."

"I can't forgive her."

"Kir... She couldn't. You know she couldn't have stopped it."

She rounded on me, anger and sadness clashing as she yelled. "She could have told me. Should have told me. You confessed everything the second you were able to. You mourned Bastian to the point of sickness in the human lands. You hated yourself every single second of that time. And what has she done? Only lied."

"You're right. I'm sorry. You're allowed to feel how you feel without me trying to justify her actions. I know it hurts."

She shook her head. "I have nothing, Rave. Not really. She was my reason for everything. It used to be me and you and Scoop against the world. And now he's gone... And you, you've got Bastian, and where does that leave me? I don't ever want to hold you back, but you can't say anything has been the same since the Trials started. You're fucking dying, and you didn't even think to tell me."

"I don't know how to say the words out loud. The Omnia was split with curses, and now the remnants are dying and I'm tied to them. Which means all the witches are going to lose their power. It started with Fire, but it's not going to end there. My problems seem so small."

"Every second since we've come back from the human lands has been to stop the Harrowing so I could save her. Save you. Do you think I give a shit about the rest of the dying witches? They sure as fuck don't care about me. Your problems are the greatest problems in the world to me. And to Bastian. And Atlas and Torryn. We're a family now. Fuck everyone else. If you're really dying, Rave..."

Her voice trailed off, but I knew what she meant. "You'll be here, and I'll be there and we'll never be together again."

Another tear slipped down her cheek, vanishing before it hit the ground. "Not a small problem. The only problem."

"I love you, Kir. You've always been the best of us. The most heart and the biggest bite."

"I love you too, asshole."

I laughed, swallowing my sadness as I turned back to my parents' house. "Together, then?"

"I'll be right beside you."

Sounds of wailing neighbors and mourning witches carried me forward. The house leaned to one side, the door hardly opening on the crooked frame. It smelled of dust and ash. No hint of the home I'd known as a child. Not a single wall held a picture, the floors creaking, threatening to sink in. The back half of the house was gone completely, ripped from the ground like it'd been unearthed by a tornado.

"Hello?" I couldn't help the way my voice cracked as I sucked in several sharp breaths, swallowing them like daggers, knowing what I'd find when I rounded the next corner. With no signs of them in the front half, they must have been outside, tending to the final crop in their garden. They hadn't had a second to hide. To scramble away from the blast of the books.

They hadn't even had time to reach each other.

The world fell silent as I spotted my mother, crumpled to the ground not ten steps from where I stood. Her favorite sage-colored apron smeared in blood, face down in the dirt. A cry swelled in my throat as I fell to my knees and crawled to her, rolling her over as if that would have saved her. She'd loved me so hard my whole life. To a fault, it seemed. Why had I been so naive to believe that smothering someone with love was the worst kind of thing? She'd protected me every single day of my life and I'd never thanked her for it. Guilt wrapped itself around me as I brushed the black hair from her face, staining my fingers with her blood.

I'd never noticed how much she looked like my grandmother. I was born to a line of fearsome witches. I was the daughter of the witch who'd first doubted the integrity of the coven leaders. Who'd gone against everything she'd known, even the advice of her own mother, to protect me. She'd jumped in mud puddles with me and then taught me how to remove the stains. She'd helped teach me how to cast a spell, though it must have killed her to see me do it. She'd made tea and sat with me for hours after I'd watched my grandmother's death, singing to me and soothing my heart.

It hurt. Everything hurt. I could hardly see beyond the pool of tears in my eyes as Kir took my hand and pulled me away. Not to take a second away from mourning my mother. Not when she let go of me to go to my mother and carry her fallen body across the garden, laying her gently beside my father.

He lay on the ground in the far corner, impaled by the handle of a garden tool, blood pooled around him turning the brown dirt into mud. The ache in my chest became an unyielding dam of sorrow. It would not break, and I could not breathe. I couldn't swallow. I couldn't make a sound beyond a sob as I looked upon his face.

Every year of his life showed there as I knelt beside him, pushing away the heartache. Reaching to close his eyes, my throat filled with daggers, the lump now a weapon against me. Those last moments I'd had with him … I'd tried to save him from Nikos at the same time he'd tried to do the same. Our relationship had struggled these past years, and it was all my fault for not seeing the truth behind the man that remained guilty of so many hateful things.

Kir laid her head on my shoulder as I clutched my father's hand, trembling and sobbing and overwhelmed with so much emotion I could hardly think straight anymore. Kirsi's tears fell as steadily as my own as we mourned our losses, and even each other. We hardly saw the sun fall from the sky. Didn't notice the men that walked up beside us, dropped to the ground and remained a constant steadying force as we held each other.

"Shall we have a pyre?" Kirsi whispered sometime later.

We looked out over the destroyed expanse of the Moon Coven to the small fires scattered throughout. So many losses, so many witches. So much destruction.

"Yes." I pushed myself off the ground, slipping the blade from my father's belt, and handed it to Bastian. "And then it's time to end this."

51

KIRSI

Standing back in the empty space where the shop had been was like opening a fresh wound. I had no idea why we'd come back here. There was nothing left. But no one questioned it when our souls led us home. No one stopped to ask where we were going or what the next plan might have been; we simply moved in numbed pain back to the only place we'd had together.

She was only a phantom at first. A beautiful witch's outline in the dust settling over the square, lit by moonlight, that powerful beast clawing at the dirt as he stretched his hind quarters, waiting for her command. The pain in my heart clutched at my throat as Nym approached, reaching into her cloak and setting a tiny black panther on the ground.

I cried out, dropped to the earth, as Scoop walked slowly toward Raven. He'd lived. Through all the chaos and destruction, he'd somehow made it out alive. The other half of my spirit blessed soul, bound to walk this world searching for me.

I could nearly see that fucking captain opening the back door and booting him out to safety the second all hell broke loose. I'd never be able to thank him for that. Though a small part of me still hoped he and Eden lived, that would hold them at the mercy of Endora and I'm not sure that was a hell anyone should have to endure. Especially after Eden's life of near solitude.

She kept her distance, watching as I reached for Scoop and scratched behind his ear, fighting the urge to take him into my arms and never let him go. The tether to him might have been severed, but I felt him in my heart just as much as I did when I was a witch. It hurt so fucking much that he didn't seem to feel the same. He couldn't recognize me from Atlas. I was simply an unknown being to him. Potential danger to his wild soul.

As Raven lifted Scoop from the ground, I shared a look with her before crossing the road to speak with Nym.

"You know, then?" she asked.

No pretenses, no bullshit. The fact that I'd always loved that about her stung.

Lifting my chin, I threw up every wall around my heart. "You should have told me. Everything I've done has been to try to protect you because I love you and you couldn't tell me."

Her words were hardly a whisper. "You love me?"

"It wouldn't hurt so fucking bad if I didn't."

She moved forward, reaching to stroke a long, brown finger down my cheek. I didn't try to feel it. I didn't want to.

"There's been enough hurt today. I can't have this moment with you right now because I need to sort it out in my mind. Thank you for finding Scoop."

Her green eyes lit with fire as she held her ground. "I'm coming with you, Kir. You know that. You can be furious, you can hate me, you can push me away, but I'm not leaving. Maybe I wasn't brave enough to tell you the truth, maybe I was trying to find the right time, I don't know. But none of this is over. Not you and I. Not the Harrowing. This is where I'm supposed to be, and you know that."

"I may never forgive you."

"Then I guess we'll just have to figure that out too, Kirsi Moondance, because I refuse to let this go. There's too much good here. Bastian found a way to forgive Raven and someday, you'll do the same for me."

When she brushed past me and joined the group, I think I loved her even more. And then I think I hated myself for it. Forgiveness was so far away, but at least she was still fighting when I was too weak to try.

"Okay?" Atlas asked, scaring the shit out of me.

"Damnit, wolf. Don't sneak up on people like that."

His smile beamed in the moonlight. "I had no idea you were such a scaredy cat. Makes sense though, really."

I rolled my eyes. "What do you want?"

"We're going to have to go to the Storm Coven and get that Grimoire from the silent witches. Bastian's magic is gone, which means the barrier around the ones in the Fire Coven is down again. We need to get them and secure them, and you and I are the fastest. Plus, the silenced witches there know you. Raven says they'll trust you."

"So, the plan is to put four books that shouldn't be together, together?"

"I don't make the rules, Wish. Just follow directions. We get the books and meet at the northern tip of the Fire Coven, heading to Moss." He paused, studying my face. "We could invite your witch, if you want. She's fast enough on the tiger."

His way of asking without asking. I shook away the sadness, unsure of anything anymore.

"It'll be quicker with just the two of us." I looked up at the moon, sighing. "Think we can make it there by morning?"

"As long as you don't slow us down again with your whining."

I lifted from the ground, closing all my feelings into a box as I looked over my shoulder with a wicked grin, so thankful for the playful heart of the wolf and the part of him that always knew what my soul needed. "I beat you last time. Don't pretend like you didn't stop to chase that squirrel."

"It's my nature, asshole."

52

RAVEN

Physically and mentally exhausted, we followed the tail of the strix. Lit by glistening starlight, he soared overhead, watching for any sign of danger while Nym, Bastian and I walked along the road, with Talon keeping watch in the back. I could feel the broken spirits of my somber company, knowing I wasn't contributing to any level of joy as I continued to mourn the life I'd once had.

Eventually, the magical bird landed, shifting into the towering man just before he touched the ground. We'd entered the Fire Coven over an hour ago and agreed the charred ground would not be a welcomed place to stop for the night. But Bastian had known of an old soldier's outpost near the border. It wasn't fancy, but I'd never needed that. Several cots in a dusty room and a lookout tower. Remnants of a brutal war that never truly ended.

Nym cast a barrier spell, warning that it would only alarm us if anyone entered, not prevent it from happening. Every part of my body screamed for sleep. The blankets were so dusty I opted to go without, knowing that if I'd breathed the dust in all night, I'd likely wake sicker than I already felt and I couldn't raise any more red flags with everyone on edge.

Bastian had hardly said anything at all since losing his magic. He'd been the hero when the witches had needed him, but that was only surface deep. Beneath all that, the wheels of his mind kept him so occupied he'd hardly been there at all, though we'd walked side by side.

When he snuck out of the hut, I followed quietly. He knew I was there, of course. He always knew. But he didn't stop me as he climbed the lookout tower. Only gave me a hand to step over the ledge so I could join him. The silvery moonlight lit the sharp planes of his face, the tips of his lashes, even the sorrow in his eyes.

"Want to talk about it?"

He shook his head, wrapping an arm around me as he studied the sky above instead of the world below. I was grateful for that warm arm on the cold fall night. The Fire Coven always smelled like a campfire and summer, even when it was chilly. But being here, wrapped in Bastian's arms, seeking warmth was far from cozy when everything else was so scarred.

"I think I am no longer the king of this world."

"Of course you are the king, Bastian. What are you saying?"

"What good is a shifter that can only turn to man. Cannot protect his family in one form or the other. What good is a witch with no magic? How will I stand before Endora with anything more than a prayer to end this? I am not supposed to be the weak one. I was the Dark King, but now, maybe I am nothing at all. Just a man."

I could have sworn I heard the tiny crack that grew in his heart as he spoke the words that must have circled his mind the entire journey here.

Holding my hand before him, I let a stroke of light dance across my skin before turning it to fire and then a vine. "Your strength has not gone. The first time I really felt the depth of your power, I was enraptured by it. I thought it was your vast power that seduced me. But it wasn't. It was always only you. Your heart has not changed. You are still a force to be reckoned with, and we will see this through together. It was never just going to be you standing there against her and her coven."

He placed both of his hands on the sides of my face, staring into my eyes. "You are not well, and I can see it." He kissed the tip of nose. "It's my job to protect you. Always."

"In case you've forgotten who you are speaking to, I've never needed you to protect me or save me. I've wanted nothing from you. Demanded nothing but fairness when I thought you to be a cruel man. It will take me a single second to put Endora in the ground. We just have to get there. Together."

He slid his hand down my body, gripping my throat with the other as I looked away. "My Dark Queen."

His rumbling voice brought my skin to life in a way only he could. He was vulnerable and lost and I knew that feeling.

"If you need to use me to feel something, then use me, King. I am yours."

He smirked, recognizing his own words before leaning over and brushing his teeth along my neck, biting only hard enough to send a flicker of pain and bliss through me. "I cannot wait to go back to the times when we can just be alone without the world ending."

I laughed before my heated lips found his. "What's the fun in that?"

"The fact that you said that with a straight face concerns me, Miss Moonstone."

I brought another flicker of lightening to my fingertips and ran them down his chest. "It's called balance. A little chaos and murder mixed with magic and pleasure."

He gripped my arm, spinning me to face him. The king kissed me with so much tenderness, so much love, I thought I'd break.

"If I could take this moment and live in it forever, I would," he said, quietly. "I've never known anything to be so unbreakable and so fragile at the same time. I think I will need you every second of every minute for the rest of forever and then five minutes more."

A blush danced across my face as he looked at me with such awe. I wondered what he truly saw.

"Every second of every minute for the rest of forever is already yours. You can have all the minutes beyond that. In every space of time, in every world, my love, I am yours. Forever."

Words laced with fear danced between us like a song as we held each other close. Though this night had ended with a renewed sense of purpose, a reminder of the future we were fighting for ... It also brought its own version of goodbye.

53

RAVEN

"He'll do something he'll regret if you don't keep yourself out of the thick of danger," Torryn warned me as we sat before a crackling fire watching Bastian pace along the northern coast of the Fire Coven, kicking at the charred ground while waiting for Atlas and Kirsi to recover the Storm Coven Grimoire.

The shifter had always been there to offer his wise counsel without prejudice, but in this, he left his warning somewhere between his careful lines of observation.

I took his hand and laid my head against his arm, soaking in the warmth. "I won't stay back when our family is in danger. I can't do it, Tor. You wouldn't ask it of him, don't ask it of me."

He chuckled. "Leave it to Bash to find someone that challenges his level of stubbornness. Just do me a favor and don't be reckless. If you can take someone out, do it. Put it in your mind now that you cannot hesitate. Hesitation is a breeding ground for—"

"Disaster. You sound like him, you know."

"I trained him. I watched him grow from a foolish little prick into a fearsome leader. But a lot of his lessons have been learned the hard way and, though that's never stopped him, it has molded him into something harder than he ever should have been. It serves him well, but you, Little Witch, have no time to learn those lessons."

I picked a piece of dry bark from the ground, snapping it in my fingers before tossing it into the fire. "I wasn't trained like you were as shifters, but my grandmother was a force to be reckoned with. And so was my mother, if she needed to be. I am a product of my raising and I'm not afraid of them."

He smirked, nudging Nym with his broad shoulder. "Please tell your friend there's nothing wrong with a healthy dose of fear."

Nym had been a million miles away, lost in her own thoughts as she stroked her familiar's spine. She smiled, though she couldn't meet my eyes. "Fear only means you will suffer twice, shifter. Once at the onslaught of weakness, and again when faced with the thing you fear. It is far better to acknowledge your fear and then conquer it."

"Wise," Bastian said, walking over to kiss me on the head before gesturing to Tor. "Might as well get some hand-to-hand in to kill time."

Tor pushed himself off the log, far less stiff than he'd been the day before. They moved away, stretching before they took opposing stances. Though I watched them intently, curious whether it would be useful in a battle against witches, I couldn't help but be mesmerized by the precise movements.

Bastian was light on his feet, faster than anything I'd ever seen. Far more graceful than he'd been on that mountain with me. But Torryn was something else. Like a mass of muscle and mind, predicting movements long before they were initiated, challenging Bastian in a way I never could.

"Do you think she'll forgive me?" Nym broke the silence with a question I wasn't prepared to answer.

I grabbed another piece of bark from the ground and picked at it with my fingers, turning them black. "Kirsi protects her heart with an iron cage. It's hard to get in, but once you do, she loves with everything she has. Equally, if she's scorned, she isn't going to easily get over it."

Sighing, she slid her feet forward, leaving a path in the black earth.

"I know. We're the same in so many ways. I need her. But ... I don't understand it. How did you get the deja to fulfill your wish?"

"If you're thinking about trying to capture another one, forget it. They're gone now."

"No. I just ... She came to you and not to me and I don't understand why."

I whipped around so fast my hair flew across my face. "What did you just say?"

"I wished for her too. Not to come back, but ... to forgive me."

I leapt from the log I sat on, mind reeling. "You wished for Kirsi to come here? To forgive you for killing her? Nym, does she know?"

She smoothed her feet over the marks in the ground, erasing them, her eyes on the small flames in the flickering fire. "She won't talk to me. Wouldn't give me a chance yesterday."

"Tell me exactly what you said. How you said it. What the deja said back."

"Ophelia attacked me in the Fire Coven because I waited for her to trap the little thing, and then I stole it before she could wish. When I got away, the deja said the stolen wish was unique. That's all. I knew I wasn't going to win the Trials when you'd already beat me in points and ran into the forest, so instead of wishing for proof that I'd caught it, I fell to my knees and begged for Kirsi's forgiveness."

"Exactly what did you say?"

"I wished that she would forgive me. That's it."

"How did the deja respond?"

"She just giggled and nodded and then said to open the jar and set her free. So I did."

I combed my fingers through my hair, braiding it out of sheer habit as I considered Nym's wish. "I'm guessing she came back for my wish and can't leave until yours is fulfilled."

Her eyes were full of tears, but her face showed only panic. Nym rose, grabbing my hands. "If she forgives me, she's going to be gone? Forever?"

"Better to live an eternity in peace than be trapped here."

She fell back down, nodding slowly, twirling the golden bands on her arms, lost in her own mind once more as we waited. I remembered how close she was to her family and the sacrifice she'd made staying with us, when she could have gone home instead of risking everything to be here.

"I've always admired you, you know. It's different being spirit blessed because everyone watches you in wonder. But we aren't unheard of. You've spent your whole life unmarked and gawked at. That's never changed your character. If anything, it's probably made you better for it. And I know how much Kirsi loves you, Moonstone. I just wanted to say thanks. For letting me in."

I smiled. "Remember that witch that came back for me in the final Trial? Commanded the skies and called the creatures from the forest to fight off Willow and Onyx? You might be losing your edge, but I'm never going to forget the moment you saved my life. You want me to help with Kir, I will. You want me to shut up and stay out of it, I will. Family is what we make of it, and you're here now. Maybe we aren't your real family, but we've got each other's backs and that's the best thing anyone can ask for."

She chucked a piece of broken wood into the fire. "It's never going to be that easy with Kir and I."

"See that brooding man over there throwing punches because he needs to feel in charge of something? You once told me I'd have to be a fool to fall for the Dark King. I don't think love is ever supposed to be easy. The work you put into it is what makes it so special. If you really want to make things work with Kir, you tell her the truth, all of it, and let her decide. If that means she forgives you and leaves this world, then find comfort knowing you gave her the peace she needed."

"So, no matter what, I lose her." Her voice cracked, and she rubbed her chest as if it would ease the pain in heart.

"We lost her the day she died in that castle. Every single moment with her since has been a blessing from the goddess, but we cannot cage her in this world."

She nodded, saying no more, and I left her to her thoughts. I didn't know if I should be the one to tell Kirsi, or if I should trust Nym to do it, but either way, if this was really the reason she was here, I wondered if Kir would truly ever be able to forgive her knowing Nym had kept so much from her. But would I have done the same? Nym had no way of knowing fulfilling that wish might have set Kir free until now. I couldn't imagine the guilt eating at her.

Bastian swung hard at Tor, not giving an inch as they fought with closed fists. The shifter dodged the blow, spinning away just in time for a giant white wolf to come in for the kill, pinning Bastian to the hard ground and licking his face.

The Dark King roared, shooting Atlas into the air with his feet as he spat into the dirt. "You're so disgusting, Atty."

"It's his *nature*," Kirsi teased, holding a transparent hand out to help Bastian up.

She'd come so far from her first day in this world in her new form. She'd broken rule after rule, still living life on her own terms. The king took her hand and moved to his feet as if grabbing a ghost, a *wish*, had been the most natural thing on the planet.

I didn't miss Kirsi's gaze at Nym as she turned away. The longing and the hurt in her eyes. She loved her. They loved each other. But this was not my battle. If Nym didn't tell Kirsi about the wish, I'd have to. It was the right thing to do for my best friend. But I would give Nym a little time to try to figure it out. Because time was precious, and we didn't have much of it.

The pluck of that magical string in my mind binding me to the Grimoires rattled. I'd known the second the book was moving out of the Whisper Coven, had felt the jerk the moment it was dropped with shifters guarding the others after Bastian's barrier vanished. Having Kir and Atty join us didn't settle the warning bells firing in my mind, didn't ease the urgency rippling over me as I thought about the book Endora had, or the ease with which she'd obliterated half our world.

"Bastian," I called, holding back the worry from my voice as I reached for the Forest Coven Grimoire in my mind, expecting to feel it nestled within the dense trees and high mountains of Xena's coven only to find it was not. "The Forest Grimoire is in the Moss Coven now. I think they crossed the bay to bypass Fire."

"Time to get moving."

A small canal passed between the Moss and Fire Covens. We hustled over the bridge without delay, entering the luscious green land of our enemy. We'd made a plan to trek through the Moss Coven from its southernmost tip, moving all the way to the north toward Endora's home. We would cut off the Forest Coven witches headed the same way and steal the Grimoire by whatever means necessary and then keep going north toward where I felt the pluck of that book. The small mountain passes we'd have to travel through to reach her had proven one thing. Her home's placement was strategic.

"Tor, take the skies. Keep an eye out for Xena. Endora can't get that book. She's likely to blow the Moss Coven off the map if she gets her hands on it."

"No." I froze. "She's not trying to destroy the land. She's trying to take out all the witches but her own. She did something in the Moon Coven. She channeled that magic somehow. How else would she have destroyed the Fire Coven's Grimoire when there's been no other record of that being possible? Give me the stone."

"What?" Bastian asked, his eyebrows drawn in confusion.

"The gem that was on the cover of the Grimoire, I need it."

He slipped his hand into his pocket and dropped the red, marbled stone into my palm. I closed my eyes and willed magic into it, pushing that amplification spell I'd had. The king's back went rigid as a hiss sounded between his teeth.

"What did you just do?"

I shook my head, the wheels of my mind spinning as the fiery stone whispered words of betrayal and poison into my mind, hardly coherent but alive, nonetheless. I thought I was destined to die with these books. Bound by them, to keep my markings hidden. But that was not the whole truth. The whispers had told me I knew what I needed to do, but I hadn't at the time. It wasn't to just accept my fate. It was a task far greater.

Tossing the stone back to Bastian, his eyes wide with shock, I started running. "If we're going to save your power, we need to move. Now."

The Moss Coven brought back a world of nightmares. The final Trial playing in my mind as we passed the phoenixes and kept going. As the forest that filled the expanse beside us reminded me of the deja and of Nikos' demand to kill Bastian. I hated it here. I hated the way it smelled of musk and foreboding. Of damp wood and witch's poison.

Still, we ran. Stopping only to drink or catch our breaths, following the owl-like creature in the sky as he led us. I'd motion occasionally, feeling for the Forest Coven book, knowing that soon we'd encounter a horde of Forest Coven witches and had no plan on how we were going to kill their leader and steal their precious Grimoire. That statement whorled in my mind until I realized I had become someone's villain. I'd wondered why Bastian had accepted the role so fully and now I understood. Like beauty, villainy was in the eye of the beholder.

54

KIRSI

Keeping pace with the witches was far slower than keeping pace with Atlas, but we followed behind Rave at a steady stride, hoping like hell she had a plan for when we came face to face with the Forest witches.

Nym didn't leave us. Instead, she ran as desperately as Torryn flew. I thought she'd go; run back to her family after I'd blown her off to leave with Atty. But she hadn't. Her heart remained with me. She carried Scoop in a satchel at her side, just as she'd have done for her familiar, taking care of him because she knew what he meant to me.

But she'd kept the truth from me for so long and I couldn't let that go. I wasn't ashamed to admit I'd fallen behind several times just to watch her run, though. She just did something for me no one else in the world would be able to do. And maybe when this day was over, I would find my way into her bed and we could discover a path to forgiveness together. I didn't even care if that made me a shitty person. Nym was a fucking queen. She was wrong, yes. But also, perfection.

Atlas spun, running backward as he moved between Nym and I, grinning. "I think you're staring."

"Mind your business, Pup."

"Are you guys fighting or what?"

"Or what."

He tilted his head like a curious puppy. "What?"

I bit back my laugh. "I hate you."

"You love me and you know …" Smile fading, he threw up a hand, releasing a short, sharp whistle.

Everyone stopped. Tor swooped low.

We moved in close, watching him as he took a deep breath, scanning the horizon. With trees to the right of us and the mossy cliffs to the left, we were wide open in a valley.

"Fuck," Bastian whispered, understanding before the rest of us. "They're here."

55

RAVEN

Atlas made a circle with his finger, and shifted into a wolf, growling as he faced the woods. A low-lying fog crept from the forest, inching toward us. We backed into each other, rotating as we scanned the trees. Torryn flew away, content to watch the sky for danger.

"Do not hesitate," Bastian ordered.

"The book is still moving," I whispered. "It might be a distraction from the Moss witches."

Atlas growled again, shaking his head. He'd smelled them. Had somehow known the origin.

"Forest, then. Good. Better that Endora doesn't know we're here yet."

I cast, pulling in a breeze to blow away the fog. Three witches stepped from the forest, while three more moved in from the top of the cliffs. Nym ran for them. She'd been here before and Talon, roaring at her heels, remembered exactly how to climb the rocks. The fiery phoenixes scattered, screeching as the white tiger tore through them with Atlas close behind.

Tor dove from the sky with his talons extended, ripping into the face of a witch who hadn't seen him coming. All hell broke loose.

Bastian caught the witch Torryn had attacked before she had a chance to cast, holding her arms behind her back as she thrashed. Kirsi had vanished, appearing behind another witch and ripping her throat from her neck.

A spell struck me in the back, turning my veins to lava as pain raced through my body. I fell to my knees, sending thick vines up the witch's legs to suffocate her, crushing her to the ground as I held back the death spell, afraid of its totality. I rose to a knee and another witch cast, her spell narrowly missing me. Halfway through the motion of a second attempt, Atlas came flying down from the cliffs, claws digging into her back as she dropped to the ground beneath him. His mouth came away bloody. I was confident the wolf still winked at me before tearing off toward Nym once more.

We'd nearly taken down every witch that had come for us. An unnecessary massacre, had they only seen reason and truth. With one final witch on the rocks, Bastian and I moved together as we waited and watched. Talon stepped slowly, like a predator hunting prey. The witch inched back, her long cloak falling over the ledge of the small cliff.

Atlas circled below like a shark in the water, waiting for her to fall. She sliced her hand through the air, her markings glowing green as the tiger was thrown to the side, exposing Nym. She cast again, but before her spell could leave her fingers, Kirsi appeared between them, plunged her hand into the witch's chest and ripped out her throbbing heart, saving Nym.

A woman from the trees screamed the name of the fallen, running into the fold as if she'd been terrified and hiding, but spurred by fury to leave her position. Bastian tried to catch her, but she was too fast. Another ran out. And then another. Until the ones that had been slain were nothing compared to those that descended upon us. A test, if anything, to see how we might fight, which powers we'd use.

Those above raced down the staggered cliffs to join us. We were effectively herded like sheep into a circle, our backs together as we faced off with the Forest Coven. Slowly rotating, studying the faces of each adversary. Atlas lunged, his massive jaws snapping at a witch that stepped too close. As if on cue, they all began casting, magic raining down on us, striking and missing.

With no other options, completely backed into a proverbial corner, I grabbed Bastian's hand as I pulled the power of death from within me and fought back. The spell that felt like cheating. Like each time I used it, Death would find me easier and easier, hunting me from the afterlife.

Animals poured from the forest on Nym's command. But it was not enough. We were not enough. The heavy fog grew thicker, and I could not focus on pushing it away and keeping myself safe from the spells that flew. Within minutes, we were nearly blinded, missing more than we were gaining.

"I can't see through this fucking fog," Bastian yelled, a witch struggling in his grasp.

I gave up my defense to bring in a gale force wind so strong, it pushed us along the ground, combatting the other witches' blinding spell. The moment we could see each other, the world grew silent. They had vanished, disappearing into the forest once more. I jerked around, looking behind me, seeing nothing but the bodies on the mossy earth. Bastian buried his knife into the back of the witch he held and dropped her, his silver eyes scanning me from head to toe, absolute death on his face as he heaved.

"Where the fuck did they go?" Kirsi whispered, appearing beside me.

"I don't know, but I don't like this," Atlas answered seconds after he shifted. "I can only smell the blood."

"Maybe if you didn't bathe in it that wouldn't be the case," Nym said, looking him over.

"I'll keep that in mind next t—"

From nowhere, a spell struck the wolf, taking him instantly to the dirt.

"Atlas," Kirsi screamed, racing for him.

But she wasn't fast enough as his giant, limp body lifted and vanished into the forest. Bastian swore, running for him. One moment he was on his feet, shouting for his brother, and the next he was out cold, falling. My ears rang, the world slowing to a stop as I yelled his name, sprinting after him. Torryn's strong arms came down around me, lifting me away as Bastian Firepool, the love of my life, was also yanked into the forest.

I bucked, kicking and yelling and fighting to get to him as the world remained silent and still. An ache formed in the back of my throat as something within me collapsed. It took every ounce of self-control I had not to cast on Torryn. Nym stepped into my view, grabbing my face and wrenching me back into this world of pain.

"We'll get them. I swear it, but you have to stop. We do this our way only, not theirs. They'd take us one by one if we let them. We cannot let them."

"Come out and fight me, you fucking cowards," I screamed, still struggling in Tor's arms until I began to cry. "You fucking cowards."

I spun, letting Torryn hug me. Letting the gentle giant speak calm words into my ear until time ticked by at a normal pace.

"They need you in the forest because that's where they are strongest. It was a trap. A very dangerous trap."

"They're in there." My throat constricted, limbs growing heavy. "They could be killing them."

"They knew what they signed up for," Nym said. "We all did."

Torryn lifted my chin, one hand still on my shoulder. "If you can promise you aren't going to run into that forest like a damn maniac, I'll check and see what I can from above."

I nodded reluctantly. What choice did I have? "I promise. Go, Tor. Right now."

We waited an eternity. And then another. Time and time again I looked into that forest, took a step, before letting Nym yank me back. I had no idea where Kirsi had gone, no idea where any of them were. And like some kind of fool, I stood there waiting for answers, for a plan from a shifter flying so high he must have been hiding in the cloud bank.

"They're alive. It was only a sleeping spell." Kirsi popped into view, floating out from the trees. "There's a witch with them that can use the foliage to amplify the power of his friends. It's better not to chase them, but cut them off. I didn't show myself, so they don't know we plan to follow."

Torryn landed behind us, agreeing. "I found Xena Foresthale. She's just over that pass," he said, pointing. "These witches were left behind as defense while she raced forward with two others. I'm guessing they plan to deliver the others to Endora, along with the book."

A pulse of lightning flickered down my skin. "Over my dead body."

56

KIRSI

Green and green and so much damn green I could have gone out of my mind searching through the gaps ahead of us for signs of movement from the Forest Coven witches like a hound. Fucking trees covered with moss. Mountains covered with moss. The path of patchy rocks covered in moss. I hadn't seen them the first time, but I'd be damned if that happened again. With Tor in the sky, diligent and watchful, and Nym racing beside us, riding her beast with my familiar strapped to her side while I hauled Raven, we covered more ground in minutes than we had in an hour with all of us walking.

It felt good to be moving again, racing along, but the scenery was so boring and repetitive I had to make mental notes just to be sure we weren't getting lost, following the base of stupid green mountains. It wasn't long until Raven hissed and Torryn was back with us. She'd seen something just as he had.

"They're up there," he announced.

Rave confirmed. "The last book isn't far away either. It's throbbing in my mind right now."

I swished myself forward to look at her. "Are you okay?"

She rolled her eyes. "No. I'm not. I won't be okay until this is over so please stop asking."

The earth rumbled beneath her, showcasing the endless rage and frustration she kept bottled up.

Leaning in, I placed my forehead on hers. "Time to let that fire out, my girl."

Her ruthless smile was all the answer I needed.

Closing the space between us and the Forest witches, deep within the Moss Coven territory, the plan was to hang back and see how many of them there were, how they were keeping our guys hostage, and then sneak in and free them. But when Raven saw Atlas tied up by his hands, out cold and being dragged behind a horse with Bastian nowhere in sight, she lost her fucking mind, broke away from the group and went charging in like a damn maniac.

The sky above darkened like night had stolen the day. Thunder rumbled and lightning charged across the world. The ground shook and the wind blew stronger than it had in that storm over the ocean. Raven held both of her hands out, fingers curled, drawing on her power like some kind of goddess cursing the world.

The first wave of witches didn't have a chance. With a single swipe of her arm, they were thrown so far, I couldn't track them. I vanished, taking advantage of her ferocious distraction to surge forward and free Atty. The witch holding him asleep with a spell must have been distracted because he woke easily when I shook him.

"Stop sleeping on the job, Pup. Unless you want to end up on someone's dinner plate."

He started, scrambling to his human feet, though he had to be sore, covered with scratches and blood from being dragged. He might have even had broken bones. "Where's Bash?"

"Are you okay?"

Holding an arm tight to his side, he shrugged. "Mostly flesh wounds. Where's Bash?"

"Help me look. Steer clear of Raven." I pointed to my best friend, pride stealing every ounce of caution. Some people fear the fire, and some become it.

Atlas' eyes doubled in size as he looked between us. "Holy hell."

"She's a goddamn monster." I beamed. "Find the king, Pup."

He tore away from me and I moved back to Raven, watching her back as she fought off every person coming her way without breaking a sweat. She'd held back before and I knew Torryn was going to have a talk with her about it. It wasn't easy to choose to be a killer. To take lives with no conscious effort and that would always be a war she fought. But when we faced the Moss witches, she'd have to bring this level of badass or we weren't going to make it. It would be us against an entire coven of ruthless bitches, their minds twisted by Endora herself for many, many years.

A crack formed in the earth ahead of us, creeping toward Raven as she cast and cast again. Spells surged for her, but she moved just in time to avoid the brunt of them. Her skin had been sliced, her cloak in tatters, but still she attacked, stalking forward, dancing over the opening in the ground to penetrate the witch's dwellings and find her missing king.

Atlas shouted, shifted and snarled as he bound forward, stopping to stand over the king that slept, discarded on the ground beside a trunk. Xena Foresthale rounded the wagon ahead, arms glowing as she sent a spell directly for Raven. She'd been pinned as the nicest coven leader by anyone that met her, but in this moment, she was anything but. Red faced and furious, she charged before Raven noticed her. Nym cut her off, stepping between them, but Xena cast her away without effort.

Raven, though? She took a glance at the approaching coven leader. The one that seemed to think she'd take that Moon Witch down with half a thought and smiled... Fucking smiled. Rave raised her arms the same second Xena did, but death was faster. Death was always the winner in a race against time.

Xena's face faded from red to ashen in the blink of an eye. One moment she stood strong, the next, a pile of bones on the ground. But the Moon witch's fury didn't end there. Not with several other witches trying to run away. Not when Atlas and Torryn had to drag Bastian behind Raven. She cast again, sending so much death into the world that the ground below her wilted. The trees to our right died. No one that stood before her lived a single breath longer, aside from one. One single witch who was allowed to run ahead and warn the Moss Coven witches that death was coming for them and there was no place they could hide from her wrath.

Raven fell to her knees, blood pouring from her nose and her ears. She coughed, body trembling. She was a force. Walking death and destruction if she had the heart to be. But she was fragile. And she'd been pushed too far. Burying her face in her hands, she began to cry. Broken in a way that perhaps none of us would understand.

Bastian woke at the sound of her cries and crawled to her, pulling her into his arms and rocking her back and forth as he whispered into her ear.

Torryn pulled her away from the king, lifted her chin and breathed fire into her soul with words that reminded her that she was still good. She was not the villain. "Whatever damage you think you've placed on your soul, you let that go. Even the sky wages war on this Earth. No one believes you hate the witches before you, Little Witch. Only that you love those standing behind you more."

When I pushed myself in, gripping the sides of her face with my cool hands, I rested my head against hers and closed my eyes. "You are blessed by the goddess. She has touched your face right here. She is everything light and pure and if you were dark, Raven... If you were anything but light, she wouldn't have been able to do that. Don't fear yourself, sister. Embrace it."

Her eyes opened, bloodshot and bruised. Tears mixed with dirt tracked down her face as she nodded. Though she didn't rise because of anything we'd said. Not because of our love. She rose because she had to. Simply that. One foot in front of the other to see this through.

The sky cleared, and the wind faded away. Bastian gripped Raven's hand as she wiped her face and led him to the trunk, kicking it open. He pulled the old, leather-bound book from the box and handed it to Torryn. Without a word, the man shifted to a strix and carried it away.

One final book. One final witch. One more battle and this nightmare would be over. Come what may. But when Raven pulled away from Bastian, shoulders down, each step forward putting a sliver of more space between us, my shared glance with the Dark King spoke a thousand words.

Raven had been irrevocably broken.

57

RAVEN

One step and then another and another, rushing through the Moss Coven until something in the world made sense beyond the toxic whispers in my mind. I'd dug into the well of power within me so recklessly, my soul had paid the price. I had stared down at the Grimoire before Torryn had taken it, only to be reminded of the task that still lay before me. Beyond stopping the Harrowing, which at this point seemed irrelevant considering the massive loss of lives, my journey was far greater. It would require far more power than I'd used on that battlefield. It would require all of it. Every last flicker of magic, and even then, it might not be enough.

"Didn't we kill her with the swamp witches?" Atlas asked, huddled beside me as we hid behind a stone hut, staring at the backside of Willow Moonhollow.

"No," I answered, all sense of conviction gone from my voice. "We let her go."

Kirsi swept forward. "And yet here she is, deep in the mountains of the Moss Coven, sucking up to Endora. What an asshole."

"She's always coveted power," Bastian said, his voice pulling me in a way I didn't know I needed.

I reached for his hand, running a single finger down one of his as our eyes locked. He'd been so worried about me. I'd been worried about myself. Overcome with fear and fury. But we needed one more push before I had to secretly break away from the group and try to fix everything that was broken. The true final task that Bastian's mother had seen in her vision. The reason she'd gifted me a portion of her power.

If I got too close to Bastian right now, though, he'd know. In that way that he always did. And then he'd try to stop me, just as the books had warned. But as the place the goddess touched my cheek burned, as the whispering incoherent voices grew louder in my mind, as the power gifted to me thrummed beneath my skin, I knew I wouldn't be able to back down.

"How about a plan this time?" Nym whispered, carefully directing her words toward me.

Kir vanished before saying, "We had a plan last time, some of us just decided to go rogue and rain hell down."

She'd said it with a lightness I knew would have pulled me out of my stupor before. But not now. Not with the guilt of those lives sitting on my soul.

"I'm going to follow Willow. See where she's headed." Kir's voice faded away as she spoke.

"Damnit," Atty said, "Why did I have to be a big ass wolf? A mouse would be so convenient right now."

"A mouse wouldn't have worked for that ugly face," Nym whispered, nudging him with a soft smile.

"True."

"Shh," Bastian hissed.

I followed his gaze to a group of men walking toward us. Without thinking, lightning moved to my fingertips, melting into fire.

Though it burned him, Bastian grabbed my other hand, pulling me away as he whispered, "Listen."

"All of them?" A voice carried to where we were hidden.

"But one," the man farthest to the right said. "She said they didn't stand a chance against them."

Another shook his head slowly. "One witch with all that power, it must be a trick of the Dark King."

"It's not a trick," a woman stepping out of the cottage warned. "She's coming this way and you're a fool if you stick around to see it. They say she is death incarnate, that unmarked one. Slept with the devil himself and stole his power."

Bastian's hand tightened on my own, but I didn't care. I hoped they feared me and ran. Better than stand in my way. Several moments of ominous silence passed.

"They're all terrified," Kirsi said into my ear. "You could probably walk right across that village and they'd hide."

"Not doing that," Atlas answered.

Bastian led us back into the trees. "Anything else, Kir?"

"Most are leaving. Willow was sent down by Endora to convince them there's nothing to fear. She's preaching about a 'reckoning against the shifters' and how Endora is supposed to lead everyone to a summit of power. Endora's claiming she has all the books."

"So, she's lying. Not at all surprising," Nym said, hand on a hip. "What should we do?"

"Well, there's something else." Kir cast a glance at Bastian. "Eden is alive and she's being held in a circle somewhere close by. Endora's in her home up that steep hill, but the witches are saying she's supposed to come down to talk to them. I guess that one Forest witch came through screaming about a death demon."

"Death demon. Nice."

"Always the child," Kirsi answered with an eye roll, though she couldn't conceal her smirk.

Nym grabbed Bastian's arm, jutting her chin toward the tree line. "Where's she going?"

Willow, creeped through the cover of trees, swatting at branches and looking over her shoulder as if to be sure no one followed. We hunkered down, watching as Kir floated away. Atlas shifted, slinking deeper into the forest next, clearly unwilling to let Kirsi go by herself when he could also hunt. We were summoned moments later, though none were prepared for the sight within the small clearing.

Eden Mossbrook hung suspended in the air by the magic of a black salt circle. Candles, unfazed by wind, melted below her arched back, hands out to her sides, fingertips dripping blood into small basins within the circle. My stomach rolled at the sight. No one spoke for several seconds, blinking and staring in shock.

"What the fuck?" Nym breathed, reaching for the comfort of her familiar, as Talon stepped closer, nudging Scoop in the satchel at her side, just to be sure he was still secure.

"Oh hell." I struggled to find words. "Could she be... Is Endora trying to split the Grimoires again?"

Nym took a step forward, but I stopped her. "Don't. You cannot break that salt circle. If you do, she could die. Thirteen candles, see?"

"So we just fucking leave her there?"

"Just... I need a minute," I said, weighing our options as I scanned the small clearing.

Atlas had Willow pinned to the ground by the throat, a single movement and he'd snap her neck. The tear that fell from her eyes was indication enough. He'd given a chunk of his life to Eden. Had left his home behind to protect her. He'd left her in that cottage and she'd been taken. Not dead, thankfully, but turned into some sort of magical sacrifice. And this traitorous soul had been sent to babysit her. To sit and watch the life stolen from her body. What kind of sick person could stomach that?

"Willow. What the fuck are you doing?" Kirsi snapped. "Endora is not the god you make her out to be."

She couldn't answer, could only let another tear drop down her scarred face beneath the maw of the growling wolf.

I walked forward, running my fingers through his coarse white fur. "Let her go, Atlas."

He snarled once, and then stepped away, leaving the trace of his fangs in her neck, a match to the scars on her face. She gasped and scrambled backward, crashing into Bastian's boots. He kicked her forward, stepping to push a boot over the wounds in her throat.

She lifted a hand to cast upon him, rasping. "You have no magic, shifter."

I struck her with a beam of lightning. Fast and controlled. She yelled, her back arching with pain. Mirroring Eden. Poor Eden, trapped in that salt circle. Half white hair and half black hanging inches above the flames of the candles.

"You will not speak unless I allow it," Bastian said.

And though they were gone, only a memory now, I could have sworn the shadows he'd once controlled seeped from him. But I blinked and they were gone. Willow nodded, her gulp audible as Atlas circled Eden's prison, passing Willow with another snarl.

She nodded slowly, staring at me.

"Why is Endora lying to everyone? What does she want with Eden?" Bastian released his foot, giving only an inch.

She blinked away another tear. "She wants you to go to hell."

I ground my teeth, stepping closer. "Specifically, what is she doing? And don't fuck with me, Willow. Today is not the day."

"She's trying to remove the ability to shift." She struggled, wiggling.

Bastian pressed his foot down until she stopped moving and then released. "Answer the question and stop fighting it."

"Eden's blood is from two covens. Her father… It doesn't matter. The shifters are killing the witches everywhere again. You don't understand," she rushed out, pleading with me. "The Storm Coven—"

The Dark King cut her off again.

"The shifters had nothing to do with the fall of the Storm Coven. Nor Whisper, nor Moon."

Her body jerked at the word Moon.

"Oh, your leader didn't tell you?" I squatted to get in her face. "Endora obliterated our beautiful covenstead, just to capture her harmless daughter."

"My parents?" Another tear fell.

Kirsi swooped in. "No one had time to check on your asshole parents. If you didn't have your head stuck so far up Endora's ass, you might have been able to see for yourself."

"Where is Endora?" Bastian asked, his voice teetering the edge of control.

"Cottage. Below her cottage." She wept.

A howl broke our thoughts as Atlas sent out a warning.

"Someone's coming," Nym whispered, adjusting the satchel that Scoop rode in. "I'll try to scare them off."

"Not alone," Kirsi answered, following her out of the clearing.

Out of the corner of my eye, I saw Eden shaking. Subtle at first, but as I spun, it turned to convulsions.

"It's your lucky day, witch." Bastian stepped back. "We don't have time to deal with you and I won't put your soul on her conscious. You run far and fast, witch, because if I ever see you again, I'll kill you with my bare fucking hands."

Willow scrambled away and I wondered where she would go. Home, or clambering back to Endora. Either way, we had bigger problems.

"We can't break the circle. We don't know what kind of mental state she's suspended in. She could die," I warned.

"If we let her bleed out, she fucking dies," Atlas said, shifting back into his human form.

The Dark King rounded on him, grabbing him by the throat. "You will remember who you're speaking to."

"Calm the fuck down, Bash." Atlas shoved him away.

"If you two start fighting, I'm going to kick both your asses," I warned. "We're all on edge, but keep it together."

Atlas moved around the circle, his eyes back on Eden. The hurt and worry he felt for the healing witch was palpable. Bastian followed him, whispering something. The wolf nodded once, then dropped his head, running his fingers through his hair. Bastian held a hand out and Atlas took it.

Eden shook with force. The two basins collecting her blood, trembling.

"Whatever we do, we need to do it fast," I said.

"Incoming," Kirsi yelled from behind.

"I'm breaking the circle," I shouted, "Kir, catch her and don't stop moving. Meet us back behind that cottage."

"Are you sure?" Atlas asked, his voice breaking.

"No," I answered, reaching forward and shoving the salt grains with my fingers.

Power blasted into me as I broke whatever magic Endora had been leaching from her daughter. Kirsi raced forward as planned, caught the witch in her arms and flew away the same second several witches stepped into the clearing. I recognized the faces of the men from before.

Pushing myself off the ground, I inched myself toward Bastian, slipped my hand into his pocket, lifting the stone and poured power into it.

"Shadows," I whispered.

All the rage and all the fear and every other emotion I'd had over this day pushed me as I shoved enough magic into that Fire Coven stone for the Dark King to rise and cast his shadows over the clearing. We didn't stop to fight, didn't give them time to see us go. We simply ran. Ran for the witch that had been a victim of her mother's for far too long, praying this wouldn't be the last of her days.

58

RAVEN

It was there. Faint, but audible, thumping in her chest. I looked around, aware that the small cove we'd found behind the cottage in the mountainside village wasn't going to hide us forever.

"Can you give me enough power to get into her dream?" Bastian asked, holding the Fire Coven stone out for me.

"It's… When I feed power into your coven, it's not just you. Everyone feels it, everyone pulls from it. I can, but I can't promise you much time."

"I'll take what I can get," he said as I put the stone in my lap. "We don't have time to wait and I can wake her."

I amplified the tiny sliver of magic nestled within, squeezing my eyes shut in concentration. Nym sat beside me, her leg pressed to mine with Atlas on the other side, holding the sleeping witch's hand.

Eden sat up with a gasp, then swayed and fell back down, the king catching her head. With eyes closed, she cast upon herself, willing whatever form of healing into her own body she could as she slowly sat up again, her face full of sorrow.

"You came?" Her broken voice was so sad.

"Of course we came for you," I answered. "Always."

She looked around, studying who was there... and who was not. "Torryn? Crow?"

Atlas dropped his head. "Torryn is safe. Crow... didn't make it."

Eden clutched her chest, trying to silence her wail as she repeated him. "Didn't make it?"

Bastian knelt, gently taking her hand. "Atty found his rings and blade in the rubble. I'm so sorry. How did you survive the blast?"

She swallowed, likely fighting the lump in her throat. "We share the same blood. I hadn't thought of it when I cast that barrier around your shop, Raven. That's how she got in. I'm sorry. She used..." her eyes flashed to Bastian. "She used the Fire Coven Grimoire as a shield to protect both of us from the blast. I'm sorry for that and the store."

His sharp jawline ticked. "Don't be sorry. Things can be replaced."

"People and magic cannot," she whispered.

Scoop crawled from the satchel and curled into Eden's lap. She lifted him, bringing his nose to hers. "You must have more than nine lives, you little devil."

"At least double that," Kirsi confirmed, though her general sarcastic tone had been replaced with something far more sad.

"Can you walk?" Bastian asked, standing. "We can't stay here."

"Let me do it," she answered. "I need to do it."

He glanced around the tiny cove before dipping his chin. "A death earned."

Eden knew the grounds of the mountainside perfectly. Though slow to start, she scaled the rocks, leading a clear and easy path toward the cottage that looked down upon the others with ease. The magic within me pulled in a different direction. The single remaining Grimoire was not in Endora's home, fortunately. I thought about breaking away from the group, hunting it while they saw Endora's death to the finish. But Bastian had no idea what my final destiny was. Didn't know his mother had halved her own power for me to fulfill it, come what may. So, I pressed on. Silently.

The door to Endora's cottage blasted to pieces, and Eden stormed forward. Her mother's taunting laughter could be heard from somewhere below. Eden wanted this moment. Had earned it many times over. But I wasn't here to play games or draw out a lifetime of revenge. She'd have her moment and if she couldn't see the deed done, I would cast and end it. The madness, the murder, all of it.

Surging into the home, an open door in the floor greeted us. Potentially hidden when she willed it, she hadn't taken the time as she ran. Though it felt like a trap, none of us backed down as we descended the steep stairwell and chased Endora through a narrow stone hall lit by floating candles.

Eden cast before her, sending a ball of fire rushing forward, crashing into the water Endora had conjured, tumbling for us. We ended up in a hollow cave carved into the belly of the mountain. I stumbled, realizing I'd been here before during the Trial that began below the catacombs of the black castle. Somewhere ahead, a fire serpent would be lurking.

We wouldn't get that far, though. Not as Endora cast, moving the discarded boulders to lock us in the room. I didn't bother proving that I could move them also. I simply took a step behind Eden, letting her flick a spell at her mother.

"Always a disappointment," Endora said, spinning, far more spry than she'd ever given hint to. "Even in death, you betray me."

"Save the small talk," Eden answered.

But rather than attack her daughter, she turned to Bastian, casting a spell that he dodged. It exploded into a green cloud of poison as it hit the dark, curved wall behind him, crumbling the stone. The stalactites hanging from the ceiling like swords, shuddered.

Eden yelled, turned to Bastian and ripped the knife from his belt before running forward and forming a small, green-tinted barrier over her and her mother. My heart dropped into my stomach as I realized what she'd done. Atlas shifted to wolf as Bastian raced forward, pounding on the hard shell. Atlas clawed and dug and growled.

We all knew Eden would never be able to kill her mother on her own. She'd fight a good fight, and we'd have her back, but in the end it would take several of us. But this was not a barrier like the one she'd placed over the shop. Her mother would only escape if Eden died, or she dropped the barrier herself. She'd learned that lesson the hard way.

Endora cackled, flicking her fingers, striking Eden across the face. An angry red welt formed where the spell had smacked her. Eden countered and, though her mother was only feet from her in the clear dome, she missed as the old crone moved to the side.

"Take it down," Bastian yelled, banging his fist.

But Eden ignored him, swiping her hand through the air, her mother falling before her. One step. One single step in. A moment of hesitation from her daughter and Endora Mossbrook struck like a snake, clutching Eden's throat with invisible hands and lifting her from the ground.

"Damnit," Bastian roared, pounding his fist into the barrier, staring at Eden as she thrashed her legs. "Bring it down, Raven."

I moved my hand over the magical wall, its texture hard as stone. "I can't."

"She's going to kill Eden. We have to try."

I looked at the ceiling, taking a long breath, considering what spell I might try. Unlock didn't work, though I knew it wouldn't. I tried casting vines to grow from below Endora, but the spell would not penetrate the barrier. Nym moved opposite of me, casting everything she could think of as well.

"Kir?" I yelled over the sound of flying magic. "Can you get in?"

She raced along the barrier beside Atlas, digging his claws into the surface of solid rock, blood coating his massive nails.

Eden dropped from Endora's blast and raced across the circle, tackling her mother to the ground with a scream that echoed in the domed room. All of her life, she'd been ruined by her mother. Every moment, overcast by the decision of a power-hungry hag with no true sense of family. All those years, we'd believed her to be mourning the loss of her precious daughter, but as she threw that daughter across the barrier, blood spattering down the wall, I wondered if even Endora knew how to keep the truth sorted from the lies in her mind.

Kir emerged beside me. "I can't break through it."

"I have an idea, but it's dangerous," I yelled.

Bastian froze, blood dripping from his palm as he'd tried to use it to break the magic. "Do not risk yourself."

"You're going to try to crack the barrier by shifting the ground beneath us, aren't you?" Nym hollered.

"You can't move the mountain, Rave." Kir swept in front of me. "It's a fucking mountain."

My limbs tingled as I could practically hear the clock ticking on Eden's life. Wiggling my fingers, I turned to Bastian. "If I do this, all hell might break loose."

He stormed across the space between us, gripping my face. "We'll escape hell together then."

I cast.

Steadying myself, the mountain rumbled, then shook violently as it roared to life.

Eden called out, arms flailing as she attacked her mother with a beet red face. Swinging her arms as much as her magic until someone's blood coated the inside of the barrier and dripped down the side. Moss and vines grew from the top, inching their way down. The fire from the sconces along the walls flickered. And then absolute dread gripped my heart as the stalactites covering the towering ceiling fell like honed weapons.

59

KIRSI

"Fuck you and your mountain moving, Raven Moonstone," I yelled as the damn world crashed down on us. Of course that thoughtless barrier remained, but the entire space transformed.

"I'm not casting anymore," Raven shouted back over the rumble, but it didn't matter. Whatever she'd started, continued. She threw her hands outward and the boulders blocking the doors rolled away.

"Everyone out," Bastian shouted, just as he tackled Raven to the ground, saving her from being impaled.

Atlas shifted, more limber as an animal. Nym screamed and my phantom heart stopped. Talon, that beautiful white tiger, one leg stained with red blood, shielded Scoop underneath him.

"Get them out of here," I yelled. "All of you need to go, now. This whole fucking room is going to cave in."

Nym shook her head, lifting Scoop from her familiar as the mountain continued rumbling, protesting Raven's attempt to save Eden. The beautiful, spirit blessed marking on her forehead glowed a golden hue, lighting her face in an ethereal beauty. Talon limped forward taking Scoop by the back of his neck and racing out of the room.

"Seriously, Nym. You too."

She shook her head, lifting her hands. The bracelets on her arms clinked together, and the melody was so misplaced in the chaos. "I need to tell you something."

I jerked my hand out. "No. Fuck no. You don't get to have serious conversations because you think something bad is going to happen. You don't."

"Kirsi, shut up and listen to me for once."

I rushed forward, pushing her out of the way of a falling death dagger. "This is exactly why we can't do this now."

"I'm not leaving this room until everyone leaves. And if I die, you're fucked."

Ice ran over me. As if someone had grabbed my physical body and plunged me into the winter tide. "Why would I be?"

Raven screamed and Bastian roared and yet I couldn't look away from her. I blinked slowly as the world faded into the background.

"I'm an asshole. But you're going to listen because if you get stuck in this world because I die, I'll be an even bigger asshole. I messed everything up. I'm sorry I didn't tell you it was me. I didn't know how or when. I couldn't lose you right when I'd gotten you back. But you're not here because Raven wished for it."

My ears began to ring as I floated steadily backward.

"You're here, Kirsi, because I wished for you, too. You might have come back on Raven's request first, but mine is what's holding you here."

I couldn't fight the slow, disbelieving head shake, couldn't help the fingers that moved to my lips or the whimper. "It was you?"

"I'm sorry, okay? I just wished for your forgiveness. I didn't think... The deja said you couldn't come back from the grave and I trusted that. It was hopeful wishing, that's all."

"Stay the hell away from me," I roared, soaring through her and vanishing.

Heart pumping as I watched pure pandemonium happening below. I allowed my shoulders to rise and fall as if I were taking breaths to steady myself. Raven limped. Bastian was trying to pull her to the door, Atlas continued to punch the god damn barrier.

And Eden? From above, I could hardly see through the moss. A back cracked against the barrier. My eyes flicked to Nym. Blood splattered along the glassy dome. I looked at Nym. Endora screeched and another round of death daggers fell from the ceiling, the mountain grinding as the earth continued to shake. I looked at Nym.

The room suffocated me. The truths and lies permeated in the promise of death, and I couldn't stay back and watch. I needed to do something. Anything. A thought struck me. I plummeted, soaring through the room, seeping into the mountain below and entering the death barrier through the floor. Eden had made a dome, not an orb. And now maybe I could save her damn life.

Everything within the space was foreign, dark. As if they'd built another world in an attempt to end each other. Eden and Endora's battle cries rang like peeling bells within the magical ball. Monstrous trees grew from the rocks of the mountain's floor. Boulders smothered in moss that continued to grow, creeping up the bloodied walls, reaching for the vines. A spell zipped past me, crashing into a large stone.

I soared to the top of the barrier, searching through the darkness for the two witches. They hid behind boulders, but Eden was clearly on the losing end of the battle. Her dress had been burned so badly down one arm, had she not been a healer, she'd be fully incapacitated. Blood smothered her skirts. The half of her hair that typically showed white was tinged with pink from a long gash in her head.

Enough was enough. I dropped down behind Endora, who'd cast upon herself just as I landed. She dashed to the side in a blur, her spell making her far more quick. And the likely reason why Eden couldn't catch her.

"I don't want to kill you, Eden. Don't make me do this." Endora closed the space between her and her daughter.

"No, Mother, you do want to kill me. It just needs to be on your timing when you've drained my power for whatever spell you're concocting against the shifters."

Eden stood from behind her rock, facing her mother. Her eyes flicked to me just as I soared forward, ready to rip Endora's heart from her back. But the black and white witch shook her head and I recognized the plea on her face. Her desperate need for the choice.

I vanished, soaring around the elder witch to stop beside Eden as Endora cast and sent her flying into a boulder behind her, then dashed away.

"Let me help you," I hissed in her ear as she tried and failed to get to her feet.

"No," she grumbled beneath her breath. "If this is how I die, then at least it's my choice and no one else's. I need this. I earned this."

She spoke directly to my only weakness. I'd not been given the same choice over my death. I backed away. Watching as Eden was broken again and again by her mother's quick wit and spells, Eden could only find enough time and strength to heal herself. She hadn't had time to break Endora down at all. A marking on Eden's neck glowed green and she thrust her arms forward, desperate to hit her mother, but she'd missed. And the knife she'd stolen from Bastian clambered to the ground.

I swooped in, Endora's counter spell surging through me as I snagged the knife before the old hag could. Eden dashed behind a boulder again.

The milky white moonstone embedded into the blade of the knife seemed to shine in the darkness of the foliage. I soared behind the boulder with Eden, shoving the blade into her trembling hand.

"You're stronger than this, dammit. You're not just a Moss witch. You're a fucking Moon witch and you have a moonstone. The Moss witches haven't had shit for power for years because you had that Grimoire, but the moon has never failed us. You're twice the witch your mother is. You dig deep, you pull whatever power you need from that stone, and you end this. I will not watch you die today."

Her mismatched eyes studied mine as she pulled the knife from my hand, running her thumb over the stone. Closing her eyes, she whispered. "As steady as the moon that reigns over the dark." When her eyes flashed open again, they seemed to glow as a renewed sense of purpose flowed through that witch's veins.

"Let me help you," I begged again.

"Maybe you can find a way to hold her still, Kirsi."

I left her behind her boulder, moving to the vines on the roof above us and ripping them away. The light beaming in gave me away.

Endora cast her own barrier and it slammed into me pinning me between Endora and Eden's magic. I was trapped. And Eden was closing in on her mother, casting as Endora did. She'd been able to catch her, honing in on power that was all but foreign to her until now. Most of her power came from healing, but she'd managed fire, burning the bottom of Endora's dress until she put it out with water.

Endora turned the floor to ice, causing Eden to slide forward, right into her mother's arms. Endora sank her claws into the wound in Eden's head, distracted by her own blood lust. Eden took the opportunity to reveal the blade she'd been hiding just before she planted it into her mother's stomach. She wiped her hand through Endora's blood and slammed her palm into the barrier that held me, shattering it.

One second I was dashing forward, while Eden yanked the blade from her mother's abdomen, the next, Endora cast a powerful spell, decimating every object in its path, sending Eden and me flying away as blinding white light filled the magical barrier.

I could hear again before I could see. The scrambling, the grunting, a gasp beyond the ringing in my ears. The world stopped. Another single sharp blast of magic silenced everything. Even the mountain seemed to bow to curiosity. Without a doubt, one witch had fallen and one remained standing.

The barrier shattered like glass, splinters of magic exploding into the cavernous room around us. I blinked once, and then twice. Eden Mossbrook stood, the victor in the center of the bloodied circle, holding her mother's entrails up in triumph like a goddamn warrior. Freed. No longer beholden to her mother's malevolence.

60

RAVEN

"You stop, you die," Atlas roared, racing for the opening of the collapsing cave.

"No shit," Nym yelled, shoving past him to get to the felines waiting in the tremoring hall below Endora's mountainside cottage.

Bastian hadn't let go of my hand, though he was furious with me for not leaving him behind in the belly of the mountain the second the daggers began to fall from the ceiling. I couldn't, though. My heart wouldn't let me leave a single one of them, knowing they would need each other one day.

Eventually, Eden limped past us, covered in small gashes and a knot on her forehead the size of a fist. She crawled up the stairs, stopping only a second to take in a home that was once hers before walking out of this cottage. A lifetime. An entire lifetime dictated by her mother's wickedness and her own personal conviction to fight it. She'd lost so much, but stepping into the sunlight, I didn't miss the way her shoulders rose, no longer holding the weight of the world.

Part of me thought the fight would come down to me and Endora. A face off she'd been cultivating for years. Since the moment she put that target on my back before I was even born. But that was not reality. I was just another witch scorned. Eden, though? Every night she'd laid her head down in the human lands, every time she'd thought to use her magic and could not, every day the sun had risen and she'd looked upon the faces of rotating shifter guards, protecting that book... She'd thought of her mother. Another tiny slice into her heart. Until years and years of slices cultivated a wound so great and scarred, even the death of her mother wouldn't heal it over.

I hoped she'd find a way through. Sadly, it wouldn't be lost in the arms of a captain. It might not even be in the heart of the Moss Coven. But she'd earned the right to settle wherever she wanted, to live the life she'd dreamed of for years.

I moved beside her, taking her hand as I pressed our shoulders together, gently.

She turned, looking down on me as a mother might her child. "We're free now."

"Almost," I whispered, closing my eyes. "Almost."

She lay her head on mine, a tear soaking into my scalp. Warmth moved through my body, racing over my veins and into the core of my bones, wrapping itself around my heart. She'd meant to heal me, but I was not the one that was sick. Not really.

I gasped, looking back at Bastian, who stood with Atlas and Nym surveying the mountainside village. "The book."

"Forget the book, Raven. It doesn't matter anymore. The Harrowing is over, Endora is gone. It's time to put the world back together."

"We have to put it back together. We need the final book."

He closed the space between us, pulling me from Eden's grasp. The anger and anxiety disappeared from his face as he gripped my cheeks, this thumb moving down to my neck as he so loved to do. "That is not a task for today, Little Witch. Today, we simply go home."

"Go on without me, then," I whispered, brushing my lips across his. "I'll be right behind you."

He closed his eyes, savoring another kiss. And another. "Fine. I concede. But only if you promise that when we get back to the castle, we spend a month together, locked in a bedroom. No clothing allowed."

My heart broke at the words he used. The plans of a future he'd already begun to make. I pushed away the small lump in my throat. The sorrow that crept up on me.

Forcing a smile, I nodded. "As soon as I finish the final task your mother has given me."

He lifted an eyebrow. "My mother?"

"Your mother had a vision. She used the power of the books to hide my markings, that's why, even in her death, they have not appeared. She also saw something, though it took me ages to figure out. She gave me a portion of her own power, knowing I would need it to put the books back together. Split by a curse, they've damned this world. Everyone is distant and fighting, even among the witches. The books are… dying."

The word 'dying' hung in the air between us, lingering as the mountain stopped rumbling below. His beautiful silver eyes shifted between mine as he tried once and then again to take a breath. I moved my fingers into his hair as he bowed his head.

"Are you also dying, Little Witch?"

I couldn't hear those words from his lips, couldn't imagine the look on his face. The world blurred as my throat burned. The moment delivered every ounce of pain I thought it might as I nodded, knowing he would not see it. Ears ringing, I swallowed. But that lump only grew as I trembled, the tightness in my chest, the weight on my limbs trumping every other feeling I had but guilt.

He shook his head, fighting the truth as he fell to his knees. "Don't say it," he whispered. "Even if it's true, don't speak it into existence."

The voice of a king, a fearsome and confident man, had been reduced to hardly a sound. Broken and gutted, kneeling before me. I dropped to the ground, taking his face in mine, forcing him to look into my eyes as he always did me. The tears were like a knife to my chest, silent as he fought them away, but he couldn't stop their fall.

"You die, I die." He spoke the words like a promise. The Dark King's vow to the world that had damned him so long ago.

"I will wait for you at the gates to eternity. You live your life and you see this world patched back together."

He grabbed me, pulling me into his arms as he buried his face into the crook of my neck. "This world can fucking burn."

His conviction. His pure anger and devastation broke my resolve to stay strong. The ache in my chest burned. I couldn't take in a full breath, remembering the short amount of time we'd had to discover love and get lost in it. To have it ripped away so soon was this world's final betrayal.

"Bash," Atlas said, kneeling to put a heavy hand on his brother's shoulder. "We have to go."

I tried to pull away, but he would not let me. Simply stood, lifting me in his arms, and turned.

"I'll go with you," Kirsi whispered into my ear, unseen by anyone else. "When this world takes you, I will go, too."

I nodded, the back of my eyes stinging as fresh tears formed. At least I wouldn't be alone.

A line of Moss witches formed at the base of the decline from Endora's home. Hands to their sides, no sign of threat. It didn't matter to Bastian, though. He needed a fight. Needed someone to punish for fate's cruel hand. He set me gently on the ground. I tried to reach for him, but he tugged away, storming down to face the witches, each step seemed to build the anger swelling inside of him.

He held his arms wide open, chest bared. "I have no magic," he shouted. "Your coven leader saw to that. I've sent food to you. I've offered you shelter. I've tried and tried to fix what she continued to break. And I fucking lost. So, I'm here now. Punish me."

"No!" I screamed, running.

None of the witches moved. Bastian surged forward, grabbing one of the men by the collar and pulling him to his face. "You want to be a hero today?"

I collided with Bastian, shoving myself between the two men. "This isn't how you deal with this," I shouted, spinning to face the witches as Atty hauled Bastian backward. "Your coven leader is dead. All of the coven leaders are dead, save one. This man has been fighting to save you for *years* and he's been villainized for it. There are no more covens. We are one now. One people. And if any of you makes a single move against anyone standing here, shifter, wraith or otherwise, I will end your fucking lives. Today is the day you make the choice. Continue to drink the poison or end your suffering and walk back down to your homes with some damn dignity."

Nym moved to my side, her tiger limping to sit at hers. Kirsi inched up to the other and then Eden beside her. Without realizing it, I'd drawn the clouds in, covering the sun. A bolt of lightning cracked like a promise waiting to be dealt. One by one, they turned, fading the rest of the way to their village. Eden Mossbrook said goodbye to us with a whisper, beaten and bruised, then followed the witches from her childhood memories. I hoped, watching her half white and half black hair fade away, somewhere along this mountain she would find the peace she'd spent her whole life looking for.

I turned, gutted to see Atlas holding Bastian back as he stared at the witches in silent ferocity, his eyebrows drawn as if a knife had been planted into his broken heart. He screamed in anger. Screamed again and again until Atlas hauled him into a hug and held him as his shoulders wracked with grief.

I couldn't handle the way my throat closed. The splintering of my own heart as I watched that beast of a man break in so many ways. An agonizing ache deep in my bones, in my core, fractured me in a way I knew I'd never be able to claw my way back from. My very soul shattered into pieces so infinitesimal they would be scattered to the wind before anyone could collect them.

He loved me so desperately, the guilt was hard to fight off. I should have never let him in. Should have fought harder those days in the castle. Should never have read a single note that fluttered from the ceiling. Never visited those gardens. I took one final look at the Dark King and turned, regret the only comfort as I walked away.

The book was easy to find when my mind was absolutely numb. Nym and Kirsi followed me silently and we traveled all the way down the mountain, through the pass, and up to a cove, easily missed if you hadn't been summoned by an ancient magical book trapped inside. Wrapped in a dark cloth to further conceal it in the back of the cave, Kirsi and Nym almost didn't see it.

But the whispers were there. Those ancient thoughts of a book cursed by the witches it had empowered. I unwrapped the Grimoire so similar to the Moon Coven book and the memories of my grandmother and then my mother slammed into me. Wrinkled fingers brushing the textured leather, beautiful hands turning the pages. I placed my hand on the cool green stone on the outside of the book and let the power soothe my aching soul.

Wrapping the book back up, I handed it to Kir. She only studied my eyes, looking for signs of life as she tucked a strand of wild black hair behind my ear. "You are not alone."

Forcing a smile, a tear fell, betraying me. "I know."

I could hear the voices of the men below the cave. They'd followed, of course, though kept their distance as Bastian worked through the hurdles in his mind. I couldn't blame him for his range of emotions. I'd lived them too.

When Kirsi disappeared with the Moss Coven Grimoire, racing it away to the safety of the other books, and far from the Fire Coven stone, I wondered if we'd find that place of power. The hidden pedestal Bastian's mother had used to bind me to those books. I had a feeling I knew where it was and maybe he did too. I couldn't ask him, though. Not now, while the world was still his enemy, and me, the reason for his heartache.

61

RAVEN

Bastian crouched beside my borrowed bed. "Can we talk?"

He'd barely been able to look at me the entire trip across the Moss Coven. He had brushed his fingers over mine several times, had paused each time I spoke to Atlas or Nym. But he couldn't look at me without breaking, couldn't figure out how to push past his own sorrow, even as we stopped to eat. Now, sleeping in an abandoned cottage just outside the border, I wondered if he'd considered mine.

I lifted the blanket from my lap and stood from the dusty floor, following him out of the tiny hut. Without a word, he wrapped his arms around me and pointed to the nearly full moon. I nodded, swallowing my sadness once again as I closed my eyes and let that milky power seep into my skin, rejuvenating me in a way I needed so desperately, it hurt.

My head throbbed with pain. Several times today, the world had blurred and swayed. I thought maybe Nym had noticed as she pushed herself to my side and steadied me, silently. But I'd lived in this torment alone for so long now, another day was not going to be the end of me.

I pulled away from Bastian's solid arms to sit on the cool ground, and he dropped the blanket over my shoulders and joined me.

"I can't handle the silence between us," I whispered. "I know this isn't the future you wanted, but this has been the hardest day. I need you to look at me. And smile. Let me feel your love, Bastian."

"I don't know how to love you and lose you, Raven. You're the only thing in this life I pine for, even when you're right beside me."

"Nothing's changed aside from you knowing what's going to happen. This had been my journey my whole life. Love me the same as you did yesterday. Start there."

He shook his head, the tips of his lashes falling heavy in the moonlight. "I can't ... Because I love you more. I'm sorry. I can't act like this isn't the end of my world. But I know it's hurting you and I don't want to add to the pain. Whatever you're feeling, whatever thoughts are swirling through that beautiful mind of yours, just know that I will still fight for you. I'm never going to accept it. But I am going to be on your side. Whatever you need, Raven. It's yours."

"I just need you. Don't push me away."

"My beautiful little witch," he said, pulling me into his lap. "You didn't deserve this day. How can I make it up to you?"

"I have a theory," I whispered. So afraid to breathe hope into his mind and steal it away, I was hardly able to say the words. "Before I tell you, I need you to promise you're not going to interfere."

"I don't like this," he growled.

"Are we a team or not?"

A deep sigh followed a single nod of his head.

"The moon will be full tomorrow. The night I was born, it was also full, and your mother placed me on a pedestal and bound my magic using remnants of power left behind by the Book of Omnia. That's why we have always had a different kind of connection. Her ancestral power feels yours, but sits within me. She linked us long ago. And now, somewhere in the heart of the castle, there's a pedestal. It's where the book was cursed and split into seven. If we place them back on that pedestal under the full moon, using this"—I pulled the Fire Coven stone from my pocket, an ache forming in my gut at the way it no longer whispered to me—"then maybe the books won't die, and I won't die."

He jerked upright. I turned to look into his eyes, the hopefulness I found there, just the thing I was so afraid of. But I needed his help.

"So that's it? We just find the pedestal, stack the books, and you live?"

"Yes," I lied. "I hope. And I can feel it as strongly as the books. It's like a heartbeat hidden below. Probably in the catacombs. It's harboring power that we will need. But this stone is nearly dead. If we don't succeed by tomorrow night, there's no chance. For them, or for me."

"Then we're leaving. Right now."

He hauled me to my feet, practically kicking down the door to the cottage, scaring the daylights out of Atlas, who shifted on instinct before he'd even fully awakened. "We're leaving. We're not stopping to rest. You fall behind, you're left behind."

He'd needed that, I realized as we tore off into the night. A renewed sense of purpose in a patchwork world. We crossed the stone bridge to the Fire Coven as I explained what that old wraith had said. Moving over charred ground, lit by starlight, I told them of the books' whisperings and sentient power, of what it felt like when they pulled me, called me.

Urgency swept over us as we ran, slowing for rest and pushing when we could. Stopping to eat, and for me to catch my breath. One step leading into another as we raced for the Grimoires. Bastian took them with no explanation, ordering everyone to stay away from the palace until word was sent otherwise. He told his coven to send what food they could spare to the Moon Coven, giving the name of the baker. Then he grabbed Kirsi and Torryn and we ran, racing for the black castle.

But as we crested the final hill of the scorched Fire Coven, the spires of the castle lit by the early morning rays of golden sunlight, my breath caught in my throat. I stumbled, falling to the ground. Bastian and Tor swooped in to grab me.

"Okay?" Torryn asked, his deep voice soothing my soul.

"It's like my dream," I breathed, staring down at the pearly white castle. No longer haunted by shadows or conspiracies of the Dark King. No longer a fearful thing to look upon. The absolute contrast of the white against the black ground was striking and beautiful.

"It's been restored by magic to its former glory," Bastian said. "This is the castle of my father's childhood. The castle my parents were married in."

I stumbled down the hill in wonder. The closer I got, the higher the sun rose until it beamed so bright, I could hardly see it at all. When we stepped into the white marble halls, I gulped, daring to touch the cool surface with my fingertips.

"The statues?" I asked, noting the various busts and beasts, sculpted to perfection.

"Mine," Bastian said, coming to stand behind me. "The catacombs were saved from the blast, and that is where I'd kept most of them."

He pulled me along, the darkness of his hair and sweeping cloak seeming misplaced in the beaming hall. He looked down at me with the tenderest smile before gesturing up to the figure of a woman in a beautiful ball gown, her eyes closed, holding her arms wide as if conducting the world in a song of life and sorrow. Tangles of wild curls fell down her shoulders. The lace details of her dress, perfection.

"Me?"

"You." He kissed the top of my shoulder, and a ripple of desire ran through me. "Every second of every minute for the rest of forever, and then five minutes more."

Those words were bittersweet now. Still, I let him wrap me in his arms, let him hold me and wish for eternity.

Until Atlas cleared his throat. "I don't mean to interrupt."

"Then don't." Bastian groaned.

"What do we do with these?" Nym asked, balancing two of the Grimoires.

Scoop yowled from his satchel and Kirsi dove, letting him out. He swirled once below her, shocking everyone before bounding away down the hallway. As if he'd been here a thousand times. But then he'd known the castle from before, so maybe he'd only gone to look for her again. As he always did when set loose and not at Talon's side.

Following Bastian through the castle, I tried to burn it to memory.

The darkened twists and turns I'd taken that night following Breya felt like a lifetime ago, walking through the lightness. Eventually, we made it to the parlor just outside the Grimoire room. Six books and seven pedestals. We placed them one by one and then the stone as Bastian looked at me, waiting for a sign.

"These aren't it. It's in the catacombs. I'm sure." I couldn't help the trepidation in my voice. The fear of disappointing him when he'd been trying so hard to move beyond his own grief.

"Raven?" he asked, rushing for me.

I hadn't felt it. The blood dripping from my nose. Hadn't noticed the turn of my stomach. I closed my eyes, swallowing down bile as the world tilted.

"Raven?" he repeated, his voice desperate.

One breath and two breaths. Steady and even. I dug my fingers into his arm, righting myself. Peeling my eyes open to see five solemn faces staring into mine. That of a wish, eyebrows drawn, sad and worried. A golden witch, her beast at her feet, holding her breath. Two shifters and a king, afraid to face a battle they may never win.

I swayed and blinked slowly. "I'm okay."

The pull from the books overwhelmed me now. Each digging their magical talons into me, desperately demanding I end this. I moved around the room silently, brushing my hand over each of them, feeling for that heartbeat to draw me.

"It's directly below this room. It's pulsing like a heartbeat. In the *heart* of the kingdom."

Again, we were moving, winding through hallways and around the statues. Past the gilded doorways and below the painted ceilings. Urgency and desperation in every footstep. I swayed again and Torryn lifted me from the ground, carrying me when I could not manage.

Down and down and down we went until we stood on dirt floors weaving around pillars of ancient stones. Bastian led us diligently, looking up numerous times until we ran into a wall. He punched the surface, looking back at me with so much dread on his face I could only imagine what I looked like.

He pulled out the stone and placed it into my hands. "Can you feel it, my love?"

Not a breath was heard as I closed my eyes and focused on the fading power of the Grimoires. The scars embedded into Moss, the faintest of whispers from fire. We were running out of time. For them, and for me.

"It's beyond that wall."

"We can't bring it down with magic," Nym said, gently. "With six books of power directly above us, we don't dare."

"Set me down."

Tor treated me like a feather, so very carefully, as he placed me on the floor. I stepped to the wall of stone, placing my hand upon it. "It's here."

"Kirsi," Bastian said slowly.

"I'm already moving, King," she answered.

"Get those books as far away from here as fast as you can. Go south, past the watchtower. At midday, you turn around and bring them back."

"I'll go with you," Nym offered, staring into Kirsi's soul.

Atlas stepped forward. "Me too."

But Kir shook her head. "No. Not this time. I'll go alone."

She vanished into the ceiling, and that was the last we heard from her.

An hour passed. I clutched the stone to my chest, eventually willing each beat of power until I was pumping my own into it on a rhythm. Praying it would be enough.

"Bastian, we have to bring the wall down. We cannot wait."

He narrowed his eyes, not giving an inch. "She's not far enough yet. There's no way."

"She's far enough," Atlas growled. "She's probably farther than you can imagine. She's faster than light and sound. She's determined and she's unstoppable. She'd have gone to the moon by now, had you asked for it."

The Dark King brought a hand to his temple, pressing as he reluctantly nodded, flashing his silver eyes to me. "Bring it down."

"Get back," I warned, holding my hands out to cast.

If Kir hadn't gotten far enough with all those books, this single spell could be total obliteration. But I had faith in her. As much as Atlas, and maybe even more. Because Kir had been the unsung hero in my story for a long time. Long before she throat punched Onyx the day of Tasa's funeral. Before we'd moved into our home, before she'd whispered the truth of her home life to me, sitting under an oak tree when we were ten.

Fighting the urge to sleep, I cast upon a statue, laying on its side across the catacombs. It lifted with ease, and I threw it like a battering ram into the wall. Dust and debris exploded around us as a crack formed. Kirsi had come through. Because of course she had.

"Again," Torryn yelled. "Same spot as before. Just one more, Raven."

Pushing away the tremble in my legs, I swung again and the wall crumpled, filling the catacombs with a cloud of dirt. A surge of power crept over me. Lightning covered my skin. Fire blazed at my fingertips. A wind I hadn't cast breezed through my hair. And there, in the center of the room, a black pedestal made of tourmaline stood erect. Humming with its own residual magic.

"We have to move it." I coughed, swiping my hand through the thick, dusty air. "This spot doesn't hold the magic. It's in the pedestal and I need the moon's power."

Torryn and Bash moved past me, the king gripping my hand as he went. We circled the stone pillar, studying the bottom and moving our hands over the top. They tried pushing it, called Atlas over to help lift it. It didn't budge.

"Can you try?" Bastian asked. "We can go slow. Moving it only feet at a time if you need to rest."

I squeezed my hands open and shut, staring at the heart of the world. "I won't need to rest."

I cast, and it lifted easily from the ground. It answered only to me. The connection of my power to the pedestal pushed another wave of rejuvenation through me. As if the sliver of magic within it recognized me. But as I passed through the catacombs, pushing that pillar to stand above ground, as it once had, many, many years ago, something deep within me jerked. Warning bells flying around in my head.

I didn't stop moving, didn't indicate the threat as I kept going. Pushing forward. Though something deep within my soul knew the ire radiating from this place of power was deep, dark, and dangerous. Smothered in sacrificial blood and cursed over and over, the pedestal had a score to settle with the witches.

62

RAVEN

"Why here?" Kirsi asked as we led her to the site I'd chosen.

I looked around the open space, just down a worn path from the pearly white castle. The black expanse of charred ground and dead trees in the distance lent no sense of ritual to this simple spot. Though the final rays of the sun setting behind us brought chills over my skin as I answered.

"This is where they forced the death spell on me. If ever there was a place of residual power used recently enough nearby, where we could still be under the full moon, this is it."

"We're not casting any magic," Bastian said, pinning me with a hard look. "You put the books together one by one on that pedestal, top it with the Fire Coven stone and then get back."

"We need a salt circle for protection," Nym added. "No magic, just something to ground us to the Earth."

Atlas reached into his pocket and pulled out a tiny glass jar, pretending to toss it to Kirsi.

She rolled her eyes. "Funny, Pup."

"No salt circle," I said, tightly. "There can be nothing binding around us."

"How do you even know this?" Kirsi asked, sweeping in to get a closer look at the pillar.

I didn't want to tell them of the visions the place of power had been sending me today. The visual of those old witches slicing the throat of innocent Meliora and draining her blood. Of curse after curse, of the screams and the sounds from the Book of Omnia as it was severed seven times.

"The old wraith told me," I lied.

All were satisfied with that answer, but Kir. She held my gaze longer, twisting her face into doubt as I turned away. Giving her my back, I crossed the outdoor space we lingered in and wrapped my arms around Bastian. I couldn't give him the goodbye I wanted to. Couldn't even hint that I was about to cast with the power of seven books, harnessing the power myself, so as not to obliterate the world.

Still, he worried, kissing the top of my head before pulling my face away to study it. He moved his thumb over my lips before kissing them with a tenderness I hadn't wanted. I wanted something painful. Something that would sit within my soul through eternity. But I supposed the look on his face in a few minutes would be enough to endure.

"Don't hug me like it's goodbye," he whispered, hardly a space between us. "It's going to work, and then we'll walk right back up to our home and lay in our bed, holding each other until the sun rises."

"I love you," I said, moving to kiss his lips. "More today than yesterday, and even more tomorrow."

He shook his head, giving me a warning. "Don't do that."

"I'm not."

That tingling in the back of my throat began again as I stepped in front of Torryn and took the book he held.

When he hugged me, lifting me off the ground, he whispered into my ear. "If you intend to break my heart right now, Raven Moonstone, you better warn me."

I didn't reply, just hugged the gentle giant back, placing my hand on his cheek for just a moment as I swallowed audibly. Fighting back the torrent of tears I could not shed.

Next was Atlas with two books. He pulled me into a hug, too. "I'll take care of him. I promise you, Rave. If this goes to shit, I've got him."

I couldn't help the struggled sigh, that tiny lump in my throat now a dagger.

Moving on to Nym, taking more books, I leaned in to hug her.

She turned her face into my curls and let out a sob. Her journey these past days had been full of heartache and hard truths, and still she stood here, a constant in this battle. A brilliant witch, never wavering in her love for Kirsi, though they still had the hardest moment to face together. Because the second Kirsi forgave her, she would likely vanish. And in true Kirsi fashion, she was brooding. Watching us, even now. As if the rest of us hadn't noticed the longing gazes and sadness in her eyes.

I took the final two books from Kir's luminous hands, grateful they weren't giant tomes.

She didn't try to hug me, only stared into my face. "I meant what I said, Rave."

I'll come with you.

Another tear fell as I nodded, forcing a smile. "You always do."

I made a step toward the center of the circle, but Bastian cleared his throat. I turned just in time to see him staring up at the night sky, mumbling a prayer to the goddess. I waited. Closing my eyes and wishing for his peace before spinning back. Each step toward the pedestal with the books in my hands was drenched in foreboding. My skin crawled, heart thundering, begging me not to move forward.

Pushing away the thoughts of self-preservation ringing in my mind, every ounce of me wanting to just run back to Bastian's arms, come what may, I knew I couldn't. If I let the books sit, they would die and so would I. We were bound. One. I had too much fight in me to give up if I had even a sliver of a chance at life.

I placed the first book. Moon Coven. The one I felt most connected to. A searing pain ripped down my spine and I fought like hell to hold myself upright. To keep that king at bay. Storm next. The coven with silent witches that had been so kind to a stranger. Another wave of excruciating pain. I stumbled.

"Raven!" Bastian barked, but he did not move.

Knowing that I could not sustain the pain and remain standing, placing each book individually, I dropped the rest of them on the pile, reaching for the Fire Coven stone in my pocket.

We are one, the books hissed.

White light blinded me. The pain coursed through my veins like a volcano eruption within my weak body. Everything that followed happened in slow motion. Like a dream. A nightmare.

I spun, placing myself behind the pillar facing the others. Before they could react at all, or race for me, though I would cast them away, if needed, I lifted my hand and shot death over the stack of powerful Grimoires.

The absolutely heart-wrenching devastation on Bastian's face as he screamed my name shattered my soul to pieces. We'd said our goodbye without saying goodbye and, as I released the sob I'd been holding back, he lunged for me, but was swiftly caught in the fighting arms of Torryn and Atlas.

I poured and poured that death spell into those books, waiting for the explosion to break the world as my life began to slip away. Drawing and pushing. That pillar took and took from me, digging into Bastian's mother's gifted power and then my own. She'd known this would happen, had known that my natural power would never be enough. But even now, beneath the kiss of the full moon, I nearly fell to my knees when I realized it still wouldn't be.

I reached forward, placing my hand on the pillar, giving what would be taken from me anyway. Praying that it would somehow save the rest of them. It didn't help my aching heart, though. Not when I looked at their faces and saw my own betrayal upon them.

Kirsi swept forward, passing through the wall of magic radiating from the power of the Grimoires.

Setting her hand on mine, she shouted to the heavens. "If there's anything you can take from me, you take it. Do you fucking hear me? She doesn't go alone."

My best friend. My sister.

Atlas screamed Kirsi's name at the same time Nym did. One pause from him, a brief distraction, and Bastian was freed, running for his life as he too broke through the magical wall and shoved his trembling hand on top of the pile.

"You go, I go," he shouted through tears of rage. "You take me, too." He commanded the goddess in the sky.

The Dark King clenched his teeth, fighting the pain that attacked him. I tried to pull away, to save him. To cast. But as the stones leeched my power, my life, I could do nothing, locked inside my own body, fighting and screaming to escape. I failed. Failed them all and myself as all the guilt in the world fell on top of my already aching heart. I should have never let them be here.

A large brown palm landed on top of Bastian's. Torryn. And then another. Atlas. They both buckled from the pain crashing over them.

"You'll die." I tried to yell, though it came out faint. "What are you doing? Please stop."

I lurched, working desperately to pull away, to push them all away. To save them, but I couldn't.

"All in. All out!" Atlas roared.

Shaking my head, my nose began to bleed. "No. It doesn't work like that."

I couldn't breathe, couldn't think. Couldn't fight them. Down and down and down I fell into a pit of despair, power ripping from me as my vision blurred again. Squeezing my eyes shut, I opened to find a final hand on top of the others. Nym.

"No," I whispered. "Not like this."

"Seven hearts, Raven. Seven."

But there were only six of us. Unless... I screamed. "Don't you fucking do it, Nym."

Wind thrashed through the air as Nym's spirit-blessed marking glowed. And then that damned tiger bowed before standing to sacrifice himself, at the behest of his golden witch.

I watched in slow motion as Kirsi turned to the love of her life, tears falling, and placed her forehead to Nym's. "I forgive you."

Pain. Indescribable, searing pain flew into my body. To everyone. The pile of books began to melt, pulling at my power, ripping me from this world, throwing me back and then doing it again. Every bone in my body turned to dust as the others screamed my name.

They'd come to save me. To give a piece of each of themselves to hold me to this world. But that Grimoire wanted me, had been bound to only me.

And I was fading.

They knew it. Bastian knew it. But we were almost there. I could feel the dissolving particles of my own life, and the rejuvenated spirit of the Book of Omnia. If I could only hold on, only give an inch more... The world slipped away. Plunged into darkness, my body fell limp. I fought to open my eyes, to go back to my Dark King.

The world was a blur as an eighth figure appeared behind Torryn, running for us. I squeezed my eyes shut and peeled them open, willing the world to be in focus. To see the form behind. My cheek burned anew. The handprint of the goddess holding me to this plane as if she were warning me of danger.

Chestnut hair.

Willow.

I could see the conviction on her face as she ran at full speed. My senses screamed. My fading heart pumped. Willow had always coveted power. If she broke this spell trying to steal it for herself, the entire world would lose all of its magic. I tried to warn the others, but I didn't have the strength for words. I was wrenched from this world again.

I hurt all over. From the bottom of my feet to the hair on my head, still, when I used the last piece of life I had to open my eyes, I saw nothing but Willow's outstretched palm flying directly for my chest.

The magic she'd thrown at me was enough to break me away from the circle, sending me flying backward. A blast of power crashed over the entire world in a giant wave of misery. They were all still there, still bound to the death spell cast upon the books.

My body was broken in so many ways, I couldn't get up. Instead, I crawled. Crying their names as I watched them all lift from the ground with that tower of books in the middle of them. We'd been robbed of a lifetime of knowing each other. Of Atlas' jokes and Torryn's guidance. Of Kirsi's loyalty and Nym's passion. Even Willow's redemption I could not, would not, ever recover from this.

I tried to cast, but I was far too weak. The Grimoire had taken everything I had and now it fed off them. I brought my hand to my cheek where the goddess had touched me. Where that bright, searing power of purity and goodness had seeped into my soul.

It was all a lie. A goddamn lie. She'd never blessed me. No one blessed by the goddess would be damned to watch every person they loved in the world die because they'd tried to save you. Bastian's legs hung limp, Kirsi had nearly faded away. My whole world was locked into that spell.

My stomach lurched as I turned and vomited, hating everything. Hating magic, hating love, hating myself mostly. The permanent lump in my throat burned as I stared, willing myself to breathe, my heart to beat. I didn't hold back my tears, nor my wails of sorrow, as something among them snapped and they all crashed to the ground.

I crawled again. Arm over arm, dragging myself to Bastian's still body. Laying my head on his chest and holding my shaking breath as I listened for a sound.

"Please," I begged. "I know you can hear me. Please let me keep him. I did everything you asked."

We hadn't had long enough. Fleeting moments of professed love among a thousand others of death and ruination. I couldn't live a life with any sense of happiness knowing what it felt like to be loved by him and to have lost it.

A gasp.

A single intake of breath filled the Dark King's lungs.

He groaned and turned, coughing, and moving achingly slow. But he was moving. Living. Breathing. The second his eyes landed on me, a whimper left his lips. He sat up, pulling me into his strong arms. He didn't cry. Not one tear.

Instead, he wiped mine away and whispered, "I'm so glad I asked for those five more minutes."

I broke, crying and clutching him as I buried my face into his neck.

"What the fuck?" Kirsi's raspy voice shattered my heart.

She'd made it, somehow. She walked around the pedestal. Walked. In full physical form, all markings... gone.

"Kir?" Nym's voice was a broken cry as she stood and raced into Kirsi's arms.

They held each other. Kissing and crying and grabbing each other's faces. Nym turned to call for Talon, but she hadn't even finished his name before she staggered and fell to the ground, clutching her heart. Kirsi swiped her hand across her forehead.

Looking down her arms in complete shock, mouth gaping, she managed, "Our power is gone. And so are Scoop and Talon."

Sucking in a sharp breath, I forced myself to sit up, reaching for my power once more and finding it still gone. Panic rattled in my chest, but I held it at bay. For now. Perhaps it was only drained from the spell.

I reached for Nym, absolutely unmarked as her shoulders began to shake, her head down. Kirsi was there first, though, hauling her to her feet so she could hug her and whisper into her ear. She'd made the ultimate sacrifice any spirit-blessed witch could ever make, and I owed her my life for it.

Every bone in my body protested as I turned to the shifters still lying on the ground. Unmoving. Swallowing my fear, I pushed myself to my feet, fighting the lack of strength so I could get to them. I held my breath as I prepared for the worst. Wondering how I would speak their deaths to their brother, who'd purposefully stayed back, afraid of what he might see.

But the shifters did not lie dead on the ground. Though I wondered how long it would take me to stop referring to them as shifters. Because, with softly lit eyes and markings appearing down their arms and over their skin, they'd clearly become witches. Both deep in a receiving.

"They live," I said calmly. "But they're changed."

Bastian pushed himself from the long green grass, moving beside me. I couldn't help but study his skin, noting the markings that were still present.

"Holy hell," he whispered, staring down at his brothers. "They're going to be so pissed."

"Can you shift?" I asked, mostly thinking out loud. "Or cast?"

Beautiful black raven wings appeared behind him. He opened them wide and tucked them tight, sending his shadows along the ground.

"The ground." I gasped. "It's... green?"

"What the fuck is happening?" Kirsi asked, staring down at the two new witches, holding Nym tight to her side.

"Grey is gone," Bastian said, his voice stricken.

Turning, I wrapped myself around him. I knew he was only a part of Bastian. That his easy smiles and quick wit were still around. But Grey had been a whole different person to me, had taken the first ride with me to the castle, had been the first one to tell me that everything I believed to be true wasn't. I'd miss him. I'd miss the dimple and calculating green eyes. The moment I'd shared with him at the cabin. Even the way he laughed with his whole body. But maybe that was still in there somewhere, buried beneath the scars and fresh wounds.

I turned to the final witch on the ground, a halo of chestnut hair laid perfectly around her. She hadn't moved at all, hadn't taken a breath. She was gone.

"Why did she...Why would she have done that?"

"You didn't hear her?" Kirsi asked, kneeling down to close Willow's eyes. "You saved her in the River Coven and the Dark King released her in Moss. Her family perished. She thought she was strong enough to pay back that life debt and live through it."

"She was a fool," Bastian said, moving to look down at her. "A hero in the final moment of her life, but a goddamn fool."

Kirsi shook her head. "She wasn't. She was brave when it mattered most. That would be Raven, if not for her. Don't forget that, King."

Looking down at the discarded body of the silent hero, I couldn't help but see my own face there, ashen and still. She hadn't been strong enough, powerful enough. The eighth heart thrust into the spell that was never meant to be. Maybe Bastian was right and she had been foolish. But so had everyone else. They'd crossed that line, throwing themselves into the fold because we were family. But Willow had done it for another reason. Maybe to save her own soul. Maybe to feel that depth of power. Regardless, her single sacrifice had changed the world forever. Had been the final drop of life to reconstruct the Grimoire that still whispered nonsense to me.

63

KIRSI

Scoop's eyes had been the same as mine, dull gray and stunning. If I looked in a mirror, I wondered if I would still see him. Still feel him, though he'd gone. He'd spent the last of his days as a tiny panther, but for years, he'd paced my mind as a great black beast, with thundering muscles that could cleave the world, should we will it. I believed him to hate that vulnerable kitten form, though he never faulted me for the name Scoop. I'd loved that piece of my soul with every beat of my living heart and every phantom sound of my dead heart. And he was gone.

I brushed my thumb across Nym's cheek, wiping the tears that fell. I'd had the time to accept the shattering of my bond with Scoop. I'd mourned him long before he'd left. But this was fresh for her. A cavernous wound on her heart.

"Will it ever stop hurting?" she asked, rubbing her chest.

I pressed my lips to hers, closing my eyes as I breathed in the tried and true feeling of her textured lips. The taste of her salty tears. The smoothness of her skin beneath mine.

"I don't think so. But I'll be here to help you through."

She gripped the ends of my blonde hair, desperate to deepen the kiss I'd teased her with. But I pulled away with a sly smile.

"Save it, pretty witch. We have a room in that shiny new castle to christen."

"Fucking hell," Atlas said with a groan.

I turned around just in time to see him studying the new markings covering his arms. He closed his eyes, tossing his head back as he swallowed. "I'm going to miss that beast."

"Oh, Atty." I fell to the ground beside him. "I'm so sorry."

He opened his eyes, studying me for only a second before wrapping his arms around me and squeezing until I couldn't breathe. And I let him. For as long as he needed.

"Plus side, free hugs," he whispered in my ear.

"Free gut punches, too, so behave yourself."

He forced a laugh, but as I pulled away, I could still see the sorrow on his face. There was nothing he loved more than being a shifter, commanding the night beneath the power of the moon.

Torryn cleared his throat, moving to his feet without a word. Turning his back to us, he hung his head for a moment, likely feeling just as lost as the rest of us. Shared misery. Raven forced herself to get up, stumbling to Tor so she could wrap him in a hug.

He bent down, his deep voice unable to soothe anyone as it cracked. "I guess this is it," he said. "We're witches now."

"It's not all bad." Raven gestured to his arms. "It looks like you have a good amount of power."

The way her eyes dropped when she said that final word struck me.

"Try it out," I urged Atlas, desperate to pull away from the tension.

He flopped his hand back and forth and a marking on his forearm turned red. A wicked smile crossed his face as a spider with long, hairy legs appeared on Torryn's beard. The beast of a man leapt backward, swiping at it while reciting every curse word known to man.

"Well, this is going to be fun," Atty said.

Tor growled and flicked his wrist, lifting the pup from the ground and hanging him upside down. Bastian stepped in, casting his shadows to cover Atlas' eyes as he hung suspended, then waited a beat before punching him in the gut.

THE UNBOUND WITCH

With an oomph, Atlas clutched his stomach. "You're such a dick, Bash."

"That was Nym, I swear," the king lied, flashing her a grin.

Dropping my hand, she moved to stand in front of Atty. When the king let his shadow magic vanish and the pup saw her standing there, he winced. She threw a hand on her hip and lifted an eyebrow.

Torryn dropped him to the ground and he jumped to his feet, dusting the dirt from his chest. All sense of sadness gone, though likely just a façade, as he swung an arm over my shoulder and then twisted his face, turning away.

"Holy hell, Kir. You fucking stink."

I shoved him away. "Oh please, when was the last time you bathed?"

He looked at Bastian and then Torryn, something sat unspoken between them. He turned and sniffed Nym, and she brought her knee up and kicked him square in jewels. He fell to the ground in pain, cursing her.

"You're shifters," he managed, grunting. "You changed just like we did."

I could do nothing but shake my head. I would have known, felt it, I thought. But there was nothing aside from that void where Scoop had been. Nym didn't disagree, though she slipped her hand into mine and squeezed. *Everything* had changed. Again.

Raven, eyes red from tears, her body still clearly weakened, limped forward. "Everybody lost and everybody gained. That's how it worked. The shifters lost the ability to shift but gained the magic of the witches. The witches lost their power but gained the knowledge to change forms. Willow gained her forgiveness but lost her life."

"And you?" Bastian asked.

She lifted a shoulder, casting her eyes to the ground. "I gained my life but lost my power."

64

KIRSI

"If you think I'm doing that fucking mountain summit climbing bullshit after we're done with this, you can kiss my ass, Pup."

"Aren't you the least bit curious?" Atlas answered, standing between Nym and me, with Torryn halfway across the open field.

Weeks had gone by and the fact that neither Nym nor I had shown any inkling of interest in what our animal forms might be was killing Atlas. I'd spent so much of my ghostly existence curious about the world, a trait common to the wraiths, I just wanted to feel content. We'd been far more entertained wrapped up with each other. Loving each other in a way neither of us thought we'd be able to. Turning into an animal to satisfy the wolf's pleading was only happening because he kept sending spiders under our bedroom door.

"I'm doing this for you, Atty," Nym said with a smile. "But if I turn into a rat or something, it's never happening again."

They'd gotten closer over the past weeks. Knowing how much each of them meant to me, they'd created a bond of friendship and teasing that mirrored what I had with Atlas. Even Raven, for all her hurt and healing, had gone out of her way to make sure everyone was comfortable, and we all had joy in our lives. Though, she also had been hard to find some days. Hadn't left the king's bed. Her bed.

Though I couldn't say I blamed her, given the way his eyes always burned for her when they were in a room together.

"I'll count to three," Torryn yelled. "The first to get to me wins a prize."

"Oh, nice. Your ass is mine, Moondance." Nym bounced back and forth on her toes, leaning in to begin the race.

"Is that a promise, witch?"

"Shifter," Atlas coughed into his hand.

"Are you guys going to do this today, or what?" Bastian yelled from the top of the small hill behind us. "Some of us have kingdoms to run."

Raven shoved him with a laugh, saying something I shouldn't have been able to hear from this far away. "Try being helpful instead of taunting."

"Taunting is Kirsi's second language, Miss Moonstone. It is helpful."

"It's really not," I shouted, bending low, ready to run beside Nym.

Atlas cleared his throat, lifting his hands. "Now, I personally had my first shift at three. Impressive, I know. But since you're a bit behind, don't be surprised if you can't make it work the first time, or can't hold your other form. It takes mental focus and strength. It's like a muscle you have to stretch."

"Ready, set, go!" I shouted, bounding off through the clearing.

"Fuck you, Kirsi," Atty yelled.

I tossed my head back and laughed as I ran beside Nym. Life lessons from a newbie witch wasn't on my to-do list for the day.

Nym wasn't holding back as she flashed me a smile. Her legs became a blur as she ran towards Tor. Turning my mind to focus on the actual task, I dug into myself, letting the core of who I was now come forward, similar to drawing power as a witch, but willing it to cover my body. I blinked once and then twice and suddenly I skidded to a halt, staring at the hindquarters of a giant white tiger, tearing through the windswept field. Talon. Only not. *Nym*. They'd been united in a different way.

Understanding melted over me as I reached for that connection with Scoop and willed it. It was different from before. Not exactly like calling him had been. Shiny black fur grew down my arms, as I dropped to the ground, still running, but with a joy and an ease I'd never known. The wild heart of the beast beat within me as I shifted to a beautiful black panther and ran. I could feel his heart. Could wrap my mind around his essence and finally embrace my familiar once more. My Scoop.

When Nym reached Tor and slowed, a renewed fervor settled within me, a playful innocence of a feline as I lowered myself into the grass and waited. She turned and I launched myself from the ground, pouncing on her until she roared and whipped around swatting at me. We rolled and played like kittens in the grass until our family begged us to go back. Even then, we didn't shift back. Neither of us wanting to leave our beast forms, the caressing of our familiars, behind.

65

RAVEN

I'd never seen so many witches in one place before. I stared out of our bedroom window, over the snowy field beyond the castle, my eyes resting on the tourmaline pedestal sealed behind a domed glass barrier, surrounded by thousands of witches. Every coven, every witch. Our entire world. I imagined if I still had magic, I'd feel the pulse of it even from this distance. But as it stood, the only time I could feel a tiny sliver of power was when I entered that dome and laid my hand upon the book that had tried to take my life.

A white rose petal fell from the ceiling, brushing my cheek before falling to the floor. Looking up with a smile, I closed my eyes as hundreds more rained down upon me. I spun, expecting to find a king clad in black leaning casually against the doorframe. He wasn't there. Instead, an ember rimmed note drifted down. I snatched it from the air, letting the cinders sting my palm.

Miss Moonstone,
  You are quite stunning.
  Turn around,
    B

I whipped around just as the windows I'd been staring through flew open. His black wings, a beautiful contrast to the snowy ground, his hair pulled back into a bun, his beard carefully trimmed. He was poised and patient as he held out a hand.

"Happy Winter Solstice, Little Witch. Shall we?"

"I'll freeze." I laughed, moving to the window.

His eyes grazed over the tight white gown I'd chosen, trimmed in a soft fur. "I can assure you, you will not."

Slipping my hand into his, I let him lift me from the opening, and as promised, warmth greeted me in his arms. He circled above the gathering as we searched the crowd for a witch with half white and half black hair. When he landed before her, she ran, smothering us in a group hug.

"How are you, Eden?" I asked, sweeping a glance over her shoulder to the small group of friends she'd acquired.

She beamed. "Things at home have become normal, though I'm scared to say it aloud."

"Normal is just the thing you need," Torryn said, joining us.

"Have you seen Nym and Kirsi?" Atty joined the fray. "I heard they're back."

"Not quite as observant as you were, Pup," Kirsi said, pushing Atlas with her hip so she could pull Eden into a hug. "Thanks again for letting us stay on the mountain. It's been just the secluded getaway we needed."

"From Atty," Nym followed, hugging Eden next.

"You girls are welcome anytime."

Kirsi took Atlas' hand and pulled him into a hug next. "Missed you, Pup."

He beamed. "Missed you too, Ghosty."

Bastian leaned down to whisper in my ear, dragging me from the happiness of our family. "Ready?"

A knot formed in the pit of my stomach, but I forced a smile and nodded. We had so much riding on this, I worried the king's words would not be received openly. I worried they'd only come to pass hatred and stare at us. I worried something tragic would happen and the shifters mingling on the outskirts of the crowd would become targets. With no power at all, how would I save them?

The witches were silently watching as we made our way to the center of the gathering. Bastian dipped his chin to an older witch in front of the Fire Coven and the man cast a spell over him, amplifying his voice. I held my breath as he began.

"It's not a small thing to travel to the center of our kingdom on the first snowfall of the year. I thank you all for coming. I know you expect us to come before you and speak of the former coven leaders, but that is not the plan for today."

He reached for me, taking my hand and squeezing. I relaxed a fraction at the smile on a witch's face directly in front of us before the voice spell melted over me.

I cleared my throat. "You've all seen now the restoration of the Fire Coven. You've seen or heard of the isles returning to the sky. Storm Coven," I said, turning to where the majority of them stood together. "You've seen the return of your powerful weather. This world was broken in so many ways. But as the Grimoires have been restored to one book, so should we become one kingdom, one people."

Wary eyes met mine as I gestured to the group of people standing together in the gathering. One by one, they stepped forward, giving their personal accounts of experiences with the Dark King. Of receiving food or coin, of his secret kindness he'd never let show on the outside. Of tasks he'd given them and trade agreements he'd made as Grey so that the people might have resources the coven leaders hadn't known about.

When they were done, they listed the names of people they'd helped in spite of the coven leaders, at the behest of the king. Pointing at members of the curious crowd and reminding them of good deeds rendered. Until all were still and silent as the truth came out one by one.

We weren't naive, though. We knew it would take more than a day, a single gathering. But the only way past the poison was to dilute it. And so we would try. Every day.

Bastian moved forward again, lifting his hands. "As I stand before you today, I would ask first for your forgiveness. I was backed into a corner at a young age and thrust into this position with the greatest target on my back, triggering the fight we all harness in our souls. I stood in a tree line and watched the death of my parents by evil hands and blamed the lineage of my people. You. Hate grew like a weapon in my heart until a little witch with a big attitude, and even bigger fight, stepped into my castle to challenge me. She didn't let me get away with a single thing. Held every grievance against me with an iron fist. She taught me how to love again and how to fight back. How to fight for each of you, even if you would not do the same."

My heart beat slowed as he spoke of me with such awe in his voice I wondered if he realized how ridiculous he sounded. Still, if no one else would hear this part, I would. Because it was our story. My favorite ever told.

"Tonight, as you dance around the fires and fill your bellies, I only ask that you share with your fellow witches and shifters alike and begin to heal the wounds etched between us. Happy Solstice, everyone."

His words were a celebration of joy and a symbol of embarking on a new journey of change. The applause was loud, the crowd was happy, and for the first time in my life, I did not fear what tomorrow would bring.

Flinging his wings out beside him, he gathered me in his muscled arms and swept us both away to the pearly white castle. When he dropped me in our room, my beautiful dress was on the floor in seconds. His hands all over me, his lips searing hot down my body.

The Dark King didn't pause for permission, nor did he take his time as he tossed me onto the freshly made bed and licked up my core before resting himself there, hard and eager. I couldn't say I was surprised. We'd stolen every opportunity to find release in each other for months.

Thrusting himself home, I arched off the bed with a cry of pleasure before melting into a puddle below him. Bastian was my weakness and my power. He pulled out, resting his tip against the folds before thrusting forward in another stroke of bliss. I needed him. Wanted him. Begged for him as he moved above me. Undulating my hips, I met him stroke for stroke, letting every bit of emotion I'd had

THE UNBOUND WITCH

working up to this day loose as he slammed against me, kneading my thighs and commanding my body with fervor.

Soft lips found mine as he kissed me, his tongue demanding entrance. Everything between us became too intense to fight. My muscles clenched around him, feeling each and every inch as he thrust, holding my gaze with those silver eyes. He drove deeper, harder, stealing a gasp with his lips as we both rose and rose. I wanted more from him. Always. I could never get enough of this moment. Could have come out of my own skin below him, exploding from the pleasure. From the way he looked at me like I was the most precious thing in his world. We rode the final wave of euphoria together, my nails digging scratches down his back as I screamed his name.

Hours later, after endless rounds of bliss, I lay in his arms, his warm breath coating my skin as we listened to the cheers and the joy of the Winter Solstice festivities outside. I rolled slowly away from him, reaching under the bed to find the small package I'd hidden below. Lifting the heavy blanket to guard myself from the frigid breeze, the fire in our room not quite hot enough to combat it, I placed the box on the bed between us, the silky ribbon long enough to drape over the sides.

"What's this?" he asked with a mischievous grin.

"A Solstice present. Open it."

Wiggling his eyebrows, he tugged on the black ribbon from the box and lifted the lid. He pulled the set of sculpting knives out and studied the deer horn handles before dragging me into a hug. "They're perfect."

"I didn't really know what to get the king who has everything."

He winked in a very Grey way. "I have something for you, too."

Slipping a hand beneath his pillow, Bastian brought forward a tiny red box. I gulped as he raised the lid. Peeking over the edge, I gasped as he lifted the necklace from the box by a long, golden chain and placed it over my head. The tiny glass ball at the end thrummed against the bare skin between my breasts.

Raising it to the light of the moon, I asked. "What's in here?"

"It's the final page from the Book of Omnia crumpled and locked inside."

My heart stopped, the tingling sensation in my nose stirring tears. "You didn't."

"Cast, my love."

A single tear fell as I flicked my wrist and a tiny candle in the corner of the room ignited. The dangerous depth was gone, but the magic, the blissful power that coursed beneath my skin had returned. Throwing my hands around him, I didn't want to ask how he'd managed it without the wrath of that dangerous book. That was a question for another day. Maybe even another lifetime. Because this one was now filled with too much happiness to bother.

That which was meant to destroy, molded me. Death had cursed me, but the goddess had blessed me. The world had broken me, but my family had strengthened me, and somewhere along the way, I'd lost myself as a broken witch, and found myself whole and his.

THE END

Coming Soon from Miranda Lyn

Want more from this world?

A romantic holiday novella surrounding Atlas will publish late 2023

Then in 2024

Immerse yourself in a dark fantasy world where the only salvation for a struggling kingdom is a betrothal.
But what kind of man wants to marry the world's cursed assassin?

And what happens when she accidentally marries the wrong man?

Subscribe to my newsletter for more inforation as it becomes available

ACKNOWLEDGMENTS

First and always most important, to the readers, the bingers and moodies. The devourers and the pacers, thank you so much for everything you've turned this world into. As a writer, every time I start a book, or a kernel of an idea enters my mind, you are there with me. I wonder what you'll like and what you won't. I wonder if you'll see it the way I do or if you'll make it brighter or darker in your minds. If you'll fall in love and cheer the way I have, or hold your applause until the end. I wonder if you'll close the book and take a moment to just let it all sink in before the characters mostly leave you. And then I wonder if pieces of them will stay. I wonder if you'll love Kirsi's fierce loyalty and Atty's wit. I wonder if you'll fall in love with Bastian, no matter the face. I wonder if you will find a piece of yourself in Raven and her courage and the decisions she ultimately made. And in all this wonder, new stories are born and the next seeds are planted. So, thank you for taking this journey with me and I'll see you within the pages, my dear readers.

To my family, my fearless daughters and my soulmate, I love you endlessly. Your support and excitement for me never waivers and I hope you all know there's a bit of each of you within these pages. My very first book I told you to never stop chasing your dreams and I hope after we've come this far, you take that into your souls and breathe life into the world around you until it becomes what you pray and wish it to be.

To Monica and Mama Kahn, I cannot find words to thank you for the work you undertook for this book. The world would have had to wait so much longer for the end of this story and you stepped in to help me see it to the end and I'm forever grateful for that and all your kind words and encouragement along the way. Self-doubt is an inevitable demon when you're on this journey and neither of you let me sit with that long once the story was in your hands. Thank you for being so willing to help.

To my dream team, Darby and Claire... It's been a wild ride. Between all the books published amongst us, it's a wonder we have time for chats, but you're always here and ever the backbone when I need it. Thank you for all the work you did on this story, but mostly for a friendship I couldn't have crafted more beautifully. I love you both even when you get too busy for me and I have to whine about it for a whole year. IT'S FINE.

To Nichole and Chloe, thank you for always having an ear for me. For riding the same waves that I seem to at similar times so this process feels a bit less lonely. For reading my book, just to tell me it's not good enough and then five seconds later telling me it is perfect (Nichole, you jerk) and for listening to hours of audio (Chloe) and sending me messages that just built me up so tall. You truly are the best.

To Ali, Andrew, Rory and Jade, my hype fam... thank you so much. There's definitely a bit of you all in this one and I'm so grateful to have had that imaginative lifeline. Girls, your letters of encouragement and all around excitement as I wrote this book that I hope you never read was such a light in my life and my dream for you both is that you keep shining. As you get older, life is going to throw you a million curveballs. You're going to think you've got it all figured out, only learn you didn't at all. But don't let that dim your spirit. Always be authentically yourself. With your mom's infectious laughter and your father's imagination, should you ever find your world darker than you like, you needn't look further than your own front door.

To Taire, my woman with a vision and an eye to always see my covers through, thank you. They say we shouldn't judge a book by its cover, but we all know that's not how sales work. You put the most beautiful faces on my stories and I'll never be able to thank you enough. I can't wait to see what you come up with next!